lso by Jeremiah Healy
Large Print:

o Like Sleep

DATE DUE

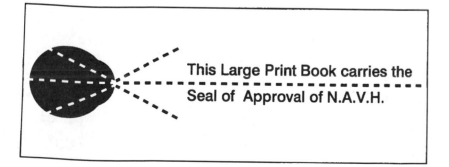

Al
in

S

STALKING

SHEILAH QUI

G·K
Hall
&Cº

THE
STALKING OF
SHEILAH QUINN

JEREMIAH HEALY

G.K. Hall & Co. • Thorndike, Maine

Published in 1999 by arrangement with
St. Martin's Press, Inc.

G.K. Hall Large Print Core Series.

The text of this Large Print edition is unabridged.
Other aspects of the book may vary from the original edition.

Set in 16 pt. Plantin by Rick Gundberg.

Printed in the United States on permanent paper.

Library of Congress Cataloging in Publication Data

Healy, J. F. (Jeremiah F.), 1948–
    The stalking of Sheilah Quinn / Jeremiah Healy.
        p.   cm.
    ISBN 0-7838-0431-8 (lg. print : hc : alk. paper)
    1. Large type books. I. Title.
[PS3558.E2347S79   1999]
813'.54—dc21   98-31443

For James Barretto,
Gary Chafetz, and Kelly Tate

PROLOGUE

It was just the way Arthur Ketterson had always thought it would be.

Dreamed it would be.

He watched Sheilah Quinn come into her bedroom. Arthur was hiding in the closet, but still he could see her clearly. Sheilah striding toward the bed in her three-inch heels, Sheilah unpinning her long auburn hair, Sheilah stepping out of her simple black dress. Even though those elegant breasts were facing away from Arthur, he knew they were perfect nonetheless.

Perfection incarnate.

And then Arthur was out of the closet and moving toward her, gliding across the carpet so quietly that Sheilah never heard him. Had no idea he was standing behind her, planting the balls of his feet just inside each of her heels and raising his hands up toward her bra.

Arthur maintained that pose — eager but controlled — flexing his fingers and preparing his wrists while Sheilah angled her arms awkwardly so that each hand could reach that clever clasp in the black lace between her shoulder blades. It was only when she unsnapped the clasp that he grasped the two ends of the bra, taking them from her as smoothly as a

7

succeeding runner receives the baton in a relay race.

Except that Arthur now whipped the bra off Sheilah's torso, looping it in a practiced motion down around her neck. He drew the elastic lace quickly and tightly against her throat, stifling any noise before the sound could reach her lips.

Lips that now parted in terror as Sheilah's spine arched spasmodically into his chest, her rump ratcheting up into his groin, her perfect, perfect flesh grinding against his massive —

At which point, the inmate in the next cell coughed like a clap of thunder, and Arthur awoke violently.

Awoke to realize that he'd never been in Sheilah Quinn's bedroom.

Awoke to realize that he was still in jail, on trial for murder.

Awoke to realize that what he'd always dreamed of was still what he only dreamed.

And for the next five minutes, it took every ounce of control Arthur Ketterson IV could muster to keep from pounding his fists into bloody pulps against the cinder-block wall next to his bunk.

ONE

Why? thought Sheilah Quinn, sitting at the defense table. She allowed her eyes to roam around the First Session. Why does trying a murder case here always remind me of being in church? Is it the high windows cut into polished mahogany wainscoting? Maybe the antique sconces glowing faintly on the walls, or the baroque chandeliers shining brightly from the exposed beams overhead. Like a little girl, I inhale that hushed silence, broken only by incantations within the altar rail of the picket-fence bar enclosure, the audience outside it on gallery benches like pews.

However, when you look a little closer, the windows get their color from sun-faded drapes, not stained glass, and the person in the black robe is a judge, not a priest. Even the people behind us aren't parishioners attending a mass or funeral but, rather, simple spectators, embracing that intense atmosphere of ritual. A ritual that begins and ends with one question: Would this troubled soul called "the defendant" be spared the executioner's tender touch?

Only there can be no more death penalties handed down in any courtrooms of this state, not since I argued and won the *Jervis* case last month on appeal to the commonwealth's supreme —

"A penny for your thoughts," said her client.

The reedy voice whispered into her ear, a grown-up trying to interest his child in a nursery rhyme by making it seem a secret just between them. Except that there was no need to whisper with the jury still excused and the judge in his chambers, the prosecutor huddled with the homicide detectives in one corner. The accused had just gotten settled with his attorney at the defense table toward the closing arguments in the trial. Only the bailiffs were paying any attention, and even then only to be sure that Arthur Ketterson IV wouldn't try to rabbit on them.

Sheilah turned her head to look at the weirdo — the description her father would have used, and it fit her client perfectly. A preppy weirdo, if that wasn't too much of an oxymoron.

Ketterson was a little over six feet, a good seven inches taller than his lawyer. He had that bristly kind of hair that never seems to lie flat after brushing, the color blond in sunlight and sandy otherwise, with bushy eyebrows that stayed sandy all the time. Clean-shaven and well groomed — even coming to the courtroom from a jail cell — his face was long, though not horsey, his physique athletic, though not muscular.

Admit it, girl. When you were in college — and probably law school, too — you'd have found the man attractive, even charming, in a campy

sort of way, including his courteous clichés —
"A penny for your thoughts".

But despite the neat-freak, "Tennis, anyone?"
aura Ketterson projected, Sheilah had a vague
unease about her client, seeing him as somehow
. . . insectlike, a praying mantis with impeccable
posture.

Jesus Mary, he makes me uncomfortable,
especially the level stare projecting from those
gray, gray eyes.

"You're probably right," said Ketterson,
picking a microscopic hint of lint from the cuff of
his suit jacket.

Sheilah turned back, away from him. "About
what?"

"About the 'penny.' I've already paid rather
handsomely for your thoughts, haven't I?"

Truth be told, he had. Accused of strangling
Jessica Giordano, a young woman he'd been
seeing, the man had forked over a retainer of fifty
thousand dollars without blinking an eye. And
his family attorney, a stuffed-shirt Ivy Leaguer
named George Lofton, had responded to every
incremental bill with return-mail promptness,
including the stratospheric costs of daily transcripts, to help her prepare better for each successive day of trial.

But Sheilah hadn't gone into criminal defense
practice because of clients' attention to the pro-
tocol of accounts payable. She turned down the
corporate law firms that would have chained her
to a desk in the library the first five years just for

this: the frequent chance to be onstage, to be the center of a drama. And you take a good role when it's offered, even if it means appearing with another actor who makes you "uncomfortable." Especially if the role also means getting to perform in possibly the last play in this grand old cathedral of a theater, because the entire courthouse was being replaced by an almost-completed new facility across the park.

"I'm sorry, Sheilah," said Ketterson in his earnest, cultured voice, the right hand fluttering up to the side of his cheek. "Here you are trying to marshal your concentration toward arguing my acquittal, and I keep interrupting your train of thought."

The man was on trial for murder, but at least outwardly he seemed to care more about his manners than his fate. A way of showing courage maybe, Hemingway's "grace under pressure."

Sheilah was about to tell him she'd worked out the closing long in advance, honing it after every day's testimony, when the uniformed court officer came into the First Session through the inner door to the judge's chambers on the left-hand side of the bench. In his early sixties and grossly overweight, Bailey had been called "Old" for decades, a nickname given the bailiff as a play on the name of the criminal courts in London. Walk into any session, and you'll see a throwback like him, intoning the "Hear ye, hear ye" that the courts in the original colonies had borrowed from the British motherland. From his chair and small table at the gallery end of the jury box, O.B. would answer the telephone or bring the judge fresh ice water, all the while ticking off the years toward retirement. Old Bailey shambled like a tired circus bear, and Sheilah couldn't imagine the court officer restraining a rowdy, short of sitting on the offender.

He said, "Before closing arguments, His Honor would like to see Mr. Mendez and Ms. Quinn in chambers."

O.B. might be a throwback, but Sheilah had to give him credit for the amenities. Despite official commissions issuing official reports with official mandates, sexism ran rampant through the system. Yet she'd never heard Bailey address anyone, lawyer or client, juror or spectator, other than formally and properly.

Sheilah stood, letting District Attorney Peter Mendez precede her toward the chambers door and waiting for the other bailiffs to hover closer to the defense table. With most clients, especially those who, like Ketterson, had been denied bail and therefore were incarcerated pretrial, she would have quickly placed her hand over his, a nonverbal, asexual reassurance that said, Don't worry, I'll be right back.

But Sheilah Quinn had never touched Arthur Ketterson after their initial meeting, when she'd tried to break the ice by extending her hand for him to shake. At first, he hadn't taken it, his own right hand just fluttering up to his cheek in the gesture she'd come to recognize as nervous habit. Then Ketterson studied Sheilah's hand, carefully, even thoroughly, as though he was doing an appraisal with his level gray-eyed stare. Finally, he lowered his hand from his cheek and closed on her fingers, causing a sensation to run through Sheilah. A . . . wobbling that she couldn't have explained competently to anyone who'd noticed her reaction (which the family lawyer, Lofton, had not but which Ketterson himself, Sheilah was sure, had). Ketterson's hands were strong, the fingers long and the palms deep, but he hadn't tried to impress her by clamping down. No, it was more that he was holding something delicate in a gentle way because he intended to . . . eat it.

Pushing away that moment now, Sheilah followed Peter Mendez toward Old Bailey and the chambers door of the First Session.

"Sheilah, Sheilah. Why have you forsaken me?"

Arthur Ketterson IV watched his attorney stride away from him, trailing that social-climbing Mambo King past the judge's bench and toward the bloated toad in blue opening the door for them. Arthur watched her legs, the calves under the hem of her skirt vibrating in the sensible heels. Watched her auburn hair — pinned up behind her head now, but down in the past, flowing over her shoulders and swaying with that stride. Then Arthur noticed the way the back of her bra strap was visible even under her suit jacket as she swung her arms, and he knew he had to stop watching her.

Arthur had to stop watching Sheilah now, because he wasn't completely certain he'd spoken the "forsaken" sentence only to himself. A man who'd always prided himself on control, he was beginning to feel a tiny seed of doubt sprouting within his chest rather than within his skull, that tiny sprout of eccentricity born of isolation that his mother always stressed to him.

"Isolation exaggerates eccentricity, Arthur" was her most pithy way of putting it. She would stress that while their position (bolstered by wealth and the power it bestows) might provide specific social encounters, on the whole he would lead a relatively solitary life, and he had to erect and maintain strong walls — "Castle walls, Arthur" — against those idiosyncracies that, untempered by social contact, might get out of hand. And so he erected those walls and maintained them, always careful to be alone before speaking aloud to himself, but allowing also for his thoughts to express themselves to him. "Internal conferences," Arthur had dubbed them.

Three months in jail, though, had tested those castle walls, tested them sorely through a kind of siege warfare unlike any other he'd experienced in his twenty-eight privileged years on the planet. Voluntary isolation at the estate was one thing, imposed isolation in a cell quite another.

The sounds, the rudeness, the . . . smells.

No, said Arthur, this time clearly to himself, the realization of which restored his spirits a bit. No, I shall not permit this parody of justice to depress me. I am used to being in control, but now events sweep me along with them. I cannot control events; I can control only my reaction to them.

And then Arthur signed off on himself, deciding that the remaining time before the jury returned to its own confining little box could be more profitably spent practicing his "trial" face, as he came to think of it. The pained, even bewildered expression that twelve citizens hale and true would find — could only find — to be that of an innocent man.

But Arthur Ketterson IV did permit himself the most controlled of smiles first.

After sending Old Bailey out from his chambers to fetch counsel — he thought of O.B. as a "retriever" of the game birds called "attorneys" — the Honorable Roger Hesterfield settled into his leather swivel chair. Burgundy leather it was, too, with peened brass tacks, matching counsel chairs in front of his desk and matching couch against the wall. Hesterfield gazed at that couch, the cushions holding fond memories of the first generation of female law clerks, back before all the absurd feminist hysteria over sexual harassment and heterosexual AIDS. And his old desk itself, the one he'd inherited from a senile partner at his still older former firm twenty — no, almost twenty-*five* years before.

Hesterfield mentally rubbed that image from his mind. Pushing sixty was no small burden, even if he still had his hair and most of it was still the original color, golf at the club restraining, if not completely controlling, his waistline. And he enjoyed the trappings of judging, the structure it gave to the day, even to the bottle of single-malt scotch in his desk's lower drawer. There was no problem limiting his intake to a swig or two during recess in an armed robbery or rape trial, smooth out a boring afternoon of computerized bank diagrams or forensic analysis of pubic hair. But during a murder? Most definitely not. Mercifully, his jurisdiction did not allow television cameras in the courtroom as a monitor on the quality of rulings from the bench, but even so, Roger Hesterfield wasn't about to risk mistrial by being two fingers of Glenfiddich slow on an objection or motion to strike testimony. No, the scotch — and the burnishing glow it provided — would have to wait.

Hesterfield looked around the chambers then. Wistfully, the way he sometimes did with a drink in his hand. The wall plaques proclaiming civic appreciation. The framed photos of "His Honor" with successive mayors, governors, state supreme court justices. Even the late, great Warren Burger himself, then chief justice of the United States Supreme Court, congratulating Hesterfield on blazing a trail away from the

Warren court's pandering to the criminal defendant while the rights of the victim — and a civilized society — withered on the vine. On a different wall, the shelves contained the commonwealth's statutes and case reporters' and bench memos, the last a kind of crib sheet to help a computer illiterate like himself still find the law when he needed it.

And he did need it. Increasingly, Roger Hesterfield realized he needed the law to give his life meaning. Or, more sadly and accurately, he needed his career to have any life at all. Never marrying, Hesterfield had played the field for years, but recently there had been precious little field to play, the currently available women either not interesting to him or — worse — not interested in him. He glanced over to the couch again. Lost opportunities were what he saw there. Opportunities for a different life, a real life outside the career.

And now the bastards were going to take away even that, his history. Roger Hesterfield's eyes came back to the desktop and the memo from the county commissioners, a piece of paper that he'd tried to squirrel under other documents but which kept crawling back out, chittering at him. The memo that detailed the "deconstruction and demolition schedule" under which the last of the "old" courthouse personnel were to "vacate," moving all personal belongings across the park to the "new" courthouse. He didn't have to consult his calendar to know that date

18

was Friday, just three days away. Only one monstrous irony appealed to Hesterfield: Rudolph Giordano, the father of the dead girl in the Ketterson case, was the contractor who had successfully bid both for building the new facility and demolishing this one. The trial of his own daughter's murderer might well be the last official proceeding in the very courthouse Giordano was destroying.

Somewhat brightened by that thought, Roger Hesterfield heard Old Bailey's telltale knock, and he squared himself to greet the combatants before the last skirmish of this particular battle.

Sheilah Quinn followed Peter Mendez through the chambers door held open by the bailiff. Mendez was in the midst of running for state attorney general, campaigning hard enough to change his features from handsome to haggard. But he was the picture of good health compared with Hesterfield.

Jesus, Sheilah said to herself, poor old Rog is really showing last night's booze this fine morning.

The brown hair still has just a few streaks of gray in it, but close up in chambers you get a perspective different from that in the high-ceiling courtroom. The capillaries bursting like fireworks at Hesterfield's nose, the ruddiness of cheek having nothing to do with the mild September air outside the windows. The judge's suspenders bowed as they rode over his paunch, and his silk pheasant-print tie was an inch wider and shorter than fashionable.

Hesterfield's hands were trembling badly as he stood, welcoming them to his lair. "Sheilah, Peter. Sit, please," he said, indicating the counsel chairs. "Unless, of course, one of you would prefer the couch?"

Sheilah just stared at him. "A chair's fine for me, Judge."

Taking the right-hand one, Mendez said, "Have you decided on your jury instructions?"

"Wouldn't have had O. B. disturb you out there if I hadn't, eh?" He handed each attorney a stapled packet of eight photocopied pages with handwritten insertions and marginal notations all over them.

Sheilah began reading what the judge would be telling the jury about the law governing their case, having to stop and go back several times to follow Hesterfield's sequencing. The man doesn't understand computers and doesn't trust secretaries, so he uses a pen to tailor specific-case instructions from preprinted, standard ones. Get with the program, Rog.

Mendez said, "Your Honor intends to instruct on both 'first degree with extreme atrocity and cruelly' and 'second degree'?"

Hesterfield frowned. He insisted upon the "Your Honor" in open court, of course, but preferred the informality of "Judge" and first names of counsel in chambers. More human, he always thought. "Yes, Peter. I don't see any evidence of premeditation in strangling the poor girl with her own bra."

Sheilah bit her tongue at the work *girl*. The victim might still have been living in her parents' home, but at twenty-one she'd clearly been a "young woman."

Then Sheilah asked what she knew to be a pivotal question. "Are you going to summarize the evidence for the jury, Judge?"

Hesterfield smiled. Sheilah had learned his preferences — he smiled wider — when she clerked for Judge Etta Yemelman before the old battle-ax had retired back into practice. "Yes, Sheilah. Summarize, but not comment."

Sheilah looked at Mendez, the candidate for higher office smiling smugly. Like the federal courts and some other states, the commonwealth allowed its judges to summarize for the jury the evidence each party offered and to comment on the weight of that evidence, kind of a "boost" from the bench for the party the judge thought should win. Occasionally, an appellate court would rule that a judge's comment had crossed the line, exerting undue influence on the jury, and so careful judges like Hesterfield would often avoid commenting on which side had the stronger case. However, even the act of summarizing the evidence could function as a crucial comment on it by what the judge selected and emphasized.

Feeling tense, Sheilah tried hard to keep her voice steady. "As guidance for Peter and me in structuring our closing arguments, could you give us a sense of what that summary will be?"

Always pushing, aren't you, Sheilah? thought Hesterfield. "I'll remind them that the prosecution established that the defendant, Arthur Ketterson the Fourth —"

Sheilah said, "Could we just leave it at 'Arthur Ketterson'?"

Hesterfield looked from Quinn to Mendez and back. He was sure Mendez would use the "IV" to remind the jury of Ketterson's aristocratic status. But Hesterfield also remembered that both of Ketterson's dead parents, Arthur Ketterson III and Madeline, had been part of his own circle from the country club. "Fine. Plain old 'Arthur Ketterson' had been dating Jessica Giordano for almost a month. At approximately seven-fifteen P.M. on the night in question, the defendant picked up the victim at her parents' house before going out to dinner — Peter, the name of the restaurant again?"

"Chez Jean, Your Honor."

"Ah, yes. Thank you. Now, where was — right. The commonwealth's fingerprint expert testified with appropriate charts that a latent on the victim's bra matched the defendant's left thumb at twenty-seven points of comparison. Unfortunately for the prosecution, that was the only identifiable print of Arthur Ketterson's anywhere in the house. The defendant testified — rather effectively, I thought, though that's obviously just between us — that the girl's previously

22

established shoulder injury would have made it difficult for her to fasten the bra. Therefore, when he arrived at the Giordano house, the victim asked him simply to help 'clip and zip' her. In any case, the couple walked into Chez Jean at approximately eight o'clock, had what the restaurant staff and other patrons testified was a seemingly uneventful meal, and departed a bit after ten-oh-seven P.M., according to the time stamp on the charge-card receipt. The defendant's version is that he then dropped Ms. Giordano back at her parents' house with no more than a good-night kiss, departing for his own."

Hesterfield looked to Peter Mendez. "The prosecution's version is — not surprisingly — quite different, though entirely circumstantial. Its version is that Mr. Ketterson thrust unwanted advances upon the victim after returning to the Giordano house, and her rejection caused a sexual rage in him that resulted in her death. Forensics established no forced means of entry at the Giordano home — the back door, in fact, standing open when the first uniformed officers responded to the scene. The postmortem vaginal examination suggests no sexual assault, much less ejaculation. Hence, no trace evidence links Mr. Ketterson with the murder."

Mendez began to speak, but Hesterfield held up his hand like a traffic cop, saying, "Sgt. Frank Sikes and Detective Gerald O'Toole of the Homicide Unit testified that upon their arrival at the scene, Mrs. Giordano was hysterical in the living room, having found her daughter's body on the floor of the victim's bedroom upstairs. Apparently, Jessica's childhood collection of puppets was scattered around her — a nice touch, that."

Hesterfield expected some appreciative reaction from the attorneys. Getting none, he said, "Sergeant Sikes noticed that the victim's watch had stopped at ten-forty-five P.M., suggesting that the struggle had occurred then. Twenty minutes was established as the approximate driving time between Chez Jean and the Giordano house at that time of night. Such a period would have given Arthur Ketterson about ten minutes of opportunity to commit the crime before driving home himself. The defendant's houseman, Parsons — I'm sorry, Sheilah, I don't remember his first name."

Sheilah said, "Howard."

"Yes. Howard Parsons corroborated his employer's time of arrival at the Ketterson estate —"

Sheilah coughed. "Judge —"

"Very well, at the Ketterson *residence* as being eleven-ten, which would have given the defendant ample time after the ten forty killing to drive there from the Giordano house in — I don't think you can quibble over this one, Sheilah — his BMW eight fifty CSI, a rather capable sports car. However, your three female witnesses, testifying on their prior relationships with Mr. Ketterson over the years, all established him as a perfect gentleman. Indeed, the one you flew in from Seattle going so far as to —"

Quickly, Sheilah said, "I believe that response about wondering whether my client might be gay was stricken from the record."

"Yes," Hesterfield replied, pondering something. "Yes, I did allow your motion, and of course I therefore won't reinforce her speculation by mentioning it in my summary. But I don't see the jury forgetting her feeling, either, do you?"

An anxious pitch to his voice, Mendez said, "Your Honor, while we're on the subject of evidentiary rulings, I'd like to revisit your decision *not* to allow the prosecution to offer evidence of the death of the defendant's mother."

Sheilah shook her head. "Judge —"

But Hesterfield held up his hand again as a stop sign. "Peter, Madeline Ketterson took her life tragically over fifteen years ago. The defendant's mother hanging herself with her bra after being diagnosed with cancer in both breasts was simply insufficiently probative and far too sensational and prejudicial for the jury to hear in another case involving murder by a similar means."

Now agitated, Mendez said, "But Your Honor is supposed to weigh what other evidence I have to establish that the defendant strangled this victim against —"

"Peter, that evidence was, and will remain, excluded."

"But Your —"

"Period," said Hesterfield, in a way that brooked no further argument on the point.

After an authoritarian pause, the judge tented his fingers on top of the desk. "Well now. Anything else?"

The lawyers exchanged glances but didn't say anything.

"Sheilah?" prompted Hesterfield. "No last-minute floating of a plea bargain, perhaps brought on by a shared 'client confidence'?"

After shutting down the prosecutor, he has to try rattling the defense attorney a little, to tweak everyone equally, she thought. From her, a very controlled "None, Judge."

"Very good. Confidences between lawyer and client should remain sacred, eh? Well, then, why don't you two return to your tables, and I'll have O.B. bring in the jury."

For what seemed like the thousandth time, Arthur Ketterson IV watched the jurors troop into their box, six against the railing, an additional six against the right-hand wall, near the witness stand (or chair), all twelve seats slightly staggered for improved sight lines. Back on the first day of trial, Arthur had thought it unfair that Mendez's table — the same distance from the judge's bench as his own, defendant's one — should be so much closer to the jury, but Sheilah had explained to him that such an arrangement was conscious, due to the prosecutor having the burden of persuading those twelve stalwarts of his guilt.

This morning, as on most days of trial, Arthur also thought the jurors appeared awfully weary, even cranky. According to Sheilah, though, they were considerably snappier than the ones she'd seen during her first years of practice a decade before. Those were the days when many categories of people — judges, lawyers, police — were automatically excluded, and virtually everyone else of any means at all was able to dodge actually serving, resulting in juries made up of four pensioners, four housewives, and four postal employees. Now the state had copied what Sheilah called the "Massachusetts model": each citizen being summoned every five years or so for one day or one trial, with the result being that lawyers and even judges served on juries when the parties ran out of peremptory (or not-for-cause) challenges to unseat them. Arthur's jury included a Chinese engineer, a Negro (Arthur's mother never used the word *colored* or *black*) schoolteacher, a retired Hispanic army officer, Armenian executive secretary, and so on. A veritable advertisement for America as melting pot, where the land of opportunity also exacted a certain reciprocal civic duty in the processing of murder cases. Not the sort that one would ordinarily entrust with even routine responsibilities, much less one's entire future. Imagine instead, though, another alternative Arthur could envision: a jury made up entirely of . . . attorneys. Given how many lawyers there now were, it was surely statistically possible, however horrible to contemplate.

As the last juror took his seat, Arthur's attention was directed to the sound of the judge's voice, the same voice the Jolly Roger used to boom in the country club's Nineteenth Hole, a double scotch rocks in his hand and drunk as a lord. After Hesterfield droned on about "he testified to this" and "she testified to that," Arthur perceived a shift in his manner.

"Ms. Quinn, you may now make your closing."

"Thank you, Your Honor."

Arthur watched Sheilah Quinn stand and move resolutely yet sensuously to the railing in front of the jurors. So confident, so capable, so . . . reminiscent.

Arthur was nearly mesmerized, watching her for — he'd lost track of the number of times he'd actually watched her, but never mind that now. She was grace in motion, subtly degrading this aspect or that of the prosecution's case, persuasively emphasizing his own credibility in testifying about the decedent — Arthur noticed that Sheilah never called the slut Giordano a "victim." He was most proud of his lawyer in the deft way she dealt with the testimony of the homicide detectives who'd come to the estate.

God, could Arthur ever forget that night? Or

early morning, he supposed, by the time they'd awakened first Parsons and then him with the "bad news" about Jessica and their request that Arthur "come downtown" with them. That fatuous Irish imbecile O'Toole: in his forties, beefy of frame, florid of face, fawning with good humor. His partner, the Negro Sikes, approximately the same age but rather athletic; given his "even" features and light skin, Sikes was probably just this side of passing for white (back when that would have been an advantage, rather than a disadvantage, to career advancement).

Both detectives had testified damagingly. But Sheilah was now deflecting that testimony ever so gently — probably so as not to offend the three blackamoors in the jury box. Harking back to her surgical cross-examination of each investigator, she recounted how each was surprised by the reaction of the "defendant" — That was me, Arthur had to keep reminding himself — when they advised him that Ms. Giordano had been killed.

"Detectives Sikes and O'Toole said the defendant smiled," Sheilah told the jury. "As though it were a joke. But wouldn't you — awakened from a deep sleep in the early-morning hours — have thought it truly was at least a misunderstanding? That the lively companion you'd dropped off safely at her home just hours before was now dead by someone else's violence?"

Ah, Sheilah, thought Arthur, being careful not to speak aloud. You were the perfect choice. I was so wary at first of . . . well, the co-*in*-cidence, I felt some trepidation at ranking you above the other options that office-bound oaf Lofton presented to me. And your professional demeanor when we first met — "I'm not going to ask you whether you're innocent, Mr. Ketterson. My job is to force the prosecution to prove you're guilty" — was just a trifle . . . off-putting, shall we say? But I'm so glad now I hired you, so glad.

Arthur became aware of Sheilah leaning forward, her palms on the jury rail. The material of her suit jacket stretched across her shoulders, the outline of her bra once again obvious to him, sitting behind her.

Sheilah, Sheilah. I envy my jurors being able to look into your eyes — *her* eyes, as I think of them. At age thirty-four, your beauty — like hers — still . . . perfect.

Though not for much longer, I'm afraid. Unless you win me the chance to intervene on behalf of that beauty. To . . .

Arthur realized he was becoming faintly aroused "down there." Then more than faintly, and he grew grateful that the defense table blocked that particular view from the twelve people in the box.

"And so, members of the jury," said Sheilah, "these are the last words you will hear from me. As His Honor will instruct you shortly, the prosecution has the ultimate burden of proving the defendant guilty beyond a reasonable doubt. Because of this heavy burden, our state allows

the prosecution to close last. I've tried to antici-
pate most of the district attorney's arguments,
but I would request one favor." She paused. "If
Mr. Mendez should raise something in his
closing that you haven't heard me discuss, please
ask yourselves, What would Sheilah Quinn have
said to that as defense attorney if only she'd had
the opportunity to speak again? Please ask yourselves that question individually in this courtroom and then collectively in that deliberation
room, and I'm confident you'll return a verdict
of not guilty. Thank you for your attention and
patience."

Arthur watched Sheilah move back toward
him, passing the prosecution table slowly,
almost languidly. No doubt to keep the jurors
focused on her and thereby disrupt the Mambo
King's timing in beginning his own closing.

Once she was seated beside him, and before
Mendez began speaking, Arthur dared lean
toward her ear — her exquisitely perfumed ear
— to say, "Loved the way you recruited them as
advocates for me."

Arthur then watched Sheilah's face turn away
from the jury, and he knew that whatever the
outcome of the trial, he'd never forget the look
those eyes bestowed upon him.

Two rows back in the audience, Detective
Gerald O'Toole tilted his head slightly toward
his partner and said, "Jesus, Frank, the hinky
bastard nearly kissed her."

31

Detective Sgt. Frank Sikes nodded tightly. As prosecution witnesses, he and O'Toole had been sequestered outside the courtroom until after the testimonial phase of the trial ended, but both of them wanted to catch the closings. Despite the suspect's print on the victim's bra, it had been a difficult case to make, and Frank almost applauded in sarcastic pantomime as Sheilah took the sting from most of the evidence they'd cobbled together. But Arthur Ketterson the fucking IV had the eyes of a man who liked to kill, that hoppy look you learn to recognize on sight to survive on the street, and evidence or no evidence, skillful cross-examination and closing be damned, Ketterson was dirty. Maybe a guy who'd acted on the dark side just the once, but somebody who listened to its siren song on probably a daily basis.

And if they didn't get him on the Giordano killing this round, Frank Sikes had a feeling the fucking heir apparent would be back in the ring again. And soon.

Pushing the campaign noise out of his head, Peter Mendez waited with elaborate courtesy until Sheilah Quinn had resumed her seat. Attorney general might be the next logical rung on his political ladder, but first he had to secure this one. And Peter didn't like the jurors' faces, including that of the retired army colonel, during Sheilah's closing. A military officer, as somebody accustomed to order and discipline, was usually a prosecutor's wet dream to have on a panel. But, Madre de Dios, even the colonel looked shaky.

Moving to the rail, Peter stole a look into the gallery audience, to be sure he could pick out the vic's parents, point them out to the people who would decide her designated killer's fate. "Members of the jury, this is a very simple case involving a very serious crime."

Peter always liked that "opening to a closing," give the jurors a sense that all the hubbub of the past few weeks could be easily synthesized, digested, and appreciated for what it really was. The worst crime the species can commit: a violent murder.

"And how violent? You heard the testimony of Detective Sgt. Frank Sikes and Detective Gerald O'Toole of the Homicide Unit about their impressions at the crime scene. It looked to both of them — seasoned, even hardened veterans of death cases — that Jessica Giordano's throat had been crushed during the killer's attack and her struggle. You heard the medical examiner, Dr. Emil Dinetti, confirm those impressions by his observations during the autopsy. The extreme atrocity and cruelty displayed in the manner of snuffing out this poor victim's life."

Peter heard a not-so-muffled sob from behind him, the direction telling him what he would have guessed anyway, that the victim's mother was about to lose it, as she had during most phases of the case thus far. Generally, Peter preferred three such outbursts: one near the beginning of the trial, one near the middle, and one now, during his closing. Punctuation marks for the jury's attention and persuasion. But he was afraid the jurors were now as tired of hearing from Rhonda Giordano as he was, a fear confirmed when only two heads turned from him and toward her.

Damn, I'm losing the majority. I can feel it.

"And the focused horror of Mrs. Giordano, returning home at eleven P.M. that night and finding her daughter. The confused horror of Mr. Giordano, returning home still later to the ghastly 'circus' he described. Of flashing lights outside his home and flashing bulbs inside it. Of the puppet collection he'd lovingly helped his only daughter build since she was a baby, now framing her body on her bedroom floor. Of the army of detectives and technicians transforming his happy family life into a lurid nightmare."

The black schoolteacher yawned. Oh my God, thought Peter, cut to the car chase.

"You heard testimony with charts, showing the fingerprint on the victim's bra matching perfectly the left thumb of the defendant. Mr. Ketterson would have you believe from his testimony that his fingerprint was applied early in the evening, when he helped Ms. Giordano fasten her bra. Now, I ask you, ladies and gentlemen" —

One of the younger women — the secretary — shot him a look of disapproval. What, "ladies and gentlemen" was pissing her off?

"I ask you, is it more credible that the finger-print was applied *early* in the evening and stayed intact all through dinner *and* a horrible struggle involving some supposed other assailant when — as all witnesses there that night testified — there was no sign of forced entry? Is it not much more believable that the defendant 'applied' that fingerprint as the struggle was going on, even accidentally after the strangulation was complete?"

Oh no. The colonel is shaking his head. He's not with me.

"The defendant leaving his fingerprints . . ." Mendez felt out of sync, knew he was drifting. Have to run the risk. "And so, given especially the violence of the crime, a violence that suggests that perhaps this was not the first time that the killer performed in such —"

"Objection!" Sheilah Quinn slammed the flat of her hand onto the table so hard, it echoed like a gunshot in the otherwise torpid courtroom. "Your Honor, permission to approach?"

Peter Mendez turned to Hesterfield, but the judge was glowering at him and waving to him while scooting his own chair toward the side bar, away from the jury.

Sheilah arrived at the left-hand side of the bench — the judge's right — with Hesterfield, both waiting for the stenographer to bring over her machine and for Mendez to catch up.

As soon as everyone was gathered at the side bar, Sheilah opened her mouth, but Hesterfield raised the stop sign. Leaning over so the jury couldn't see his face, the judge's features contorted grotesquely at the prosecutor.

Mendez tried to jump in first. "Your Honor, Ms. Quinn's interruption of my —"

Hesterfield's voice was a low rumble, the jury no doubt able to pick up his tone, if not his actual words. "Mr. Mendez, I'll hear no argument from you. None! There wasn't a shred of evidence during trial that the defendant is responsible for other deaths. The only even remote connection would have been his mother's suicide, an incident that I explicitly ruled inadmissible as evidence. Ms. Quinn might be well within her rights to move here and now for a mistrial."

Sheilah thought, Hey, Rog, how about letting me make my own argument on that?

"However," continued Hesterfield, "given that we're at the closing stage of this case, I'm inclined to advise the jury to disregard that last comment, and to give them an additional corrective instruction once you're finished. And Mr. Mendez, I hope you are very nearly finished."

Sheilah would have liked to contest Hesterfield's decision, but she couldn't blame him for making it. Allowing her motion now would mean a waste of the current trial and the cost of a whole new one, with the press going after Peter Mendez, candidate for higher office, pretty doggedly for why all this had happened. On the other hand, if the jury came back with a not guilty, then there could be no appeal by the prosecution, and Mendez's gaffe would be reduced to a harmless error that would never be reviewed.

"Your Honor," said Sheilah, "I'd still like to lodge a continuing objection to the district attorney's argument. He —"

"So noted. Now, let's put this one to bed, shall we?"

Everyone went back to their places. Hesterfield instructed the jurors briefly that there was no evidence of any other crime in this case, an instruction that was technically correct but which rang hollow, given what they'd just heard from the prosecutor. Mendez finished his closing quickly, if haltingly, Hesterfield then lecturing the jury on the law and repeating the corrective instruction. Which Sheilah feared only reinforced an impression the twelve people in the box might draw: that maybe they hadn't been told all there was to know about Arthur Ketterson IV, accused murderer.

"Is it typical for us to wait like this?"

Sheilah looked at her client. They were still seated at the defense table, the bailiffs being very careful but keeping their distance to allow for confidential communication between attorney and client. Most of the audience had filed out. The homicide detectives stayed, as did the

Giordanos, and even George Lofton. The Ketterson family attorney, from one of the main-line firms, had congratulated her ("Splendid performance, very solid") before returning to his seat and opening an unrelated file, double-billing another client for his downtime in the First Session. Media representatives and retiree court-watchers were out for a smoke or drink or bathroom break, and Sheilah had noticed Peter Mendez beating a hasty retreat with them, dodging the Giordanos before the bereaved couple realized he was gone.

"Well, is it?" said Arthur.

"Typical to wait?"

"Yes."

"Most juries come back in a few hours, and Hesterfield is a judge who always wants the defendant and attorneys nearby when that happens."

"Really?"

"Really?" said Sheilah.

"Yes. A few hours seems so . . . brusque."

Brusque. Jesus, Dad, he's a weirdo for true. "Sometimes they take longer, make it look good."

Ketterson nodded. "May I say — on a somewhat different note — how good you look?"

Sheilah didn't reply.

"In front of my jury, I mean."

Sheilah continued to watch him. Before the initial client conference at the jail, when Lofton introduced them, she'd known that Ketterson

38

already had interviewed other attorneys. Some male defendants charged with a crime against a woman want a female lawyer for public-relations reasons. However, others — the Neanderthals — say to themselves, Hey, public relations is all well and good, but what if she gets her time of the month during *my* trial? Then where am I, huh?

Just seconds into her interview with Ketterson, though — in fact, the moment he had released her hand — Sheilah knew that he'd decided she was the one.

As if reading her mind, Ketterson now whispered at the defense table, "I'm so glad that you represented me during this absurd ordeal."

Sheilah said quietly, "And it's not over yet."

"When you objected during the prosecutor's closing argument, he was trying to sneak the jury something about my mother's death, wasn't he?"

"Yes."

"Do you think the jurors got that?"

"Directly, no. But the innuendo was there, and one of them will pick up on it, maybe raise it during deliberations."

"But that's so unfair."

Sheilah gave Arthur the same look she had after he'd complimented her on the closing argument. As if sensing she was tired of discussing the point, he closed his eyes for a moment, his voice changing pitch. "By the way, how is your father?"

Sheilah stared for a full five seconds. "My father?"

"Yes." Ketterson opened his eyes. "George told me that you had to put him in some sort of rest home."

Sheilah felt uneasy. "Why do you want to know this?"

A shrug. "You were being very protective of my mother's memory, and I appreciate that immensely. I just wanted to reciprocate the . . . solicitude."

Again, Ketterson had managed to throw Sheilah off balance with his combination of preppy charm and, well, old-fashioned courtesy.

"Thank you for asking, but —"

The door to Hesterfield's chambers opened, and Old Bailey shambled back into the courtroom. "His Honor says everybody can pack it in for the night."

It had taken Peter Mendez all of five minutes to cross the park to the new courthouse, where the district attorney's office had moved a month before. He made his way upstairs to the modern layout, with computer-friendly wiring behind shiny paneling, ergonomic furniture, and even a couple of showers to reflect the heightened physical conditioning of the current administration.

"Madre de Dios," said Peter, breezing by Veronica at her secretarial workstation and scooping up the paper message slips they still employed instead of voice mail. "I could use about a three-mile jog to clear the head."

"Better answer that top one first."

Veronica had drawn a red Flair arrow on the first message slip, Mort Zussman's telephone number under the arrow.

Inside his office, Mendez closed the door. Settling behind the new desk and losing himself in a cluster of computer and telecommunications devices, he hit the speed-dialer button for his campaign manager, lifting the receiver rather than putting the man on the speakerphone.

"Zussman."

"Mort, it's Peter."

"Hey-ey-ey, Petey, how's the boy?"

Talk about your old-time pols. "Been a tough morning, Mort."

"That Ketterson thing still?"

"Yeah. But we wrapped it up, so what's going on?"

"Wrapped it up? You mean you won?"

"Not yet." Mendez thought about the calculated risk he'd taken, the chance that his improper argument would win the case. Or at least hang the jury so nothing more would happen until well after the November election.

"Not yet?" said Zussman.

"Jury just started deliberating."

"Oh. When're they due back?"

A great campaign manager, but not your keenest sense of litigation. "No way of telling, Mort."

"I mean, it'd be real nice if we had something

41

positive for you to get asked about come Thursday night."

The fund-raising dinner, two days away. "I'll keep my fingers crossed."

A different tone crept into Zussman's voice. "What I mean, Petey, is something that would make people feel good about you."

No, Mort, thought Mendez, what you mean is something that will make them feel good about my chances come November. Something that would make them open their checkbooks as well as their hearts.

Veronica stuck her face inside the doorway, frowning.

"Mort, can I get back to you?"

"Nothing else hitting the fan, is there?"

"I hope not."

Hanging up, Mendez said, "What?"

The secretary looked apologetic. "The Giordanos."

Can't duck the survivors again. Reluctantly, Peter rose. "Show them in."

Veronica didn't have to.

Rhonda Giordano beat her husband through the door. Right behind her came Rudolph, the father of the victim. They were both about forty-five or so, and they gave the impression of having known each other since grade school. Actually looked a little alike, with dark curly hair, she kind of squat at about five three, he sturdy and nearly six feet, just an inch or two shorter than Peter. The woman wore a simple dress; Mendez wasn't sure if it was the same dress every day, but the Giordanos had some money, so he doubted it. And he'd seen the husband around, supervising the job site on this new building. Even in what looked to be a good suit, Peter thought, the man could never be mistaken for anything but a hard hat.

Nobody seemed interested in sitting down.

Around her handkerchief, badly smeared with makeup that used to be on her face, Rhonda Giordano said, "Oh, Mr. Mendez, that Quinn woman is just so hateful!"

"She's only doing her job, Mrs. Giordano."

"Yeah, well, how about doing your job?" said her husband.

I do not need this right now. "I thought I did, Mr. Giordano. You watched me."

"Yeah, I watched you all right. I watched you get yelled at by the judge like some third grader stepped out of line in the schoolyard."

"The judge was concerned about an implication in one of my arguments. I explained to you both how the system has to protect the defendant constitutionally from —"

"And who was protecting my baby?" Nearly a wail from the mother. "Answer me that."

"Mrs. Giordano, what happened to your daughter is a tragedy, and believe me, the homicide detectives and I have done —"

"Yeah, well, at least those guys hung around, see what'd happen. You beat it back over here."

"Mr. Giordano. I care about your case.

43

Deeply, believe me. But it's not the only one on my plate." Mendez motioned helplessly at the stacks of files already topping the new desk.

Rudolph Giordano raised his hand, pointing the index finger as though lecturing a lazy child. "Well, it's the only case 'on *our* plate,' get me? It's all my wife lives with, day in and day out. And there'd better be justice from all this."

Mended looked at both of them, knowing there was nothing further he could do. "It's in the jury's hands now."

"Yeah, well, if it'd been in my hands that night, we have a gun in our bedroom —"

"Mr. Giordano —"

"And if I'm there, the bastard's dead before we have to worry about somebody else's justice."

"Mr. —"

"Back in June, you told us that you were gonna send that baby-killer to the chair, remember?"

"I said I'd seek the death penalty, but —"

"But you lost that other case last month to this same lawyer Ketterson's got. Well, listen up: Now you got just one thing on *your* plate, too. And you'd better hope this jury comes back the right way."

"The system's not perfect, Mr. Giordano, but usually it works."

"Yeah, well, it better work for Jessica Giordano, understand? Be goddamn sure you get my wife and me justice out of all this here."

The father turned on his heel, the mother following in tow as though someone had tied a hawser around her. After they were gone, Peter Mendez slumped back into his desk chair.

It had been awhile since he'd thought of his job in terms of justice.

TWO

After the bailiffs led Arthur Ketterson away through the door at the bench end of the jury box, Sheilah Quinn slung the long strap of her briefcase over a shoulder. Outside the double swinging doors of the First Session, most of the media had evaporated, a couple of print reporters halfheartedly shouting questions at her they really didn't expect to have answered. A parapet curved around the second-floor perimeter offices, now mostly abandoned, their occupants and equipment already moved to the new courthouse. Sheilah walked along the parapet to the wide stone staircase and took that to the lobby's rotunda level.

She used the time to review a mental checklist of things to be done back in her office. Nodding to the court officer at the security desk tucked into the closeted foyer of the main entrance, Sheilah went outside and descended the wider stone steps — thirty or more of them — connecting the main entrance to the street level below. She glanced across the park to the old building's successor, nearly finished now. Sheilah had been by there many times, but only twice actually inside it, both times visiting the DA's office. To her mental checklist, she added a trip to see the new courtrooms before she actually had to appear in one for a trial. Always know an arena before you compete there.

Preserving a tradition established before Sheilah was born, the parking lot behind the old courthouse was free. Her car, a red Mazda Miata convertible, sat sprightly in the row of those who, like her, had arrived prior to the convening of court that morning. Since it was only half a mile from her office to the courthouse, Sheilah often would walk the distance for both exercise and — given the traffic patterns — speed. But it was over four miles from her apartment building to the courthouse complex, and so she'd come in by car that morning for the Ketterson trial.

Driving a little five-speed toy. One of the few pleasures I've had these last few months, what with Dad and his . . . No. No, shake that off, girl. Doesn't help anybody.

The Miata started right away, an even hum the only engine noise. After ten minutes of bumper-to-bumper, her office building came up on the left, just before the shops in Bing Square.

Sheilah and Etta Yemelman, the retired judge for whom she'd clerked right out of law school and with whom she now shared a suite, each enjoyed a reserved space on the side of the building, though Etta's was always empty. Sheilah repressed a smile as she pulled in, thinking of the older woman's belief that it was ecologically unsound to drive when the subway system — straddling the city like a daddy longlegs — was so efficient.

The elevator moved slowly, as usual, but whisper-quiet as it opened on Sheilah's floor, the suite door down the hall open. Sheilah and Etta both thought their door onto the corridor should be closed whenever possible, less for security and more for appearances. However, their secretary, Krissie Newton, complained she was "going, like, brain-dead from the lack of cross vent, you know?" A little rough around the edges, Krissie, but a whiz with computer technology and, for a twenty-year-old, remarkably good in handling the wide variety of clients Sheilah's and Etta's diverse practices attracted. To avoid losing her, they'd conceded the door point months ago.

Krissie was clacking away on her computer keyboard. One of Etta's long inter vivos trust agreements, from the single paragraph sprawling over the screen. Sheilah was computer-competent for legal research and word processing — at least the initial creation of documents, if not the final formatting. But Etta was old school, and so Krissie had on the desk in front of her an equally old-school tabbed Rolodex so that the retired judge could find an address and phone number without having to take an "ax to that burping piece of electronic shit."

Ever notice, thought Sheilah, that every "progressive" person has an Achilles' heel about some aspect of progress?

Krissie looked up from her keyboard. Squarish face, big eyes, and hair the color of breakfast biscuits, cut in layers that showed off three rings through her right ear and a single pendant hanging from her left. "So, did you, like, bring them to their knees?"

"Jury hasn't come back yet." Sheilah picked up the small stack of phone messages on the left side of the reception desk, the pink slips another concession to Etta's refusal to join the twentieth century. "These all of them?"

Krissie went back to the computer. "What, you want *more* work to do?"

Etta's door in the right corner of the suite was closed. Sheilah glanced at the telephone console, one of the older lawyer's two lines glowing red, then walked toward her own office in the left corner. Both attorneys had offices the same size, Etta feeling strongly that "equality breeds quality" in any operation, legal or otherwise. In fact, probably the major reason they had settled on this suite as Etta retired from the bench and Sheilah relocated was that the offices were mirror images of each other. As the more senior player, though, Etta had slightly the better view, a sweep up the street toward the old courthouse, while Sheilah faced a skyscraper and the Bing Square subway station several blocks farther down.

Sheilah dropped her briefcase on the floor at the side of her desk and clicked on her computer, the screen blooming into the animated opening of a rose. Before she could sit, her phone began bleating, and she called out to Krissie, "Who?"

"Him," said Krissie, stretching the word into two syllables with a lilt at the end.

Smiling, Sheilah used the toe of her right foot to kick the door shut as she picked up the receiver. "Hi."

"Congratulations on a good job today."

She made her way behind the desk and sat down. "Haven't won yet."

"And here's hoping you don't. But you still did a good job."

"So did you."

"Thanks, I think. Look, I'm a little pressed here. We still on for the weekend?"

"Unless."

A quieting of the voice. "Your dad?"

"No." Sheilah forced her own voice to mask what was in her heart about the man who'd raised her. "I mean, I guess that's always possible, but I'm going to stop by and see him tonight."

"Then what's the 'unless' part?"

"Maybe the jurors won't return a verdict in *Ketterson.*"

"A verdict? Sheilah, it's Tuesday. You don't think they'll be back by Friday?"

"I think they will be. That doesn't mean it's a lock."

"Well, even if they're not, let's go anyway."

"Right, and have both of us be reachable at the same number if there's a verdict over the weekend?"

A pause from his end. "You make a good point, but —"

"Let me make another. If I win this trial, the weekend's my treat."

"You're on a contingency fee?"

"We both know that would be unethical in a criminal case. I just mean, if I win, I should treat us."

"Does that mean I'll have to repay you with sexual favors?"

Sheilah tried to growl deep in her throat but came off coughing.

"Sheil, you okay?"

"Yes . . . just got something . . . caught in my throat."

"Maybe we should save that kind of thing for this weekend."

"Stop. . . ."

"Okay, okay. I'll be pulling for a verdict, just not in your client's favor."

Sheilah coughed again. "Get back in touch on Friday."

"You know I will. 'Bye."

Sheilah hung up, feeling her toes curl a little inside the medium-heel shoes.

Old Bailey stuck his head through the chambers door. "Everything okay, Your Honor?"

Roger Hesterfield looked up from his desk, making no effort to hide the crystal tumbler, nor to cover how little was left of the several amber ounces he'd poured into it not five minutes before. "Fine, O.B." Hesterfield glanced at the clock on his wall. "Closing up?"

The bailiff nodded but seemed uncertain. "You leaving, too?"

Hesterfield thought about visiting the country club, the mindless banter like a vaudeville show held over too long in the same town. Then he thought of his empty house, where there'd be no show at all that the cable box didn't provide.

Hesterfield realized Old Bailey was watching him, a strange expression on the court officer's face. The judge held up the scotch, which caught the day's fading light through his window, firing the liquid with a translucent glory. "I think I'll sit awhile longer, O.B. Rushing the Glenfiddich tends to bruise it, you know."

The bailiff nodded again, even more uncertain as he closed the chambers door.

"So, when are you gonna let me in on who he is?"

Sheilah looked up at Etta Yemelman standing against the doorjamb, her hip cocked and her arms folded across her chest. Etta's face was creased with the worry lines of deciding litigants' fates and the years since burying a loving husband, but her white hair was cut in a stylish helmet and her body, framed by benevolent genes on the thin side, still carried almost no excess fat.

Sheilah put the next message slip back on her desk. "Who?"

"Who? Who? The mystery man, that's who." Etta glanced behind her, then coarsened her voice before saying softly, " 'Hehimmm.' "

Sheilah laughed. "Krissie doesn't know. You don't know. Nobody knows."

Etta dropped her arms to her side, coming into the office far enough to rest one hand on the top of a client's chair. "All right, it's a state secret, and you can't trust your closest colleague with the information. I understand."

The "I'm only your surrogate mother" guilt voice. "Etta, when it's time to tell you, I'll tell you."

"And it's not time yet?"

"No."

A sigh. "Just so he's ringing the right chimes for you."

"Aren't we the salty one."

"Salty. That's a good word. My Irv — may he rest in God's peace — when we'd . . . Well, let's just say he used to call me that and worse." Etta's look became motherly, too, but now showed real concern. "Which also reminds me — I haven't been by to see your father in awhile. How's he doing?"

Third person to ask me that today, Sheilah thought, quickly dismissing the first, Arthur Ketterson, from her mind. "He has good days and bad ones. I'm going to see him before heading home tonight."

A nod. "Give Jack my best." Etta moved toward the door. "I'm on my way out, too."

"You don't mind riding in a fossil-fuel, air-polluting private vehicle, we could see my dad together."

The older woman stopped but didn't turn around. "Sorry, prior commitment."

Sheilah smiled. "I've been noticing you bugging out a little early on Tuesdays and Thursdays."

Over her shoulder, she replied, "So?"

"So *you* wouldn't have somebody on the side that *I* don't know about, would you?"

"At my age, Sheilah, I had somebody on the side, everybody would know about him. Give your father a hug for me, huh?"

Trying to picture hugging Jack Quinn as he was now, Sheilah found one more thing to put out of her mind.

"You want to know where was I?" replied Rudolph Giordano.

"Yes," said his wife. "Where were you?"

Her husband got into the driver's side of the Cadillac Coupe de Ville and pulled on the calf-skin driving gloves he favored, regardless of the season. "I told you when we left that DA jerk — I had some questions to ask Nick."

"The day our daughter's killer ought to be condemned, you're asking your construction foreman about toggle bolts?"

Turning the key in the ignition, Rudy shook his head, trying to keep his temper. Toggle bolts. Where'd she remember those from — that parking-garage project years ago? And then forgets me sitting next to her in a courtroom the last two weeks, holding her hand while poor Nick tried to juggle both the on-site and the admin for the new courthouse. I mean, process the change orders, haggle over the punch list, rush back-ordered items from suppliers who couldn't give a flying fuck I got a delay-damages clause in my contract with the county commissioners.

Rudy shook his head some more. Nick was a good guy on-site — one of the best — but he liked to build things, not play office, too. The admin was Rudy's job, except for the renovation stuff he liked to take on himself. Work with the old things, maybe even transplant them to a new place, give some old craftsman's handiwork a new lease on life, you know?

"So?" said Rhonda.

"So it wasn't toggle bolts. It was the million and one things that've gone sour since this farce of a trial started."

Rhonda turned away, facing the windshield now, a hankie dabbing at the corners of her eyes. Left, right, left, right. Rudy turned his head toward the traffic, too, pulling out toward their house in a part of the city still within the boundaries but as suburban as you could get. Rudy liked the house — hell, built it for himself and Rhonda and . . . He always thought of Jessica as "the baby," even though his daughter was already seven when he started excavating toward pouring the foundation. They'd never had any other kids, so Jessica would always be "the baby." His baby.

"You don't have to yell at me," said Rhonda.

Rudy took a breath. "Look, I'm sorry, okay? It's just . . . this hasn't been easy on me, neither." Try to change the subject. "How about we go out for some dinner, get our minds off things for awhile?"

He could feel his wife swiveling her head toward him, knew he'd said the wrong thing the instant it was out of his mouth.

"I can't go to a restaurant in this condition. And I can't cook, either."

Which meant the same routine for tonight as every other night. I drop Rhonda off at the house, go get us some takeout — you ever stop to think about it, after enough nights in a row, there aren't a whole lot of really different things *to* take out? Then, by the time I'm home with the food, she'll have the photo albums on her lap, the ones of the baby from all the way back to the shots in the maternity ward at the hospital. I'd lay money on it.

Rudy said, "What kind of takeout you want tonight?"

"Doesn't matter. Just be sure it's not something that'll slop all over the pictures."

The photo albums again. What'd I tell you? I built my baby the puppet collection, but you don't catch me going up . . . No. No, it's like a knife through the heart, thinking about that.

Rudy just shook his head some more, not

saying anything as he steered the Caddy toward home.

At her office desk, Sheilah adjusted the strap of the briefcase on her shoulder, the bag mercifully lighter without the Ketterson file in it.

Okay, mental checklist again. Returned phone calls . . . went over pocket calendar . . . made note of the research to start tomorrow on the computer so I can get away for the weekend, assuming the jury comes back by Friday. Which reminds me of something I forgot to ask Etta before she left.

Krissie was clicking off her computer's power button and bending over the lower right drawer of her desk. A flashy dresser and good-looking in a baby-fat sort of way, the young secretary was as quiet about her social life as Sheilah was about her own.

"Krissie, do you know if Etta's going to be around this weekend?"

"She had me make a reservation on Amtrak for New York."

Sheilah thought about that. "One person, or two?"

Krissie paused, straightening up from the drawer and holding her handbag. "I'm thinking Etta'd for sure want that kept confidential, don't you?"

Sheilah had to smile. A little rough around the edges, "for sure," but Krissie really was a treasure, protecting her bosses even from themselves. "Fair enough. It's just that I might be going away, too, and somebody has to feed Quigley."

"You stocked up on cat food?"

"Plenty, in baskets by my kitchen counter."

"Then not a problem. I can do it."

"You sure?"

Krissie opened her handbag, fishing off the snap clatch a set of two keys on a ring with a little white tab attached to it. "Still got your keys from that Caribbean vacation you took last winter."

"You sure those are mine?"

Krissie sighed heavily, dangling them in front of her. "See?"

Sheilah read the initials S.Q. on the tab, frowning.

"Now what's the matter?" said Krissie.

"I'm not sure if you should have that attached to them."

Krissie looked down. "The tag's so I can keep your keys straight from my mom's and my sister's and my —"

"I mean, someone else might know, too."

Krissie sighed more heavily. "They're just your initials, right?"

"Right."

"No real name. No address. No nothing, right?"

"Right."

"So," said Krissie, putting the key ring back on the clatch, "like who's gonna know from initials?"

THREE

A game show, thought Arthur Ketterson IV, shaking his head stoically. My future — my life — rests in the hands of twelve people I've never met, and tonight I'll have to endure a . . .

Arthur could hear squeals of video joy and audience cheering as a young deputy sheriff named Vinnie — or Timmy, or some such ethnic nickname — led him through the double-trap barred doors and back into the county jail's Administrative Housing Control Unit. Which was just a euphemistic elaboration of *cell block* for the alleged perpetrators of capital crimes.

Arthur's immaculate flannel suit, custom-tailored at Harrod's on his last trip to London, had to be left in the "court-clothes closet" on the "civilian" side of the "trap" — is there any bureaucracy in the world that doesn't have its own idiosyncratic argot? As always, the guard had coughed impatiently while Arthur carefully fitted the plastic cleaner's bag over the hanger to protect the material from the other garments of more questionable pedigree around it in the closet.

According to Sheilah, the sheriff's office usually allowed a defendant but two sets of court

clothes. However, George Lofton had interceded with some functionary and won Arthur
the modest dispensation of having three outfits
in his rotating wardrobe.

Arthur now wore a cotton jumpsuit,
short-sleeved and without pockets. The color
code of red showed he was no longer a recent
arrival (tan) or a nonviolent pretrial detainee
(powder blue) or a convicted and sentenced
offender (green), but, rather, Admin Unit.

Situated on the top floor of the new courthouse building, the unit's capacity was twelve,
and it currently held seven inmates (the word
prisoner being frowned upon for some reason
Arthur couldn't fathom). Each inmate had his
own cell on the long north side of the building,
the interior bars facing the opposite, south, wall
of the corridor. Arthur had asked several times if
there were any female offenders in residence,
but he had never received a civil answer to the
question.

Each cell had a single steel bunk on the west
wall and a stainless-steel sink and hopper on the
east wall. A narrow window fashioned from
some sort of plastic offered a dismal view of
industrial squalor until the air pollution blurred
against the horizon. The window had vertical
bars designed to mimic Levolor blinds, a writing
surface jutting out below, with one plastic chair
for the correspondence-minded. Frankly, given
the stories he'd heard about homosexual rape in
correctional institutions, Arthur wasn't sorry

about the solitary-confinement aspect of the sleeping arrangements. But trust a governmental contractor like pig Giordano pater to put the only window on the north wall, not appreciating the aesthetic mien that southern exposure might have lent to the surroundings.

The guard walked Arthur down the corridor, past the cell of one Willie T. Eggers and the three widely spaced television monitors mounted on the south wall. The door to his own cell slid open and Arthur entered. As it clanged shut, he said, "I take it I've missed the community vote on tonight's entertainment options?"

The deputy said nothing, but Arthur really didn't expect an answer to that question, either. And even if he'd received one, it wouldn't have mattered. His own vote hardly mattered. Seven inmates in the unit meant seven votes, and his the only educated mind in the lot.

All three video monitors carried the same programming, and guess what options carried the day. The Weather Channel? Irrelevant to life "on the inside." Headline News? Only by rare accident. No, in the Admin Unit, the screens were filled with soap operas, followed by talk shows, followed by endless and mindless game shows, like the one on now.

Arthur suspected that half the talk shows were rigged somehow, actors and actresses slyly recruited to play the roles of the ridiculous cretins appearing on them. However, at least they offered a certain bizarre variety. The game shows, on the other hand, were mind-numbing in their redundancy, and only Willie would vote with him for *Jeopardy*, both of them losing out to some pap in which a vapid housewife might win a washer/dryer "combo" to the enthusiastic response of the Admin Unit's appreciative "home" audience.

As the guard turned to go, Arthur said, "I haven't eaten, you know."

"You missed chow."

"I was before a judge. Specifically, the Honorable Roger Hesterfield. And there is an equally specific institutional regulation requiring the staff to serve out of order an inmate 'detained by court appearance.'"

The deputy wavered, and Arthur was again amazed at how quickly he'd mastered the ways of "jailing." Thanks, in part, to the aforementioned Willie.

The guard said, "I'll see what I can do."

Which meant not only would the food be late and cold but probably not even the meager fare Arthur had come to expect. Pork chops on Monday, beef stew on Tuesday, and liver — *liver!* The week's menu was enough to make one retch. At least the beef stew ought to be warmable, if there was any left. However, an establishment that served its major meal of the day at 5:00 P.M. certainly wasn't to be trusted on any other aspect of culinary planning.

Stretching out along his bunk, Arthur settled in with one of the novels that George Lofton had persuaded a publisher friend to send to the jail for him. The only outside goods allowed in the Administrative Unit were those shipped directly from the publishers involved — fear of a "file in the cake" ploy, presumably — but fortunately, George's friend was at a house that did a lot of mainstream fiction, biographies, and books on "women's issues."

Arthur didn't especially enjoy books in that last category, but he felt honor-bound to read some of them. It was part of the obligation he had welcomed every day for countless years. No, not countless. Fifteen, to be precise. Ever since the night his mother had told him of her cancer. When he realized what she was obliquely requesting him to do for her.

For *her*. Which was exactly how Arthur had lived each day since. Partially, at least.

For his mother.

Jack Quinn gripped the M1 tightly, his muscles having developed since basic training to the point that the steel pot on his head felt almost natural, even in the pitching, yawing landing craft. Then the man to Jack's left threw up. You couldn't hear it over the artillery barrage from the navy's big guns farther out in the Channel, but you sure could see it, all over the backpack of the GI in front of him. Jack swallowed hard, thinking to himself, Jesus, and this'll probably be the best part of the day.

Then a German shell from an emplacement somewhere above Omaha Beach howled like a banshee over head, sparing his platoon for at least a few more seconds. As the landing craft chugged through the choppy water, you could feel things bumping against the metal sides, wreckage from prior waves of men and equipment that never made it to the sand. Jack swallowed harder.

Then suddenly somebody was yelling behind him, and the ramp of the landing craft fell forward in front of him. The first rank of soldiers plunged ahead, disappearing as the second joined them, and then everybody was just pushing forward, every mortal soul wanting to get the hell off the tin —

And Jack was in the water, almost over his head, floundering from the weight of the gear, the stench of oil and blood and somehow something even worse in every mouthfull of salty liquid he inhaled and sputtered to spit out. Bullets rained on the surface all around him, making that peculiar, awful sound somewhere between a whistle and a hiss. And worse sounds from the wounded men drowning around him, drowning among the bobbing corpses.

"Dad?"

And then Jack was stumbling over a dead GI, and another, but stumbling on sand. Dry land, sort of, if you didn't count the blood seeping downward. He fell forward, the ground quaking from the seismic rumbles of the big German guns. Jesus, have to get away from the waterline, have to reach the cliffs to make it. And he got up and somehow kept his legs moving, the boots churning through the sand until he got far enough —

"Dad?"

What the hell? A woman's voice. And a woman's hand on his arm, the fingernails on the hand all trimmed with care and painted with some color polish he'd never —

The hell was a manicured woman doing on Omaha Beach, 6 June 1944?

At some point during a particularly slow-moving passage in the novel, Arthur became aware that a nature show had come on the air. There were some questionable regulations about the programming that inmates could choose, but fortunately many of them enjoyed entries such as *World of Survival* and *National Geographic*. Arthur closed the book and watched the monitor, the screen depicting first a lioness stalking an antelope, then the parallels of a house cat stalking a mouse. Most surprising, the show then segued to a "community" of chimpanzees, remarkably humanoid in their social structures and strictures. Including the propensity of young males to act in concert to isolate and then ambush some smaller monkeys, unfortunates from a genus named *Colobus*. Arthur watched, fascinated, as the male chimps tore one trapped colobus literally limb from limb, then offered the gory pickings to female chimps in exchange for sexual favors.

And they accuse me of "extreme atrocity and cruelty," Arthur thought. He tried to tune out the exhortations of his fellow inmates, many of whom, he thought, rather resembled the

65

courting males on the screen.

Eventually, the nature show ended, followed by some sort of thunderous and chaotic automobile racing involving what appeared to be go-carts with metal scoops as their roofs. Arthur returned to his novel. There would be no further "entertainment" worthy of the name this night.

At least not until after lights-out.

For the third time, Sheilah Quinn said, "Dad?"

Behind her, in the doorway to the room, Lucille Wesley spoke in a quiet voice. "Jack been like that most of the last two days now, child."

Sheilah stayed seated on the edge of the bed, but she let go of her father's left arm and turned toward the stolid black woman. Wesley had processed hair that ranged in shade from brown to honey, the small curls and smaller kinks lying almost flat against her head. A bulldog in a starched pink uniform, her features were imposing until she gave you her warm smile, the gold teeth catching lamplight in a way that sent a sparkle from her mouth. Sheilah had come to think of Lucille as her father's personal aide, even though Valley Nursing Home didn't assign staffers to particular residents. Jack was the "resident" and Sheilah the "customer," paying five thousand dollars every thirty days, in advance on the first of each month.

"Like what, Lucille?" said Sheilah, placing the

nurse's call button on its cable near her father's head so that he wouldn't reflexively push it and unnecessarily summon another harried night-shift attendant.

"Hard to rouse up once he be sleeping a time. I think he going back."

"Going back?"

"To other times, other places in his life. They do that, old peoples like Jack. They go back, maybe to happy times, make them feel good. Or exciting times, make them feel important."

Sheilah nodded tentatively, then turned back to her father.

"God, Dad, but you look so worn-down."

The black hair she remembered as glossy and thick — "I'm black Irish, Sheilah, descended from the Spanish sailors that shipwrecked off the Armada and intermarried with our people. Never forget that." And she hadn't. But his hair was now barely wispy, the age spots on his scalp showing through beneath individual strands. Jack Quinn's forehead was lined, less from pain, Sheilah thought (or hoped), and more from frustration over the stroke. The furrows under his eyes were deep and almost blue, as though tears had eroded the flesh from that part of his face. The stroke had taken Jack's speech and most of his motor skills, only the left hand still retaining a minimal dexterity, just enough to press the nurse's call button. Or to communicate face-to-face in crude code. The index finger would tap against the sheets, once for yes and twice for no, if asked a leading question —

Jesus, girl, you can take the lawyer out of the courtroom, but . . .

Sheilah laid her hand once more on his left forearm, shaking it gently. "Dad? Dad?"

And then Jack Quinn opened his eyes, the lids managing to shed thirty years and their aggregate toll on body and spirit, and the man lying in the bed was almost Sheilah's father again.

"Welcome back," she said, smiling.

His lips only twitched, but the eyes smiled for them.

"Are you feeling okay?"

The left forefinger tapped once against the bed sheets.

"No pain, Dad?"

Two taps.

"You sure?"

One.

"That's good. Did you enjoy dinner tonight?"

Two taps, but the eyes were smiling.

From the doorway, Lucille said, "Jack, you tell your daughter now. The cooking in this place is better from what they give you in the army, right?"

One tap, and the eyes somehow shrugged, as if to say, Small compliment.

Sheilah smiled, then looked back at Lucille and nodded. The "customer" really appreciated the way Lucille catered to her father, but over the months, Sheilah's backward look and nod had become the unspoken signal that the

68

daughter would like a little private time with her father.

"Well, I be leaving you peoples alone, catch up on things. Child, you ring that button, you need me."

"I will."

"And Jack, sweet dreams now."

One tap and a cast of the eyes toward the door as Lucille closed it behind her.

Sheilah waited until she had her father's undivided attention again. "The Ketterson trial's almost over, Dad. We closed this afternoon, and the jury's still out. They'll resume deliberations tomorrow."

Jack's eyes asked her the question.

"I've certainly seen stronger cases, but I've seen weaker, too. Could go either way."

His eyes asked a different question.

"Do I think Ketterson did it, you mean?"

A single tap.

Sheilah tried to frame an honest answer, found there was only one she could give. "I don't know."

"Fifteen minutes," boomed the guard's voice. "They're out in fifteen."

Arthur Ketterson sighed deeply, skimming through the current chapter in the vain hope that something — *any*thing — might happen in the characters' lives. But no such luck.

Marking his place with a sliver of toilet paper (he couldn't stand to dog-ear the pages of even a bad novel), Arthur placed it on the writing surface behind him and waited until he could no longer hear the guard's footsteps in the corridor. Then he said quietly, "Willie?"

No answer.

As quietly, but more insistently, Arthur whispered, "Oh Willie?"

The voice came back at him. "Not till the light's gone, man. Bull might be back while's he can see, but not once it's all dark and the night demons come out, bite his little white-bread dick off for him."

The "night demons"? A pity Mr. Willie T. Eggers never made it through grammar school, thought Arthur. He'd give Koontz and King a real run for their money.

Ah, well. Fifteen minutes wasn't that long, was it?

Lucille Wesley measured out the last bit of her midshift break, sipping decaf from a mug in the staff lounge.

She tried to rest as comfortably as possible in one of the plastic chairs the home must have gotten some kind of deal on, since they sure bought enough of them. Down the table from her, Orville sat slump-shouldered in another of the chairs, a cigarette at the corner of his mouth doing little bitty nip-ups every time he sucked some of that poison down into his lungs.

Man's just a janitor, not an aide, but he still ought to know better than to mess with those things. Stringy dishwater hair and enough pimples on his face, a body'd think he was farming for them. Look at him now, trying to read that printed paper on the table, a foot in front of his eyes, lips moving as he sound out some of the words in between puffs of smoke from the cigarette and swigs of Mountain Dew from a can.

I know that paper be a racing form, account of that's all Orville ever read, white trash that he is. Just like that no-account Willie T. Eggers I used to take to my bed, back when I worked at Mercy Hospital. What could I have been thinking of? Well, I guess I know what I was thinking of, but that was before the Good Lord saved me. And I heard somebody say Willie was back in the jail, for killing two womens like he might have killed me, I didn't find Jesus first.

Lucille noticed Orville reaching down to scratch himself around the crotch. Scratch longer than he had to, strictly speaking.

She glanced away. Lucille also knew Orville liked working the night shift for two reasons. One was that it let him shag his sorry butt over to the racetrack during the day, where he could insult the fresh air and sunshine with his cigarettes while he did his gambling and other sinning against the Good Lord's way. The second reason Orville liked the night shift, Lucille didn't want to think on, account of what he might do around a resident who passed away without other people's being there, protect the poor soul's things.

That reminded Lucille of something she did like to think on, that brave old soldier, Jack, and his good daughter, Sheilah. The last few weeks, Lucille had been composing what she'd say to that child, hoping her words would carry the meaning she wanted them to have. The meaning that Jack wasn't going to be around all that much longer, so there wasn't no need to —

At the other end of the table, Orville belched like a blast furnace, not even bothering to cover his mouth or say an "Excuse me." White trash.

Lucille sipped some more decaf. No, I done learned to see the end coming in the eyes of the old ones over the years, learned to see it better than any machine. Or any doctor, for that matter. They get a look in their eyes, the old ones do, a look that say they been back in time, spending some of their last days on this earth in the company of the peoples and times they remember as special. They knowed the Good Lord was coming to take them, and they shared it with you, you knew what to watch for.

Lucille glanced up at the clock. Her fifteen-minute break was gone. Orville now, he was in his chair when she got there, and he'd be there when she was gone. But Lucille wasn't a supervisor, and just because Orville didn't do his job right didn't mean she wouldn't do hers.

Heaving herself out of the plastic chair, Lucille Wesley moved to the sink and washed out her cup.

The corridor and every cell darkened. The way night must fall on the moon, Arthur remembered thinking his first evening in the unit.

He said, "Do you feel safe now, Willie?"

"Night demons don't bother me none, but they just love white-bread ass like yours."

A real charmer, Willie T. Eggers, in the Admin Unit for beating his wife and her sister to death. So far as Arthur understood it, the man and his spouse had completed their nightly ritual of animalistic sexual satisfaction and were engaged in recurrent recriminations when Willie simply began to beat the woman with an empty liquor bottle, the contents of which they had managed to drain earlier in the evening. The contents were probably suspect, but the bottle must have been engineered like the nose cone of a rocket, because it didn't break even after Eggers had fractured the poor woman's skull in numerous places and then did the same to the sister when she attempted to intervene.

Willie had approached Arthur the first time they and the other Admin Unit inmates were in the exercise yard under the watchful eyes of three guards. Eggers suggested that Arthur might want to learn "how to jail from somebody knowed the ropes, seeing as your white ass is likely to be in county for a while and maybe the big yard for a good while longer after that." While Arthur did not like to think in those terms, he had readily agreed that he could use the tutoring of someone schooled in this particular art, and was neither offended nor shocked by the money Willie expected Arthur to arrange confidentially for the support of the three children he'd had with his dead wife and the two born without benefit of wedlock to her dead sister. The total was a paltry five hundred per month, which Arthur instructed George Lofton to pay by postal order per Eggers's instructions, no one in the extended family apparently having a checking account to receive more typical deposits. In exchange for the payments, Willie had instructed nightly on the finer points of jailing until Arthur himself had heard enough. That was when he'd told his tutor that the postal money orders would be stopping unless the curriculum moved on to other skills, as well.

"So, Willie," said Arthur in his reedy voice, "what can you teach me tonight?"

"I'm seeing a guy, Dad."

Jack Quinn was frustrated, finding it hard to follow his daughter's thoughts for some reason. Maybe it was him — Jesus knows, he was losing his grip in more ways than one. Just try having all kinds of thoughts, all day long, and dreams you remember when you wake up like you'd been living them — not just dreaming them — and then have nobody to tell them to unless the person asked you just the right question, yes or no. *Frustrated* just didn't cover the waterfront, nossir.

74

Sheilah had finished with the story of the murder suspect she was defending, the type of practice she'd developed never sitting well with Jack and him telling her so plenty of times before his stroke. "Thank God your mother isn't here to see you defending killers and rapists," he'd say, though he hadn't really meant it.

The part about Sheilah's mother not being there, that is.

And not just because his wife would be another caller in this room. Jack knew how hard visiting him had to be on Sheilah, that one and only baby born to them in middle age, long after they'd given up hope of conceiving one. Jesus the poor girl was here nearly every day. At least, that's what he thought, his count on the days not being so reliable since the stroke. And except for that colored woman, Lucille, nobody else in the place gave a damn about him. He wished that Sheilah hadn't had to sell his old house to help pay for his care at Valley, wished that Lucille could somehow have been hired to look after him in his own living room, sitting in his own chair in front of his own TV. Maybe even rest in the shade of the apple tree in his own small yard on the nice days. And tuck him into bed at night like the helpless little kid he'd become again.

But those thoughts were more childish still. Sheilah's mother was gone, and his house was gone, and the colored woman Lucille worked only part of the day and had to have a life of her own somewhere. Everybody should have a real life.

"So, even with all that, I think you'd like him, Dad."

Jack Quinn wanted to use his eyes, ask who the hell Sheilah was talking about now, but that would show her he hadn't been paying attention, and Jack Quinn hated to do that to her — how hard it must be for his daughter the trial lawyer to come visiting him at all. So he just lay there, spacing out the taps with his left forefinger until Sheilah leaned over and kissed him on the forehead. Then she replaced the nurse's call thing in his palm so Jack could get Lucille to come running, if he needed her.

Had to give Lucille credit that way. She wasn't a small woman, but she *would* come running. Lucille cared about her job, cared more than most he'd ever met. And Jack Quinn had met his share of people who had important jobs to do, especially in the service.

Which reminded him — he'd never told anyone about what happened in the war. It was the part of his life that made Jack the most proud, but he'd never told his wife or his daughter about it when he could, and now that the stroke meant he couldn't, Jack kind of wished he had. The things he'd seen, they shouldn't all die with —

Jack Quinn suddenly realized Sheilah wasn't sitting on the edge of his bed anymore. Taking a breath, he closed his eyes, and a single tear rolled down the length of his nose and onto his upper lip, quivering there before dropping down upon his tongue, the taste like . . . seawater.

Bullets rained on the surface all around him, making that peculiar, awful . . .

"I tells you how to hot-wire a car?"

"You did, Willie."

"How about getting your white-bread ass past a burglar alarm?"

"Ditto."

"Say what?"

"Yes, Willie, you told me about the alarm trick, too."

A pause. Eggers's memory patterns were scrambled, Arthur certain that the defect resulted from some sort of substance abuse.

"I tells you the way to know did a bank teller step on her panic button?"

"No, Willie," said Arthur, finally perking up. "No, you haven't."

"Well, then, listen up, white bread, you gonna learn something." Eggers shifted around on the other side of the darkness. "Most people figure, you watch the bitch's eyes. Those eyes, they gonna stay on you the whole time, account of that's how they be taught in like bank-teller school, you hear what I'm saying?"

"I hear you, Willie."

"That mean you watch the bitch's eyes, you gonna get fooled, think she just so scared, she gonna go along with whatever you say. So instead, you gots to watch her nose."

"Her nose?"

"Right, right. She go to press the button with her foot, her nose gonna get bigger."

Not the jungle's most articulate émigré, Arthur thought, but with a little prompting, really quite a talent for teaching. "Like Pinocchio, you mean?"

"Say what?"

Slowly, Arthur said, "The woman's nose gets longer, as though she's telling a lie?"

"The fuck you saying, man?" A pause from the adjoining cell, Willie clearly being thrown by all this. "Don't nobody's nose ever get longer."

"Then what *do* you mean?"

"I mean, the holes in the bitch's nose, they gonna get bigger, account of she gots to take in more air, pump herself up for the risk, dig?"

Ah. "You mean her nostrils will flare."

"They ain't gonna light up, man. They just gonna get bigger."

"Got it."

"All right, then. That's what you look for. Course, it don't work that way with a judge."

"A judge?"

"Them judges, they got panic buttons, too."

"Really?"

"Up there behind their benches someplace, I don't exactly know where. But I was in a courtroom for arraignment this one time, and the judge, he just have this sleepy-looking bull don't know shit about who to watch for, and this brother next to me, he all hopped up on some good smack, and he flying so high, he take a run at that bull. Well, I seed the judge move his hand some, but I just sit back, figure might's well enjoy the show, you hear what I'm saying? Then, the brother finish up with the bull and decide to try the judge, too, but before you know it, they's three different bulls in the room now, whupping the living shit out the brother before he gets up to where the judge's at."

Arthur thought about that, visualized going after Jolly Roger Hesterfield if the jury came back with an unjust verdict. But such an action surely would tie Sheilah's hands on any appeal, and he quickly discarded the otherwise-enjoyable image.

Willie said, "So, that be enough for now?"

Though the teacher couldn't see him, the student had to smile. He's like Scheherazade, thought Arthur, trying to stretch his tales over a thousand and one Arabian nights. And not even to save his own life. Just for five hundred dollars a month distributed among as many little Negro yard apes.

"No, Willie, it's not quite enough."

A snort. "Okay, here's a real good one, then. You know how to kill a body so's it look like a heart attack?"

"No," Arthur said, sitting up as well as perking up this time. "No, but it sounds good."

"You got that right. This nurse bitch Lucille I used to hump, she tell me about it once. She seed it happen in that Mercy Hospital where she work."

"Seen what happen, Willie?"

"Well, first thing, you got to get this nice fluffy pillow, dig?"

Leaving her father's room, Sheilah walked toward the home's lobby, the corridor heavy with the cloying scents of disinfectant and air freshener. Small improvement over the smells they were intended to mask.

A handrail ran the length of the corridor wall, stopping only at the doorways to individual rooms. When Sheilah had come by during the day on weekends, she would see some residents moving slowly along that rail, like skiers clutching an old-fashioned rope lift, waiting for their turn to go down the mountain. Others would scuff along in wheelchairs or shuffle along with the aid of walkers. Most would wear mismatched outfits, dressed haphazardly by the staff from whatever was passably clean in the elder's bureau. Their facial expressions would break your heart if you looked at them long enough.

Sheilah had learned not to look long at all.

Passing the rooms, she could hear night noises coming from many of them. Snoring and coughing, moaning and whimpering, even the unmistakable sound of some poor soul evacuating without the echoing sound of toilet or bedpan.

Sheilah walked a little faster.

In the lobby, she gave a weary wave to the brown-shirted security guard behind the office window. He was reading a magazine and didn't wave back, possibly wasn't even aware Sheilah was there. No doubt a time once existed when Valley's visiting hours were strictly enforced, but in these days of everyone from the later generation working and trying to find time to see residents from the previous generation catch-as-catch-can, such restrictions would be bad for business.

Sheilah went through the unlocked front entrance and out into the parking lot. Put the roof down on the Miata, let the cool night air blow away the nursing home scent that clung to her hair and clothes like briers. She didn't want to think about having to drive home come winter, with the smell of the home surrounding her in the little car's cabin.

Six miles later, Sheilah turned into the reserved white-lined space behind her apartment house. Watchful of the darkness around her, she secured the convertible roof and locked the doors. Sheilah knew that, in an exceptional wink of fate, the Giordano house was only four blocks west of her place, and in the event — the *unlikely* event — that her client really hadn't killed Jessica, someone else clearly did, a crazy who might still be working the neighborhood.

Carrying her briefcase and squeezing three keys between her fingers like a medieval mace,

Sheilah walked quickly around the corner of the building and used one of the keys to open the downstairs door, waiting for it to close behind her before moving to the elevators. Pushing the button for the eighth floor, she missed the luxury of a doorman, particularly given her erratic hours, but with the monthly nut of Valley's care, that class of building was out of the question.

In fact, lots of things were out of the question. Her student loans all paid off and the law-office overhead manageable, Sheilah used to enjoy dinners out with friends, tickets to the symphony and shows, even real vacations, like her trip to the Caribbean the prior winter. But she'd bought the Miata new, just before her dad's stroke, moving to this apartment soon after. Her life had pretty much devolved into covering her cases and visiting Jack Quinn. And Sheilah wouldn't be doing much for entertainment until his situation . . . resolved itself.

The elevator opened onto the hallway outside her apartment. Sheilah knew few of her neighbors, and none of them well. Another casualty of the job and her father's condition.

She shook her head, forcing herself not to dwell on all these lost opportunities. Sheilah had Etta as staunch colleague-*cum*-surrogate mother, and Krissie to feed Quigley while Sheilah went away — okay, only for a weekend — with a man whom she was coming to love and believed loved her as well. People can have worse lives, you know? Besides, there was a time and place to deal with sorrow, and Sheilah had learned to close the door on her hurt just as she'd learned to "compartmentalize" a loss in court, sealing each watertight compartment so that losing one case didn't "sink" her performance in the next. And the next.

As Sheilah inserted the upstairs key into its lock on the apartment door, a scratching noise started near the sill. "It's okay, Quigley, just Mom."

Pushing the door over the nap of the carpet, Sheilah nearly caught one of Quigley's claws. The animal cried out, then ran three loping strides down the hallway before turning its head back to blink at her.

"I'd think a creature as clever as you are would learn by now."

Quigley, an orange-striped tabby with an enormous head, just blinked at her. Blinked the way Sheilah remembered Tom Selleck blinking out from the movie screen in *Quigley Down Under*, hence the cat's name.

"Well, wouldn't you?"

Quigley blinked again, and Sheilah suddenly realized it was the same kind of yes/no question she'd been using with her father. Shaking that off, too, Sheilah dropped her briefcase by the foyer table and moved into the kitchen.

"Who's ready for some yummies?"

Quigley bounded around the corner, skidding a little where the carpet gave way to linoleum. Sheilah noticed his ceramic food bowl

(QUIGLEY stenciled in blue on the side), real- izing that she'd forgotten to clean it that morning. After washing out the bowl and refill- ing it with dry cereal, Sheilah opened a small can of "gourmet" food for his dinner, mashing the minced beef into the dry stuff to make the best part of her cat's day last a little longer.

That done and Quigley occupied with eating, Sheilah went to the refrigerator, six ounces of chardonnay looking just right sliding down the inner surface of a wineglass. She glanced into the living room long enough to ensure that plants, furniture, and knickknacks all looked as she'd left them at 7:30 A.M.

After taking a sip from the glass, Sheilah car- ried it with her down the hall to her bedroom. Setting the wine on the night table that held her answering machine (a zero glowing in the mes- sage window), she went into the bathroom. Just as she would have liked to be in a doorman building, Sheilah would have loved a Jacuzzi- style bathtub, but she couldn't afford it, either. So she made do with a substitute that consisted of a low white platform like a small surfboard that suction-cupped to the bottom of her tub, a detachable white plastic hose running at a ninety-degree elbow angle from the platform to a small globe-shaped motor near the toilet. The whole thing had cost her less than a hundred bucks, and once turned on, it sent forced air from the motor through the hose to the platform, where holes allowed for the air to bubble up and create the illusion, if not quite the sensation, of a real spa.

Drawing hot water from the tap, Sheilah sprinkled some bath oil into the tub, the oil quickly foaming and smelling of juniper. Then she went back to the bedroom and stripped, chucking Mr. Fuzzums under the chin as she always did once she was naked. The stuffed animal was a bear, with grizzly fur now pretty much threadbare, his triangular ears poking up through slits in the brim of a derby hat. Mr. Fuzzums had been the last "girl" present Jack Quinn had given his daughter, on her ninth birthday. Sheilah remembered rolling her eyes in embarrassment, and her father had gotten the message, but secretly she loved the bear more than any of his other gifts.

Sheilah even remembered a game she and her father used to play in her parents' old house. Whenever Jack Quinn thought his daughter was oversleeping and was going to be late for school, he'd come into her room and rub Mr. Fuzzums across her face until she woke up, giggling from the tickling sensation of the synthetic fur. Then, when Sheilah was older, she'd do the same to him, get her father to drive her wherever —

No, enough of the memories for now, girl.

Back in the bathroom, Sheilah set the wineglass on the lip of the tub, knowing she should buy plastic cups for this part of the ritual but always forgetting to. Then Sheilah pictured the rest of her night. After nuking a Healthy Choice entrée in the microwave, she'd sit down to dinner in the living room, listening to some Melissa Etheridge or Annie Lennox on the CD player and enjoying a second glass of wine. Following which, she'd climb into bed, cuddling with Mr. Fuzzums and being mushed on by Quigley's front claws until she let him cuddle, too. Then she'd fall asleep, seven or so precious hours of peace before going off to battle again the next morning.

First, though, the bath I promised myself all day long during a long day indeed.

Turning off the tap, Sheilah pushed the power button on the motor and set the timer for twenty minutes, the sound of air burbling up like a hot springs behind her. Eyes closed to enhance the sensual feeling of entering the foaming water, she felt her way over the wall of the tub. An inflatable travel pillow served as makeshift headrest, and while not all of her body would fit under the surface, easing into the aeration already started to soothe her.

Eyes still closed, Sheilah let her hand find the wineglass, and she brought it to her lips, taking a deep drink. Feeling the steam rise around her cheeks, Sheilah let her muscles and nerves dissolve into the bubbling water, become part of it.

The timer on the motor beeped once at the ten-minute mark, which was the signal Sheilah had trained herself to follow. Trained herself through lost causes and shattered affairs, through a stricken dad and everything else in life that tore her to pieces each day.

And then she began to cry. For poor Jack Quinn and, to a lesser extent, for poor Sheilah, as well. Cry until her stomach hurt for the little girl, receiving her last childhood present from the father she'd loved so deeply and now was losing so slowly but so clearly.

It wasn't until Arthur Ketterson awoke with a start that he realized he'd been crying. First, he cautiously listened in the dark to the breathing noises of Willie T. Eggers and the men in the cells past him. Amazing what one can discern through the eardrums when stimuli to all other senses are cut off. Arthur had ended the lesson with Willie some time before. So far as he could tell now, all the other inmates were asleep, and none had heard him.

With a supreme effort of will, Arthur tried to recall what he'd been dreaming about that would have brought on such an episode. It couldn't have been Sheilah Quinn, because the emotion was wrong. No, it had to be some- thing —

And then he grasped the thread that, once pulled, illuminated the subconscious scene he'd been replaying. A birthday party, his ninth, he believed. Yes, yes. The present of the pony that he loathed on sight, expecting a first sailing dinghy, the Fatty Knees design, perhaps. But the mount was a present from his mother, the dearest Madeline Ketterson, and so he hid his convulsing disappointment until, in the privacy of his own bed, he could cry his eyes out with the supreme justification of the monstrously deprived.

Odd that I never felt such sadness, verging on crying, about Mother's death. Wistful, to be sure, that thrilling memory still the strongest impression of my life. But never actual . . . tears.

Wondering about that, Arthur realized he was fully awake. The night sky outside his window gave no hint of dawn, and therefore he would need some sort of release before being able to sleep again.

Easing out of the bunk, Arthur moved stealthily to the stainless-steel hopper. He began to exercises his wrists isometrically against the steel, curling and stretching and stressing them as best he could to retain that tensile strength so important to his ultimate challenge, the exhilarating joy Arthur loved best. At one point, the hopper creaked a little, and he froze, one of the men in the other cells coughing, then snorting and apparently dropping back to sleep. Shoddy construction work by pig Giordano pater was Arthur's assessment of the situation.

Finishing his exercise, he washed up birdbath-style in the sink. A man who strove for perfection in all things, Arthur felt being permitted to shower but once a day was simply insufficient, especially given Willie's "jailing right" warnings about "not dropping the soap, white bread." Arthur recalled several winks from prep school classmates in a similar context, and he felt the revulsion he always did about them wanting to touch his body in any way.

Easing back into the bunk, Arthur found himself immediately, perhaps even naturally, thinking about the provocative slut Giordano. Her request when he arrived at the house that he help fasten her brassiere. Which he did, musingly, not being able to see how that could possibly come back to haunt him. No, to be fair, not even thinking about it. Then what she suggested later — No, it was simply too frustrating to think about her, in any context.

However, thoughts of Jessica Giordano necessarily brought back memories of the young women who had testified *for* him at trial, two coming through nicely, emphasizing what a gentleman he was. But then the third, the one he had actually paid to fly in from Seattle, testifying that Arthur had been so polite to her while they were seeing each other that she'd wondered, just fleetingly, if he might be gay. Arthur Ketterson IV, a homosexual, of all things.

No, said Arthur to himself, and firmly. No more thoughts of that witness. Better to think of the ones who satisfied him, the ones he painstakingly — and lovingly — scouted, selected, and stalked before . . . enjoying. Arthur had intended to review them slowly, and in order, but he found his wrists flexing in the manner he trained them toward, and his sexual tension could not survive merely the memory of his first woman, his own dear mother so many years ago. The look on her face, in her *eyes,* when she realized what he was doing with —

Arthur suddenly found himself all wet and sticky, so he moved stealthily once again, but this time to the sink. Performing a modest hygiene, he slipped back into bed, his body telling him that it was now ready to resume sleeping.

Just before dropping off, though, Arthur Ketterson allowed himself just the most controlled of hopes. A hope that, thanks to Sheilah Quinn's good offices, he would be free to enjoy many more such women in the years to come.

Starting with Sheilah herself, of course.

FOUR

District Attorney Peter Mendez had a headache. Only 9:30 on Friday morning, but a real screamer. "Like Steve Martin shot an arrow through your ears," as one of his fraternity brothers would have phrased it.

Peter even knew what the headache was from, had felt it coming on the night before at the fund-raiser. The jury in the *Ketterson* case was still out after having deliberated Tuesday afternoon and all of Wednesday and Thursday. Such a long deliberation in a pretty straightforward trial was usually bad news for the prosecution, suggesting the jury might be stuck on some aspect of the commonwealth's evidence or the judge's instructions. Peter had gone so far yesterday as to ask Old Bailey if he was sensing any vibes, which was a waste of the DA's time. O.B. took his job seriously and would never leak gossip about what he might hear said (or yelled, for that matter) from the jury room.

Peter had delivered his dinner speech beautifully the night before, but the question-and-answer period afterward had made him nervous. So, he'd had a few hard-liquor drinks, always a mistake after 9:00 P.M., especially when he wouldn't be able to squeeze in a run the next morning before heading into work.

Maybe I can do a few miles at lunchtime, now that I've got a shower in these new offices.

Then Peter's mind drifted to the Q&A after his speech the night before. It hadn't been a disaster, and he'd trotted out perfectly acceptable dodges ("Given that the *Ketterson* case is now under submission to the jury, it would be inappropriate for me to comment upon it at this time"). But although the baby spotlight on him at the podium on the dais had prevented his seeing the audience clearly, Peter had been able to sense people fidgeting uncomfortably in their chairs, turning to one another. A low, steady murmur here, an abrupt squelched laugh there. Not the signals a candidate hoped to get from the people whose money he needed to buy all that TV time in the important two to three weeks before the election, when Mort Zussman said most of the voters really made up their minds.

From the podium, Peter could see Mort, too. Sort of in the wings to the right of the dais, directing the woman with the mobile video cam to catch this aspect or that for future campaign use. Mort was sweating, though, and not just from exertion.

Which was born out on the late news. Both network affiliates in the city ran a piece on the fund-raiser, and both featured Peter's dodges instead of the campaign sound bites. Even the surviving city newspaper, a constant supporter in the past, shortchanged his one-line zingers on "the crime that has become our culture" and what he'd do as attorney general to protect all the commonwealth's citizens from the "drug dealers haunting our neighborhoods." The last paragraph of the morning edition hinted there was some question whether as district attorney Peter Mendez could even put away one homicidal aristocrat.

The problem, the prosecutor decided, wasn't so much Ketterson as his attorney. Truth be told, Peter hated going up against Sheilah Quinn. There was something so . . . calm about the woman, even at the appellate level. When they'd argued the death penalty challenge, and she'd come up with the constitutional hole in the commonwealth's capital punishment statute, the forehead of the swing justice on the state supreme court creased ever so slightly. Peter cringed inwardly, thinking — no, *knowing* — that he was croaked. And at trial, any trial, the jurors couldn't take their eyes off her, one of those rare women who get more attractive the more you hear them talk. Peter had lost another homicide case to Sheilah just before the supreme court argument. If Ketterson went the wrong way, too, it would make three in a row. A record Peter Mendez couldn't stomach as a litigator, and a trend Mort would read as very bad tea leaves for statewide office.

Yet Ketterson was guilty. Granted the evidence was thin, granted Peter'd had to run the risk of tainting the jury just a bit during his closing to round out the proof, but goddamn it, just look at the man. Frank Sikes from Homicide had said Ketterson had freaky eyes — no, not "freaky." What was it Sikes . . . Right, right, "hoppy" eyes. The look that was fine until you saw that little jump in them. And Peter had seen that jump, seen it when he'd first interviewed Ketterson before the man was even arrested. Seen it moving around the courtroom, too, examining other witnesses but glancing back at the defense table from time to time. Even seen it up close when cross-examining Ketterson during the defendant's own day on the stand.

Only one problem: The jurors were probably far enough away that they hadn't see it. What they'd seen instead was a composed, respectable, highly educated, and articulate white — there it was, *white* — man who just didn't seem the kind to cap off an innocuously pleasant date by strangling the young woman he'd just treated to dinner.

Peter was massaging his temples with the middle finger of each hand when Veronica stuck her head in the door. "I think you want this call."

"Who?"

His secretary told him, and Peter Mendez quickly picked up the receiver.

Sheilah Quinn was at her computer, composing the rough draft of a brief in a drug-trafficking appeal, using the word processor's editing function to cut and paste electronically the happy passages of appellate court opinion she lifted, usually not out of context, with the help of her CD-ROM drive. It really was amazing, what had happened over the last ten years. Instead of something like fifty running feet of library space to hold thousands of dollars' worth of volumes containing case opinions, Sheilah could just push into the CPU tower a CD tinier than her dad's old 45-rpm records. And voilà, all the cases decided by the commonwealth's highest court could be comprehensively searched by computer command, then easily uploaded into the word-processing file that was the brief.

The phone made its frightened-sheep noise. She knew Krissie was "down the hall" — Etta's kinder, gentler phrase for the bathroom — so Sheilah picked up. It was Joey Trask, the attorney representing a codefendant in the armed robbery of a liquor store. The nub of the case for trial purposes was identification, because the two Latino kids, Pablo Diaz and Cundo Borbón, were virtually indistinguishable from each other and dozens of others in the neighborhood both as to hairstyle and dress code (half the teenagers in a three-block-square area adopting the colors of the Dallas Cowboys, "America's team"). She had Pablo as her client, and for plea-bargaining purposes, the case turned on who was the gunman and who was the wheelman. So far, both Pablo and Cundo were claiming to have been in the car, not the store. But Sheilah really thought they had a shot at insufficient ID, particularly if she could get Trask as Borbón's attorney to stay the course and let her handle the cross-examination of the eyeball witnesses if and when it came to trial. However, now Joey — notorious among the defense bar for avoiding juries whenever he could — was whining in her ear about his client having the longer record and therefore the greater risk if they went to trial over this one.

Sheilah cut the other attorney off in mid-sentence. "Joey, Joey. The only problem is, we both have this sense that somehow if our clients were the perps, your guy Cundo is the one with the gun. And the one with the gun terrorized not just the owner of the store but also a pregnant customer of said owner who nearly miscarried twenty minutes after the boys peeled away."

"Sheilah, honey —"

"Joey —"

"Sorry. Look, the woman shouldn't have been buying liquor in the first place, how far along she was."

Sheilah pinched the bridge of her nose with the index finger and thumb of her left hand. Jesus Mary, when will this kind of shit end?

"Joey, the woman's statement says she was buying a boxed bottle of Chivas Regal for a gift. A gift, Joey. You want to try and show the jury that they should discredit her on that?"

No response at first. Then, "It's just that

96

Cundo's getting kind of nervous."

Uh-oh. "Meaning he's thinking of rolling over on his best friend since boyhood?"

"Just nervous, Sheilah. Maybe we could kind of drop in on Mendez together, get this thing straightened out."

"Joey, hold on, okay?"

"What, you got another call coming in more important than this one?"

"No. I meant just hang in there. I still think we can beat the ID, and both the boys will walk."

"I'll talk to my client."

Sheilah replaced the receiver and thought about it. Good chance that Cundo will roll, especially given Joey, the gutless wonder, as his attorney. If Cundo rolls, Peter Mendez would welcome going after her Pablo as the gunman, and most judges would sentence accordingly. But Peter would have to offer Cundo an awfully nice deal, an inducement that she could use to cross-examine Cundo on the stand, bringing out his rather impressive rap sheet to impeach him even further by criminal conviction. Only problem there is that the jury then realizes it can't convict Cundo — a real bad guy — but can convict Pablo — a bad-enough guy — of something, get him off the streets regardless of what role he played in the robbery. Unless the eye-witnesses both realize —

The phone bleated again.

Sheilah glanced at the computer and killed the screen showing part of the drug brief to avoid burning an image. Shelving the immediacy of the Pablo/Cundo problem also, she momentarily envied herself being on trial in the *Ketterson* case for the last two weeks.

Second sheep noise.

Laypeople generally assume that trying a case is the most stressful part of a litigator's life, given what might be at stake. Frankly, Sheilah always felt relaxed during a trial. In the office, people can expect to reach you regarding any one of fifty matters, but on trial, nobody could expect you to deal with anything — including your father's situation — except that one case. There actually were times during necessary though unobjectionable testimony elicited by her opponent when Sheilah had to pinch herself to keep from falling asleep.

After the phone sounded a third time, she picked up. "Sheilah Quinn."

"Ms. Quinn, this is Deputy Bailey speaking."

Always the formal manner. "What's up?"

"Your jury's coming in."

That quickening in the blood. "My client there?"

"I called for him first thing."

"Thanks, O.B." Walking would be faster than driving. "Be there in fifteen."

"I'll so inform His Honor."

"Rather exciting, isn't it?" whispered Arthur Ketterson IV into her ear from his chair at the defense table.

Not for the first time, Sheilah Quinn looked at her client with amazement in her mind, if not on her face. But, the fact was, she had to agree with him. Waiting for Roger Hesterfield to ascend the bench and call for Old Bailey to bring in the jury, an undeniable tension filled the air. It reminded Sheilah of an exam room just before the proctor hands out the papers.

Ketterson said, "I feel as though we've been through a blazing, humid summer afternoon, thunderheads rolling over the horizon and descending toward us." He stuck out his tongue. "I swear, the ozone is actually condensing on my taste buds."

Sheilah thought, You poor weird fuck. Or rich weird fuck, correcting herself.

Arthur reveled in that sense of connection he experienced frequently with Sheilah, this time over the impending-thunderstorm metaphor. It reminded him deliciously of another time, that last night with his mother. Arthur also thought it showed Sheilah how confident he was that her efforts would produce the right result in his case. But now he turned from her, albeit reluctantly, to survey the courtroom.

Arthur didn't think the upwardly mobile Mambo King looked all that well. A touch of prosecutorial hangover? Or perhaps just a little dyspepsia from the prospect of the verdict.

The "I could pass" Negro detective and the Irish clown white one were standing in front of a pew bench in the audience, watching him. Drink it in, *cerebrae minutaie,* because soon I will be free of this room and beyond your ken.

Oh, and there was the grieving family. The sow Giordano mater, with her ever-gauche dress and ever-present hankie. The father, shooting daggers toward the defense table, but not directly at me, at least not at this moment. I wonder, does the pig Giordano pater despise Sheilah, as well?

And George Lofton, giving me the thumbs-up. Such camaraderie, as though we were fighter pilots in the same command, facing a common enemy with élan. But do tell, George, how many five-hundred-dollar hours have been racked up while you've just sat through my trial like a bump on the proverbial log and watched another attorney *really* earn her keep?

The remainder of the seating area was occupied by people whose faces Arthur recognized but couldn't match with names. Media jackals, some of them, with little pads for the reporters and large, rather comical ones for the sketch artists. Others were merely professional watchers with nothing better to do.

One thing did stand out, though. There were additional bailiffs today. Arthur counted five, two more than the usual trio of the bloated toad and the more capable Vinnie and Timmy — or Timmy and Vinnie. Who could keep track of these uniformed bouncers? Arthur thought about the reason for extra manpower. Probably

100

to prevent a riot, should the jury —

"Cooooo-urt. All rise, please."

Everyone in the First Session stood as Old Bailey opened the door to the judge's chambers on the left-hand side of the bench. Roger Hesterfield moved deliberately to take his raised seat while his bailiff moved even more deliberately to the jury door, opening it and stepping aside to allow the twelve to file into the courtroom and reach their staggered chairs within the box against the right-hand wall.

Hesterfield addressed the audience. "You may be seated."

Everyone settled back down.

When the air was completely still, the judge said, "The defendant will rise."

Sheilah tugged on the sleeve of Arthur's suit jacket, to bring him up with her. Arthur found it a most affecting gesture, and he had to restrain himself to keep from responding to it.

Then Hesterfield addressed the jury. "Mr. Foreman?"

The juror seated in the first-row chair nearest the judge rose.

"Has the jury reached a verdict?" intoned Hesterfield in a practiced manner.

The foreman glanced around him, to the side and behind. Then in a small voice, he said, "Uh, no, Your Honor, we haven't."

Hesterfield seemed about to speak, but instead reacted to the swelling growl from the audience by banging his gavel once, then squinted at the foreman. "What was that?"

"We can't reach a verdict. The vote is —"

Hesterfield's voice cracked like a whip. "I do *not* wish to know the current state of your deliberations regarding any votes." He took a breath. "Mr. Foreman, you may sit."

Hesterfield turned to the audience and said, "Defendant may sit as well, but counsel to the side bar."

As the attorneys and court reporter walked toward the side bar, Gerald O'Toole tilted his head toward Frank Sikes, who tilted his as well, so the two almost touched at the part line. "Where would you put this one on the we're-fucked-o-meter?"

In spite of what he felt inside him, Sikes nearly grinned. "Nine-point-oh." Then he stole a quick look at the Giordanos.

"Rudy?"

"Ssssshhhh."

"What's happening, Rudy?"

"I don't know, Rhonda. All right?" he said, thinking, This better not mean what I think it means.

Sheilah knew what was coming at the side bar, but she let the judge run the show.

In a voice low but cold with anger, Roger Hesterfield spoke to the court reporter. "For the record, I'm going to give this jury the dynamite charge."

No surprise there. The jurors claim they're split, the judge puts a stick of "dynamite" under them — a speech from the bench about their duty to resolve any differences among them, and therefore the case, as well.

Hesterfield looked at Sheilah. "Ms. Quinn, I assume you wish to note an objection for the defense?"

"Yes," she replied, wondering, Rog, why are you being so nice to me?

"So noted."

"Thank you, Your Honor."

Peter Mendez said, "Perhaps also you —"

"Mr. Mendez," Hesterfield's voice growing colder, "I will additionally note for the record that, in my opinion — formed after nearly twenty-five years presiding over trials for this commonwealth — your closing argument may very well have been the cause of our current problem."

Sheilah didn't watch Peter's face, but she was sure it was turning red, like a law student caught unprepared during class. However, she sensed that Hesterfield was sending her an oblique message, too. What was it?

The prosecutor got out "But your —"

"That's enough, Mr. Mendez. Given the current hour, I would appreciate counsel remaining in the building while we see if the supplemental charge produces a verdict."

Sheilah said immediately, "Certainly, Your Honor."

Hesterfield eyed her. For a beat longer than necessary, she thought.

Then the judge said, "Very well. Step back."

His right hand fluttering up to his cheek, Arthur Ketterson IV watched Sheilah walk toward him again. He understood winning, and he understood losing, but this was . . . neither?

As Sheilah reached her chair, and before he could speak, she whispered to him, her breath scented with mint and something underneath, something . . . muckier. "The judge is going to give the jurors a pep talk about reaching a verdict."

Arthur wanted to know more, but he heard Roger Hesterfield begin, and so he watched him instead.

"Members of the jury, it is my duty to reacquaint you with certain concepts I covered in my earlier instructions. You twelve are the best possible deciders of this case. Each attorney has worked hard to present the best evidence available on the issues involved in this case, and no other jury will be better equipped to discharge the solemn . . ."

Something Arthur had once read came back to him: the hung jury. If these wretches don't reach a verdict, guilty or not guilty, there'll have to be another trial, with a whole new jury. The prospect nearly nauseated him: having to endure another interminable proceeding, with Lucifer knows how many more months wasted living next to Willie T. Eggers. Or worse.

Hesterfield continued: ". . . and so the law protects the defendant by a 'reasonable' doubt, not 'all' doubt and not just 'any' doubt. It is important that each of you reexamine your conscience, then determine whether or not there is room for agreement on a consensus verdict."

Arthur didn't like the slant of that, as though the Jolly Roger was endeavoring to bulldoze any jurors leaning toward acquittal into joining the majority favoring a verdict of guilty. Shaking his head, the defendant then tried to gauge the jury, the impact the judge's words might be having on them. Arthur's gaze flitted from one face to the next. He thought he saw a consistent, if not universal, message there.

The pep talk wasn't going to help this particular team. Not . . . at . . . all.

"So, if I may ask, where exactly do we stand?"

Internally, Sheilah was still trying to decipher Hesterfield's oblique message to her. "I'm sorry?"

Ketterson smiled. Or his version of a smile, the corners of his mouth just going up, no teeth, like Dick Van Dyke on Nick at Night, the goofy look her father once told Sheilah was a mime of Stan somebody from one of those old thirties comedy teams.

Jesus Mary, Dad, I hope I won't be having to see this weirdo much longer.

She said, "The judge asked counsel to remain. Sometimes the pep talk" — Ketterson doesn't have to know it's called "the dynamite charge," she thought — "works, and sometimes it doesn't."

Her client now frowned. He really is transparently readable, thought Sheilah, rapidly losing that sense of dread she'd felt earlier with him. Put even a supremely arrogant man at the defense table, make him stand to face what he thinks will be a verdict of murder one, and he reverts to being a little boy, waiting in fear outside the principal's office.

Still frowning, Ketterson said, "I thought it sounded rather one-sided, that the judge was spurring them on toward finding me guilty."

"Which is why I lodged an objection to the supplemental charge at the side bar."

"But what if the jury still can't make up its collective mind?"

"Then the prosecutor has to decide whether or not to retry you."

A deeper frown. "And if the prosecutor does, will I have to sit in jail *until* he does?"

Sheilah stared at her client. Could that be what Roger had meant at the side bar? That he'd actually consider setting —

The door to the jury room opened, and Old Bailey came into the First Session. "Where's Mr. Mendez?"

Sheilah looked around. "Down the hall, maybe?"

Old Bailey spoke to one of the younger bailiffs. "Hey, Vinnie. Go see if Mr. Mendez —"

"Right, O.B.," said the younger man, moving off toward the doors to the corridor.

"And Vinnie?"

"Yeah?"

"Let the press know, too."

As Old Bailey went to the chambers door and knocked, Sheilah Quinn squared her shoulders.

Quietly, Ketterson said, "Is the jury coming back, then?"

She didn't even glance at him this time. "We'll be the first to know."

Arthur Ketterson watched the jurors troop into the courtroom for the second time that Friday. Eleven took their seats, while the one who'd spoken earlier stayed standing.

Roger Hesterfield's voice still conveyed the pep-talk tone as he said, "Mr. Foreman, have you reached a verdict in this matter?"

"No, Your Honor." His next words, nearly drowned out by the audience as well as by the judge's gavel, were, "We're deadlocked. It's hopeless."

When the courtroom was once again silent, Hesterfield — rather fighting to maintain his temper, Arthur thought — told everyone to be seated. After a moment, his eyes turned toward the twelve people sitting against the right-hand wall. "Very well. The jury is thanked for its service, and you are all dismissed. Bailiff?"

As the bloated toad motioned the jurors to stand up and file back out, the judge faced the lawyers. "Mr. Mendez, does the commonwealth intend to retry?"

The prosecutor rose, a tad green around the gills. "At this time, Your Honor, that determination hasn't been —"

Hesterfield simply turned away from him. "Ms. Quinn, I'll hear you now on the question of setting bail pending retrial."

Arthur wasn't sure if he actually believed his ears, but hc was pleased to see Sheilah standing up and smiling confidently, as though she'd somehow anticipated all this.

"Bail?" said Mendez.

"Mr. Mendez," said the Jolly Roger, fairly bellowing, "you had an opportunity to inform this Court of your office's intentions in this matter. Now it is Ms. Quinn's turn." Hesterfield came back to Sheilah. "Proceed."

"Your Honor," said Arthur's lawyer, "the defendant has been put to trial in what at best was a barely sufficient case, and now would have to wait, given the upcoming election —"

Oh, Sheilah, my Sheilah. A *deft* needle, that.

"— for many months before retrial is possible. Accordingly, I ask that my client be released on one-million-dollar surety, no cash alternative."

Mendez looked positively stricken. "But, Your Honor, a million dollars to a man of Mr.

Ketterson's means is . . . is a joke."

Arthur felt himself sniffing involuntarily. As though the Mambo King ever saw that kind of money outside of some drug deal.

"Mr. Mendez," said Hesterfield, "I assure you, that amount is not a joke to anybody. Bail is set at one million dollars, no cash alternative." The judge glanced Arthur's way. "Mr. Ketterson, your lawyer may inform the clerk if you can post such a bond."

Now it's Hesterfield who's being insulting, the pompous prick. As though *he* has no idea of my net worth.

The next sequence blurred somewhat for Arthur. As he leapt up to congratulate Sheilah, a stricken sow Giordano mater shrieked loudly enough to shatter crystal. Pig Giordano pater rushed the prosecutor, of all people, cursing like a sailor and even grabbing the man by the lapels before the two homicide detectives caught up to the grieving man and pulled him off. Arthur did manage the presence of mind to see if the Jolly Roger went for a panic button, as Willie had intimated. Arthur thought he noticed an ever so slight flicker of the right hand toward the panel of the bench closest to the chambers door, what the judge had been calling "the side bar."

So, Willie proved right. Again.

By the time Arthur next turned to Sheilah, the media jackals were already making a din outside the picket-fence bar enclosure behind them, clamoring for him to make a statement. His lawyer was stuffing papers into her briefcase.

"I'm free to go, then?" asked Arthur.

Sheilah looked up with those eyes, those . . . enchanting eyes. "If George Lofton can get a surety company to post the million for you."

"Oh, I would imagine that's no trouble. He sits on the board of at least one of them, I'm sure."

Sheilah, his Sheilah, seemed about to say something else, then shook her head instead. "Well, call me if you have any other questions."

"Just one for now."

"Go ahead."

"My tie, is it straight?"

Sheilah looked at him with undisguised wonder, obviously impressed by his insouciance. "Yes, but there won't be any cameras until you get outside on bail, and I have to advise you to say nothing about the case to the press other than that you're glad the presumption of innocence has finally been recognized."

" 'The presumption of innocence . . . has finally been recognized.' Oh, I like that," said Arthur, the soul of sincerity.

"Well, I'll contact you if and when the DA gives me a new trial date."

Arthur nodded. "You know, Sheilah, there's only one thing about all this that truly bothers me."

She nodded, too, seemingly united with his thoughts. "That you'll have to go through another trial."

Out of respect for their relationship, Arthur tried, heroically, not to frown. "Not exactly. My only regret is that I can't share with you as yet whether or not I actually killed that wretched slut."

Ah, thought Aruthur. Sheilah needn't say another word. That look on her face is eloquence incarnate.

Sheilah was almost over the wobbly shiver, the first time in a while she'd felt it, when the polite voice of Old Bailey brought her back.

"Ms. Quinn?"

She turned to him. "Yes?"

"His Honor would like to see both Mr. Mendez and you in chambers."

"Now?"

Old Bailey nodded solemnly.

Peter Mendez tried to sit in one of the tacked leather chairs across from Roger Hesterfield, but he simply could not stay still. Pacing, the prosecutor delayed saying anything until Sheilah Quinn joined them.

"Your Honor," Peter began, "with all due respect, you just made me look like a horse's ass out there."

Hesterfield finished hanging up his robe on the coat tree, then sank judiciously into his desk chair, motioning Sheilah to the other seat. "Peter," he said, the coldness gone from his voice. "I am not the advocate who argued specif-

111

ically prohibited evidence to the jury in my closing."

"But, Your Honor. Look —"

"No, Peter, you look. We aren't the fucking Rotary Club here. The three lawyers in this room all know what you did, and even why you did it. You were afraid an acquittal in this case wouldn't play too well toward election day, so you decided to go outside the rules a little to get a conviction — or, at worst, the hedged bet of a hung jury. You get crowned AG, and some other poor bastard has to prosecute the probably soured cream of the city's social register for murder a second time. You're not going to disagree with me on any of that, are you?"

Peter glanced at Sheilah Quinn but didn't respond, his hardest decision of the week. She kept a poker face.

"Good," said Hesterfield. "As far as I'm concerned, what I did out there on the bail issue was proportionate to what you tried to pull. Even fair, all things considered. I'm not sure I wouldn't have voted Arthur Ketterson not guilty myself."

Peter glanced at Sheilah again. Her eyes were aimed at her lap. Looking back to the judge, he couldn't help himself. "But Your Honor, think of the media coverage."

Hesterfield dropped his voice an octave, to the point where it rumbled. "I'm appointed for life, Peter. For *life*. I don't give a rat's ass about media coverage. But I do care that what you did out there sullied this court, the First Session, with a stupid ploy in what was almost certainly the last capital case she'll ever see."

She? Peter shook his head. I can't believe this. Arthur Ketterson is out on bail, and I'm going to be roasted by two network affiliates and a major urban daily, all because I insulted a WASP judge's courtroom?

Hesterfield adjusted his voice. "I didn't want to see a hung jury in my last big one here, Peter." A beat. "Surely you can understand that?"

Peter reined himself in. Not going to win this round, he thought. "Anything else, Your Honor?"

"Regarding the *Ketterson* case, no. But Sheilah, I wonder if you'd mind staying to discuss another matter?"

Peter Mendez felt something in Hesterfield's request go by him, but when he looked at Sheilah Quinn, all he saw was a woman again playing poker, and perhaps with a pat hand in front of her.

George Lofton said, "And Arthur, if you'd just be so kind as to sign . . . there, and . . . there."

Arthur Ketterson couldn't believe how smoothly this process seemed to be unfolding. George might not have his sea legs in a criminal courtroom, but give him some densely printed legal documents to have executed and he was comfortably in his element. And the little twerp sent by the surety company nearly rubbed his hands together with glee. Not surprisingly, given the percentage of the $1 million bond George told Arthur the issuing company demanded as a premium — unintentionally disclosive choice of word, that — for providing it.

George handed several copies of the documents to the twerp and several more to the young bailiff — now clearly named Vinnie — George retaining several, as well. Then a few more signatures on some county documents would be followed by a short ride in the sheriff's van back to the jail — Vinnie insisted that no one else could sign for the books in the cell or the suits in the court-clothes closet. A chore that, frankly, Arthur was happy not to delegate. In an hour, perhaps less, though, the previously detained defendant would be a provisionally free man.

As Vinnie hunted up the keys to the van, George said to Arthur, "I'll tag along in the Mercedes."

"Why?"

George's face betrayed that perplexed look, the one he always seemed to display when Arthur asked him perfectly reasonable questions. "So I can give you a ride home. Or anywhere else to celebrate."

"Actually, George, you should come to the jail, in order to take my things to the estate. But I think I'd rather spend the afternoon in the city and on my own."

The perplexed look still. "On your own?"

As though three months of such company would be too much for even me to tolerate, mused Arthur. "Yes, George. I'd like to sample some genuine sunlight, breathe some relatively fresh air." Arthur treated his family lawyer to his most ingratiating grin. "I also have an errand or two to run."

"Sheilah, let me put my cards on the table."
Since she'd been consciously trying to maintain a poker face, Sheilah Quinn actually found Hesterfield's remark almost laughable, but she just nodded.
He came forward in the swivel chair, elbows on his desk. "I've been thinking about" — he cast a sidelong glance toward the couch — "us."
I don't believe this. "Judge —"
"How about 'Roger' again? Please?"
Sheilah chose her words carefully. "There is no 'us.' "
"There was for a beautiful Christmas — what, can it be eight years ago, already?"
Nine, you son of a bitch. Sheilah had closed the watertight door on that incident long ago, but now she found it cracking just a little. The courthouse Christmas party in the lobby rotunda downstairs, everyone letting down their hair, the distinguished Roger Hesterfield inviting Etta Yemelman's starry-eyed law clerk to stay "just a bit longer, Sheilah," perhaps enjoy a nightcap in quieter surroundings? I was flattered by his private guided tour of the First Ses-

sion, even him showing me the little pivoting panel he'd rigged under the side bar of the bench, a snub-nosed revolver mounted on the reverse side of the panel. "Just in case," Roger had said gravely and with just the right note of manly reluctance to use deadly force. Yeah, sure. And then the Hesterfield chambers, and the "Hesterfield" couch. "As though we just dropped the c from the front of the name," he joked at the time, then had to explain to me that the design of the tacked leather furniture was known as chesterfield.

And there was no forcing of affections. Hell, admit it, girl: You developed a crush on the man the first time Etta had an out-of-state conference and "lent" you to Roger for some research he needed done. But the interlude on the couch was vulgar and messy and over within twenty minutes, and I vowed that would be the last time I made love — no, don't romanticize it, had sex — with a man I didn't love.

Roger had broadly hinted at subsequent dinners or "perhaps just a ride along the coast, Sheilah," but she'd consistently declined, years ago assuming that if he hadn't forgotten about the incident, he at least saw it as clearly a part of history, as she did.

"Sheilah, don't try to tell me you don't have any feelings for me still?"

Her stomach turned over. The deterioration of the man was a vivid, tangible reality. Almost pitiable. "Judge, I —"

116

" 'Roger,' remember?"

"Judge," she repeated, a little more juice in her tone? "I think that our memories of that one time —"

"Not my fault there weren't —"

"— diverge significantly."

Hesterfield's face hardened, draining of color in the cheeks, if not the permanently ruddied nose. "I remember how much you wanted it, and how much I wanted to give you more. And not just sex."

"Judge —"

"Like today, for instance."

Like . . . Jesus Mary, so that was it. Rog set bail on my client not just to tweak Peter for insulting his "lady" of a courtroom but also to pave the way for . . . "Judge, this conversation is over."

"Sheilah —"

She stood and turned to leave.

"Sheilah, please?"

She paused at the door, turning to face him, a sad, aging man.

"I'm lonely," he said.

"I'm not," replied Sheilah Quinn, and let herself out of his chambers.

FIVE

Sheila Quinn walked back toward her office building. No, she thought, I'm not walking; I'm stamping. And from the way people are getting out of my way, I must be giving off steam, too.

And why shouldn't I? Fucking Roger Hesterfield. The case stays in limbo because Mendez argues unfairly, and even the minor victory of my client being released on bail is tainted by old Rog implying (hint, hint) that he ordered bail to grease the skids for hitting on me. Bastard!

Entering the office suite, Sheilah went by Krissie, picking up her stack of pink message slips without saying anything.

The secretary looked up from another of Etta's endless trust documents on her computer screen. "Well?"

"Don't ask."

"Sorry I did."

Sheilah stopped. I'm pissed off at Hesterfield, but that doesn't give me the right to take it out on her. "No, Krissie, I'm the one who's sorry."

"Like, forget it. What about the case?"

"We drew a hung jury."

Krissie looked genuinely sympathetic, biting her lower lip the way she almost never did. "Hey, at least it doesn't go in the 'loss' column, right?"

"Right." Sheilah flipped through her phone slips. "Hold my calls till I assess the damage already in these."

Krissie leered. "Including him?"

Heh-immm. Sheilah didn't bother looking for his number in the messages. "He tried to reach me?"

"Only like three times in the last hour."

"He tries again, put that one through."

"You got it."

Sheilah noticed her suite mate's door was closed. "Etta off to New York already?"

"No. Conference call."

Nodding, Sheilah went into her own office, leaving the door open. She kicked off her shoes and began wading through the stack of pink slips, returning the three most urgent of her messages, reaching only one of the attorneys on a Friday afternoon but leaving cover-her-ass callbacks with the voice mails of the remaining two. Dialing a fourth on a matter that could wait till Monday, Sheilah saw the other button on her phone light up and then heard Krissie's singsong of "Guess who?"

Sheilah cut off her outgoing call and pushed the second button. "Hi."

"Hi," said the smooth, low voice on the other end. "We set for the weekend?"

"What happened back there wasn't exactly a verdict."

"Yeah, but you won't exactly be held hostage

119

by phone for the next few days, either."

"I don't know," she said, feeling her tone more as "Persuade me."

"When's the last time you saw your father?"

"Last night."

"So no guilt there, right?"

"Right. The guilt comes from other places."

A pause. "We can talk about that."

"Over a pillow?"

"My favorite conversation piece."

God, the man does make my toes curl. Is that the right omen?

"Sheil?"

"Still here."

"You shouldn't be. You need the rest. Change of scenery, change of pace. And we're going far enough, nobody's going to recognize you."

All probably true.

"Sheilah?"

"Yes?"

"Go home and pack. I'll see you at the inn around . . . seven?"

"You're on." Try a different tone. "Don't forget the vitamin E, now."

"Counselor, you constantly underestimate me."

After hanging up, Sheilah decided she liked the way all this felt. Stacking the unreturned messages, she left her briefcase in the corner and went out to the reception area. No Krissie, probably "down the hall," since the suite door to the corridor was closed and Etta's document instead of the screen saver was on the computer screen.

Sheilah scribbled a quick note to Etta and another about Quigley to Krissie, then walked through the door, closing it behind her.

And closing off a miserable week, all things considered.

Arthur Ketterson found himself actually strolling down the busy street, five hundred dollars of George Lofton's cash in his pocket. And hadn't George looked pained to be parting with it at the ATM, as though the family attorney hadn't netted that much and more from just the time spent helping his client make bail. Now, on the sidewalk, the pedestrians milled around and past Arthur, preoccupied with their own lives.

They don't even see me, don't recognize the presence of an accused murderer in their midst. Not so different, really, from the colony of ants depicted in another nature program on the Admin Unit's television monitors. I have to admit, the experience of "jailing" has brought certain new perspectives to my life.

For example, how blue the sky when not seen through Plexiglas or chicken wire. How fresh the air when not strained through the body odor, and worse, of guards and other prisoners. How — and Arthur had to smile at this one — good to know you really are talking to yourself, and not out loud. To be able to rely once more on the confidentiality of an "internal conference." Amazing, really, the insecurities bred from being perfectly safe behind bars.

121

Unfamiliar with the part of town around Sheilah Quinn's office building, Arthur wandered past a locksmith, two Yuppie fern bars, and three gourmet coffee establishments before finally finding what he sought. Inside the florist's, the smell of fresh blossoms was nearly overwhelming, like the viewing room at a funeral. Arthur felt a sensation ripple through his body almost instantly.

The sensation of feeling . . . at home.

A sizable poodle came dancing toward him, its fur cut resembling nothing so much as an albino baboon. Another metaphor from the "animal kingdom."

Will the Admin Unit culture never leave me?

Behind the poodle, a woman's voice said, "Etienne? Etienne, heel!" A modulation of voice. "I'm so sorry if he's bothering you."

"Oh, no bother." Arthur actually stopped to pet the cur's unnaturally clipped head. The middle-aged owner struck him as an executive cow who'd been glass-ceilinged before pulling the rip cord on her golden parachute. Probably used the money to buy an entrepreneurial little "shoppe," only to have now the severest of second thoughts about the decision.

The woman gave a treacly smile. "Etienne is a champion."

"Even if he weren't, I've rather come to like bizarre creatures."

The woman looked at Arthur strangely. "Can I help you with something?"

"Yes. A striking arrangement of flowers, if you would. In a nice vase."

"A gift, then?"

"More a floral expression of gratitude, but with just a breath of what's to come."

The cow was acting nervous now. Her dog, who had been absolutely silent to this point, began whining.

Arthur realized he'd have to answer for her. "Well, let's just include some lilies, shall we?"

"Lilies." The woman rubbed her hands on the smock she wore over some garish blouse. "And how much did you wish to spend?"

Arthur pulled out the ten fifties and peeled off two of them.

"Certainly, sir." A cow's eyes can light up, can't they? "We provide a simply smashing arrangement for ninety-five. But I'm afraid there'll be a delivery charge, as well."

"Ah, no," said Arthur, carefully separating and creasing the bills before laying them on the counter side by side, like miniature pup tents. "I'll be delivering the bouquet myself, you see."

At home, Sheilah changed into casual clothes — jeans and a blouse for driving — then turned to packing with a fury. Jack Quinn had always commented on that. When she was six, he'd told her, "Sheilah, girl, you take your time coming to a decision, but once that mind's made up, you're like George Patton scenting a river." She'd had to ask her father just what that meant, of course, and he'd said it had to do with being an "aggressive tanker."

Quigley made a throaty, crackling noise behind her, the same one he let loose when she hauled out the canvas overnight bag from the closet. He's not stupid: He knows when I'm leaving him.

"Don't worry, Quig. Krissie's going to be feeding you good stuff tomorrow."

The crackling noise again. Not convinced, are you? Better remember to close the shower curtain, or my little tabby cat will drop a turd or two there instead of in the litter box, upbraiding me for being a neglectful parent.

Then Sheilah moved to the lingerie drawer in her bureau. After only a little rummaging, she found the piece she wanted: red satin and black lace, with pull strings in strategic places. "I'm not too broad through the beam for this teddy, am I, Quigley?"

No response. When Sheilah turned around, the cat was nowhere in sight.

The word *teddy* did make her think of Mr. Fuzzums, though. She'd taken the stuffed bear on trips occasionally, the little girl in her happy that the grown woman could indulge herself once in awhile.

Sheilah glanced at the teddy on the comforter, then back at the one in her hand. Then she thought about which image she'd rather be projecting this weekend.

Folding the lingerie under the blouses in her

bag, Sheilah went to the bed. She hid Mr. Fuzzums under the blanket, making a slight bulge but hopefully protecting him from Quigley, since the cat had whacked the poor thing around out of frustration in the past. One time, he even dragged the little bear off and hid him, Quigley's other form of revenge for her leaving him alone.

Then Sheilah opened the top drawer of the night table for some of the condoms she'd bought when her new relationship had begun. Ultrathin, lubricated, handy receptacle end.

A boxed dozen. Optimist that I am, she thought.

Arthur Ketterson got on the elevator in the lobby of Sheilah Quinn's office building, a woman smiling sweetly as she looked first at the cellophaned flower arrangement and then at Arthur himself, up and down. Heavy through the legs and hips, she walked off toward the main entrance, slowly enough that he was sure she expected him to speak to her.

Another cow. The city's just chock-full of them these days.

The elevator doors closed almost silently, and Arthur found himself impressed by Sheilah's surroundings. He had half-expected some tacky walk-up with linoleum floors and pebbled-glass doors badly stenciled with the names of talent agencies and tax preparers. Instead, the building had been beautifully restored, its directory displayed between mirrored panels in the lobby. And the modern elevator was blessedly spared the music for which such conveyances were justly infamous.

When the doors opened with a barely audible *whoosh* on the sixth floor, Arthur could hear an older woman's voice quite distinctly. He pressed a finger against the hold button on the elevator's panel and peered discreetly around the door.

The voice — raspy, even grating — belonged to an old crone with the dried, leathery face of a persimmon, at least in profile. Profile was all Arthur could appreciate, the woman standing in the open doorway to a suite, turned to whomever she was addressing inside the offices. She wore a granola lover's backpack and some sort of cross-training shoes that looked so new, she couldn't really have exercised in them even once.

The Persimmon Queen said, "Krissie, I'll be back from New York Sunday night."

"Fine, Etta." The voice of a tired, rather bored young woman.

"I'll need that trust you're working on first thing Monday morning, but if you don't want to stay tonight, you can come in over the weekend."

Slave driver, thought Arthur as the young Krissie just said, "I'll stay."

"Sheilah's gone already?"

"Uh-huh."

Arthur sighed. Drat the luck.

"Remember," said Etta, "you're supposed to feed Sheilah's cat tomorrow."

Well, well. Sheilah, does that mean you're taking a little trip without me?

"I'm gonna go over there before dinner," said the secretary.

"Just don't forget."

An exasperated sound from the young Krissie as Arthur heard a metal desk drawer clunk twice as it opened, the sound of something heavy thunking on a surface.

The Persimmon Queen said, "You pull up on the handle, the furniture won't make that noise. Last longer, too."

Krissie, rather petulant, said, "Handbag." Followed by a tinkling noise and "Keys." Followed by more tinkling and what sounded like "Ess Cue."

"So all right, all right," said the older Etta. "I get the picture."

"Then, like, clue me, okay? Why does everybody around here think I'm some kind of airhead?"

"I apologize, Krissie," said the Persimmon Queen. "Enjoy your weekend."

"You, too, Etta," a relenting note in the young woman's reply as Arthur heard the desk drawer's clunking sound again.

When the old crone hiked on one strap of her backpack, Arthur ducked his head back inside the elevator and quickly released the hold

127

button, pressing the number 7 instead as the doors closed silently.

On the seventh floor, he stepped out into a corridor of seemingly emptied offices. Arthur placed the heavy vase on the floor and waited a full two minutes, the light outside his elevator blinking 6, then descending through the intervening numbers to L, for the lobby.

Arthur waited one minute more, going over his next few steps mentally before pushing the elevator button and lifting the vase again. When the doors opened, he stepped inside. Plucking from the cellophane the tiny note he'd penned at the florist shop, Arthur stuck the envelope in his jacket pocket and pressed another button.

For the sixth floor again.

"Good-bye, Quigley," said Sheilah, hefting her overnight bag.

He looked up at her, a little cross-eyed, his way of playing on her sympathy.

"I left you an extra dish of dry food and double the water, just in case Krissie doesn't come through tomorrow."

A tilt of his head and the throaty, crackling cry.

"Oh, okay." Leaning the bag against the front door of the apartment, she reached down and picked up the tabby, his fur soft as acrylic, his purring throat a seductive vibration against her breasts.

"I'll miss you, but don't tear the place apart,

okay? And leave Mr. Fuzzums under the comforter."

Then Sheilah Quinn set the cat down and warded him off with her bag while she opened the door to the hallway.

"Ohmigod!"

Arthur Ketterson relished the impression he inspired, realizing that since he'd met Sheilah only in jail, this was, of course, the first time her secretary was seeing him in the flesh.

So to speak.

Arthur rested the vase on the corner of her desk. "Well, I guess it's obvious you know who I am. Would you be Krissie?"

The blond cow — with a terraced coiffure and cheap metal rings through various parts of her ears — nodded once. A coarser version of the slut Giordano, but something more there, too. Indefinable.

Arthur made a ceremony of looking around the suite and its closed office doors. "I wonder, could you ring Sheilah? These, probably not surprisingly, are for her."

The poor cow made no movement.

"Krissie?"

"Sheilah's . . . gone . . . the weekend."

Good Lord, she is positively terrified of me. Positively delicious, too, that emotion, but what does it say about her employer's display of confidence in my innocence?

"A pity." Arthur decided not to let the young

Krissie off the hook quite yet, so he asked her a question he didn't really need answered. "Perhaps you could give me Sheilah's home address and I could drop them off there?"

An involuntary glance toward the old Rolodex near her telephone. "I . . . can't."

"Well." Arthur could sense Krissie's mounting desire to get away from him. "Here's what we do, then. I'd like to leave these for Sheilah. If you could just put them in her office, I'll have done the best I can by way of expressing my deepest thanks."

The cow stood and carefully lifted the vase while eyeing him. Krissie first backed, then tentatively headed toward the nearer of the two closed inner doors. She opened the door — with some difficulty, given the weight of the vase — and disappeared from sight past the corner of a large desk.

"Oh, Krissie?"

Her head popped around the doorjamb like something in a Marx Brothers skit. Marvelous, simply marvelous.

Arthur said, "Could you perhaps take a scissors and cut the cellophane from around the blossoms? I'm afraid otherwise they'll smother and wilt."

"Uh, for sure."

The head popped back into Sheilah's office. As soon as Arthur heard the crinkling and shearing begin, he slipped open the bottom right drawer of Krissie's desk, being careful to follow

Etta's suggestion of pulling up on the handle. Quiet as a mouse.

Delving into the pocketbook — one of those drawstring affairs — Arthur saw a little flapped hook holding several rings of keys and pursed his lips, then noticed one ring had a white tab on it and "S.Q." written in script. Ah, thank you, Krissie.

He pulled those keys off the hook and drew the strings on the bag. Replacing it in the drawer, Arthur flipped the *Q* tab on the Rolodex, finding a card marked "S.Q." between "Quayle" (no doubt one of the Persimmon Queen's trust clients) and "Quinones" (not much doubt which lawyer was handling that, was there?). Arthur already knew the address, of course, but the apartment number and telephone were helpful, so he memorized them.

Flipping the Rolodex back to where it had been, Arthur returned to the visitor's side of the desk with ten seconds of crinkling and shearing to spare.

Krissie came toward him from Sheilah's office, still holding the scissors. Probably subliminal, thought Arthur, but at least her subconscious is attuned to potential danger.

"Thank you so much, Krissie. I'll be off now."

"Right. Uh, like, congratulations on getting out of jail."

"Why, thank you. Again."

How touching, thought Arthur, closing the door behind him. Not sincere, certainly, but really quite professional of the young Krissie to think of saying it. That was the indefinable quality I noticed in her, and I'll have to compliment Sheilah as employer.

The next time I see the dear woman, of course.

The Miata cruised easily on the interstate, Sheilah beating most of the rush-hour traffic commuting out of the city. A New Age cassette by Suzanne Ciani lifted her spirits, the piano music from the tape player pinging clearly through minispeakers in the headrest despite the chilly wind whistling past her ears. Kind of a contradiction, having the top down and the heat on, but it seemed just the combination of opposites that she hoped would work well over the next forty-eight hours.

Reaching up to pull off the barrette holding her hair, Sheilah hesitated. I'll look blown to hell by the time I get there, she thought. On the other hand, it's early enough, we won't be going out to dinner right away.

Thinking about how they'd spend that hour or so, what he would do to her hair and everything else he'd touch, Sheilah Quinn experienced a subtle tingle below the seat belt. A sensation from the "right chimes being rung," as Etta would say.

Unclasping the barrette, Sheilah shook her head. The wind whipped her hair horizontally behind her neck, the tug on the roots like the urgent touch of an ardent lover.

She felt her weekend beginning already. Beginning the way she'd envisioned it, and Sheilah Quinn decided she was very glad to have decided to follow through on the invitation.

Standing on the platform under Bing Square, waiting for the subway to the Amtrak station, Etta Yemelman thought back to her ride down in the elevator at the office building. She'd enjoyed that, the scent of flowers in the car, as though somebody had just gotten a bouquet delivered. Etta was born and bred a city girl and always enjoyed being in any urban area. But there was something about the smell of flowers, the possibility of romance —

No. Enough already. You're daydreaming like that old woman next to you at the hairdresser's.

Etta believed in just a shampoo and a cut, keep it simple, but the woman in the next chair was having what Fritz, her hairdresser, called "the works." The woman kept going on and on about how the scalp massage from Fritz was the only sensual contact she still experienced at her age. Truth was, Etta had to agree with her, but she would never express such a thought. You give up hope like that in this life and the nursing home was just a cab ride away.

Which was not the reason she didn't take cabs, mind you. No, if a client matter was hanging in the balance, she would. But in addition to the ecological waste of the engine to carry just one passenger, Etta always felt that having to take a cab betrayed a failure of planning. Just like using the damned fax-whatever. Nobody planned ahead anymore, everybody relying on technology to bail them out of professional oversights.

A couple of teenagers, both black males, came down the steps into the station. One had his hair shaped so that it was wider at the top than over his ears, like the front view of an aircraft carrier Etta had once seen in the harbor. The other boy had a striking pigmentation problem, an imbalance of some kind that made most of his complexion brown except for virtually pink rings around his eyes and mouth.

Every white face on the platform studied them briefly, though Etta didn't believe the reaction had anything to do with either boy's distinctiveness. No, we're all thinking, Are they trouble? If so, am I going to be a target?

God forgive me, thought Etta. I remember a time when it wasn't like that. Or it was, I guess, the shoe just being on the other foot, the blacks being afraid of how the whites would treat them. But even with the uneasiness I feel now, they're citizens, I'm a citizen, and we're all entitled to be waiting here for public transportation. Those boys aren't challenging me, and if they do, I stand my ground. Better to be killed with your head held high than scurrying away like some frightened rat.

Now, where was — oh, right, the technology dreck. That's the problem: Kids today, they don't read. All they watch are screens. Movie screens, TV screens, video screens for the games and all. Even Krissie at work, all the time looking at the computer screen, talking about "uploading" this and "downloading" that. Nobody under the age of thirty has a book in their hands anymore.

The two black teenagers were now circling the crowd, the people on the fringe edgy as Strange Hair jostled Stranger Skin. For something to do, Etta glanced down to be sure the third rail, the high-voltage one, was still where it was supposed to be. Then she leaned over the tracks a little, looking up the tunnel for the telltale headlights of her subway train. No sign of it.

Pulling the backpack off her shoulder, Etta undid the side flap and removed the book recommended for the class she was taking — the class that required her to sneak away from the office early every Tuesday and Thursday. Etta looked at the title on the book's cover. Computer gibberish followed by *for Dummies*.

She knew how Krissie — and even Sheilah — thought about her. A dinosaur, the *Ettasaurus*. Well, maybe she was. A creature, a species, even, whose era was passing. Somebody who sat next to old women — all right, all right, to *other* old women — at the hairdresser's. And who took the train to New York to visit yet another old woman, a college classmate who'd lost her husband the year after Etta had lost Irv. Romantic? No, but a fine dinner tonight, a walk through a couple of museums tomorrow, and a Broadway show for Saturday evening. Not so bad for a retired judge in her seventy-sixth year.

And — Etta was sure of this — she'd learn about the computer screens. From this book, which she had to read every page of at least three times before each class and twice afterward. You can't learn about books from a computer, but you can learn about computers from a book.

So long as you don't quit.

Etta opened the "dummies" volume. Glancing around once for the black boys, and seeing them now joshing harmlessly with each other, she found her place on page 32. Sighing once, Etta Yemelman began to read slowly, haltingly, about "Setting Printer Protocols."

Arthur Ketterson came through the doorway, and the man behind the counter in the closet-sized shop near the florist looked up from a vise in front of him. Unlike the young Krissie, the locksmith showed not a flicker of recognition. Or intelligence, thought Arthur. A troll with grease-stained hands and grease-stained pants.

Which came first, I wonder, the chicken or the egg? Did the hands stain the pants, or did —

"What can I do for you?"

Arthur held out the keys with the S.Q. tag removed. "One of each, please. Quick as you can."

The troll took the keys and brought both to his eye in a maddeningly slow manner, a jeweler appraising the rarest of stones in an exotic setting. "These yours?"

"No. A friend's."

"Well, I gotta tell you, this one's no problem. But this other here, it looks like a downstairs security door."

"Meaning?"

"Meaning they're a bitch to match from a copy like this, instead of the master."

"Very well," said Arthur. "In that case, give me three of that downstairs one."

"Three?"

"Increases the odds of a copy working by several hundred percent."

The troll just stared at him.

"Look, my good man, I'm in a bit of a hurry here."

"Gonna take me awhile. I gotta —"

"Twenty dollars for you if all four are done in five minutes."

"Let's see it first."

Arthur laid one of George Lofton's fifties on the counter. "I'll expect change from that."

Staring at the bill, the troll nodded but gave no evidence of hopping to.

Arthur used the palm of his right hand to push back on the cuff of his left sleeve. "I'll time you." A thought pleased him, and he smiled. "Pretend you're on a game show," Arthur Ketterson said, pointing with an index finger at the locksmith and saying, "All right . . . go!"

Just like the inane hosts always used to do on

the television monitors in the Admin Unit.

Off the interstate and onto the winding country lanes, Sheilah drove more slowly now, but it was more fun to put the little Miata through its paces. Upshift to fourth, downshift to third before winding around a sharp curve, then accelerate and upshift again. And once more into fifth.

God, I love this little car, and I don't do this kind of driving often enough.

The foliage on the hillsides was just starting to turn. The sugar maples red, the birches yellow, the oaks orange. Long, flat clouds tracked slowly through a bluer than blue sky, their shadows undulating over the slopes like giant earth-worms.

Music still poured from the headrest, now Yanni's concert at the Acropolis, which Sheilah had recorded from a CD onto a ninety-minute cassette. She ran a quick check on her inner self: The *Ketterson* case seemed a million miles away and a million years ago. The music and scenery was relaxing her by the mile, the driving just challenging enough to keep her alert, on the edge of excitement.

Exactly the contrasting images I want to project tonight, she thought, checking her watch against the failing sunlight.

"Oh, I'm so glad you're still here."
Krissie jumped, her jerking fingers hitting ten

keys at once, making the goddamn cursor freeze again. Her brain racing, she thought, Like, you scared the shit out of me last time. Once a day isn't enough for you?

What Krissie said was, "It's still . . . Friday."

"So it is."

"What I mean . . . Sheilah's not —"

"No, no, I didn't think she would be. But" — he reached into his pocket, even that little gesture just so totally creepy coming from him — "I'd gotten nearly halfway home before realizing I'd forgotten the note."

"The note?"

"Yes. When I picked up the flowers, you see, I was afraid the card would fall out of the cellophane on the walk over here. So, I stuck the thing in my pocket and then completely forgot about it when you were kind enough to receive them earlier. I wonder," he said, extending the baby-size envelope to her, "would you mind?"

Krissie took the note from him, then stood up and went into Sheilah's office again. She put the card down on the desk, thinking, He's like that Bela guy with the eyes from that awesome Johnny Depp flick, *Ed Flood*, or whatever it was. Only this guy is American and kind of good-looking. Even preppy, like some of the other lawyers Sheilah or Etta have over here.

A vampire preppy. That would make a totally bizarre flick, wouldn't it?

From outside by her desk, Krissie heard "I wonder, could you perhaps tape the note to one of the flower stems, just to be sure Sheilah notices it first thing?"

Yeah, like she's gonna miss the fucking garden growing next to her phone. "Uh, for sure."

Pulling out a drawer to find Sheilah's tape dispenser, Krissie heard a slight echo of the sound from near the suite's front door.

Funny. I wonder if my desk does that for Sheilah in here?

After attaching the envelope to one of the stems, Krissie put the dispenser back and walked through the inner doorway. Ketterson was sitting on the edge of her desk, but he stood up as soon as she came near him. The first guy Krissie could ever remember doing that for her, and he had to be Sheilah's creep client.

Just bizarro. Totally.

"Krissie, you've been such a big help. Thank you."

She pretended not to see his hand extended toward her. Touching him was com-*plete*-ly out of the question, at least during this incarnation. "You're welcome. Like, enjoy your freedom, huh?"

"Oh, I am." Krissie thought those Bela eyes got just a little softer for a second. "But thank you for taking the trouble to concern yourself." He turned to leave. "Good-bye."

God, I hope you really mean it this time.

After Arturus the Vampire Preppy left, Krissie decided she had to go to the bathroom before dealing with the frozen cursor. Then there'd be another hour or more of entering Etta's revisions for the trust document, depending on how many of Krissie's changes the computer had saved before the keyboard seized up.

Etta, I admire — no, tell the truth — I love you. Like you were my grandmother or something. But I gotta say, sometimes the work you ask me to do is an awesome pain in the ass.

Krissie opened her desk drawer and lifted out her handbag, making sure she had an extra light-days pad in there. Good thing, too, because the S.Q. tab was nearly falling off its ring, all the times she'd handled it recently.

No, after the shit I've taken — and dished out — over feeding Sheilah's cat, it would be like totally embarrassing not to know which were the keys to her place.

Right?

SIX

It was almost 7:00 P.M. when Sheilah Quinn pulled the Miata into the wide driveway of the Brook Farm Inn. Loose gravel crunched under the tires with a sound and feeling that Sheilah realized was strangely reassuring, as though the ride really had brought her someplace far different from a city paved over long ago. It helped that the other car she was hoping to see was already parked near a utility shed.

The inn itself, which Sheilah had picked sight unseen from a guidebook, was constructed of yellow clapboard. White fretwork bordered the eaves and roof gables, with shrubbery trimmed and shade trees looming over everything. Still sitting in the driver's seat, Sheilah looked up at the arcing limbs and took a deep breath. Letting it out felt so good, like when she was a little girl and knew all her chores for the day were done.

Except one. Sheilah raised the roof of the Miata to avoid sap and dew falling on the upholstery, then carried her single piece of luggage up the leaf-flecked path to the main entrance of the inn.

The screen door was closed, the inner wooden one open. Next to the jamb, someone had tacked a xeroxed WANTED poster, a calico cat's sly face in full front and profile as the "criminal.' The poster read: IF HE'S OUT, DON'T LET HIM IN. IF HE'S IN, DON'T LET HIM OUT.

Sheilah found herself smiling. We're going to like this place.

Glancing both inside and out but seeing no cat matching the one on the poster, Sheilah opened the screen door. A little bell tinkled over her head, a woman's voice calling out, "Come on in. Around the corner toward the library."

Sheilah followed the voice and saw a fortyish woman standing beside a Dutch door, the top half open to the kitchen area behind her. The door had a flat counter on the lower half, and the woman looked up, smiling, from a recipe box she'd been holding. "I'm Anne. My husband, Joe, and I are the proud owners of this establishment." She hefted the box. "Which includes making sure I have what it takes for tomorrow's breakfast."

Sheilah walked toward her, swiveling her head to take in the books on the shelves. Dickinson, Ginsberg, Keats, Longfellow. "All poets, Anne?"

The woman smiled, but differently this time. "Yes. When Joe and I were looking to make career changes, this place was on the market, and the thought of having all these beautiful verses around us . . . I don't know, it was sort of reassuring, I guess."

Sheilah remembered how she'd felt parking the car, then glanced around the room, drinking

143

it in like another deep breath. "I agree with you."

"Good. And you are?"

Sheilah smiled herself. Anne obviously didn't recognize her, the television coverage out here either thinner or ignored. In fact, isn't there a poem about that, the fleeting something of fame?

"Sheilah Quinn, Anne."

A nod as she shook hands. "Your friend's already here. Room four, upstairs and end of the hall. Our most private suite."

"I'm glad. It's kind of a special occasion."

"Well, please let us know if we can make it any more so. If you'll step this way, we can get you registered."

After finishing with Anne, Sheilah carried her bag up the central staircase. The room in front of her had a brass 3 on it, so she followed the hall to its end. The bag started feeling lighter somehow.

Sheilah knocked on number 4, the door swinging open immediately, as though the person behind it had been waiting for her.

She looked at him; he was naked except for a towel doubled over and tucked in at the waist.

He said, "What took you so long?"

"I drove the speed limit."

"Why?"

"A trooper scopes me, I can't just tin him or her to avoid a ticket."

Frank Sikes grinned at Sheilah, the cant of his eyes making a little part of her begin to melt.

"Maybe it's time an agent of law enforcement did catch up to you."

Sheilah Quinn brushed the fingernails of her free hand lightly over the lower front of his towel as she moved by him into the room. "I'll come quietly, Officer."

"I hope not," said Frank, having to clear his throat to say it.

The cabbie craned his neck to take in the red-brick mansion with the white pillars holding up the front porch of the estate house known as Woodmere to generations of Kettersons. "Hell of a place you got here, buddy."

"It's quite comfortable."

Which was more than Arthur could say about the man's taxi. The backseat's upholstery was shabby beyond belief, and the interior fairly reeked from a flatulence born of garlic. Penance for not hiring a car, Arthur thought, but the marvelous jolt he'd derived from visiting the young Krissie had left him feeling . . . spontaneous.

The driver slowed to a stop in front of a marble fountain, the one Arthur's great-grandfather had stripped from Florence and shipped to the States when such coups were still feasible. "Fare comes to twenty-seven-ninety."

Getting out of the taxi, Arthur gave him thirty dollars of George Lofton's cash and suggested the cabbie use the difference to buy an air freshener.

"Fucking rich pricks make me fucking sick,"

said the driver, peeling rubber as he shifted into gear.

Arthur turned casually, watching the cab careen down Woodmere's macadam drive, disappearing into the privacy grove just before the gated stone fence. Redundant little toad.

"Welcome home, sir."

Speaking of toads. Arthur turned again. The door behind him had opened silently, and Parsons stood in the doorway, dressed as always in the modified livery of tweed sports coat, regimental tie, and cavalry twill slacks. When his mother died, Arthur had inherited the estate, oodles of money, and Howard Parsons, though but for the man's signature on household account checks, Arthur wouldn't have been able to recall his butler's first name. The job title "butler" also was a bit misleading, because shortly after his mother's death, Arthur dismissed all the other servants Parsons had supervised. However, Madeline Ketterson had called the man her "butler," and Arthur would no more dishonor her choice than —

"Sir?"

"Ah, beg your pardon, Parsons. Lost in thought." Arthur changed his tone. "Wise of you not to tax yourself by attending the trial."

"Thank you, sir. Aside from my testimony in your favor, I couldn't see how I might be of service in the courtroom, and I was concerned, of course, about the house and grounds."

Parsons, the perfect windup toy, with Thursdays and Sundays "at leisure," which he spent God knows where. But reliable enough, and actually rather nice to come home to, in an android sort of way.

The butler twitched his head almost imperceptibly. "I thought you might enjoy beef Wellington tonight, with perhaps one of the first growths?"

The true aesthetic of wealth, though Arthur. The best wine matched to the finest food.

Arthur shook his head.

Parsons frowned ever so slightly. "You'd care for something else, then, sir?"

"No, no. You're right on target, Parsons, as always. A Haut Brion, one of the brighter vintages, though."

"And the osso buco, I think," said Sheilah Quinn.

Frank Sikes looked at her over his menu, but Sheilah was smiling at the ponytailed little waiter, handing him back her own menu. She and Frank had strolled hand in hand from the Brook Farm Inn to the Italian Grotto, and now she'd ordered the most expensive item the restaurant had to offer.

Going to take me awhile to get used to her treating, he thought. But then again, I'd better, because Sheilah's going to have to do that for a while, at least until my almost-ex-wife, Pam, and her divorce lawyer get finished picking over the financial carcass of our marriage.

"And for you, sir?"

Frank broke his train of thought. "Prime rib, medium."

The waiter nodded and didn't write it down, as though he'd pegged Frank for a prime-rib guy the minute they'd walked into the place.

And quite a place it was, too. White linen tablecloths, twisted iron candlesticks on the tables echoing the grating over the windows, as though this restaurant in the middle of rural nowhere had to worry about break-ins or rocks through the glass. The walls were covered by some kind of scrolled, scored paper in dark red, pastoral scenes of shepherds and lakes and —

"Hey, stranger?"

"Sorry, Sheil. I was just thinking."

"About?"

"How this place doesn't remind me of home cooking."

Frank immediately regretted saying that, afraid it would remind Sheilah of his wife still being technically in the picture. Or remind her of the fact that they couldn't easily entertain each other at their apartments, especially while the case of Arthur Ketterson the fucking IV was hanging fire. Frank's own place was more anonymous, but a real dive in a grungy part of town. And if they went to her place, all it would take would be one reporter who knew them both doing a badly timed drive past Sheilah's building, and HOMICIDE DICK VISITS DEFENSE ATTORNEY IN LOVE NEST would be the lead headline neither of them would want to see.

Instead of being put off about the "home cooking" remark, Sheilah reached across the table, sandwiching one of his hands in both of hers. "Thanks for showing a girl a great time back at the inn."

"Must have been the African-American side of the gene pool."

Frank heard a gruff laugh from the bar, and he realized he might have spoken a little too loudly. Looking over there, he saw one white guy nudge another in the ribs, not even bothering to glance away when his and Frank's eyes met. Dressed in office clothes, the men had some size to them but they struck him as a couple of yahoos who might have to —

"Frank?"

He came back to her again. "Sorry."

"Don't let anything spoil this, okay?"

"Okay."

The waiter brought the wine Sheilah had ordered, some kind of red, which Frank guessed might go more with his meal than hers, though all he knew about osso buco was that veal figured in it somewhere. Sheilah sampled and approved the wine, the waiter pouring for both of them before leaving the table.

She clinked her glass to Frank's, a musical sound that hung in the air. "To the beginning of a great getaway."

He tried the wine.

Sheilah said, "What do you think?"

149

Frank was going to say it tasted like the smoothest cherry cough medicine he'd ever swallowed, but instead he remembered a line some English actor had said in a Peter Sellers film. " 'Impertinent little claret.' "

She laughed, like the musical sound their glasses had made, only deeper. "Where'd that come from?"

"What makes you think I didn't make it up myself?"

"Because only the British call wine 'claret,' and then only some French reds."

"I got it off a movie. We didn't have much opportunity to enjoy wine with dinner when I was growing up."

Frank watched Sheilah roll her lower lip under her upper teeth, the way he'd learned she did when she wanted to put a question but was weighing how to phrase it.

"Ask," he said.

The lip came back out. "All right. My family didn't have wine at home very often, either."

"That doesn't sound like a question."

"It was a preamble. The question is, How come if we both grew up in houses instead of mansions, you seem to take offense at some things I had to learn on my own?"

It was a good question, because Frank knew he was guilty of doing exactly that. "You're a lawyer; I'm just a cop."

"The difference being one more level of education?"

"And maybe some other differences, too."

"For instance?"

Frank drank a little more wine, worked over how to explain things. "Sheil, I told you my dad was African-American, my mom white, right?"

"No news so far."

"Well, they didn't go out much, and not just because of the money thing. If we all went to a restaurant — like for my birthday or anything — I'd see the people watching us. Sometimes we couldn't get served, even in this bastion of liberal thought."

"Frank, that was what, thirty-plus years ago?"

"So?"

"So now we're here, not there."

"Sheil, we didn't exactly pass the 'no blink' test with those guys at the bar."

"That's their problem."

Frank thought about it. Thought back, too, to the time he was a rookie and two white officers — the Clooney brothers — decided they didn't like the way he talked with the white female dispatcher. Or the way she flirted with him. So they caught him in the locker room after shift one day and tried to stretch adhesive tape over his pubic hairs, then tear it off, give him a "wax job," as they called it. Only the brothers had underestimated him, almost to the point of becoming the Clooney sisters.

"What's so funny?" asked Sheilah.

"Nothing. You're right. Let's enjoy the dinner, the fortune you're spending on it."

"It's not a fortune, Frank."

He decided to push a little. "And besides, a truly rich client is basically paying for it?"

"Frank —"

"Sheil, we have to talk about this guy. Ketterson —"

"Please, not now."

She squeezed his hand, and Frank Sikes said, "All right."

"Dinner was satisfactory, sir?"

Arthur Ketterson dabbed the damask napkin against his lips, then sighed. "Truly magnificent, Parsons. Your handling of the sauce was impeccable, as always."

"Thank you, sir." The older man reached for the crystal decanter, the plate under it sterling silver. "More wine?"

"No. No, in fact, treat yourself to that last glass." Arthur looked up at the short wall of the dining room to the portrait of his paternal grandfather. His mother's portrait had been displayed there when she was alive, but after her death, he'd had it rehung — Arthur couldn't help but smile a little at the convergence of verb — in her bedroom. "I believe I'll take a snifter of grandfather's Napoléon to Mother's Dell."

"I may have to open a new bottle, sir."

"That's all right." Arthur thought back upon the extraordinary events of the day that followed three months of tedium. "After all, it is a rather special night, isn't it?"

"Quite, sir," said Parsons, a bit dryly even for him, Arthur thought.

"Sheil, that was one hell of a dining experience."

"I'm glad, Frank."

They were walking arm in arm with a lazy, swinging gait toward the Brook Farm Inn. The little shops in the village were closed for the night, display windows barely backlit to allow for wishful browsing. They'd lingered over dessert at the Italian Grotto, finishing the last of the wine. Sheilah was glad the two guys at the bar had left earlier, apparently being able to afford to drink but not eat at the restaurant. Yeah, right, thought Sheilah, like I really can. But it was a special kind of night, and she wanted to learn more about the man next to her.

Sheilah leaned into Frank a bit with her next step. "Can I reopen a previous line of questioning?"

"You may, counselor."

Frank intoned the words, as if he was mocking Roger Hesterfield.

Sheilah almost giggled, but she stifled it. As lightly as possible, she said, "How come you always use 'African-American' instead of 'black'?"

Sheilah felt Frank tense against her arm, drawing it closer to his rib cage. "Couple of reasons. One, it's more descriptive."

"Descriptive?"

"Africa's where we came from, Sheil."

"Even though your mom was white."

"Sheilah, let me tell you something, you haven't already noticed it. I'm not saying there isn't any skin-tone discrimination among African-Americans. Hell, before the sixties, I was what a young sister would love to have as her boyfriend. 'Lighter was righter,' you know? Then came the assassination of Dr. King, and suddenly 'blacker was better.' But to the majority of people in this country, if you're colored at all, you aren't even a little white, okay?"

Okay. "What are the other reasons?"

"For not using 'black'?"

"Uh-huh."

"Well, 'African-American' is more consistent."

"With?"

"Everybody else. You say 'Irish-American,' right?"

"No. Usually, just 'Irish.' "

Frank smiled without showing any teeth. "O'Toole, too, but I kind of hoped he was just a moron."

"Okay, I'll grant you 'Irish-American' and 'Italian-American' and enough other hyphens to sustain the 'consistency' reason. Anything else?"

"Yeah, but I think it's a little more subtle."

"What is?"

"When people write 'African-American' — or even in the way they say it — it gets capitalized."

Sheilah thought that over. "And 'black' doesn't."

154

"Right. If everybody else gets capitalized, we'd like to be, as well."

Sheilah laid her head against Frank's shoulder, riding in rhythm with his stride. "I think that makes a lot of sense."

"Good." Sheilah felt him shift inside. "Can I open a previous line of questioning, too?"

"What's good for the goose . . ."

"Arthur Ketterson."

Sheilah jerked her head away from its resting place. "Aw, Frank, cut it out, huh?"

"Sheil, the guy worries me."

"He's my concern, not yours."

"You ever really watch the guy, see that hoppy look in his eye?"

"I watched him with the jury, while he told his side of things on the stand. I didn't see any 'hoppy' look then."

"Granted the guy's a great actor. But other times, when he doesn't think you're watching him, he kind of breaks role, you know?"

Sheilah did know what Frank meant, and the same wobbly chill she'd felt at the initial client conference with Ketterson went through her.

"Sheil, you okay?"

"Yes . . . fine. You ever stop to think he might be innocent?"

"Ketterson tell you that?"

Now Sheilah slid her arm out from Frank's. "Come on, you know I can't talk about what he's told me in confidence."

"But you really think the guy's not a killer?"

"I've been around a lot of bad ones, Frank, career criminals facing serious time. And that makes them very serious about what happens at trial, what happens to their lives as a result. Ketterson is . . ."

"Is what?"

"He treats it more like a game that amuses him, like it doesn't really involve him."

"So, great. He's nuts, too."

"Nobody — not from your side of the aisle or mine — has ever questioned his competency."

"I don't mean he's legally insane, Sheil. I mean the guy's not right, like spoiled milk. And shit, we found his print on the Giordano woman's bra."

"Frank, he explained that from the stand."

"Well, I still think he did it."

"Which is why cops investigate and juries deliberate."

When Frank Sikes didn't respond, Sheilah Quinn knew she'd won the argument, but that didn't make her feel any better.

Brandy snifter cradled snugly in his right hand, Arthur Ketterson walked through the garden and onto the path down into Mother's Dell. The path was lighted by small solar-powered ground lights, but with each step, he found he had to contain his stride.

Three months away from the holiest of places. It's no wonder I feel the impulse to hurry.

When Arthur reached the copse of trees, he

paused, breathing deeply. There was enough moonlight to see that the dell was just as he'd left it except for a few scrub bushes and predictable weeds. Deal with those in the morning.

After a moment, Arthur moved toward the miniature wooden shed he'd painstakingly fashioned as the weatherproof holder for a folding chair and a white resin cocktail table. He brought the table out first, setting his snifter on top of it. Then Arthur went back and carried the chair to the left side of the table before unfolding it. He realized he'd arrogated these little procedures to the level of ritual, but repeating them gladdened him more than he could have guessed.

Settling into the chair, Arthur looked to the headstone marking Madeline Ketterson's grave. Fifteen years ago, the authorities had objected to his mother being buried on the estate, some stupid regulation or other. However, George Lofton saw to it, which, of course, was what he was paid to do.

Lifting his eyes from the gravestone, Arthur took in each of the fruit trees that, at a measured radius, surrounded it. Then he smiled, as he always did, and not just a controlled smile, either. No, this was the fulsome reflection of something rising from deep within, the beatific smile of the satisfied soul.

"I'm home, Mother," said Arthur Ketterson IV, savoring the sound of each syllable as it left his lips.

The rest of the walk back to the inn was awkward, Frank feeling a little guilty about having brought up the *Ketterson* case, but not knowing quite how to handle it. Once in the room, Sheilah said, "What's this?"

When Frank turned, he saw her looking at the mantel over the fireplace at the foot of the four-poster bed. "Is that a card?"

Sheilah lifted the tiny envelope that lay between the two thimblelike glasses of amber liquid. The card inside read, "With the compliments of the Brook Farm Inn."

She said, "It's a gift from Anne and Joe."

"The owners?" Frank moved to the glasses, picking them up and sniffing over one. "Smells like it's made from some kind of nut."

Sheilah leaned toward him and sniffed hers. "Sherry."

"Good as a nightcap?"

Sheilah's eyes smiled back at him. "Or we could pool them."

" 'Pool them'?"

"As syrup for a . . . second dessert?"

It took a minute for Frank to realize what she meant.

Sipping his brandy, Arthur said, "So, while the ordeal is far from over, I'm really rather impressed by my lawyer. Despite her father being quite ill, a stroke victim, according to George . . ."

158

Arthur paused, nearly coughing on the brandy now as an image came to him. An image of Sheilah speaking to her father as Arthur spoke to his mother. What a striking parallel to conjure, another omen of what was meant to be. But, back to reality for the moment.

"I'm sure you'd like her, Mother. She's what you might have been like if you'd attended law school instead of art school. In fact, I think that calls for a toast." Arthur raised his glass in the direction of the headstone. "To all the attractive women who've enjoyed higher education."

Swallowing a soupçon of brandy, Arthur thought back to that night of nights, fifteen years before. His mother asking him to come to her suite after dinner, no doubt feeling the intimacy of the bedroom preferable to the more severe furnishings of the parlor. Madeline Ketterson fixing her son with those eyes, telling him, flat out and oh so bravely. "I'm afraid I have cancer, Arthur. In both breasts. The doctor . . ."

He recalled her voice showing just the slightest patina of cracks then, but she continued. "They're going to have to do an operation, Arthur. Mother won't be . . . beautiful anymore."

And then she turned, and began to cry. He knew her so well, how important the perfection of beauty always had been to her. And Arthur knew also what she was asking of him — so subtly, so obliquely, so . . . Mother. Asking of him as "the man of the house," which he'd been since his father's death in a car crash. Madeline Ketterson needing the help of her son to prevent his first love from becoming ugly to herself. Instead, to keep her beautiful, and perfect, in his eyes and hers.

Forever.

Then Arthur's gaze fell upon the apricot tree he'd planted. For Diana, the first one after his mother, back in . . . Can it be six years already? Yes. Yes, his senior year of college, when he'd heard about the neighbor of a woman he'd been seeing. Just the whisper of poor Diana's affliction, but no doubt of the eventual result. Gross imperfection. So tragic, yet so . . . familiar?

And thus it was that Arthur found his niche. Scouting Diana so "innocently," so subtly each time he visited the neighborhood of the woman he was seeing. He was wise enough, after "helping" Diana avoid imperfection with her own bra, too, to see to it that she merely . . . disappeared, so no embarrassing body could turn up to trigger piercing questions.

Following that experience, he was to discover also that the affliction itself wasn't the key. No, the key was to find a beautiful woman of approximately his mother's last age, thirty-four. Someone teetering on that cusp, the delicate metaphysical membrane between being perfect and . . . not. To observe her, to stimulate her, to cause her to envision the gratitude she'd feel toward him. And finally to help her avoid the inevitable ugliness of growing old, allowing himself exquisite enjoyment in the process.

Arthur sighed. Then, so as not to slight anyone, he raised the snifter first toward the apricot tree and then individually to the cherry and the plum, each of which he'd planted and, naturally, named after the woman buried beneath it.

"To Diana . . . and Hedy . . . and Lorraine."

Aglow with the sense of both accomplishment and anticipation, Arthur Ketterson downed the remainder of his brandy.

They both lay naked in the four-poster under just a sheet. Sheilah had hoped that the atmosphere and the after-dinner drink would have dispelled the bad feelings associated with their walk from the restaurant, but she could tell as she'd used Frank's sherry and her mouth making love to him that it wasn't to be.

The first time we've been together that he hasn't responded to me sexually.

Oh, we both made appropriate noises of pleasure, each of us comforting the other with excuses of "too much food, too much wine," but the passion just hadn't been there. We weren't "feeling" each other the way we had before, like I can "feel" a witness in the courtroom sometimes, the rapport that's almost like making love. Then again, maybe twice in six hours was a little much for a man in his forties, even his early forties.

But Sheilah didn't think that was the real

reason, and she noticed that even the cuddling afterward — after nothing, really — didn't last very long.

Arthur entered the house from the back patio, Parsons already, he was sure, asleep in his quarters. However, the butler had left on the little night-lights at the baseboard of the central staircase, like a sprinkling of fairy dust guiding Arthur's way up the steps.

At the top of the staircase, Arthur turned left, to his own suite. It consisted of a drawing room, full bath, and sleeping room with a sleigh-style queen-sized bed flanked by Oriental rugs and covered by a rather colorful quilt that his mother had bought for him sometime before he was ten.

"Purchase the best, Arthur, and it will repay your investment by wearing well."

Inside his bedroom, he moved to the walk-in closet. Upon arriving earlier, Arthur really hadn't taken the time to remind himself of the pleasures of touching his wardrobe. His real wardrobe, not just that subset the judicial system had permitted him as court clothes. Arthur's fingers grazed a shoulder here, a sleeve there. The finest materials carefully tailored so as to be eternally stylish, rather than momentarily fashionable. To attain and retain . . . perfection.

That was one an aspect of "jailing" that Willie's otherwise sound advice simply couldn't address. For many of the inmates, Arthur realized, being imprisoned was rather an improvement on their native environment. Meals and exercise provided as scheduled, some degree of structure in general and protection in particular. Yes, for such creatures, the death penalty would be appropriate, the termination of a life on the inside that was better than they'd had on the street. For someone like Arthur Ketterson IV, however, the experience of jailing was worse than death, due to the deprivation of precisely the things he'd enjoyed since his return home. No, for a man of wealth and taste, any prison stay, even the relatively manageable three months of pretrial detention he'd endured, bordered on the unconscionable.

Arthur stripped to his briefs before donning pajamas, the uniform his mother had always insisted upon when putting him to bed as a child. Then he stole quietly across the corridor and into her suite. The portrait she'd once commissioned — the dear Madeline wearing an evening gown and admiring her favorite lithograph of Degas dancers — hung above the high sconces on the long wall, illuminated by them like a museum piece. Arthur was struck, as always, by how well the portrait artist had captured not just his mother's appearance but also her mien, that quality that even the best photographers managed just to miss.

He was also struck, again as always, by how vividly the placement of the portrait on the wall brought back the images of that night so long ago. The night when his mother was hanging from one of those very sconces, her bra tightly around her neck, the ends of the straps wrapped around the arm of the fixture itself. A matter of luck that the sconce was so solid, a mark of the fine workmanship that had gone into building Woodmere in the first place.

Arthur thought of the look on Parsons's face as the screams of the thirteen-year-old son brought the butler into his employer's suite. How Arthur had clambered up onto the wheeled serving cart the police believed poor "suicidal" Madeline Ketterson had used as her stool, so to speak. How Arthur and Parsons frantically tried to undo the bra straps from the sconces, the woman's neck already so terribly abraded by the bra closing off and crushing her windpipe that her body simply sagged to the carpet below.

Rather a lot for a thirteen-year-old to manage, thought Arthur, as he had countless times before. Manage in more ways than one, however deceptively strong he might have been at that age.

Then Arthur looked up at his mother's portrait, the eyes speaking to him even now. He remembered vividly how each of the others had that same mien. How Sheilah's eyes had exhibited even more of Madeline Ketterson's essence the day George Lofton first brought the well-regarded criminal lawyer to see him in that godforsaken interview room at the jail. It hadn't been Arthur's first view of Sheilah by any means, but it had been his closest, and even now he shuddered giddily from the experience.

"Sheilah Quinn has your eyes, Mother. And now I have her keys."

Arthur suddenly realized how exhausted he was from the emotional ordeal of being released and coming home. Postponing the infinite pleasures of revisiting his mother's lingerie drawer, source of both her sorrow and his inspiration, Arthur walked flat-footed to her bed. He drew back the curtains that hung over the side of Madeline Ketterson's old four-poster and slipped between the sheets, pulling the covers up to just under his eyes, like a veil.

"Murder suspect successfully stalks own defense attorney," said Arthur Ketterson IV in the Headline News sort of tone only rarely heard from the video monitors in the Admin Unit. Then, more intimately, he whispered, "I wonder, Mother, could that be a first?"

SEVEN

Buttering a piece of toast, Sheilah Quinn said, "We can let last night sour the whole weekend, or we can move past it."

They were sitting by themselves in the dining room of the Brook Farm Inn, Frank wearing a corduroy sport coat and black turtleneck, Sheilah under a bulky cardigan sweater, despite the Saturday-morning sun streaming through the windows and making shimmering patterns on the hardwood floor around the table. Joe and Anne had served them, then discreetly disappeared when it was obvious the two "special occasion" guests weren't talking to each other.

Frank set down his orange juice. "Sheil, it's just that —"

"This doesn't sound like moving past it, Frank."

"Can I just say one thing?"

"One."

"Last night, you treated me to the best appetizer and dinner I've had in the last ten years."

"We had salad, not appetizers," said Sheilah.

Frank just looked at her.

"Oh," she said.

He raised the glass again. "Then I had to step

on it by bringing up your favorite client."

"Frank —"

"Not once, but twice. And it bothered me that I ruined the mood, and it bothered me enough that . . . well, you remember the rest. I'm embarrassed, and really sorry."

Sheilah nodded slowly, thinking, A man who can apologize. Be still my beating heart.

"So," Frank said, "I'm past it. How about you?"

"Me, too."

He finished his orange juice, tilting the empty glass toward the window. "The weather looks great. What would you like to do?"

Sheilah fished the color brochure out of her sweater pocket. "While you were using the bathroom, I got this from the rack by the mantelpiece."

Frank opened the folded paper. After scanning it, he looked up at her. " 'An authentic Shaker village'?"

"Broaden both our horizons."

A smile appeared under the thin mustache, and Sheilah felt a blushing quiver in what Etta would call "the right spot."

Frank said, "You're on."

Anne came into the dining room, her manner a little tentative. "How is everything?"

"Excellent," said Sheilah, meaning it.

Arthur Ketterson watched Parsons delicately remove the platter that had held three kinds of pastries. Then, without being asked, the butler poured five more ounces of fresh-brewed coffee into the bone-china cup.

"Anything else, sir?"

"I think not, Parsons." Arthur sipped appreciatively. "At least not in terms of food."

The butler waited for instruction.

"However," continued Arthur, "I thought I might drive out to the club, try something I haven't enjoyed for three long months."

"Tennis!"

Rudolph Giordano jumped a little, but he tried to concentrate on the stock quotes in the newspaper he was reading at the kitchen counter. Still dressed in his robe, Rudy hooked his feet on the bottom rung of a cocktail stool. They'd bought a set of six after he'd built the place fourteen years before.

"Oh, Rudy," his wife yelled again from their living room. "I'd forgotten how much Jessica liked tennis. Why, this one must be around the fifth grade."

Rudy closed his eyes, not from the newsprint and not for the first time, either. Rhonda with the old photo albums. Every day.

"Oh, and here's a shot of her actually playing. My God, she was so . . . graceful."

The sound of a tissue being torn from a box. The albums and the Kleenex. Morning, noon, and night. Maybe it was just a phase Rhonda had to go through. Rudy wanted to believe that.

Wanted to, but didn't.

"Graceful like a swan, Rudy. Remember?"

He did remember. Would always remember. But looking at pictures wouldn't bring Jessica back.

"So . . . graceful."

Another tissue. Another leaf of the album being turned.

"Oh, come look at this one, Rudy."

It was enough to drive a man crazy.

"And the structure in front of us is a round stone barn." The tour guide, a woman with a friendly face and a commanding voice, didn't have to shout in order to reach all the people huddled around her. "The Shakers got their name from their ecstatic religious dancing, which other people thought was just a whole lot of shaking."

Polite laughter.

"However, the Shakers focused more on farming than dancing, and in the early 1800s, they learned that feeding hay to many cows could be a time-consuming process."

To Frank Sikes's nose, especially as they entered the barn, it seemed that those cows hadn't moved out yet, though he couldn't see or hear any.

The guide, whose name tag read MOLLY, pointed upward. "So what the Shakers did was build this barn into the berm behind us. The cows entered on our level, and the hay wagon came in upstairs, from the top of the berm. The wagon would then go around the perimeter above us, one man driving the team, others forking or even just throwing the hay down over the edge for the cows to find and eat."

Frank looked toward the second floor as Sheilah Quinn said, "This is amazing."

He thought it was barely to the interesting side of okay, but he could see her point. They'd already visited a machine shop and laundry built over a millstream so that the running water could power the lathes and washers. Clever folks, these Shakers.

"And," said Molly, "since the barn was round, the wagon never had to stop and turn around. It could come in on the second level, do a circuit, and head back out again, team first onto the berm. If you walk on the planks upstairs, though, be careful. They're not nailed down."

"How come?" asked a teenaged boy with four pens in his shirt pocket.

"Another thing the Shakers learned. The spark of a horse's shoe striking a flooring nail could set off a spontaneous combustion of the hay. This way, there was no metal-on-metal possibility."

Sheilah said, "Absolutely amazing."

The tour guide swung her hand around the barn. "Spend as much time here as you'd like. Then I'll show you the communal cooking and baking facilities in the Dwelling. As most of you probably know, the Shakers are famous for their furniture design and their selling of seeds — they were the first to package seeds in envelopes for retail sales. Unfortunately, though, as you'll see from the sleeping accommodations, they were doomed to die out."

"How come?" asked the same teenaged kid in the same tone.

Molly smiled kindly. "The Shakers themselves believed in celibacy, so there was no procreation, no natural children born to the sect. They could continue on only through accepting orphans and converts."

Frank leaned close to Sheilah and whispered, "After last night, you bring me to a place where nobody had sex?"

From the way Sheilah laughed, Frank felt the rest of the weekend was going to be just fine. Maybe even "amazing."

Fascinating. That was the only word for it, Arthur Ketterson thought repeatedly during his first hour at the club. From the valet who took the keys to his BMW — and what an unfettered joy it was to be back behind the wheel of that superb machine — everyone gave him a different reaction.

On the front veranda, some pumped his hand in an absurdly overboard way, babbling good cheer at seeing him again. Others were merely polite ("Arthur" and a curt nod typical of these). Still others picked exactly the moment of his approach to lose themselves in admiring a

171

recently clipped shrub or other pedestrian aspect of the club grounds. Most fun were the ones inside the main building, where they couldn't easily escape or plead distraction. Especially the Mambo King, District Attorney Peter Mendez, no doubt talking campaign fund-raising with a couple of primping dowagers at the coffee bar, then managing to turn his back on Arthur's path. Most irksome of all was Roger Hesterfield, though, who stared at him intently from the library, something alcoholic in his fist even at 11:00 A.M. A stare, but not even a nod for a member of another old family.

Well, Jolly Roger, it all goes down in the big book, doesn't it?

On the back patio, Arthur experienced several variations on the earlier themes of welcoming before spotting the tennis professional, a rather dazzling fellow with the broadest of shoulders, the tannest of hairy forearms, the tightest of little tushes. Arthur had watched him give lessons a few times but otherwise had not paid him much mind. Must drive the pubescent girls wild, though.

Arthur knew only the pro's first name, Larry, but the man came a-running when summoned, blue eyes and hundred-watt smile gleaming. He also would be more than happy to work Mr. Ketterson into a cancellation at 11:30.

"I'll be wanting a genuine workout now, Larry."

"Yes sir."

"I've a long spell of inactivity to burn off."

The smile dimmed only a bit, consistent with what Arthur took to be the faintest of brain waves flickering behind the tanned forehead. "Just making a little joke, Larry. You may laugh."

Larry did, then briefly squeezed Arthur's arm at the bicep, a gesture the latter found almost genuine, and therefore both surprising and endearing.

Rather like — what was it? Yes. Yes, the young Krissie at Sheilah's office, congratulating me on my release.

Good service people, both. Rare finds, these days.

Rhonda Giordano set her coffee mug on the kitchen counter. "Oh, Rudy, does this bring back that week at Atlantic City?"

Christ, he thought. Give it a fucking rest, huh?

"Remember, we stayed at that great resort hotel, with the funny-shaped beds? And Jessica, how she loved to play in the surf."

Actually, Rudy could picture that. Holding his daughter's hand, running with her into the waves, her . . . the fuck do they call it? Those sounds a little kid makes, like she was already getting —

"Oh, look. This was Jessica in her first bikini."

Rudy had to get out of the kitchen. Get out before he exploded. "I'm going, Rhonda."

"Going? Going where?"

Rudy pictured one of the bars he'd visited the night his daughter died, but he said, "I have that puppet show."

"Show?"

What do I have to do, spell it out for you? "Over in the mall there," he added, walking stiffly out of the kitchen.

From behind him, Rudy Giordano heard "Wouldn't you rather look at the album from the lake?" but he kept on moving, as if he hadn't heard anything at all.

"Quite a collection, isn't it?" Sheilah said.

She could tell from the questions Frank had already asked her that he didn't know much about museums, other than to allow he'd covered a homicide at one. But Molly, the tour guide lady at the Shaker village, had recommended both a café — where they'd had a nice lunch — and this museum, so Frank had agreed to go with the second suggestion, as well.

Sheilah noticed him looking at a harbor scene. "That's a Turner."

Frank stared at it, assessing something as his eyes went over the storm light, playing on the quiet water inside the jetty but fracturing on the raging sea outside. "I like it, the way the guy — Turner was a guy, right?"

"Right."

"I like the way he uses the light to make his point."

"Me, too."

As they moved through the interconnected galleries, Frank commented on a few more seascapes by other artists and a couple of waterfalls by Bierstadt.

Then they reached a portrait exhibition. Sheilah could tell Frank wasn't nuts about the head shots, except for one of a bishop by El Greco.

"That stand for 'the Greek'?" he asked her.

"Yes. All his stuff I know about was done in Spain."

"I like the way the guy kind of floats in space."

Sheilah looked up at Frank. "You ever take art history in school?"

"I got my degree in criminal justice, Sheil. There wasn't much time for 'Great Painted Faces of the World.' "

But he said it lightly, and Frank was the first to move on to the next gallery, Sheilah smiling slightly behind him.

Lying on a lounge at the pool, Arthur sipped the piña colada. A frivolous drink, he'd always thought, but then, he was in a frivolous mood. And damned deserving of it, too, after three months in that concrete box with Willie T. Eggers and worse.

On the court, Larry had proved to be a human ball machine, consistently making Arthur hit the same shot from only slightly different foot positions. Exactly what the doctor ordered, but an hour was enough, despite Larry's offer to extend. After a handsome tip — actually earned, Arthur conceded to himself; even more rare these days — he took a steam bath and cold shower. The day had warmed up nicely outside, so Arthur had put on swimming trunks, determined to lose some of the prison pallor alongside the pool.

He took another sip of the coconut drink, then began contemplating the evening ahead. Which caused more than a slight bulging under his trunks, he was pleased to note. However, Arthur didn't want to broadcast that reaction at the club, and so he casually rolled over to hide it.

Without discouraging it, either, of course.

His armpits resting against the leaning rail of the bridge, Rudy Giordano rocked the main control bars in each hand to make the Desi and Lucy figures move toward each other on the stage floor five feet below. Pitching his voice to imitate Lucy giving a lame explanation, Rudy manipulated the main bar of Desi to have the male marionette's hands fly to his face in shock, the squeals of laughter from the audience in the mall an indication of how well the puppets in the theater were playing to the children Rudy couldn't see through the screen.

He'd originally begun playing with hand puppets for Jessica when she was still a toddler, finding that their games wore well even as she got older. But Jessica had insisted that her father put on shows for her friends, too, and as the circle of kids grew up, Rudy tried more sophisticated figures. Like rod puppets, the rods being thin umbrella ribs attached to the puppet's hands for movement.

Eventually, he got into doing public shows in the city library, then the mall, which led him to marionettes for a number of different reasons. One, the younger kids were still captivated by them, while the older kids weren't bored by them. Two, marionettes were bigger, so you could have a larger audience that could all see them. And three, marionettes had come over from Italy something like four hundred years ago, and Rudy liked that aspect of his heritage.

Hey, who am I kidding? he'd also think to himself. The reason I do marionettes is because it's like construction. You have to build yourself a little theater, with the stage floor for the puppets to walk on and the leaning rail five or so feet higher for you to brace against, manipulating the things. Then there was the making of the marionettes themselves, including hollowing out most of the frame in the chest or hips to ease up a little on the weight. You ever tried manipulating two of the bastards for ten minutes or so, you'd get the point of weight as a consideration.

And Rudy often did manipulate two puppets at once. It meant simpler control bars and therefore simpler movements, as well. Once in a while, he'd even have to hang a puppet from another horizontal bar he'd installed in front of the leaning rail in order to use both hands on one of the marionettes. But simpler control bars also meant Rudy could work alone, not have to coordinate with anybody else doing his shows, especially once he found that mimicking a lot of different voices came naturally to him.

Rudy finished the Desi and Lucy segment and lifted them up from the stage floor to cheers and applause from the audience. Christ, I love this shit, he thought. It keeps me sane, the way things play out like I want them to — every time.

Rudy hung the sitcom marionettes from hooks behind him on the bridge, then did some flexing exercises to relimber his hands and fingers. For the finale, he lifted, one at a time from other hooks, his *Beauty and the Beast* puppets from the Disney movie. The Desi and Lucy ones went over a little bigger with the parents than with their children, but now the kids went wild with recognition. Rudy used his own voice for the Beast, but he'd always adopted Jessica's voice for the Beauty. He started doing that years ago because it appealed to him, and now he couldn't change, especially after what had happened in his house and that fucking courtroom.

Rudy went through selected parts of the story from the animated movie, the bowing of the Beast not that hard — even though the kids loved it — the head and leg movements tougher to control. Tears welled in his eyes at certain points of the sweet love story, but, as he did every week, Rudy blinked them back.

After the final scene, Rudy lifted the two marionettes from the stage floor and over the leaning rail, hanging them back on their hooks. Then he came out front, the boys and girls all jumping up and down for him, the mothers and fathers shaking his hand. In low voices, the adults would tell Rudy how much they appreciated his courage in continuing to do the shows, especially those parents who had known Jessica well enough to recognize his imitation of her voice for the Beauty.

That went on for maybe ten minutes or so, like always, and Rudy felt as good as he'd feel for a week. He knew why his wife kept looking back at the photos of Jessica in the albums. He couldn't stand it, maybe, but he understood what she was doing. The photos were Rhonda's way of proving to herself that their daughter had been real, actually a part of their life for twenty-one years. Well, Rudy didn't need fucking photos for that. He had these shows, where he could talk to Jessica in the *Beauty and the Beast* segment, and he could go in her room back at the house anytime he could stomach it, look at the puppets Rhonda had replaced around the headboard of his baby's bed.

And after he got tired of schmoozing with all the mall parents and their kids out front, Rudy could walk alone behind the puppet theater — back by the leaning rail, where the marionettes hung from their hooks like so much wooden meat.

And then, when he was pretty sure nobody else was around, Rudy Giordano could use his own voice to cry his fucking heart out.

EIGHT

Sheilah Quinn swayed just a little too much with her next step, throwing Frank Sikes almost off balance. "Nice recovery, Sergeant," she murmured into his ear.

"This is dancing the way it was meant to be."

They'd just finished Saturday supper in a small jazz club a few miles from the Brook Farm Inn. The trio on the bandstand played a slow piece every third number or so, at which point many of the people at the spindly cocktail tables would get up to dance. An older crowd in a college town, there were even a number of other interracial couples on the floor.

God, thought Sheilah, this is what life is supposed to be like. Not just courtrooms and nursing homes, computerized research and elder-care bills, but real enjoyment in the embrace of a growing relationship.

She brushed her lips against Frank's ear again. "We're like those dancers from the old movies, Fred Astaire and Ginger Rogers."

Frank grunted a little laugh. "Only we're more Lionel Ritchie and Nicole Kidman."

Liking how he thought of her, Sheilah nevertheless said, "Except they aren't dancers."

"Right. But I always thought I looked kind of like Lionel, especially when I was younger. And I always envied him some, too."

"Envied? You're a lot more handsome."

"Not what I mean, Sheil. You old enough to remember the Summer Olympics back in '84?"

"I was in college then, Frank, not kindergarten."

"Okay, so picture the closing ceremonies at the L.A. Coloseum. When Lionel appeared at the top of the stadium steps like that spaceship effect just dropped him off, and he came down the stairs singing?"

"I remember."

"Well, I see that on television, and I realize, Hey, the man's performing in front of a billion people, worldwide. A billion, Sheilah, and they're all going to identify the song he's singing with the event on their screens. And I envied him that kind of . . . historical achievement, I guess."

"Frank the First, Philosopher-King."

"Hey, you expect us insensitive males to share things, you can't make fun of us when we do."

"Point taken," said Sheilah as the trio segued to an even slower tune. "God, I'm enjoying this. Could it be only five years ago that I was still going to discos?"

"More like fifteen for me, Sheil. I don't think I'd feel real comfortable in those places anymore."

She pressed her pelvis into Frank, suddenly but gently, and the sensation of him hardening against her rose from there up into her heart. "Just as well."

"Why?" he said.

"I'd rather save your energy for later."

Frank Sikes responded by drawing her in tighter to him.

Arthur Ketterson told Parsons to postpone dinner until a European hour. Arthur didn't say that given his tasks during the interim, he wished to feel light and sharp, not heavy or even logy. And besides, he needed to give the young Krissie time to discharge her catty duties and be gone.

Dressed in dark casual clothing, Arthur drove the BMW to a parking garage on the outskirts of the city — one that he'd found while seeing the slut Giordano. Within walking distance of the address Arthur wanted, the garage was as anonymous as possible while still remaining relatively vandal-free. And he certainly didn't want some overzealous minion of the law spotting his car parked anywhere near his eventual destination, there being no acceptable excuse for its being there.

Arthur retrieved from the trunk a little Coleman cooler, that model many tourists carry. Perfect for cans of soda to keep the kiddies amused, perhaps a Budweiser or two slipped in to keep Dad from growing too grouchy.

Leaving the garage, Arthur strolled with the cooler nearly half a mile to Sheilah Quinn's apartment building. No one was in sight as he approached the front entrance. Arthur had brought all three copies the locksmith had made of her downstairs key, but happily, the first one he tried fit the building's entrance door and opened it smoothly.

Ah, a good omen for the night.

Inside the empty lobby, Arthur moved to the elevator. A car was awaiting the touch of his finger to the call button, and he rode up to the eighth floor without burden of companionship.

When Arthur stepped into the corridor, not a creature was stirring, and he made his way to Sheilah's apartment. There were two locks on her door, but after a missed effort, he realized that one turned clockwise and the other counter-clockwise. As the door cracked open, a rather overfed orange tabby scurried out between his legs.

Arthur was startled, but he recovered quickly. The cat didn't go far; in fact, it immediately followed the new visitor back into the apartment. Arthur closed the door and secured both locks, then turned to survey the abode he'd so often imagined.

Kitchen to the left, living room in front, short corridor with bedroom and bath to the right. Moving past the kitchen, Arthur took in the furnishings: nubby sectional sofa the color of oatmeal, some splashes of color he'd always associated with the Southwest in the small rugs and wall hangings. Simple and tasteful, but hardly an expensive decor.

Sheilah, Sheilah. Am I the only high roller in your stable of clients?

The cat stopped at the kitchen and meowed. Arthur came back to it and looked down at the linoleum. There was a fired-clay food dish with QUIGLEY on the side and a plastic water bowl.

Arthur said, "Tell me, little wretch, is your name really Quigley?"

The tabby meowed again.

Arthur inspected more carefully. The food dish was clean, but it appeared to be more licked than washed. The water bowl was only half-full.

"So you've already devoured the ration young Krissie provided you, eh?"

Another meow.

"Well, you'll get no more from me. Gluttony is a disgusting characteristic — in any species."

More crying.

Arthur bent down, the tabby coming over to rub against his angled shins. "Count yourself fortunate that I admire predators of the genus *Felis*, little wretch."

Then he set the cooler on the counter near the sink and opened the refrigerator. Rather sparse, but a carton of milk sat on one of the shelves.

Skim milk. Watching our fat intake, are we, Sheilah? Good discipline, even if ultimately only a futile tactic in the fight against . . . imperfection.

Arthur then permitted himself a sliver of memory. Pursuing the first one, Diana, he'd put the contents of his cooler in a carton of orange juice. Arthur had asked her later if she'd ever reported it, and Diana swore she hadn't. Given her circumstance at the time in question, he was fairly certain she wouldn't have lied to him. But picturing that circumstance had the usual effect on Arthur, a tremor of delight rippling down his spine, spurring another swelling under his zipper.

Yet he stayed the hand that reached toward the milk. Perhaps there was a better place to leave Sheilah her "present." And besides, Mother always counseled against mixing-and-matching experiences in life.

Particularly the best ones.

From the driver's seat, Vinnie said, "Hey-ey-ey, Krissie, I gotta have this limo back to my uncle's garage by ten-thirty."

"I know, Vinnie. You told me."

She said it from the passenger's seat beside him, sitting kind of close to the window, not real cozy. Christ, you'd think I was still wearing my bailiff's uniform or something, taking that psycho fuck Arthur Ketterson back to his cell.

Vinnie shook it off. That's what I get for trying to put some money aside so's maybe we can take a real vacation, Caribbean somewheres. It's not enough I been working double shifts at the sheriff's — eight to four in the First Session, then four to midnight on the security desk downstairs, keeping the sewer rats company in the old courthouse. No, I also been spending my weekends helping Uncle Phil with the car service.

Hey, you ever drive a limo? Let me tell you, it ain't all it's cracked up to be. I mean, granted you're not chained to a courtroom or a fucking security desk all the time, and if you're some-body's into reading, there's plenty of time — for books, magazines, whatever — while you're waiting for the clients. Which is what Uncle Phil wants us to call them, "clients," just like we're chauffeurs, make the clients feel like they're Rockefellers. And boy, do the guys with the plat-inum charge cards ever go for the sixty-inch stretch jobbies. Which is really funny, you think about it, because all the factory does is put five extra feet of steel in each side of the car just behind the front seats, make the thing look like a walrus instead of a seal. And if the client rents it figuring he'll have half a load on before he gets into the back, he'd better be sure to sit facing the front, like the driver does. Otherwise, it's a fucking–what'd Uncle Phil call it? Oh, yeah. "A disconcerting experience." A fucking discon-certing experience for somebody half in the bag to face backward, see where he's been instead of where he's going and maybe getting to see the last couple hours of food and drink coming back up, too.

Not that it's any picnic being the chauffeur, either. I mean, you're constantly checking the side-views, making sure you got the right clear-ances. And the reason you get to read a lot, you can't fucking leave the limo sitting by itself. You even go off to take a leak, and, sure as shit, some asshole's gonna be breaking into it for the radio or boosting the hubcaps or just running a fucking key along the side of it, ruin a two-thousand-dollar paint job because his mommy didn't love him or his daddy wouldn't play baseball with —

"Hello?" said Krissie, kind of pissed off.

"What?"

"You gonna take me there or not?"

Vinnie glanced over. "So what're you saying now, we got to go to your boss's place?"

"No, that's what I said like five minutes ago, before you spaced out on me. I told you, I have to feed her fucking cat."

"Why didn't you do it before I picked you up?"

"Because I was getting ready for you."

"Can't the cat wait till tomorrow?"

"Vinnie, I don't feel like going over tomorrow by subway to do it just so's she'll know I was there when she gets home, awright? I've got you and a ride tonight, so it'll take like fifteen minutes and then we can get started."

Again, Vinnie glanced over at her, all done up Madonna-style in black lace. Krissie had obviously spent some time on the makeup and the ear studs. Then he used the rearview to scope out the client part of the limo, picturing how Krissie was going to look lying back there. Her legs up and spread, him hammering away between them.

Vinnie shifted part of himself under the

steering wheel. "Awright, so what's your boss's address?"

The bartender said, "Another, Rudy?"

"Yeah, why not?"

The bar prided itself on a dozen different drafts, half from microbreweries nobody ever heard of, but great stuff just the same. Another hundred or so cans and bottles were in glassed-front cold cases behind the bar, samplers for people who preferred their beer recently opened. But this bar had cherry wood — not veneer, mind, but solid wood — to lean an elbow on, and a wide granite block floor. A couple of women in their early thirties were sitting a few chairs down, drinking Rolling Rock from bottles. Upscale place like this one, Rudy couldn't imagine anybody not sticking with the taps. He eyed the two women a little but got nothing back.

As the bartender drew his ale, a dark stout, Rudy tried to remember what time it was. He didn't like to wear a watch when he wasn't working, but he knew he was drinking his dinner. Rhonda would kind of miss him, but ever since she came home that night and found Jessica dead in her bedroom, his wife's sense of time was off.

"Here you go," said the keep. "Shame about that fucking lawyer getting the jury all confused like that."

"Fucking lawyer is right, the bitch." Rudy

took a good hit of the stout. "And fucking judge."

"Hey, what do you expect?"

"I don't follow you."

"Rudy, judges were lawyers themselves once, right?"

"Christ, that's right, isn't it?"

"Leopards, Rudy."

Another swallow. "What?"

"Leopards. You can call them different names, but that don't change their spots none."

"Fucking right."

"I mean," said the bartender, "they had the guy's fingerprint on her . . . on the thing there, right?"

"Right," a third, deeper gulp of stout, trying to wash away the memory. Didn't work.

The keep shrugged. "So, they ought to lynch the guy, not let him walk."

Downing the last of the glass, Rudy felt some of the tension leaving his chest, the way it always did with the right kind and amount of booze. If he couldn't get justice in a courtroom, he'd find a substitute for it in a barroom.

"Another round, Your Honor? Why not?"

In his own house — alone, as always — Roger Hesterfield didn't mind speaking out loud once in awhile. Not so eccentric, and certainly not crazy to do that. He reached for the bottle of Glenfiddich, then paused when he thought he heard a snapping noise. Hesterfield was sitting in his study, its brass-tacked leather chairs nearly identical to the furniture in his chambers. But just as the old courthouse had rats, the old house had mice, and he was forever setting traps for them, a swifter and more satisfying brand of justice than the Constitution — state or federal — allowed him to dispense from the bench.

Legal argument turned his mind toward trials in general, and the most recent toward Sheilah Quinn in particular. Hesterfield thought about her face, and body, and even voice. It would be good to hear her voice, anyway. I could call her —

"No, you old fool." He brought himself up in his chair. "It's Saturday night, and after the way Sheilah cut you off in chambers, you're not about to give her the satisfaction of knowing how lonely you really are."

Roger Hesterfield nodded once, then shook his head and poured another three fingers of scotch into the glass.

God, but it's good to hear her laugh.

Frank had told a small joke as they got to the front steps of the inn, and Sheilah laughed at it all the way through the door.

Anne was just inside the library, smiling at them as they reached the staircase. "You're back early."

Sheilah said, "We kind of danced ourselves out."

"What time would you like brunch tomorrow?" asked the innkeeper.

"Late," said Frank, before Sheilah could answer, but she didn't seem angry he'd decided for them.

They walked up the stairs, his arm around her shoulder, hers around his waist, but they broke apart so Sheilah could go through the door to number 4 first. Once in the room, Frank ran his thumb and index finger down the sleeve of Sheilah Quinn's dress.

Once in the closet, Arthur ran his thumb and index finger down the sleeve of Sheilah Quinn's dress. No residue of feline fur on any of the fabric, and Arthur thought he knew why. The doors to the closet were louvered, folding ones, with a catproof latch halfway up that had to be flipped to gain entry. So, unless the tabby could reach it with a front paw, Sheilah's clothes were safe.

But only from her cat.

Arthur buried his face in the suits he'd seen on her during the long days of trial. He was certain Sheilah must have perspired during tense moments in the courtroom, but also certain that she must patronize the cleaners often, for only one or two of the garments had the sweet pong of sweat and perfume that was so strong and yet at the same time so feminine. Arthur forbade, of course, the removal of his mother's clothes following her death, and even after all these years he fancied he could still smell Madeline

Ketterson on them when he browsed through her closet.

Ah, but mustn't be mixing memories again. Concentrate on the present.

Arthur opened drawers in the bureau. Poking here, probing there. Very carefully, of course, so as not to disturb anything. The lingerie drawer was particularly fruitful, but taking something from it was too great a risk. Not to mention . . . premature.

Then Arthur heard a noise behind him and turned quickly, but it was only the cat, leaping onto the bed and pulling down the covers over a stuffed bear in a silly hat that was propped against a pillow. Young Krissie and the Persimmon Queen had implied that Sheilah was going away for the weekend, but nothing about a male companion. Could the bear be a gift from —

At which point, the cat clamped its teeth onto one of the animal's ears and dragged it over the surface of the bed, trying to carry away a prize.

Arthur intervened and rescued the bear, the cat scampering from the room in defeat. Up close, the stuffed creature wasn't just tattered from attack but obviously old, as well. Arthur's free hand fluttered to his cheek, a smile creasing his lips. It must be. A childhood gift from her father. A keepsake she sleeps with while he wastes away in some nursing home.

Internally, Arthur Ketterson put on his thinking cap. Now, how can I use this?

Channel-surfing with the remote in his right hand, Roger Hesterfield watched the different ways the light from the television screen danced through the single malt in the glass held high in his left hand. Occasionally, he would glance at the screen, invariably disappointed in what he saw. Dare not go to a video store to rent or buy a porno movie, because he might be recognized. Couldn't even subscribe to the Playboy Channel, because some busybody at the cable service might spot it on his account and leak the information to the Judicial Conduct Commission. They ought to come up with a plain brown wrapper for videos anyway. Maybe — what was his name, that dago publisher at *Penthouse?*

Penthouse. That was the way Roger pictured Sheilah sometimes, as a Pet of the Month. She'd done well in law practice after the long-ago clerkship, kind of "outhouse to penthouse" herself. Roger even thought of a joke to tell Sheilah, one he'd heard at the club. Describe the offspring of insomniac, dyslexic agnostics: The child stays up all night, wondering if there's a dog.

Roger Hesterfreld laughed once, harshly, then looked over at the telephone before taking another slug of scotch.

Arthur was standing at the doorway to Sheilah's bedroom, about to move on to her bathroom, when the cat meowed from the kitchen area. Instinctively, Arthur suppressed an urge to tease it by walking down there with the stuffed bear. And a prudent instinct it proved to be, too, as the next sound was a key turning in the locks of the front door.

Startled now, Arthur stepped back into the bedroom, uncertain what to do. Then he heard the front door open and the young Krissie's voice calling out, "Awright, you little creep. Back off."

The cat meowed again as the door closed.

"Back off," repeated the voice, now from the kitchen by its echoing. "You want food, I guess."

A chocky, rummaging sound, as though Krissie was looking for something in a box or basket.

"Well, according to the label, the shit in this can isn't too ucky. Let's see — huh?" A pause. Then she said, "What happened, Sheilah leave her picnic lunch behind?"

Arthur could hear Krissie shoving his Coleman cooler along the counter, a faint scraping noise. Her unfastening the lid would produce a distinctive popping. Which would, of course, mean she'd be able to see what was inside the cooler itself.

Arthur stayed stock-still in the bedroom, listening very carefully to determine whether or not he'd have to kill young Krissie.

The sounds from Sheilah's throat weren't exactly words, but they were all she could manage, and she sensed they were exactly what Frank wanted to hear. He began thrusting harder, deeper, the walls of her tunnel now so slippery with welcome that there was just the barest friction from the condom against them. He suspended the weight of his chest by leaning on his elbows against the mattress, and all she felt of him was the rhythmic, exquisitely varying arcing inside her.

Sheilah had the disorienting sensation that the four-poster was rocking off the floor. Then the arcing inside her rose higher and drove deeper just as Frank grunted against the hollow of her throat. When he finally released himself, Sheilah experienced such a powerful orgasm that her whole body clenched, beyond ache or even pain.

Five, ten seconds before she felt his chest finally sag onto hers, and Sheilah Quinn just caught herself before she began to sob.

"Hey, Rudy, how's it going?"

This was the second-shift bartender talking to him at a different place, a butcher-block and fern meat rack on a trendy street. Rudy'd already knocked back a few Bass ales, the selection of draft not as varied as the first bar but the clientele a little more interested in some action. He'd been commiserating with a guy on a corner stool who was going through a bloody fucking divorce, Rudy repeating things people had told him in the first gin mill as though he'd thought of them himself.

Rudy ordered another Bass, then was about to

take a hit from it when he saw a woman, just inside the front door of the place, shaking out her hair. Big hair, and the same broad he'd picked up the night his daughter died. The woman worked for an answering service or some fucking thing, lived with a roommate on the other side of the city. But Rudy couldn't remember her name right off. He did remember her telling him she'd just gotten back from a trip — to Toronto, of all fucking places. Her going on and on about white college boys in the theater district there, pulling little wooden rickshaw with the names of Broadway shows on the backs. Plus black ground squirrels — "Can you believe it, Rude, black as pitch." And cars that had their headlights on all the time, day/night, sun/rain, you name it.

I can remember that shit, but I can't remember her name. No, wait, she made a joke about it. The fuck was . . . Yeah, Como, Terri Como, like the old-time TV singer, except spelled different.

Then Rudy thought about what the cop had told him — that good guy, O'Toole — about their interviewing Terri after Rhonda found Jessica. Christ, when I picked Terri up that night, she was drunker than I was. How the fuck much could she remember to tell them?

Rudy Giordano set down his Bass ale on the bar and looked back toward the door, toward where he'd just seen her shaking the hair. But Terri Como was gone.

Krissie thought, No sense in opening this. Sheilah left it here yesterday, whatever's in it would be spoiled garbage by now, anyways.

Leaving the lid sealed on the cooler, Krissie pulled back the tab on the can of cat food, using one of Sheilah's little forks to shovel the glop into Quigley's dish, which seemed to focus him. Now that he was chowing down, Krissie could slip out easily.

She started toward the front door, then stopped herself. Sheilah forgot the cooler like that, probably be a good idea to look around the place, make sure she didn't leave a window open. Vinnie could wait ten more minutes. Don't want to give it to him too quick, anyways, or he might not be back for more, and that limo is the coolest car I've ever been in, even if it does belong to his uncle and not Vinnie himself.

Krissie walked down the hall, glanced into the bathroom. Everything looked okay. Then she crossed the hall into the bedroom. A stuffed bear was lying on the bed, kind of old and scuzzy.

Sheilah, with a little kid's toy. Huh, who woulda thunk it?

Krissie checked the window, then hesitated at the bureau.

Well, you're here because Sheilah asked you, right? Maybe just sneak a peek at what, like, lies ahead, you work as hard as she does. There's a name for it when the department store people do it: comparison shopping.

Opening each drawer in succession, Krissie didn't see anything so different from her own bureau, except for some of the colors Sheilah liked to wear underneath. All the reds and pinks were kind of surprising, but otherwise, not much to impress.

Of course, most of the really good stuff was probably in the closet.

Roger Hesterfield got up a little shakily, surprised to see how much farther down the Glenfiddich in the bottle looked from a higher perspective. He'd had a friend at the telephone company very quietly obtain Sheilah's unlisted home number for him a few months ago, when some ideas first began suggesting themselves to him.

Now, if I can just find where the hell on my desk here I put that slip of paper.

At the back of the closet, a faux fur collar tickling his nose, Arthur Ketterson thought all would be well. His ears had told him that except for moving the cooler aside — probably to gain counter space for opening the cat food — the young Krissie had left the Coleman alone. Now she'd come down the hall and into the bedroom, though she was probably just playing caretaker as well as cat sitter.

Rather like my recurring dream about Sheilah, though. However, best to save the . . . actualization of it for —

He heard the bureau drawers begin to be opened, and some unintelligible comments muttered by Krissie. Arthur had closed the closet door in such a way that the latch slipped naturally into its slot, child's play to flip it up again from where he stood by using a credit card through the slight separation between the doors. But now Arthur could see a shadow come across the louvers and stop. Peering downward at their imposed angle, all he could see was black lace.

Ah, young Krissie. So considerate of me and my "freedom" yesterday. I'd really rather not kill you.

Really and truly.

This is the kind of place my father would have called a "joint," thought Rudy Giordano, himself already what his father would have called "three sheets to the wind." A dugout with one half window giving onto the avenue, worn mahogany bar, stools from everywhere. There were framed and autographed black-and-white photos of boxers you never heard of on the walls around a — Christ Almighty, a genuine rotary-dial pay phone.

For the last hour or so, a guy Giordano barely knew from one of the trades — plumbing, if he had to bet on it — had bought him drinks, but now the bartender was making noises like he wasn't serving any more if they were going to Rudy.

The trades guy said, "Hey, that's okay. Time

to head home anyway. Right, Rudy?"

Giordano wasn't sure what the guy meant at first. "What do I want to go home with you for?"

A smile that Rudy didn't like. One of those bleary, condescending smiles you got when the other guy realized you didn't finish college or something. "No, Rude, what I'm saying is, we both ought to go home. You to yours, me to mine."

That made a little more sense, but when Rudy got off his stool, he stumbled. Fucking way they wax the floors, oughta be a law about that.

"Fix your floor," said Rudy to the bartender.

The keep said, "How's about I call you a cab, buddy?"

Rudy got his feet under him, waved that off. "I got my car."

The plumbing guy was up off his stool. "Hey, Rude, I can maybe give you a lift instead?"

Christ, he's reaching out his hand, like he's trying to steady me or some fucking thing. Rudy shrugged the hand off angrily. "What are you, deaf? My car's outside, I told you."

Climbing the steps up to the entrance, Rudy had to use the banister. Fucking steps are so steep, they gotta have these things. Who designs bars, anyway?

Walking the half block to his Caddy, Rudy fumbled with the computer fob thing on his keys so the door'd unlock, make that chirpy sound. Gonna have to drive a little more careful than usual. Cops are getting tough on drunk driving, and I'm maybe a shot or two over the line.

Getting behind the wheel and pulling on his calfskin gloves, though, he had a different idea. Fucking system screwed me, the judge, the lawyers. Screwed me over good.

Turning the key in the ignition on the third try, Rudy Giordano thought, System screwed me over with Jessica, it can fucking well cut me some slack tonight.

Krissie stood in front of the closet, her hand on the knob. She tugged, but the door didn't open, even though it was one of those folding types. Then she noticed the small piece of hardware on it, a latch.

Probably to keep the cat out of there. Good idea, too. Little bugger probably sheds over everything.

Krissie reached up, flicked the horizontal bar over, and put her hand on the knob again, cracking the door open. "There we go."

At which point, there was a plaintive meow behind her.

Krissie jumped and turned. "Quigley, you fucking little creep. You scared the shit out of me."

The cat looked up at her, licked its lips, and then began shuddering like it was hiccuping, backing up awkwardly on its feet as its head pecked toward the carpet.

"Oh no," said Krissie.

The cat began to throw up a huge hair ball,

part of it starting to peek out at her.

Krissie clamped her eyes shut. "Eeeeeww!"

Tilting her head to the ceiling, she opened her eyes again but focused on the top of the doorway to the hall. Edging slowly around where the cat was still hacking, Krissie went into the corridor and down toward the kitchen.

At the front door, she undid the locks. "Sheilah thinks I'm supposed to clean up cat puke, they can, like, find another secretary," said Krissie Newton to the apartment as she slammed the door behind her.

In the dark, Sheilah Quinn lay on her back next to Frank Sikes, the sheet and part of a blanket over them. Well, the blanket was actually over her, not him.

"You cold?" he said.

"Not really."

"Then how come the blanket?"

"I've always been like this after making love," said Sheilah. "I think it must have something to do with the blood moving to different places, you know?"

Frank nuzzled her ear, the mustache tickling in a different way than it had earlier. "I can vouch for that." His voice changed tone. "That was really special."

"For me, too." Sheilah turned to him, enough moonlight from the curtained window to allow her to make out his features. "Did you do something . . . different?"

A small laugh. "What do you mean?"

"I mean, like some different . . . technique?"

A bigger laugh. "Despite the myths, Sheil, we don't know more about doing it than white guys."

"Uh-oh. Another balloon punctured."

"What you do . . . what I do anyway is close my eyes and go with the feeling."

Sheilah shivered next to him.

"Something wrong?" said Frank.

"No, it's . . . What do you mean by 'feeling'?"

"Mean?" Frank hesitated. "I don't know that I can explain it, exactly. Sometimes, you just feel something's right. In sync, like. And you go with it, the way it happens sometimes interrogating a suspect."

Sheilah almost froze.

"Now what?" he said.

"Nothing. Really. It's just that I was thinking something so similar earlier."

"When?"

Rather than tell Frank it was the night before, after their unsuccessful efforts following dinner, Sheilah rolled over, giving him a deep, lingering kiss as she let her hand slide down his stomach. Breaking the kiss, she said, "I'm getting a little reaction here."

"Little?" he said, swinging his legs out from under the sheets and standing for inspection.

"You go rinse yourself off, and I'll try to" — Sheilah gestured vaguely — "expand on that."

Smiling, Arthur Ketterson walked into the

bathroom. Ah, little wretched kitty, you of nine lives saved another's tonight.

Once standing on the tile floor, Arthur took a deep breath, as he had in the closet. The scent of Sheilah emanated from everything in the room.

From the towels and facecloth.

From the soap and bath oils.

From the half-empty bottles of cologne and perfume.

However, what one sense provided, another derided. Opening his eyes and examining the fixtures, he was once again rather disappointed. Pedestrian in every way, especially that embarrassing substitute for a "spa," with the platform in the tub and a kinky plastic hose running from it to a globular motor next to the toilet.

Arthur was about to turn away when an idea struck him. Kinky. He leaned over the tub, noticing the right angle in the hose at the bottom. Probably bent from hot water coming in contact with the flimsy plastic.

Now, let me see if I can extrapolate the program here. Sheilah would fill the tub with hot water, sprinkling in some bath oil. And the motor unit has these labeled buttons on it. She'd push them for intensity of airflow and duration, say twenty minutes or so. Then Sheilah would step into the tub, sinking into the water. Possibly even with her eyes closed, for maximum relaxation.

Oh, yes, thought Arthur, this should work very

nicely. And uniquely. No mixing and matching of experiences.

Singing softly to himself, Arthur Ketterson walked toward the kitchen to retrieve the frozen cubes from his Coleman cooler.

Rudy Giordano sideswiped the oak at the entrance to his driveway. He felt the scraping noise, but on the whole, he counted himself lucky. Four, maybe five miles from the last place to home, and he hadn't hit anything or even passed a cop.

Opening the driver's side, Rudy looked up at the house. His dream house.

He'd bought the undeveloped lot over twenty years before, when he knew this would turn into a good neighborhood. A lot that backed onto a city-owned strip of conservation land with its hiking trail there. Then and now, you could walk past the lawn and flower beds and be in what felt like wilderness, the trail winding through the trees for three blocks before coming out on another suburban street.

Six years after buying the lot, Rudy had scraped together enough money to start the house itself. Picked out the design, picked up the material, picked where every board would go. Every nail and screw, even.

When Jessica was home, there'd always be a light on in her room, like a candle burning in the window from one of those old stories they made you read in school. But without his baby, and with Rhonda knocked out by Christ knows how many sleeping pills, tonight the split-level looked more like haunted house than dream house, even to Rudy.

He closed the door of the Cadillac, feeling himself sobering up. Too soon. Walking toward the stoop, Rudy tried to remember if he'd bought more ale after the last time, didn't think he had.

Because of his gait, the dress shoes made a skittering noise on the flagstone path. The sound reminded Rudy Giordano of some poor little animal, returning empty-handed to its emptier den.

"There you are," said Roger Hesterfield to himself after lifting off his desk the book covering the memo slip from his friend at the telephone company. Hesterfield's eyes went from paper to keypad three times to ensure he punched in Sheilah Quinn's unlisted number correctly the first time.

Then Hesterfield heard the ringing begin on the other end, and he stared hard at the telephone itself.

Arthur Ketterson was in the kitchen, resealing the cooler, when the phone rang next to his head, startling him nearly as much as having heard Krissie opening the apartment door earlier. Now he fought the instinct simply to pick the receiver off the wall, then remembered noticing an answering machine on the night table in Sheilah's bedroom. Arthur went quickly down the hall, just as her outgoing tape cut off the ringing sound.

"Hi," said Sheilah's voice, "I'm sure you know what to do."

Ah, thought Arthur, closing his eyes. Now the sense of hearing, as well. I should have thought of that. Simply press the button labeled OUTGOING TAPE ANNOUNCEMENT, and I could have —

"Sheilah, Roger here."

Arthur opened his eyes, cocking his head and frowning. Familiar, but the only Roger I know is —

"I was just . . . well, thinking of you," continued the voice. "Have a joke you'd like, I think."

My God, it *was*. The Honorable Roger Hesterfield, and unquestionably in his cups from —

"What do you get if you cross an . . . No, wait a minute. No, what would be the offspring of an agnostic and an insomniac who had dxylexia? . . . No, that's not it, either."

Good Lord, the man is making a complete fool of himself.

"Well, Sheilah, let's forget about the ice-breaker and get straight to the point. I just was wondering if you were in tonight, because if you were, maybe I could come over there, or you could come over here, and . . ."

Disgusting, thought Arthur. A man of Roger's age and decrepitude, seeking a rendezvous with . . . perfection.

"So, when you get a chance, why don't you give me a call?"

The phone went dead, and the tape machine clicked and whirred a moment, showing a 1 in green neon through a little window before settling back into silence.

Carefully, Arthur lifted the lid of the machine. There appeared to be two cassettes, helpfully labeled OUTGOING and MESSAGES. Carefully, he again opened the drawer of the night table, quite pleased with himself to see several spare message tapes looking back. Still carefully, Arthur replaced the cassette in the machine with a spare one, pocketing the captured voice of Roger Hesterfield.

A final look around the bedroom brought into view the stuffed animal on the comforter. Cradling the bear in the crook of his arm, Arthur Ketterson moved into the corridor, being careful to step over the impressive hair ball deposited near the threshold.

"God, I can't believe how badly I botched that," said Roger Hesterfield, wiping damp palms on his pants at the thighs. "Like a frightened high school kid who needed a date for the prom."

He tried to push that analogy from his mind as he reached for the Glenfiddich. Hesterfield wished he hadn't thought to call, hadn't found the memo slip with the number, hadn't left any message at all.

Then Roger Hesterfield poured himself another three fingers of single malt, picked up the remote control, and went back to whatever the cable might offer a lonely old man late on a Saturday night.

Frank Sikes slipped back into bed, Sheilah Quinn waking with a start.

"I thought it was only us males who were supposed to fall asleep afterwards."

"I was basking in the glow."

Lying on his back, Frank looked at her. "And the glow made you drop off."

"Just for a wink."

Frank turned his face toward the ceiling. "If you'd rather, we could just cuddle for a while, instead of —"

"Hush," said Sheilah solemnly, leaning over, licking his chest. "Remember Lionel Ritchie."

"Lionel Ritchie?"

"The song he sang at the closing ceremonies." Hooding her eyelids, Sheilah looked up at Frank. "All Night Long?"

They both laughed as Sheilah's lips ranged southward, each lover going with the feeling and knowing it was right.

NINE

"So, Peter, I trust there are no hard feelings about the Ketterson trial?"

Burying his hangover in a distant corner of his mind, Roger Hesterfield spoke as Peter Mendez watched the foursome ahead of them tee off at the first hole. The club's course wended in a serpentine manner over three low hills, the front nine by far the less challenging half of the eighteen.

Look at him, thought Roger, trying to contain that fiery Latin temper of his.

Mendez said, "Hard feelings? Of course not, Your Honor."

Your Honor. Not merely "Judge," even on the golf course. Can't teach this Chihuahua any new tricks, can I? In which case, best to remind the dog of his "treat." "You know, Peter, you're still my man for the AG slot."

Roger liked the way Mendez swallowed that. Almost see it going down.

"And I appreciate your support," said the candidate.

Damned well better. Mendez hadn't a prayer with the informal but essential group that decided the nomination for his party long before the convention was called to order. But Roger had interceded for him, impressed with the young man's malleability as a district attorney. Mendez knew when to push for a headline and when to look the other way to repay a sponsor, and Roger had become convinced the party was far better off nominating a co-opted, suburbanite minority lawyer than risking a loss in the general election to the bomb-tossing ghetto practitioner the other party had put up at its convention three weeks earlier.

Now, if only we also controlled the county commissioners who run the courthouse complex.

The foursome in front of them was taking forever to play the hole. Roger was justly proud of the way the club held his Sunday-morning tee time, whether he was going out with three others, two, or just one, as this morning. The judge looked at the younger hopeful, wondering how long it would take for Mendez to vent over —

"Can you believe how slow those idiots are?"

Roger smiled, pleased with his understanding of the man. "Did I ever tell you the story about the minister, the priest, and the rabbi, waiting like this to play?"

Roger sensed Mendez clenching at what would be a joke he couldn't tolerate if others were around but couldn't duck so long as a principal patron was telling it privately. Still, the "I don't think so," took its own sweet time coming out.

"Well," said Roger, "on a glorious sunny morn', the three clergymen are following a foursome that's doing everything wrong. Can't seem to line up shots, find balls, even keep track of one another. So the trio starts making rather pointed — and increasingly louder — comments about the people in front of them. Then suddenly, the club director comes rushing over to the three clergymen and says, 'Gentlemen, please.'

"And the minister says, 'What's the matter?'

"And the director says, 'That foursome in front of you is . . . blind!' "

Roger could see Mendez wincing already. Excellent.

"At which point," said Hesterfield, speaking faster, "the minister looks to heaven for forgiveness, the priest drops to his knees, crossing himself, and the rabbi says to the director, 'So, they couldn't play at night?' "

Now Mendez was forcing a smile. "Good one, Your Honor."

Roger clapped him on the back lightly, lapsing into mental reverie. Damn but I do enjoy mentoring a younger man. Especially on the golf course. Not like tennis, where it's all grunting — or, at best, shouting — across a net for all to hear. No, with golf you can speak to someone confidentially, and at necessary length. Impress upon him what he's doing right or wrong. And if he's wrong . . . Well, spare the rod, spoil the candidate. Take that incident during the Ketterson closing, for example.

Which reminded Roger once more of Sheilah Quinn. I wouldn't mind being her "mentor," again. But then, it was unlikely she played golf.

There's just no justice in this world.

Rudy Giordano shuffled into the bathroom off the master suite. Just no fucking justice.

In the mirror, he tried to see the hangover, couldn't understand how his head could feel this bad without nails sticking out of his eyes. You get burned, you see it on the skin. You get punched, you see the bruise. How come you can't see a headache like —

Rhonda yelled up, "You want scrambled or fried?"

The tangy scent of bacon came into the bathroom, seemingly with her very words, and Rudy felt his stomach turn over. All the magazines arriving at the house, he wondered if his wife ever read an article on healthy eating.

"Rude? Scrambled or —"

"Fried, over hard," he yelled back, immediately paying the price for it. Using the pain to organize his thoughts, he said to the mirror, "Today: Watch the ball game, outside on the portable. Tonight: Hit a couple, three places, have some laughs for a change. Tomorrow: Get started on the old courthouse. Knock the —"

"Rudy, you want catsup or Tabasco on top?"

He closed his eyes but decided against shaking his head.

Dressed casually in duck pants and a pink Ralph Lauren Polo shirt, Arthur Ketterson bounded down Woodmere's central staircase toward his butler at the bottom.

"I trust you slept well, sir?"

"Yes, Parsons. The unfettered sleep of the innocent."

As usual when he was being teased, Parsons never so much as blinked. Old toad, thought Arthur, you are a treasure.

"Would you be caring for breakfast, sir?"

"Yes. Yes indeed."

Parsons turned toward the kitchen.

"Oh, and a picnic lunch, as well."

The manservant turned back. "Certainly, sir. You'll not be going to the club, then?"

"No, Parsons."

Sitting at the inn's dining table, Frank Sikes ate the last of his muffin, looking up at Sheilah Quinn until he finished chewing. "Any preferences for this morning?"

"Just a drive, I think. Somewhere in the area." Sheilah raised the coffee cup to her lips. "This weekend's been more like a week's vacation."

"Know what you mean."

She let out a deep breath. "Frank, I really like the way I've felt here."

"I like the way *we've* felt here."

Sheilah Quinn smiled over the brim of her cup. "That's what I meant."

"Ach, too bad, Peter. Have to do something about that slice of yours."

Peter Mendez grinned, jaw shut tight, as a way to keep from screaming. Madre de Dios, he wanted to scream. Something like: I hate golf, you pompous fart, and I hate you, too. The living example of all that's wrong about the way the world works. All that I'll change, once I'm sitting in that attorney general's chair.

Well, no, thought Peter, let's be reasonable here. Even as AG, I wouldn't be able to touch the Honorable Roger Hesterfield. Only the chief judge of the superior court could give him orders administratively, and only the state's highest court could remove him disciplinarily. And even that august body would have to wait until after enough other judges or lawyers complained to the commonwealth's Judicial Conduct Commission to trigger a formal inquiry.

Which would never happen. No, Hesterfield was an arch asshole, but he also was careful to spread his abuse around, never seeming to help or hurt any lawyer or class of lawyers — or even class of litigants — all that much. You might know where Roger Hesterfield's heart lay — if it lay anywhere at all — but you'd never be able to prove it during an investigation. And as the old saying goes, If you set out to kill a king, make sure you kill him, lest he —

Peter watched Hesterfield's next swing, the head of the club striking the ball with a solid crack, the shot trajecting seventy-five yards down the middle of the fairway.

The old bastard isn't a big hitter, but, despite the booze ravaging his body, you have to give him credit for consistency in his swing. Of course, he also likes the game, which has to make a difference.

Hesterfield replaced the club in his bag, smiling benevolently.

"So, Peter, I've decided to give you a chance to redeem yourself."

Uh-oh. "How's that, Your Honor?"

"Against Sheilah Quinn, in the eyes of the electorate and the deeper pockets you appeal to for that green paper fuel of campaigning."

"But redeem myself how?"

"I'm calling a certain liquor-store robbery for trial on Tuesday."

Peter had the sensation of holding a seashell to his ear, an ocean storm raging out of control. "The *Diaz/Borbón* case?"

"Not anymore. Joey Trask managed to let slip over a martini in the Nineteenth Hole yesterday that his client was going to exemplify the maxim 'No honor among thieves.' "

Peter knew Borbón had decided to roll over on his partner, but he wasn't pleased that Trask had been broadcasting it. If Hesterfield knew about the plea bargain, then Sheilah Quinn couldn't be far behind. And besides, Peter would have to go straight from the golf course to his office to prepare the case, especially after what had happened with the Ketterson trial.

"But Your Honor, I'd need time to —"

"Oh, come, come, Peter. Thanks to what I've just said, you're effectively getting a good twenty-four hours more notice than Sheilah. And anyway, we know how this little morality play will unfold, don't we? Simple armed robbery, with Sheilah's client left holding the proverbial bag-a-roo. Plus, this should give you a nice last performance in my favorite theater."

So that's it, thought Peter. We're back to his "lady," the fucking First Session. He just doesn't want to let go of her.

It, Peter reminded himself.

"Your Honor, maybe we shouldn't begin the trial in one courthouse, only to have to switch the proceedings to —"

"I doubt any 'switch' will be necessary, Peter."

Something about saying that seemed to bother the old bastard, though. A lack of . . . certainty, which produced the only consolation Peter Mendez was deriving from the day's activity.

Rudy Giordano lay on a lounge chair in his backyard. He'd built a nice deck off the rear of the house, but this was still baseball season, and he liked to sit out in the grass to enjoy it, grass like the game was meant to be played on.

The grass. It's high enough, I ought to be thinking about getting on the John Deere, give the lawn a good cut. Only the thought of straddling all that engine and mower vibration makes me sick, and I'm holding down Rhonda's choles-terol special only by the skin of my teeth as it is.

Rudy had a battery-operated Japanese TV and a quart of spring water on the cocktail table next to his lounge chair. He took a long draw from the quart. A bartender once told him, "Rudy, you're an everyday kind of drinker, your body needs fluids. Plain water, now, that's best. Give the body back what it lost last night."

What it's gonna lose again tonight.

Rudy finished with the water for now and adjusted the TV's contrast button so the sun didn't screw up the image on the screen too much. A batter who'd just joined the team as a free agent was stepping into the box. What, twenty-three, twenty-four years old? Twenty-five at the outside, and making $2 million a year for hitting .260 as a right fielder last season. I mean, give me a fucking break, huh? Two mil-lion for .260?

"Rudy?"

Rhonda was calling to him through the sliding screened door that led from the house onto the deck.

"What?" he yelled back.

"I'd kind of like to visit the grave today."

Christ on a crutch, not again. "I'm watching a game here."

A pause. "Can we go at halftime?"

"This is baseball, Rhonda."

"So?"

Rudy could feel the headache building again,

reached for the water. "So that means no halftime."

As he swallowed from the quart, Rudy could hear her crying. Quietly, so she thought he wouldn't notice.

Rudy closed his eyes, trying to figure out what had happened to his fucking life. Then he thought, I wonder what that satanic sonuvabitch Arthur Ketterson IV is doing today?

Arthur was "touring," as he liked to put it, on the two-lane roads that wound through the horse and manor country to the west of the city, lost in the glory of driving the candy apple red 850CSi. His little hop into town to visit Sheilah's apartment the night before really hadn't done the car justice.

It was possible that some entity other than Bavarian Motor Works made a better vehicle, but Arthur tended to doubt it. He'd had a classic 2002 in prep school, liking it so much he'd kept it through college, though suffering some gibes from classmates who'd "traded up." Arthur had owned two more BMWs since, the most recent an 850i that had cost over seventy thousand with a 5.0-liter V-12 churning out 296 horsepower. This newest Beemer also sported twelve cylinders, but the price had jumped to nearly a hundred thousand — thanks to the dollar's deplorable slide against the deutsche mark — and the engine size to 5.6 liters, horsepower now rated at 372. The slut Giordano had absolutely loved it, he recalled, hinting rather bluntly at certain "favors" that would be his should he let her drive it.

Arthur shook his head ruefully. Ignoring the vulgar barter implied, can you imagine trusting a twenty-one-year-old girl with a six-speed Teutonic missile?

Sunroof open, he took in the marvelous day, truly his first breath of real fresh air other than the Woodmere grounds since he'd been released from jail on — Good Lord, was it only two days before? Arthur shivered, then noticed some rather indistinguishable roadkill at the edge of the pavement. One night in the Admin Unit, Willie had told him about a café that had its menu printed as though the meals served actually were roadkill. "Smear of Deer," "Poodles and Noodles," just to name a few. When pressed, however, Willie could not say that he'd actually eaten at the establishment to judge the authenticity of its offerings.

Arthur shivered again, but more from the thought of being back in jail. Then he put a nicely orchestrated violin concerto into the CD player, humming along as he watched for an appropriately pastoral spot to picnic with the basket Parsons had packed for him.

"You know something?" said Frank Sikes, finishing yet another meal with Sheilah Quinn.

"No, what?"

"Your hair is a different color, depending on

what kind of light we're in."

"Is that a compliment?"

"Variety is the spice of life, right?"

They'd had a beautiful morning driving through the countryside in her Miata convertible, roof back. Now they were lingering over a late lunch of salad and wine on the open porch of a converted railroad station that hadn't been recommended by anyone.

A place they'd found together.

I'm finding something else, too, Frank admitted to himself. I like the rhythm of spending quality time with this woman, both in bed and out of it.

"So," he said, "where to now?"

"Home, I'm afraid."

Frank put down his fork. "Already?"

"With the *Ketterson* case over, Hesterfield could call Diaz/Borbón anytime, and since somebody persuaded me to take the whole weekend off, I need to spend a full day in the office tomorrow, catching up on everything else."

"Yeah, but that's tomorrow, right?"

"I also want to see my dad. I try not to miss a Sunday night with him."

Couldn't argue with her on that score. No way to win.

Frank kept quiet as Sheilah settled up the bill. He listened to the small talk dwindle between them as she drove him back to the Brook Farm Inn.

They both got out of the Miata, hugged and kissed, Sheilah breaking it off sooner than he would have.

"See you again?" Frank heard himself saying.

"Count on it."

"When?"

She got back into her car. "I'll call you. At your apartment."

Then Frank Sikes watched Sheilah Quinn drive away from him.

"No, thanks, Your Honor, I really have to be going."

Leaning with his back against the bar rail of the Nineteenth Hole, Roger Hesterfield smiled for effect. He could smell Mendez's nervousness, the body odor that came through the younger man's golf shirt having nothing to do with the tension of the match they'd played that day.

I've pressed the perfect button on you, haven't I, Peter? This armed robbery, precisely the right challenge both to test the man and please the crowd. A victory in a Latino defendants' case just before the general election would show that the candidate was impartial and even merciless where his own people were concerned. A solid conviction — coupled with a maximum sentence from the righteously indignant trial judge — might even eclipse some of the bad taste left by the Ketterson nonresult.

Roger rested his hand lightly on Mendez's

shoulder. "I understand why a young husband and father might be needed at home, Peter. Thanks again for giving up part of your weekend to join me."

The prosecutor turned to go.

"Oh, and give my regards to your lovely family." *If you ever get to see them this afternoon, that is.*

Mendez visibly forced himself to turn back and smile before hurrying along and out.

From behind Hesterfield, a male voice said, "The usual, Judge?"

Roger merely nodded. He could tell from the swishing of the club steward's sleeve and the clink of the bottle off the top shelf that the man was reaching for the right stuff, and Roger Hesterfield permitted his mind to leave Peter Mendez for sweeter contemplations.

"Do you think we should have gotten roses?"

Standing to the side of Jessica's grave, Rudy Giordano always got misty if he looked at his daughter's headstone, or even the grass over where she was. This time, he'd been distracted by a girl who looked about fourteen, bending over another grave three rows down. A girl with hair the color of Jessica's. "What?"

Rhonda looked up from where she was kneeling, a towel under the knees themselves. She'd learned that trick from the first time here, Rudy remembered. After it'd rained the night before.

His wife said, "Roses. You think we should have gotten roses this time?"

Jesus, Mary, and Jo— "Look, Rhonda, we brought roses last time. That mixed bouquet there, that's nice, too."

"You really think so?"

"Yeah. Nicer even."

Bouquets. That reminded him of wreaths, and wreaths reminded him of Jessica's funeral. Rudy had served as one of the pallbearers. Insisting on it, but surprised, too. Surprised by how fucking . . . light the coffin seemed to be.

Rudy shook his head. For a while — what, four, five years before all this here? — he'd had a cop moonlighting on one of his residential projects. Good carpenter, too. One time, over a couple of beers, the cop told Rudy about how an autopsy worked. About the pathology doctor cutting the scalp and pulling off the face. Cutting into the chest past the rib cage, too, taking out all the organs, the liver, the stomach, the . . . heart, everything. Everything that gives a body its weight, a person her spirit. "Rudy," the cop had asked, laughing into his beer, "why do you suppose they call these pathologists 'canoe makers'?"

Rudy's eyes went involuntarily past Rhonda to the grass above where his daughter's coffin lay. They fucking hollowed her out in the autopsy there, like I do with the wooden bodies of my marionettes, make them lighter, easier to manipulate.

"Honest?"

225

Rudy turned to his wife. "What?"

"You being honest, saying the bouquet here is nicer than roses?"

"Maybe." He struggled to find words. "I think so, yeah."

Rhonda went back to arranging the flowers on the grave. "I don't know. I think we should have gotten roses this time, too."

Rudy Giordano felt the tears fill his eyes, then looked away, back toward the Caddy parked on the narrow macadam path. After I drop Rhonda home, I'm gonna fucking work my way backward through all the bars I hit last night. Hit the last place first.

If I can remember which fucking one it was.

Well, better a late picnic in a perfect spot than settling too early.

Arthur Ketterson had spread the plaid stadium blanket so the sun fell across it warmingly. He sat down, approving once again this site on the slope of a variegated hill, with evergreens behind and a mixed stand of oak, maple, and poplar beneath him. Affording a view of the valley farther below, the spot also allowed Arthur to keep an eye on the Beemer, parked just off the road to his right.

Having laid out the contents of Parsons's basket on the blanket, he used a levering corkscrew to open the wine, a lovely Pouilly-Fuissé that had been drinking awfully well just before his arrest. Pouring a dram into the glass and tasting it, Arthur was delighted to discover the vintage hadn't lost anything during the intervening months.

Having filled his glass, Arthur was about to reach for a plate to hold the chilled game hen when his peripheral vision caught a slight movement at the edge of the woods to his left. He froze, then turned his head ever so slowly, forcing his eyes to strain a bit in coming to bear.

A small brown rabbit, evidently oblivious to Arthur's presence, hopped twice through the grass toward him. It paused now on hind legs to sniff the air. Adorable. Nose twitching, ears cocked this way and that.

But, unfortunately for the rabbit, not every which way.

A shadow under one of the evergreen limbs shifted subtly, then shifted again. The rabbit seemed unaware, dipping its head down sideways to snap off a stalk of grass.

The bobcat chose that moment to streak out from under the evergreen, accelerating as it approached the feeding rabbit.

Arthur was quite sure he could have stood up in time. Or he might have yelled. Given either alternative, the predator would have veered off, the prey fleeing — panicked, but safe — toward a different point of the compass.

Of course, Arthur did no such thing.

The rabbit had just begun to tense when the bobcat, its front paw no more than a mustard-colored blur against the brownish fur, brought the smaller creature down and clamped its jaws on the rabbit's neck. There was a nerve-tingling squeal — not unlike that of a child on an amusement ride — as the prey twisted in agony and terror, the bobcat both holding it down and shaking it ferociously with wicked cleaverlike movements of its head.

Then Arthur heard a distinct snap, and the rabbit suddenly went lifeless. The bobcat shook it several more times before dropping the body onto the ground and sinking its teeth into the neck area again. Half-prancing, the predator carried the rabbit toward the tree line. Like Sheilah's orange tabby with the stuffed bear. Or, better, like . . .

Arthur wiped a tear from the corner of his eye, for one of the few times in his life thinking sincerely about another. "If only Willie could have seen this," he said softly, but aloud.

And then, when Arthur was sure the bobcat was far enough away not to be frightened into abandoning its hard-earned meal, he began to clap enthusiastically, shouting, "Bravo!" three times before returning with gusto to his own, if tamer, repast.

Sheilah drove east toward the city, the afternoon sun slanting behind her, the cool September air jet-streaming over the windshield and above her head.

I know I was a little . . . abrupt with Frank back there, but Jesus Mary, if he'd hugged me another ten seconds, I'd never have wanted him to let go. Which would have meant coming back into the city together and risking being seen at his place or mine.

On the other hand — face it, girl — you feel better now than you have in years. Frank's married, technically, but he won't be for long. And then, potential conflicts of interest or not, you and that man come out into the open with the relationship, and build something special into something permanent.

Several hours later, Sheilah approached a simple directional decision. Her apartment house was closer than Valley Nursing Home, but there'd be weekender traffic flowing — or slowing — into the city, clogging up most of the major roads like a workday rush hour. Plus, she knew her father still worried about her, and it might be nice for him to see his daughter earlier in the evening, while she was happy and bouncy for a change.

It might even make Lucille feel a little better.

As soon as Rudy Giordano walked in the bar, he realized it wasn't the last stop from the night before. No, this was the butcher-block and fern place where he'd seen the woman, Terri Como. Rudy realized that because he saw her again now, sitting on a corner stool, some drink in front of her that looked like Hawaiian Punch with one of those stupid paper parasols in it.

Terri spotted Rudy a second or two after he

noticed her, and she waved him over. Best not to piss her off, no question there.

When Rudy got close to her, Terri slipped off the bar stool like a ballet dancer, moving a step toward him and giving him a big hug.

"God, Rudy, I heard on the news the jury let the guy go?"

"Kind of. The fucking DA has to decide about going after him again somehow."

"That sucks."

"Plus, one jury doesn't convict the bastard, I can't really see another . . ." Rudy seized up.

Terri tugged his arm, patting the stool next to her. "Here, sit. Let me buy you a drink for a change."

So, she remembers that much from the other time, that I was standing for the drinks. Having to use the little cash in my side pocket because I left my wallet with the credit cards and even the ATM card home that night.

Home. That night. Rudy shrugged off the memory.

The bartender took his order, and Terri said, "Just got back from Atlantic City."

"Atlantic City." Receiving his ale from the keep, Rudy clinked his glass to Terri's. "You were just back from Toronto when I met you, right?"

"Yeah, but Toronto don't have the gambling. My ex, Jimmy, he was — did I tell you about him last time?"

The mileage on her, Rudy had figured Terri must have been married at some point. Maybe more than once. "Uh-uh."

"Well, the clink was from Philly, and he loved driving to A.C. The casinos there, they've done a lot for the retired people, give them a place to go? But not much for the city itself, which is still a fucking slum — pardon my French. Anyway, Jimmy loved to gamble, but he wouldn't always cash out at the end of the night."

"How come?"

"Scared of being followed from the cashier's window and then mugged on the way back to our hotel. So he'd just leave with some high-denomination chips — like hundreds, say. Only thing was, Jimmy'd peek into the bedroom, and if I was asleep, he'd try to wake me up by flipping the chips at me through the doorway."

"Flipping them?"

"Yeah. He thought it was romantic, the clink. Like Romeo throwing pebbles at Juliet's window on the balcony there."

Rudy didn't think people had glass windows back then, but Shakespeare wasn't exactly his strong suit, either. "Sounds like a good way to lose the chips."

"You got it. I'd wake up, and then have to get down on the floor with him, try to find the little things in the shag carpet like a contact lens somebody dropped."

"So how'd you do?"

"You mean at the gambling this time?"

"Yeah."

"Not so bad. I gotta tell you, though, the

casinos are all crowded now, even during the day when it's nice outside. Everybody wants to lose their money." Terri sipped her drink, then got a serious sound in her voice. "The cops, they were after me about that night there, you know."

Here it comes, thought Rudy. "I'm real sorry about that, but I had to tell them where I was when . . . at the time."

"Yeah, I know, and believe me, I'm not blaming you. It's just that, well, I had to tell them . . . what we were doing and all."

"The Irish cop, O'Toole, he let me in on that."

Another sip. "And you're not mad or anything?"

"Hell no. It was kind of bad timing, you and me being in the car . . . getting acquainted. I mean, I'm back at the house instead of with you, none of this . . ."

Rudy felt himself starting to seize up again, the way he did whenever he thought about that night, much less tried to convince somebody that fucking Ketterson —

Terri all of a sudden had ahold of his arm, squeezing it. "Look, I know all this shit — pardon my French — has been just terrible for you. But I liked you then, Rudy, and I still like you now."

He felt her squeeze change from sympathy to more like a grope, and he thought, I'm over it. "Hey, same here, Ter."

Not letting go of him, she glanced at her watch. "I got another commitment tonight, so I have to leave now. But how about we see each other again?"

"Sounds good to me."

"Maybe around six Friday, here at the bar?"

"Sure." And why the fuck not? Something to take my mind off the fucking world for a change.

It wasn't until after Terri Como had left that Rudy realized she'd stuck him with the tab for three of her parasol punch drinks and his ale to boot. But somehow it didn't piss Rudy Giordano off like he would've thought it might.

Frank Sikes left the car against the curb a block past his apartment house. Walking back to the entrance carrying his overnight bag, he was struck by how ratty the street looked. The trash, the broken bottles, the untrimmed bushes. A couple of surly teens in Oakland Raider colors dissed him from a stoop.

I pass this way twice a day, but I never really noticed it all before. Must be because of the inn, how nice everything was by comparison.

Upstairs, the apartment seemed even rattier, with no one to blame but himself. Just three rooms, and Frank hadn't so much as straightened the place up — much less cleaned it — for he couldn't remember how long.

Setting the bag down next to his threadbare couch, Frank sank into it. He turned on the TV, then turned the set off almost immediately.

Is it the place that's bothering me? Or is it that Sheilah's not here with me? The pang from leaving her back at the inn had gotten worse on the drive home, and worst of all just now, coming up the ratty street and back to the ratty apartment.

Frank looked around him. Not much he could do about the street, but the apartment he could fix, at least enough so he wouldn't be ashamed to have Sheilah come visit.

Long as you drive her to and from, security wise.

Frank got up to start cleaning. Ten minutes later, he thought, No, this rathole is just a small part of what's bothering me. Another part's her case with Ketterson, but every time I tried to bring it up over the weekend, Sheilah slammed the door in my face. The guy's dirty, I know it. But she can't see it, probably because he's her client.

So, okay. You can clean up the apartment, you can clean up the other thing, too. You probably weren't at your best those weeks, anyway, trying to build a case against Ketterson while also trying to get through the divorce stuff with Pam. But the file on Jessica Giordano is still at the office, and you can go back over it, make sure that candidate Mendez remembers that District Attorney Mendez ought to retry it.

Maybe even find the man some new ammunition, too. Something he didn't have before.

Frank Sikes decided he had a program now, both professionally and on the home front. Whistling, he put on a jazz CD instead of the

234

tube, then went into the kitchen to fill a bucket with soap and water.

"Peter, is that you?"

"Yes." Mendez came in the front door of his house, still in the golf shirt. Which, he'd noticed, was giving off a slight stink but which he also hadn't seen trying to change at the office, given nobody else had been there on a beautiful Sunday in September.

"I was worried about you," said his wife, Elena. A pleasingly slim but forgettable woman in her early thirties, she didn't like playing the candidate's wife, but nevertheless, she tried her best to support her husband's effort.

Peter gave Elena a hug without meaning it, dog-tired and dispirited. "I told you over the phone that I had to go through a case file for tomorrow."

"Yes, but it's nearly eight o'clock."

He sniffed. "What's for dinner?"

"Chicken."

"Again?"

"It's good for you" is what Elena said, but it sounded more like she meant, This hour, you're lucky there's anything.

Mendez didn't want to push it. "Let me just hit the shower first."

"Well, hurry, okay? The kids are starving."

He looked in the family room, the boy and girl transfixed by some kind of action animation on the forty-two-inch screen. Peter had always taken pride in being able to remember the names of witnesses, pro and con, even months after a trial had ended and he was involved in one of many new cases. However, there were moments, like just now, when he realized he wasn't dead sure of his own children's names.

Those moments used to bother Peter Mendez, but lately they hadn't. Which he knew should bother him even more.

But didn't.

"Jack's not having hisself a good day, I'm afraid."

At the doorway to her father's room, Sheilah Quinn searched the eyes of Lucille Wesley. "How bad is he?"

"Don't seem to want nothing to eat. Always had his appetite, that man, but now . . ." She looked helplessly into the room.

Sheilah entered, more shadows than light coming through the window onto the bed. Jack Quinn lay under a sheet and blanket, his left hand outside them, with the nurse's call button lying perpendicular to his index finger.

My God, she thought, it's like he's aged a year since I saw him last week.

It was just a piddly little French town, not much more than a village, really. But Jack Quinn's platoon had been ordered to secure it, and secure it they would.

Some German panzer tanks had been through — *you could see their treadmarks on the dirt road. The enemy infantry had left their dead as they retreated, one poor devil run over by one of his own tanks. Flattened like a pancake, he was, like a cartoon cat after the mouse runs over him with a steamroller, you know?*

"Dad?"

Anyway, we entered the little town midmorning, moving down the main street toward the plaza. But some Germans, they'd been waiting for us. A machine gun in the upper window of a stable opened fire, killing two men in front of me. But you don't think of your buddies then. Nossir, you think about you, and getting down on that ground, and wishing to Jesus your fatigue buttons weren't so goddamn thick, you couldn't get lower even.

"Dad?"

I empty the clip from my M1 into the ceiling of the stable, and a body comes pitching out and down. Jesus, he's just a kid. Fifteen, maybe.

A kid in a gray uniform, trying to kill me. I hope to God I never understand war.

"Dad!"

And now somebody's tugging on my sleeve? Forget that. I've got more Germans on the upper level of this stable, the machine gun rattling again, chopping up my buddies.

Hey, quit with the tugging, will you?

Sitting on the edge of the bed, Sheilah dropped her father's arm. Taking his left hand in her own, she shook it gently. A little contraction from the fingers, but that might have been just reflex. Then his eyes opened, the pupils still rolled up inside his head.

"Dad?" Come on, be yourself for me. "Dad?"

The pupils rolled down, seemingly independent of each other. Jack Quinn's head was turned toward her, but no awareness shone in the eyes.

"Dad. It's me." Oh God, please let him recognize me. "It's Sheilah, Dad."

From the door, Lucille Wesley said firmly, "Jack, it's your daughter, come to visit." When Sheilah didn't turn to look at her, Lucille stayed in the doorway.

Jack Quinn seemed as though he wanted to speak, a little drool trickling from the corner of his chin, but no sound came out. Sheilah put his hand back down on the sheet, to allow him to tap once for yes, twice for no. If he could.

"Dad, are you okay?"

Nothing.

"Are you in pain?"

Same.

Then Sheilah thought of something, the game they used to play with Mr. Fuzzums. Reaching across her father's chest, she took the spare pillow from beside him. Holding it in both hands, Sheilah rubbed it across his facial features. No reaction from the man in the bed.

Fighting the tears, Sheilah fluffed up the spare pillow and replaced it beside her father's head. Then she picked up his hand again, the skin dry, the bones standing out almost as much as the veins and not feeling much stronger.

This is the hand that helped me learn to tie my shoes on the back porch. Taught me how to fly-cast between the lily pads on a small pond. Slapped cooling mud on my shin when a bee stung it.

The hand that now feels me caressing it. If the man who was my father can feel anything at all.

"Don't you worry, child." Lucille Wesley let out the breath she'd been holding ever since the daughter had picked up that pillow. "Peoples like Jack, they bounce back from bad days. I seen them."

A nod from the lawyer woman, but no signal from her to leave. Lucille waited until the spare pillow had gone back where it belonged, then stepped out into the hall and closed the door on the room. And on her own bad memories of relatives hurrying along their sick ones back in that Mercy Hospital.

Daughter's not gonna do nothing foolish this night. Give her some privacy.

Roger Hesterfield believed it was bad form to drink too much at the club. Or anywhere public, so to speak. Three, four maximum on a weekend day, then into the car and home before his blood-alcohol level would confirm the Breathalyzer registering a presumptive .10 from the air inside his mouth. The police aren't as deferential to those in the judiciary as they once were, after all, and a DWI would do a lot more damage to the sinecure of presiding judge than renting a simple porno movie.

Which Roger had seriously considered on the way home. In the past, he'd taken out some of the safer, so-called artistic erotica movies, but he'd found them both exciting, in that they left something to the imagination, and unsatisfying as well, for the same reason.

Depositing his golf clubs in the front closet, Roger skimmed through the mail he'd ignored the previous day. All the important correspondence goes to the courthouse, anyway, he thought. Always has. Then Roger went back into the study, sitting down in his chair before picking up the cable remote. Next to the phone.

You called Sheilah Quinn's number last night. Not one of your smartest gambits.

On the other hand, what harm could there be in contacting someone I find attractive? Especially since I show her no favoritism whatsoever in the courtroom.

Well, maybe just a bit on that Ketterson bail issue.

No, no. You're letting your judgment grow clouded here. Not a good idea to have called her like that, and especially not to leave a message that you remember as being . . . well, unfocused, shall we say? No, best to apologize to Sheilah for the call next time you see her.

Which should be tomorrow, after she finds out

about the liquor-store case being called for trial come Tuesday.

Smiling at the prospect, Roger Hesterfield poured himself an extra finger of the Glenfiddich and used the remote to click on the cable box.

"Hey, Al? Al! Two more here. This man's money's no good, you hear what I'm saying?"

Rudy Giordano was vaguely aware of being back in the bar with the boxers on the wall, but a different keep pulling the taps. And there was this black guy — big black guy — buying him drinks, not letting Al take his money.

"System shafted you, man," said Rudy's new friend, laying a twenty next to a coaster on the worn mahogany. "Shafted you good. Give you an idea what it's like to be a person of color in this world."

Now the big guy's saying I'm black? Rudy shook his head. Met this bastard at a construction conference once but can't remember his name. I do remember him getting some jobs account of minority-hiring preferences over the years. Guy's probably scared shitless, too, now that old Newt in Washington's letting the preferences run out.

"So," said the black guy, "You need any help on that courthouse thing, you give me a call, you hear what I'm saying?"

Rudy heard him all right, and he tried not to laugh. Except for stripping the interiors of the old building for salvageable fixtures, like the chandeliers and wainscoting there, most of the remaining work was just demolition. Rudy had already made up his mind to save for last the courtroom where his daughter's case had been wrecked, to do the work himself. Tear down the fucking joke that sucked his heart through it. He was going to enjoy that, in a way. Taking apart the one place in this world he knew there was no fucking justice.

"Hey, Rudy, my man. You ready for another round?"

"Why not?"

The big guy's money buys just as good ale as anybody else's, right? The fuck, I'm not prejudiced.

Sheilah Quinn opened the door to her apartment, drooping more than when she'd left it. As though forty-seven hours had been spent with her father and only one with Frank Sikes. Quigley greeted her at the door, but he didn't cheer her very much.

"So, was Krissie good to you?"

A meow.

Sheilah moved to the food dish, which was licked clean. That reminded her of the meals she'd enjoyed with Frank. Smile, girl, she thought. And did.

After emptying a new can of food into the dish, Sheilah freshened the water bowl. Going back toward the bedroom, she had to step quickly at the doorway. "Ugh. Thanks, Quig."

Sheilah pitched the overnight bag onto the bed, then returned to the kitchen, pulling some paper towels off the dispenser. The cat looked up from his dinner. "Yes, I meant you, Hair Ball Central."

In the bedroom once more, Sheilah cleaned up the mess and dumped the towels into the bathroom wastebasket next to the tub. Consider your priorities: You can unpack first, or you can relax with some wine and a bubble bath, then unpack later.

No contest. Sheilah began running the water for a bath, waiting until there was an inch or two above the perforated platform before adding a dollop of bath oil, the bubbles frothing up immediately.

Back in the kitchen, Sheilah poured herself half a glass from the chardonnay bottle in the refrigerator, then carried it to the bedroom, Quigley following her down the hall. "More lonely than hungry, huh?"

The cat rubbed a moist nose against both her calves.

Sheilah sipped some of the wine, then stripped, tossing the clothes toward the bag on the bed. Naked, she brought the chardonnay into the bathroom, setting the glass on the rim of the tub before testing the water. Perfect. Turning off the tap, she reached over past the sitting Quigley to the motor, pushing the buttons for high speed and twenty minutes' duration. Then, eyes closed, she eased into the tub.

The water felt wonderful, the aeration seeming to clear some of the thoughts clouding her mind. I've got to shake off this feeling of dread about Dad. I didn't make him sick, and I can't make him well. It's not my fault.

It's not my fault.

It's not my fault.

Even through that little mantra, the tears began to come. Sheilah willed herself to postpone them for a while, at least until she enjoyed another sip of wine.

Opening her eyes and reaching for the wineglass simultaneously, Sheilah wasn't aware of her hand flying out, knocking the glass over. She wasn't aware of the glass shattering on the tiles or of Quigley racing from the room as though he'd been scalded. The only thing she was aware of was screaming.

Screaming as she clumsily rose to her feet in the tub, the scarlet liquid coming up with her.

Screaming as the slimy redness clung briefly, horribly, before running in rivulets down breasts and belly and hips and legs, eventually joining the darkened water below her.

Screaming as Sheilah Quinn whisked her hands over her flesh.

"Am I bleeding? Oh God, Jesus Mary, am I bleeding to death?"

Sitting on Woodmere's patio in the twilight,

Arthur Ketterson said, "I wonder if Sheilah thought —"

"Sir?"

"Oh, sorry, Parsons. You asked me a question?"

The butler, standing next to the wrought-iron patio furniture, looked down at him. "I asked when you preferred dinner, sir."

"Dinner. I think just a snack, rather than a full meal. Your picnic lunch was not only delicious but also quite filling."

"Thank you, sir."

After Parsons went into the house, Arthur made his way down the path toward Mother's Dell, carrying a glass of Cakebread's best reserve chardonnay. Taking the table and chair from their shed, Arthur arranged them and settled in. The lightning bugs began to twinkle like Christmas decorations in the trees.

"I must be more careful around Parsons, Mother. Deep in what I thought to be an internal conference, I found myself speaking aloud about Sheilah where he could hear me."

Arthur dipped his tongue into the chardonnay. Still a bit too chilled for full appreciation of its nuances.

Nuances. Sheilah, my Sheilah. That word captures perfectly the way you're different from the others. Have been, from the moment I first spotted you on the street five months ago and followed you like a lovesick puppy back to that office building. The other women might have had Mother's eyes, but only you have her compleat mien as well, a combination of nuances as evident on a public sidewalk as in a criminal courtroom. With the others, I'd always maintained a careful distance, and an equally careful "cover story," as spies might say. And each cover story worked beautifully, no hint of suspicion directed my way over the disappearance of Diana, or Hedy, or Lorraine as I kept my attentions on other women in their neighborhoods, the women who testified at my trial.

But fate seemed to intervene in the matter of you, dear Sheilah, throwing the two of us together over the death of the slut Giordano, my cover story for *you*. Fate never once intruded upon my stalking of the others. . . .

Arthur allowed his gaze to move from tree to tree around the dell. Slowly, nostalgically. Diana never reported the blood in the juice carton, preferring to believe something had simply gone terribly wrong in her refrigerator and certainly not willing to make a "federal case" out of a ninety-nine-cent quart. Hedy never reported the blood she found in —

No, that won't do. I must not lump the memories together like that. Much better to recall and revere each as a separate episode, a major chapter in . . .

Arthur stopped again. I should have been about to say "in my life," but what was on the tip of my tongue was "in my career."

He considered the implications of that subconscious clue. The stalking of all these women, his delivering them from imperfection. Efforts less akin to the mere passage of one's existence than to the pursuit of a professional career.

A career that had evolved from its genesis in soon-to-be-mutilated women to include as well the lovely, reminiscent ones. A career that still *was* evolving, if one thought about it. Witness the spontaneity of planting the frozen cubes of blood in the hose of that crude bathroom spa.

Which brought Arthur back once more to Sheilah Quinn, as most of his thoughts seemed to lately. She wasn't merely different from the others: She was better in every way. For the first time since he'd strangled Madeline Ketterson, Arthur really had . . . improvised spontaneously. As a target, Sheilah had the power to catapult his career — there, "career" again — in a revolutionary way, the catalyst that would carry him to the pinnacle of his chosen art form.

Of course, it was also just possible that Sheilah might report what she experienced the next time she bathed. However, given her extraordinary intestinal fortitude as a trial attorney, Sheilah would more likely keep the incident to herself. Perhaps run the pitiable little apparatus in her tub three or four times as an experiment, to determine if the incredible would happen again. When it didn't, of course, Sheilah would assume it was simply some malfunction of plumbing, either the spa's or, more likely, her apartment's. Unexplainable, but not particularly . . . disquieting, come the cold light of day.

Arthur sampled the chardonnay again, now just warmed enough to give off its best flavors of vanilla, oak, and butter. No, if I had to wager on it — and to at least some extent, that's exactly what I *am* doing, wagering — I'd have to say that I'll be able to move forward, because Sheilah will not be reporting her little interlude in the bathtub.

"I would, however, be grateful to have your thoughts on the subject, Mother," said Arthur Ketterson IV as deferentially as possible.

TEN

My God, thought Sheilah, standing in her office doorway. Then out loud with, "Flowers?"

She'd opened the suite on the sixth floor at eight on Monday morning, Krissie not yet at the reception desk. Sheilah wanted to be in early, and she hadn't gotten much sleep the night before, anyway. Once the initial shock of the bloodlike stuff in her bath wore off, Sheilah had let the tub drain and then showered for ten minutes. After examining herself carefully, she refilled the tub and turned the motor unit back on. No more discoloration. Just some kind of freaky malfunction. Calming down, Sheilah had called the apartment building's management company, leaving a message on the answering machine to please check her pipes the next day.

When she did get to bed Sunday night, she couldn't find Mr. Fuzzums. Quigley must have dragged him off somewhere and hidden him again, probably to retaliate for her spending the weekend away. After visiting her father and dealing with the tub, though, Sheilah just didn't have the energy to begin searching for the little bear.

But flowers, now, they could salve those problems and then some.

Sheilah reached for the note, taped kind of oddly to the stem of a lily. When could Frank have arranged for these to be here?

After tearing open the little envelope, she read the handwritten card:

To my dear Sheilah,

For a job well done. However, luncheon at Monday, noon, will be an even more tangible expression of my gratitude.

I'll stop by then.

Devotedly,
Arthur Ketterson IV

Wobbling a bit, Sheilah Quinn crumpled the card and dropped it into her wastebasket.

The moment his telephone rang, Arthur Ketterson felt a chill ripple through his pajama-clad body.

Venturing a hand from under the covers, he depressed the blinking intercom button on the machine next to his mother's bed and lifted the receiver. "Parsons?"

"Yes, sir," came the tinny response. "I was wondering when you might care for breakfast."

"Before we get to that, it's rather cold in here this morning, don't you think?"

"So sorry, sir. I'm afraid the thermostat may never master the vagaries of a stone mansion."

Parsons, ever the droll troll. "Well, try your best, would you?"

"I will, sir. And breakfast?"

"Just some cereal. I'll be going out shortly."

"Very good, sir."

Then, recalling his note on Sheilah's floral arrangement, Arthur said, "Oh, and Parsons?"

"Sir? "

"I don't want to be available by telephone today."

"Certainly, sir."

Arthur released the intercom button, hand gladly retreating back under the covers. Given the chilliness of the air, he came to the conclusion that he should decide which clothes to wear for his luncheon with Sheilah before taking any further action.

In chambers that morning, Roger Hesterfield noticed a patch of plaster dust on his pant leg. Pushing back from his desk, he brushed away at it, muttering.

Goddamned workmen — downstairs, at the lobby level — tearing off this light fixture or that piece of wainscoting, not caring who's trying to walk by them. Grave robbers. They're no better than grave robbers.

Roger was just about to return to the docket entries on the liquor-store robbery when Old Bailey's signature knock rattled the door to the courtroom. "Yes?"

The bailiff stuck his head in the door. "Your

Honor, Mr. Rudolph Giordano here to see you."

And waste my time. "Didn't you tell him that I can't discuss his daughter's case?"

"He says it's not about the case, Your Honor."

"So, how was the weekend, Frank?"

In the Homicide Unit's squadroom, Gerry O'Toole watched his partner look up from a case file, then look back down.

"It was okay," said Frank.

Kind of overcasual for him, Gerry thought. "Well, mine sucked. Had the mother-in-law over. Last barbecue of the season, wife says we gotta invite her, you know? Fucking woman, she talks even while she's eating."

"Not a pretty picture, Ger."

"No shit. I swear, I couldn't believe it when she had to go in for that surgery, remember?"

"I remember you pissing and moaning about having to visit her."

"Hey, before the operation, I don't have a problem with it. She's old, she's weak, she probably won't make it off the table. So I figure, No harm in wishing the old bag bon voyage on the journey ahead, you know?"

"Uh-huh."

"Only she pulls through. I mean, Frank, can you believe this shit? Fucking doctors can't kill her with knives."

"They ought to spend some time with us, bone up on it."

"What, we get a fresh stabbing?"

252

When his partner looked up again, Gerry inclined his head toward the file.

Frank said, "Uh-uh. Giordano."

Gerry shook his head this time. "You heard whether the DA's gonna retry that hinky bastard Ketterson?"

"No. But I thought I might find something to help Mendez make up his mind."

"Good luck."

At which point, the phone rang.

Gerry said, "We're catching this morning, right?"

"Afraid so."

Trying to be optimistic, Gerry O'Toole reached for the receiver.

Peter Mendez gathered the papers on the liquor-store robbery into his briefcase. Joey Trask, the lawyer for Cundo Borbón, had called him first thing that morning, confirming Roger Hesterfield's report that his client was rolling over on Pablo Diaz, Sheilah Quinn's boy.

I saw this coming — hell, a child of three could have seen this coming — but maybe Sheilah will request a continuance, claiming surprise and the need for more time to prepare her defense. No. No, that hope is wild fantasy. The woman's a litigational Amazon, requesting no favors and granting none. And, despite yesterday's golf match, I'm still on thin ice with Hesterfield, anyway.

Thin ice. Bad metaphor. Mort Zussman had

used it over the phone the night before, saying that he didn't like the way Peter was skating with the moneybags. Saying they needed something big.

That's what Hesterfield thinks this trial is, but it's just a piece-a-shit armed robbery. No, I need to do something dramatic, something that'll move the media off this and onto matters of life and . . .

Sure. Of course.

What could be more dramatic than the death penalty? I call a news conference, then make the pitch that what this commonwealth really needs is a new capital punishment statute. Never mind that, thanks pretty much to Sheilah, the state's supreme court invalidated the existing statute on state constitutional grounds, and it'd take more than waving a magic wand to make those disappear. But get a couple of legislative hacks up for reelection to swing with me on it, and we all look like heroes.

At least through ballot-casting time.

Time. Look at the watch. Got to get over to the First Session.

On her way out the open door to the corridor, Sheilah Quinn said, "First Session."

Krissie Newton glanced up from the computer screen. "What case?"

"Diaz/Borbón. I just got a call from Old Bailey that Hesterfield's starting it tomorrow. Oh, and thanks for looking after Quigley, by the way."

Yeah, right. No souvenir from the weekend or "I hope it didn't fuck up your plans." Sheilah, you're a good boss, and if I love Etta like a grandmother, I love you like an older sister. But not even to bring me a bunch of — "Hey, what'd you think of the flowers? Awesome, huh?"

Sheilah's face kind of scrunched up. "When did they arrive?"

"Friday afternoon. Your client, like, really outdid himself."

Sheilah's eyes went funny. "How did you know who they're from?"

"That Ketterson guy, he brought them himself."

Sheilah's face got worse, if anything. "Arthur Ketterson was here?"

"Yeah. You, like, got him out on bail, remember?"

Huh, now Sheilah's face looked like she was maybe gonna hurl her cookies or something. "Krissie, I want you to call him at his home number, tell him I can't make lunch at all, today or this week. Got it?"

The lunch thing must have been on the card. "Got it."

"Etta in yet?"

"Haven't seen her."

"When she arrives, be sure to tell her that Ketterson might be stopping by —"

Ohmigod. "He's coming here again?"

"Maybe. Let Etta know to tell him the 'no

255

lunch' message, too. Okay?"

"Okay."

Sheilah's heels clicked down the hall toward the elevator. Turning back to her computer, Krissie Newton said quietly, "Etta better fucking be here when Arturus the Vampire Preppy comes through that door."

Roger Hesterfield had no intention of accepting the piece of paper Rudolph Giordano was foisting upon him, mainly because he already knew what it would say.

Using a thumb to hike the blue hard hat a little higher off his forehead, Giordano ignored Old Bailey moving closer to him and then used the thumb again to point at the dateline on the memo. "You should have got one of these from the county commissioners. Couple, three weeks ago."

"Mr. Giordano, the needs of the criminal justice system —"

"I don't know about the 'system,' Judge. Other than what I seen of it outside the door there. I just know I'm supposed to be dismantling the courtroom and chambers in here, and for that, I need you out."

Roger felt his blood pressure surging. The hubris of this dago hod-carrier, issuing ultimatums to me in my own chambers. "Mr. Giordano, I will be leaving the First Session when doing so will not prejudice litigants before this Court."

256

Giordano grinned. " 'Litigants'? Was I one of those? I don't know. All I know is, this memo from the county commissioners says you were supposed to have your stuff boxed up and labeled last Friday for the move."

A stupid man who believes he has the upper hand. And, God help me, perhaps he does.

"The county commissioners . . ." Roger heard his voice rising, not in strength but in pitch, and he fought to lower it. "The county commissioners do not run this courtroom."

"Maybe not. But they do run the building it's in, and they got a contract with me that says I can start tearing down this Friday, and that's what I'm gonna do." Giordano turned to leave, Old Bailey shadowing him.

Can you believe the unmitigated gall of this —

From the door, Rudolph Giordano said, "That contract I got with the commissioners, it's like 'the law.' Right, Judge?"

Neither Roger Hesterfield nor Old Bailey said anything as the man in the blue hard hat left them.

Arthur didn't want to trust his choice of restaurant to telephonic inquiry. No, better to reconnoiter on foot, since he hadn't exactly been out and about over the last few months. And he certainly had no intention of ever returning to Chez Jean after what happened with the slut Giordano afterward.

Not to be superstitious, but as Mother would

say, "Fool me once, shame on you; fool me twice, shame on me."

And so at 11:00 A.M. Arthur was knocking on the glass door of an Art Deco establishment, its menus for lunch and dinner posted prominently in the window. A portly man dressed better than a waiter but not as well as an owner waddled out from some darkened recess and opened the door a crack. "We are not as yet able to seat you, sir."

"I understand that. But today is a special occasion for me, and I wondered if I might see the available tables before returning later."

The portly man, probably the maître d', knit his eyebrows. Rather comical, actually. As though he was truly attempting to think.

To spare the toad's synapses of intellectual overload, Arthur held forth a folded ten-dollar bill, the denomination drawing rather immediate attention from widening eyes under the now unknit brow.

"Of course, sir. Please."

The ten disappeared in a flourish of door opening.

Arthur found the interior of the restaurant almost charming. Chrome tables decently spaced. A functioning fountain in the middle of the room, under a skylight. The pungent smell of burning wood — mesquite, perhaps? — wafting from the rear of the establishment.

Arthur walked around the room, but only to confirm what he'd initially decided. "The table on the south side of the fountain."

"Of course, sir. And for what time, please?"

"I'm not sure as yet. Say noon onward."

The brows went at it again. "But sir, surely you must understand. That is one of our finest tables. To hold it empty for an entire afternoon would not be fair to the staff assigned —"

This time, a folded fifty, which seemed to strike the current member of the staff as eminently fair, and, given the impression Arthur wished to make on his luncheon companion, money well spent indeed.

Either old Rog got less sleep than I, Sheilah thought, or he's drowning in the sauce. Look at the expression on his face. It's like he just lost his best friend.

Sheilah followed Peter Mendez and Joey Trask into the judge's chambers, each taking a counsel chair in front of the desk. Old Bailey, as usual, stayed by the door.

"Well," said Hesterfield, seeming to recover a little. "What's our status here?"

"Judge" — Trask leaned forward, earnest — "my client has decided to cooperate fully with the commonwealth in this matter."

"Where do I register my surprise?" said Sheilah.

Hesterfield looked at the prosecutor. "Peter, I trust you're ready to go forward against Mr. . . . ah, Borbón, is it?"

"Diaz," said Peter, no inflection to his voice at all.

Trask leaned back. "Borbón's my guy, Judge."

"Ah, yes. Honest mistake, eh?"

Joey laughed with Roger, Peter forced a small smile, and Sheilah didn't do anything.

Now Hesterfield glanced over to her. "Under the circumstances, Sheilah, are you ready to go forward, as well?"

Give it half a beat, just to get Peter looking my way, hope in his eyes. "As soon as Mr. Mendez gives me the parameters of the deal his office struck with Mr. Borbón."

"Well, then," said Roger, rubbing his hands together, suddenly a little overeager, Sheilah thought. "No sense putting off till tomorrow what we can do today, is there?"

Mendez appeared shaky. "Your Honor?"

"Let's impanel the jury this afternoon, so we can plunge right in come morning."

"Suits me," said Sheilah. God, Peter looks sick, even just nodding.

"Anything else, then?" asked Hesterfield.

Sheilah shifted in her chair. So long as he's being expansive, it's a good time to lay some groundwork. "Just one request, Judge."

"Yes?"

"I'd like the prosecution's witnesses not to be sequestered."

"What?" said Mendez, turning toward her.

"I want everybody who's testifying for you to be in the courtroom during your direct case."

"Just one big happy family, eh?" said Hesterfield. "Well, Peter, you certainly can have no objection to that."

Peter Mendez shook his head, and Sheilah Quinn felt sure the DA was worrying that he should have thought of one.

Arthur Ketterson stood in front of a mirrored panel in the lobby of Sheilah's office building, checking to be sure the Windsor knot in his tie was snugged perfectly up to the collar button. The way his mother had taught him so many years before, standing behind him at the full-length mirror in her bedroom. The lovely Madeline's elbows brushing the saddles of his shoulders, her breasts caressing the shoulder blades themselves as her hands demonstrated the proper twists and flips of silk that made the knot perfectly symmetrical to —

No, I can't drift off here. Better to postpone such memories and focus on the present. And the future. Like making certain the little cassette player in my jacket pocket doesn't betray itself by ruining the drape of the fabric.

Frequently checking his watch, Arthur waited in the lobby until precisely 11:55, then took the now-familiar elevator to the sixth floor. Impress Sheilah with the punctuality of a fellow professional.

Even if the visitor practiced a substantially different profession.

The corridor door to the office suite was open again, though nobody was walking through it.

Must be their policy, thought Arthur as he made his way there, seeing the doors to both inner offices were closed. As a courtesy, he knocked lightly on the jamb, still standing at the threshold.

The young Krissie jumped in her desk chair, but not as badly as when he'd first appeared, the previous Friday. Marshaling her resources bravely, she actually managed a smile. "Mr. Ketterson?"

"Yes, Krissie. And how are you today?"

"I'm fine. But I called —"

"And did Sheilah like the floral arrangement?"

"Yeah, loved it, but —"

"Oh, I'm so glad. Is she nearly ready for our luncheon engagement?"

"That's what I'm trying to tell you." Krissie paused, perhaps thinking her last sentence had come out a bit harshly. "I'm sorry, Mr. Ketterson. What I meant was, I called your house, and I told the man answering to let you know. Sheilah can't make lunch, today or this week."

Arthur knew he had been right not to be available by telephone. "Death in the family?"

The young Krissie looked distracted. "Death?"

"In the family. Or perhaps a close friend or colleague?"

Krissie just shook her head.

Arthur said, "As the reason Sheilah can't have lunch with me?"

"Oh. Oh, no. She's on trial."

"At the courthouse here?"

"Yeah," Krissie replied, as though she really wanted to say, Where do you think trials are held, cretin?

"Well, then," Arthur moving toward one of the chairs in the reception area, "I'll just wait for her."

"Wait?"

"Yes." He sat down, laying one arm over the back of the chair, his long hand dangling, twitching a bit.

"But Sheilah . . . she'll be, like, hours."

"Not a problem, believe me. I've cleared my calendar for the entire afternoon."

As Arthur reached for a magazine on the table in front of him — *Redbook*, a publication his mother used to favor — he noticed in his peripheral vision that Krissie's hand was moving almost imperceptibly toward the side of her telephone. She seemed to press something.

An interesting development. Might lawyers have panic buttons, too?

Within seconds, the door to the office that wasn't Sheilah's opened, and the Persimmon Queen came out. She wore a shapeless dress of some peasant-spun material, black stockings, and sensible shoes. As Arthur stood, the wrinkled face regarded him carefully.

Interesting as well. I sense genuine antipathy here.

Krissie said, "Etta this is Mr. Ketterson."

"Yes, I know."

"I'm afraid I haven't had the pleasure," said Arthur.

"Etta Yemelman, Sheilah's partner." The old crone made no effort to shake hands "Can I help you?"

"I was to meet Sheilah here for a luncheon engagement, but unfortunately, she's been spirited away for a trial."

"Then maybe you could leave a number where she can reach you."

"Krissie already tried that. I'm rather difficult to pin down, communicationswise."

"Etta, Mr. Ketterson wants to wait here till Sheilah gets back."

The young Krissie said it rather bleakly, thought Arthur.

The Persimmon Queen shook her head. "No, I'm afraid that's not possible."

Arthur did a slow, graceful pirouette, keeping his arms at his sides. "There appears no shortage of seating."

"This is a functioning law office, Mr. Ketterson. Krissie and I have to be assured that the confidences of other clients will be protected, communicationswise."

The old crone quoting me against myself. Usually, I'm tolerant, even admiring, of such cleverness in others. Why do I intensely hate her for it now?

Krissie said, "And when you were here with the flowers last Friday, I put them in Sheilah's office just so you wouldn't accidentally see anything confidential."

Almost humiliating, being outflanked by both of them. Best to retreat gracefully and regroup.

Arthur addressed the Persimmon Queen. "I can certainly appreciate your point, Miss . . . I'm sorry, I seem to have forgotten —"

"Ms. Yemelman. Please leave your number with Krissie, and I'm sure Sheilah will contact you when she can."

Contact. The proverbial bum's rush, is it?

With great dignity, Arthur said, "Since I am Sheilah's client, this office has my number."

Walking back to the elevator, Arthur Ketterson IV thought about specific, satisfying things he could do to the old crone. Not terribly exciting things, perhaps, but satisfying nonetheless.

"Another false alarm," said Gerry O'Toole, putting down the phone.

Frank Sikes looked up from the document he was reading. "What this time?"

"You know Donna the Dominatrix?"

Works the computer at Missing Persons. "What about her?"

"She got this burr under her blanket about a missing kid. Twelve fucking years old. Turned out him and a friend of his just took off. Kid finally called his family. From Newark, no less."

"What about the other kid's family?"

"They never even noticed their little prince was missing. Nice, huh?"

"Lovely." Frank went back to the Giordano file. Which was how he thought of the case, even after they arrested Ketterson.

Everybody's always saying how cops are heartless, but we're the ones who call the case by the name of the victim, while it's the lawyers — both prosecution and defense — who use the name of the defendant, like "the *Ketterson* case." Granted, those attorneys don't usually get involved until there's at least a solid suspect to be indicted, but they think of the opponent or the client in the courtroom, while we're focussing on the victim. And, until there's an arrest, the surviving family, too. Which just goes to show —

O'Toole said, "I'm gonna grab a sandwich, bring it back here. You want me to pick something up for you?"

"Yeah. Ham and cheese on rye, mustard, no chips, Mountain Dew."

"Need the caffeine?"

Just a nod.

After O'Toole left, Frank went over the incident report filed by the patrol officers the night Jessica Giordano died. Responding to the 911, they were the first on the scene. Back door open — not just unlocked, but wide-open. Like somebody bolted through it and down the hiking trail behind the yard, a substantial part of Sheilah's "reasonable doubt" argument. No sign of forced entry on any windows or doors.

Frank himself had interviewed the mother,

Rhonda. Hysterical, she'd ruined the immediate area of the crime scene in her daughter's bedroom, cradling the body in her arms, even rocking it. Most people, they come on a nightmare like that, they're repelled, don't go close to the corpse. Not Mrs. G, though. Just our luck, thought Frank. And, when the uniforms got there, the puppets the decedent had collected were tossed all around the bedroom, no prints other than hers on them.

Gerry had interviewed the father, Rudolph, or Rudy, when he got home. Half-drunk and ashamed, from what Gerry told Frank later. The father had been at some Yuppie meat rack, trying to slap the make on this woman he'd picked up while his daughter was being strangled. Gerry tracked the woman down, miracle of miracles. Name of Terri Como — what can parents be thinking?

I mean, what if mine had named me Ike Sikes?

Anyway, Como confirmed everything Giordano had told them about getting her back to his car, then giving up on finding a motel because "he was just so hot for me." The father ought to feel ashamed, thought Frank. And feel real fortunate that Sheilah Quinn, who by court rule had gotten a copy of Giordano's statement, didn't bring it out at trial. Of course, it wouldn't exactly help Ketterson for the jury to hear that the married father of the victim was looking to get his ashes hauled by a pickup from a singles bar.

Still, Rudy Giordano was a good lesson for the rest of mankind. When you're doing anything, you always have to be wondering what other somethings might be happening at the same time.

"Chicken salad and lettuce, wheat, mayo."

Sheilah watched the man wearing the unappetizing combination of goatee and hair net as he made her sandwich behind the glass counter of the cafeteria in the new courthouse building across the park. But even the county can't screw up chicken salad, right?

Back when I clerked for Etta, she always told me, "Eat something before any aspect of a trial. You need energy to be your best, especially during the crucial phase of impaneling the jury. Talk to most experienced litigators and they'll say that over half the cases they try to verdict are won or lost at the voir dire — literally, "to speak the truth" — questioning of prospective jurors.

And it wasn't just who you got into or kept out of the box, either. No, it was more the relationship you built up with each man or woman, even as you might be questioning one of the others. The impression you had to give of wanting to know the jurors, how each felt, why each was a good citizen, performing his or her civic duty by sitting on the case. Yes, done right, the jury got to know and respect you during voir dire, wanted to find for you. Which really meant finding for your client.

The entire purpose of the exercise, if you thought about it.

"Pepper on your tuna, sir?" asked the waiter.

"Just a little," said Arthur Ketterson.

The waiter ground the fresh pepper from a mill that had a miniature spotlight on the bottom of it, like a bomber searching its target.

"The tuna, sir, it is to your liking?"

"Yes." Mesquite-grilled, the steak was so rare in the center as Arthur test-cut it that a bystander might call it "sushi."

Now the wine steward approached and reached for the bottle. "Some more of the pinot gris?"

Always trying to empty the first so you'll order a second, even at lunch. Employ the flat tone. "I'll pour for myself, thank you."

Getting the hint, the toad backed away a step. *"Bon appétit."*

Which left Arthur Ketterson alone again, mulling over his options for action.

Peter Mendez knew the jogging wasn't much help to him. It never is if you have to concentrate on where your running shoes are going to strike the ground.

As a warm-up, he'd already done one circuit of the park between the old and new courthouse buildings, the sweat sliding inside his singlet toward the waistband of the shorts. Usually by this point of a run, Peter's mind had become emptied of thoughts, just synchronizing the ratio of eight strides to a drawn breath, then the blowing out of air in three harsh grunts. Eight strides, three grunts. Eight/three, eight/three, until that ratio was the whole world, the only thing that mattered in life.

Except for Sheilah Quinn.

Damn her! I would have been ready for the *Ketterson* case — read*ier*, anyway — if it hadn't been for all the campaign bullshit, the late nights and the long drives and the bad food, too many drinks thrust into my hand by people who would notice if I tried to dispose of the excess by pouring it into a potted palm, the way they did in old movies. No, the campaigning was bad enough, but having to kiss Roger Hesterfield's ass was worse. God, but I hate golf, and the Nineteenth Hole especially, which takes longer to "play" than even the back nine.

Another mile, and Peter reached a long wooded stretch of road. The only place in the city without much traffic, because there was nothing to pull into or out of. Oh, the shoulder was fifteen feet wide and gravel, so you couldn't really believe you were on a secluded country lane. But the gravel was smooth, like a groomed track alongside the pavement, and if you closed your eyes, the fresh pine tang of the evergreens could make the world slow down, fool you into believing you had time to accomplish everything you ever wanted to do.

Time. It always came back to that. Just not

enough hours in the day recently. Not enough time to eat right, exercise regularly, even think straight. Instead of having to slog through the Diaz/Borbón armed robbery, he needed something big as an antidote to all the negative publicity on the Ketterson fiasco.

Peter Mendez spent the next mile trying to think of who at the legislature he should call, set up that press conference on the death penalty.

"Well, O.B.," said Roger Hesterfield, "not too many more of these ahead of us."

Old Bailey nodded politely, placing the tray he'd carried over and up from the new cafeteria on the judge's desk in front of him.

Hesterfield looked around the chambers. "I'm going to miss this place, you know."

Old Bailey looked around with him. "Lot of history here, Your Honor."

Hesterfield thought about extending the conversation, actually wanting to, which surprised him a little, but he also knew there was a tray with soup and a sandwich waiting for Old Bailey outside the chambers door. Always the faithful servant, feeding his master before himself.

"Thanks, O.B. Let me know when the attorneys arrive."

"Yes, Your Honor."

After the door closed, Hesterfield looked down at the turkey club sandwich. The woman who used to work in the old cafeteria downstairs had been a genius at making the sandwiches, each a tailored masterpiece, particularly if she knew that the next was intended for the presiding justice of the First Session. One of those old hags who undoubtedly had never married and therefore transferred both romance and maternal urge to the nearest, most attractive male. But she'd retired, gone as the cafeteria was moved to the new courthouse building.

Still looking down at his tray, the presiding justice of the First Session tried to remember the last time he'd had single malt scotch with turkey. No memory, which seemed a propitious omen for the day.

Roger Hesterfield opened the lower drawer of his desk, hoping that Sheilah Quinn had noticed how nicely he'd treated her that morning.

"Coffee or dessert today, sir?"

"No coffee," said Arthur Ketterson, lingering over the last of the wine. "But perhaps something from your dessert selection?"

"I'll wheel the cart over, sir."

Obsequious toad. How much tip can anyone reasonably expect for an afternoon of service?

Then Arthur allowed his attention to return to the internal debate he'd been having over Sheilah Quinn. He understood from his involuntary involvement in the criminal justice system that one's schedule was never really a matter of certainty. Arthur's own case had been postponed several times, even though he'd not been informed until after Vinnie dragged him to the courthouse in that fetid van the jail guards referred to as "the vegetable truck." Accordingly, it was quite possible that Sheilah simply had had no choice in the matter of missing luncheon with him but, rather, had been a victim of circumstance, perhaps even a circumstance initiated by Roger Hesterfield.

It wouldn't surprise me, thought Arthur. I sensed something afoot between them in the courtroom, even during the trial. Some . . . friction, a crackling static in the air. Including that churlish jury instruction, trying to pep-talk my jury into finding me guilty. No, the Jolly Roger had proved himself a traitor to his class, and — based on that pathetic message left on Sheilah's telephone machine — he probably would have kept Sheilah from seeing me out of spite.

So resolved: Arthur Ketterson IV will provide Miss Quinn another chance. A second bite at the apple, so to speak.

Apple. Sheilah, the Apple Tree? No. No, not quite right.

As the waiter trundled the dessert cart in front of him, Arthur Ketterson glanced down at his watch. It was 3:00 P.M. Plenty of time for a leisurely torte before "heading back to the office."

As Peter Mendez questioned the juror who'd be number eight if not successfully challenged, Sheilah glanced up at the clock on the wall of the First Session. The minute hand ticked to three o'clock. Then she looked back to the bench, thinking, I wonder how many pops Old Rog had over lunch.

Oh, not that he was blasted. No, if anything, he's still being overly solicitous of me. Even asked for the proper pronunciation of my client's name. And loudly enough that the prospective jurors, seated in the audience at the back of the courtroom, could appreciate his concern for all participants in the trial process.

Shifting slightly, Sheilah took in the profile of Pablo Diaz. Nineteen, he looked years younger, some acne pitting the hollows under his cheekbones. Inside the conference room just before they began impaneling an hour ago, his slim body had been shaking visibly, legs jigging his heels against the floor, hands trembling. Pablo had enough experience in the system to know this was the big time, and enough of a rap sheet to go "upstate," the silo into which the commonwealth dumped the worst of its violent offenders. Like the ones who threatened pregnant customers during liquor-store holdups. Pablo's record tagged him as a joiner rather than a leader, though, and he swore to Sheilah that he'd been in the car, thinking his friend Cundo was just going to use some fake ID to buy them beer. Sheilah believed the car part. The trick was getting the jury to believe it in the face of the prosecution's citizen witnesses and Cundo the Judas without putting her own, highly impeachable client on the stand. She hoped the nonsequestration tactic would be the key, as the witnesses who fingered Pablo Diaz got a look at —

Peter Mendez passed the juror to her. Sheilah looked up again at Hesterfield, who seemed to be dozing now.

Jesus, Rog, pull it together at least when you're in public, huh?

"Your Honor?" she said.

Hesterfield started a bit, focusing on Mendez before he swung over to Sheilah.

"Your Honor, may I inquire of the prospective juror?"

"Yes, counselor. Yes, you may."

Sheilah Quinn turned toward the man tentatively assigned to seat number eight and tried to figure which way a toupee the color of cream soda might tilt him regarding the case.

Standing in the open doorway of her own inner office, Etta Yemelman said, "How are you doing on that inter vivos trust?"

"It's coming," said Krissie Newton.

"I'll need the final draft by tomorrow morning."

Like that's a real shocker. "Then I'll stay to finish it."

"Sheilah back yet?"

"Uh-uh."

"Has she called in?"

"Uh-uh."

"Well, give her my best. I'm GFTD."

Yeah, right, thought Krissie. *Gone for the day.*

Like she's so cool, grammy with her anagram-mies.

"What if that Ketterson guy, like, shows up again?"

Etta swung the knapsack so she could slide her other arm through the strap. "I doubt he will."

"Yeah, but if he does?"

"You're in charge. Deal with it."

Yeah, right. Lucky me, in charge of myself. I love you, Etta. No shit, I really do. But some-times you gotta remember, I'm a secretary two years out of high school, not fucking Wonder Woman.

As Etta left, Krissie thought about closing the door behind her. Then figured, The Vampire Preppy can probably walk through walls, so, like, what's the point?

Frank Sikes turned another page in the Giordano file.

Good, the statement Gerry and I took from Arthur Ketterson the night of the murder, before the crime-scene guys had matched the print on her bra. He'd been in bed when we arrived at his mansion, the butler — a geek named Parsons, almost as weird as his boss — getting him via some internal phone. Ketterson came down-stairs in a robe, pajamas in a paisley pattern vis-ible where the robe wasn't. And wearing those old-style scuff bedroom slippers.

Christ, when was the last time you ever saw a pair of them?

To Frank, Ketterson at first had seemed . . . aloof. A little fancy, as words go, but right on the button. They introduced themselves as being from Homicide, then asked him to describe his actions that night. When he wanted to know what this was all about, Frank told him that Jessica Giordano had been killed.

Ketterson's reaction was what did it for me, and Gerry, too. The guy's hand kind of fluttered up to his cheek — like Jack Benny used to do — and his eyebrows arched, with just a little twitching, too, at the corners of his mouth, as if he wanted to grin but knew he shouldn't. And Ketterson said, "Really?"

Like somebody had just told a dyed-in-the-wool baseball fan the final score of a soccer game.

They asked him to come downtown with them, and then did a question-and-answer session in front of a stenographer. You could tell Ketterson was smart, but he didn't want a lawyer, which was dumber than dirt, in Frank's opinion. That was the way some people were, though — confident to the point of cocky. We can handle this problem ourselves, guys, no need to bother with attorneys. Only this time, it seemed to be even more than that.

With Ketterson, it actually seemed like he was playing a game against them. For stakes he could afford to lose, which in a homicide case made no fucking sense whatsoever.

Skipping the preliminaries in the first few

paragraphs, Frank began to read the transcript of the Q&A.

Q: Now, Mr. Ketterson —
A: Sorry, but I'm afraid I've already forgotten your name.
Q: Sikes. Sgt. Frank Sikes.
A: And against the wall . . . Detective O'Doule?
Q: O'Toole, with a *t* and two *o*'s.
A: Ah, yes. Sorry about that, as well. Now, you were saying, Sergeant Sikes?
Q: How long had you known Ms. Giordano?
A: About a month.
Q: Can you be more specific?
A: Not without a calendar.
[Stenographer's note: Detective O'Toole leaves the interrogation room to get a calendar.]
Q: While we're waiting, Mr. Ketterson, can you describe your relationship with Ms. Giordano?
A: We were seeing each other.
Q: "Seeing"?
A: Dinner, the theater, though I'm afraid Jessica found that somewhat less smooth than the television programs she raised as comparisons.
Q: Less . . . "smooth"?
A: Yes. I would always reserve orchestra seats — center, first five rows — but

278

Jessica kept complaining that she could see the makeup on the actors and actresses. That it interfered with her suspension of disbelief — my term, of course, not hers.

[Stenographer's note: Detective O'Toole returns with a calendar.]

Ah, thank you. Now, if you'll allow me just one minute . . .

Q: [Pause] Mr. Ketterson, directing your attention to —

A: It was in May, Sergeant. The tenth of the month, I believe.

Q: What was?

A: When I met Jessica. Purely by chance, at a function for one of the charities. I bumped into the girl, partially spilling her drink, and I insisted on getting her another. Then we made some small talk.

Q: "Small talk"?

A: Oh, you know. Where do you live? What do you do? That sort of thing. We rather hit it off, despite the fact that I'd been invited to the event, and Jessica was "crashing" it — her term, by the by.

Q: And that was when you first met Ms. Giordano?

A: Haven't I been "specific" enough?

Q: Did you two see each other exclusively?

A: I've always devoted myself to one person at a time, Sergeant.

Q: And did Ms. Giordano feel the same?

A: I wouldn't know about Jessica's predilections there.

Q: You wouldn't?

A: Of course not. Not the sort of thing one discusses.

Q: [Pause] Mr. Ketterson, were you intimate with Ms. Giordano?

A: In our wide-ranging conversations, yes. But if you mean sexual intercourse, no.

Q: Seeing her exclusively for over a month, you and she never had sex together?

A: It's not unheard of, Sergeant.

[Stenographer's note: Detective O'Toole said something indecipherable off the record.]

Q: Gerry, please? [Pause] All right, Mr. Ketterson, you'd take Ms. Giordano to dinner, the movies —

A: The theater. There *is* a difference.

Q: The theater.

A: And the ballet, even the symphony. But I'm afraid she didn't enjoy those much, either.

Q: Then why did you keep dating her?

A: I wonder, Sergeant, could we use a different word?

Q: "A different word"?

A: Than "dating." It's just so . . . common.

Q: [Pause] If Ms. Giordano didn't enjoy the events you took her to, why did you continue "seeing" her?

A: I enjoyed her company, Sergeant.

Refreshingly different.

Q: In what way?

A: Attitude. Outlook. Jessica was real and substantial, not as . . . sheltered as some other women I've met.

Q: Did Ms. Giordano ever indicate that anyone else was interested in her?

A: I may have misunderstood an earlier question of yours, but I believe you've already asked if I was aware of anyone else she was seeing, and I replied that we didn't discuss it.

Q: [Pause] And you didn't find out in any other way?

A: Oh, very good, Sergeant. Nice way you have of actually listening to my answers. But no, I was not aware of anyone else in her life, romantically speaking.

Q: Now, about that night itself —

"Hey, Frank, you going deaf on me or what?"

Sikes looked up from the Q&A transcript as his partner was putting down the phone.

O'Toole said, "Shelve Chatsworth Osborne the Third there and get your coat. We got a fresh one down by the river."

"Spare any change?"

"Not today," said Arthur Ketterson in an almost-pleasant voice from the park bench. He was still basking in the glow of a fine meal — though one that would have been better shared

— and it seemed rather chilly for anybody to be panhandling.

As the derelict moved away, it occurred to Arthur that it was also rather chilly to be sitting on a concrete bench, watching the main entrance to Sheilah's office building. However, while Arthur believed another visit with the young Krissie would be no real trouble, he preferred not to confront the Persimmon Queen again.

At least not so soon.

And then a stroke of good fortune, as Arthur had often experienced when undergoing some self-inflicted privation in the past. The old crone came out the front entrance. Knapsack on back, athletic shoes on feet, and therefore evidently headed home.

"Arthur, sacrifice and patience are always rewarded," his mother would have phrased it.

Arthur Ketterson waited until the knapsack bounced out of sight before standing and walking toward the office building.

"Well, I thought that went quite well."

"Yes, Your Honor," said Peter Mendez.

Shrugging out of his robe, Roger Hesterfield beamed at Sheilah Quinn before looking over to Mendez, who was seated next to her in chambers. "Now, Peter, any problems to raise before the state begins putting on its case tomorrow?"

"I hope not, Your Honor."

Hesterfield sat behind his desk. "And Sheilah, how about you?"

Why the "kindly-uncle" treatment, Rog? "No, judge. The defense is ready."

"Excellent. I believe that concludes our work together for the day, but I'd appreciate it, Sheilah, if you'd stay for a moment regarding another matter."

She felt Mendez glance nervously at her before he rose and left, closing the door behind him.

"Now, Sheilah —"

"Judge, that's the —"

" 'Roger,' please."

Stay in control, girl. "Judge, that's the second time in two cases that you've done that."

The soul of innocence. "Done what?"

"Excused the prosecutor and asked me to stay on another matter."

"Oh, I see." A cocking of his head. "Well, I wanted to apologize, you see, and it didn't seem appropriate to . . . call again."

Sheilah stopped a moment. "Call *again?*"

"Yes. About my phone message Saturday. I was a little under the weather, and —"

"What phone message?"

Now Hesterfield stopped. "On your tape machine."

"We have an answering service at the office, and there was nothing logged in from you."

Hesterfield smiled. "Your home phone, Sheilah."

Bastard! "That number's unlisted, Judge."

"Yes, well, I happened across it somehow, and I dialed you to share a joke that —"

"I didn't get any message from you. And if I did, it might force me to file a motion to recuse you from this case, and neither of us would want that, would we?"

She stood and turned for the door.

"Sheilah —"

"No more, Judge. Please."

After she closed the door, Roger Hesterfield went into a slow burn. Here I've been feeling so goddamned guilty, and my message never even registered on her goddamned machine? Little bitch probably doesn't know how to work it — that's what must have happened. And after I lavished all that courtesy on her during the impanelment today, sweetening her toward accepting my "apology."

To the closed door, Roger Hesterfield said aloud, "No more Mr. Nice Guy, Sheilah."

Then he opened his bottom drawer.

"Knock, knock."

Jesus fuck! The Vampire Preppy doesn't even make any noise. Can he fly, too?

Krissie Newton sat staring at Arthur Ketterson, who was standing in the doorway to the corridor, knuckles still over the jamb.

"Hello, again," he said.

Like, try to slow the heart rate. "I'm sorry, Mr. Ketterson, but Sheilah isn't back yet."

" 'Yet.' that does give one hope, doesn't it?"

"Hope?"

"That she will be back eventually. I'll just

sink into one of these chairs and edify myself with a periodical from your extensive collection."

Of all the words he used, *edify* was the only one that gave Krissie Newton trouble. But then it wasn't the guy's vocabulary that really worried her.

Peter Mendez was barely going to be on time for the bar association's cocktail party, even given the state trooper — conscripted as a political favor — who'd been his assigned driver for the last month. The party was ostensibly social, but Mort Zussman had it rigged as an informal fund-raiser.

Madre de Dios, I have to make a good showing tonight, and yet I don't —

"This is it." The trooper, in plainclothes, pulled the unmarked black sedan to a stop between the granite pillars holding up the portico of the bar association's headquarters. "When do you want me back?"

Peter was already out the rear door. Over his shoulder, he yelled, "An hour, and right here, understand?"

Slamming the door, candidate Mendez didn't catch what the trooper muttered under her breath.

Coming through the open doorway, Sheilah saw the look on Krissie's face before registering the tall man rising to her left.

Arthur Ketterson said, "Sheilah, I virtually just arrived."

Bracing herself, she turned to him. "Krissie was to call you to —"

"And she did, I'm sure. But it was simply impossible to reach me this morning, and when I came by at lunchtime, I thought, Why not stay downtown for the afternoon, then enjoy a cocktail with Sheilah instead? And so here I am."

"Look, I don't have —"

"Just one drink. That's all I ask."

Sheilah thought about it, trying to maintain her poker face. I keep putting him off, he's not going to quit. And cocktails in a public place might be better than waiting for the weirdo to pop up anywhere.

Or anytime.

"One little sip?" said Arthur.

"Just one."

"A toast." Roger Hesterfield spoke out loud as he raised the glass to the four walls of his chambers. "To all the time in this room, all the justice meted out to those deserving of it and more."

Roger had kept a journal over the course of his years as a judge. No, not so much a journal, he realized, the scotch gliding down his throat. More a . . . tally sheet. Yes, a tally of my tenure. Tally, tenure. Nice alliteration, that.

And mark this well: In almost twenty-five years on the bench, I've sent 2,013 miscreants to prison. Of those, fifty-one got life, and seventeen were sentenced to death. A proud record, except that half the lifers got paroled, and only three of the death-row scum were unable to cheat their fate, the rest hanging fire for as long as twelve years. Twelve bloody years. And that was before Sheilah took poor Mendez over the coals on the constitutionality of the death penalty last month. Now none of the other fourteen I aimed at the chair will ever sit there, thanks to "our Ms. Quinn."

The bitch! I pour my heart out to her, and she can't even make her answering machine function properly. Well, I can take people over the coals myself. And pretty effectively, if I may say.

Roger Hesterfield tossed off the rest of the scotch like a shot of tequila, which required him to reach for the bottle again toward proposing another toast.

"Do you approve of my selection?"

Sheilah Quinn looked around the lounge of the old hotel, the antique phone booths at the entrance, the chandeliers and fluted wallpaper. "Quaint," she said.

Arthur Ketterson laughed as they placed their orders with a tuxedoed waiter who had to be seventy-five if he was a day. Sheilah, Sheilah, a sense of humor, as well.

After the waiter moved off, Arthur leaned forward conspiratorially. "This is where I had my first illegal drink in public."

"Illegal?"

"Yes. My mother brought me downtown shopping when I was eleven. I remember every detail of that day vividly, but especially our sitting here, when she ordered a cube libra — that's rum and Coca-Cola, twist of lime?"

"I know."

"Well, I asked the waiter — perhaps the same one serving us today — for a simple cola with lime. After our drinks were delivered to the table, I waited patiently for Mother to turn her head away. Then I switched the glasses. And she never even noticed."

Arthur cherished the look Sheilah gave him, so much like . . . hers. Those eyes — the lovely Madeline's eyes.

The waiter arrived with their drinks. A glass of chardonnay for Sheilah, a vodka sidecar for Arthur, unmixed, the old pensioner pouring the lime green concoction from a small beaker onto the ice in the sugared glass.

As soon as they were alone again, Arthur raised his cocktail. "To the finest trial attorney of her time."

Sheilah somehow failed to clink her glass to his. "So, what do we need to talk about?"

Ah, straight to the point. Just like Mother, no shilly-shallying. "I think it would be mutually beneficial for us to see more of each other."

A long sip of wine. "I have a rule. Lawyers don't see their clients socially."

"But, perhaps . . . romantically?"

"Especially not romantically."

"Well, think of this as preparation for my becoming a former client, then. Surely there's no problem with that? And besides, you heard our own witnesses verify what a gentleman I am."

She put down her glass. In a slightly different voice, she said, "Let's just say there are too many complications in my life just now."

" 'Complications'?"

"Yes. My father's —"

"In a nursing home. I remember. How is he faring, by the way?"

Sheilah seemed to feel the need to take a breath. "He was a hero during World War Two, and very active since then. Now the man's reduced to lying flat on his back in a bed. That's how he's 'faring.' "

Arthur nodded solemnly, thinking, Struck a nerve there, didn't we? Does explain her teddy-bear fetish, though.

"And," said Sheilah, "I have obligations to my partner, and the judge from your case has me on another trial already."

"So long as there's not another . . . beau, as well."

"That's an issue you and I don't have to reach. I'm too busy to be able to stay here any longer, or to see you again, other than professionally. I appreciate the gesture of the flowers — and this drink — but I really have to get back." Sheilah stood. "I'll call you when Peter Mendez tells me whether or not he's going for a retrial."

Arthur looked up at her, into those eyes. "I doubt he has the stomach for it."

"Don't be too sure of that."

"Oh, but I am. You scared him."

"Mendez has a lot on his mind, but he's hard to scare."

"Perhaps, but I know one thing, Sheilah."

"What's that?"

"You certainly scare me."

Without smiling, she turned and strode away, her bra strap enticingly pushing out in bas relief under the material of her suit.

Arthur's feelings of arousal provoked another internal conference. Sheilah, Sheilah. Perfection in your every performance. That rare blend of grace and power Mother always projected. The blend that bobcat displayed as well, stalking and killing the small rabbit at my picnic.

His heart nearly bursting, it was all Arthur Ketterson could do to keep himself from again applauding and shouting "Bravo" three times.

"Okay," said Gerry O'Toole. "So it's not exactly a 'fresh' case."

Squirting gasoline from a little vial onto a handkerchief and holding the cloth to his nose, Frank Sikes nodded at his partner and the ashen uniform who'd led them to the river's edge. Squatting near the body, Frank looked it over quickly. A floater, washed up on shore, soft tissue — eyes, lips, and earlobes — already eaten away, the torso bloated in a grotesque parody of the human form.

Christ, what a mess.

Gerry squatted on the other side of the corpse. "Nothing like a floater just before dinner, I always say."

Focusing on anything but food, Frank Sikes began the preliminary investigation.

Nursing the vodka sidecar, Arthur Ketterson thought about what he'd learned from Sheilah's eloquent description of "complications."

That's something I've mostly been spared. The real-life troubles of real-life people. Family, work, opponents, et cetera. Poor Sheilah, set upon from every direction.

And yet Arthur sensed a message in the description, too.

An oblique one, perhaps, like Mother telling me that night so long ago about her breast cancer, how the doctors were going to have to cut . . . *them* off. The destruction of her beauty, her perfection. Drinking a bit more than she should, Mother was still, like Sheilah, quite eloquent about it, her words so moving. Moving me, in fact, to —

Of course! Arthur nearly slapped a palm to his forehead. Good Lord, how could I have missed Sheilah's implication? Her implication about her "complications." The girl couldn't come straight out and ask me to act for her, especially given all the money I've paid her thus far for representing me. But that must be the reason she shared her burdens with me.

In the hope that I could alleviate them. As I had with Mother's.

Arthur set down his drink.

Dealing with Sheilah's complications would require a change in the usual pattern. So far, I've stalked the women themselves, discreetly and imaginatively, while using my little dinner or opera companions living nearby as masks for the game. As I'd planned to do with Sheilah after meeting the happily located Jessica Giordano at that charity event. At least until the slut propositioned me like a common whore, and in her own parents' house!

No. No, I never told Sheilah that, of course, since bringing up sex solicited by the slut Giordano could hardly help defend me against a charge of sex-crazed murder. But even just thinking about that night is causing me to slip off the point, and I can't allow myself to be diverted by tangents of my own creation. No, I must focus on the functionally uncharted waters ahead, which undoubtedly will require a modicum of improvisation.

Arthur felt his mind taking a philosophical turn. It may be that improvisation becomes appropriate once one reaches a certain plateau in any . . . professional career. However, improvisation will carry with it unpredictable problems, as well. And it does seem that my next step should be to intensify Sheilah's burden of "complications" a bit before diminishing any of them. In order to heighten, in turn, her eventual gratitude for my intercession.

And for my rendering permanent Sheilah's own . . . perfection.

Arthur Ketterson rose from the table and went to one of the antique phone booths, closing the door. Once the light above him came on, he removed from his jacket pocket the little cassette player. Dialing the home number he'd memorized as though it were his own, he waited for the outgoing announcement to end and the beep to sound before pushing the PLAY button on his own machine and holding it up to the pay phone's receiver.

Home at last.

Sheilah Quinn felt Quigley pushing his face against her shins, but she ignored him. Krissie had been pissy — I almost have to laugh at the rhyme now — when I'd gotten back to the office, though I didn't want to do any more work anyway. After that surreal drink with Arthur Ketterson, driving out to see Dad seemed to make more sense.

Except that at the nursing home, Jack Quinn wasn't much better. Only half-conscious and not very responsive, even with the finger tapping. Lucille stood in the doorway to his room, saying, "Let's hope God takes him soon, child," which was as defeatist as Sheilah had ever heard the aide sound.

Shake it off, girl. Pour some wine, put on some music, take a bath.

Back in the bedroom to change, she saw the number 3 lit in the message window of her tape machine. The first call was from her dry cleaner, saying the suits she'd brought in were done. The second was her apartment building's management company, confirming that a plumber had checked all Sheilah's bathroom pipes and found no problems.

Just as she was feeling relieved that the malfunction Sunday night had indeed been just an unexplanable freak, the third message began.

"Sheilah, Roger here."

Scratchy and kind of faint.

"I was just . . . well, thinking of you."

At first, the voice didn't click, even with the given name. But then it did.

Hesterfield.

"What do you get if you cross an . . . No, wait a minute. No, what . . ."

That slimeball! The nerve of him today, apologizing for a message he hadn't even left yet. And calling me at home to do it after I told him —

Ripping mad, Sheilah opened the flap of the machine and pulled out the message tape. Something to hold on to, in case Roger is so far gone that he keeps this up. Then she opened the drawer of her night table to replace the tape from the machine with one of the spares she kept there.

Behind her, Quigley mewled for his dinner.

294

Turning on him, Sheilah yelled, "You'll get fed when you bring back Mr. Fuzzums."

The cat scampered up the hall, and Sheilah Quinn required three deep breaths before feeling calm enough to go after him with an apology of her own.

ELEVEN

"Objection, Your Honor," said Peter Mendez.

"Sustained."

Standing behind the defense table next to Pablo Diaz, Sheilah Quinn looked up at Hesterfield. "Your Honor, may I ask the grounds for sustaining the objection?"

"No, counselor, you may not. Proceed."

Sheilah tried to keep her temper. It had been going like this all morning, old Rog riding her, Dr. Jekyll turning into Mr. Hyde after the chambers "conference" the prior afternoon. His behavior wasn't just erratic; it was borderline schizophrenic, especially given the call yesterday to her apartment number. But, to avoid prejudicing her current client in the eyes of the court, Sheilah had resolved not to mention it unless something further happened.

The only problem was, Peter Mendez had stopped bothering to state any grounds for his objections, since Hesterfield was routinely sustaining any challenge the prosecutor raised. Still, though, Sheilah knew she'd been scoring points with the twelve people in the box.

Following his opening to the jury, Mendez had put one of the arresting officers on the stand.

The uniform and his partner had chased Diaz and Borbón after the boys ran a red light later that night. Their low-rider had crashed into some garbage cans and stalled out, but both boys had left the vehicle and were running when the officers collared them — at the time, just for reckless driving. Sheilah had gotten the uniform on the stand to admit he couldn't identify which suspect had been the driver and which the passenger.

The prosecution probably would offer Borbón as its last witness, since — unlike the liquor-store clerk and the pregnant customer — Borbón was in custody and therefore not in the audience. After the uniform, Mendez called the clerk, a retired Water Department worker named Muncie. From the stand, the man solemnly identified Pablo Diaz at the defense table as the one who had waved a gun in his face and threatened the pregnant customer. Sheilah was using her cross-examination to bring out how scared Muncie had been, how little time he'd had to view the robber, and how sketchy his original description to 911 had been ("A Spanish kid — I don't know, eighteen, maybe?").

"Now, Mr. Muncie," continued Sheilah, "you never saw the person who robbed you prior to that night, correct?"

"Correct."

"Yet you're sure that my client is that person."

"Objection," from the D.A.'s table.

"Sustained," said Hesterfield. "Move on to

new ground, Ms. Quinn."

"Mr. Muncie," she said, "the arresting officers never brought the defendant and his companion to your store that night, did they?"

"No, they didn't."

"So the first time that you actually saw my client after you believe he held you up was the next afternoon at a lineup, correct?"

"Yes."

"And how many lineups did you see that day?"

"Uh, two, I think."

"You think? Mr. Muncie, how many have you *ever* seen?"

"It was two. I remember now."

Sheilah paused. Another question along that line about Cundo Borbón would be nice, but too dangerous in tipping her nonsequestration strategy to Mendez. "And the next time you saw my client?"

"This morning."

"At the defense table."

"Right."

"As the accused in this trial."

Muncie shifted in the witness chair. "Yes."

Sheilah turned toward the bench. "Your Honor, I have no further questions at this time. However," she added, reaching inside a file on her table and extracting a folded paper, "I would like the opportunity to recall this witness to the stand as part of the defense case, and I have a subpoena here to ensure his continuing attendance."

Hesterfield frumped. Oh, Rog, you don't like this, do you?

Mendez said, "Your Honor, what possible purpose could this serve?"

Reluctantly, Hesterfield said, "Extending a witness's attendance is defense counsel's right." He turned to her. "However, Ms. Quinn, I would certainly advise you to be respectful of the patience of both the jury and this Court."

"Of course, Your Honor," said Sheilah, handing the subpoena to the confused Mr. Muncie, who clearly, but mistakenly, had thought he was finally done with all this.

Arthur Ketterson lifted the pay phone outside the Goodwill clothing store and waited for an obese woman in bulging peach-colored slacks to walk by him. Disgusting, he thought. Ought to be fed in her room.

If at all.

Looking down at the sheet he'd ripped from the Yellow Pages in the hotel's antique booth, Arthur dialed the first listed number. Alphabetically seemed as good a way to proceed as any.

"Beechwood Nursing Home. How may I direct you?"

A woman's voice, formal tone.

Dropping his own voice an octave and coarsening it, Arthur said, "My name is David Mills, and I'm calling from the airport. A friend of my grandfather from World War Two is in a rest home somewhere in the area, and since I had this layover, I thought I'd try to visit him."

"I'm sorry, sir, but we don't give resident information over the telephone."

"Hey, I understand, really. But I served in the Persian Gulf myself, and it made me realize how important contact from someone else can be."

A softening. "I don't know . . ."

"Tell you what. Just let me know if he's there or not, so I can at least send a card?"

"His name, then?"

"Quinn."

"First name?"

"I don't have it, but I believe Grandpa said Mr. Quinn has a daughter who's an attorney."

"Hold on a minute."

Arthur could tell the woman was going to check for him, and he allowed himself a controlled smile.

Two minutes later, the formal voice came back on. "I'm afraid we have no resident with that last name, sir."

"Oh," said Arthur, genuinely disappointed. "Well, thanks anyway. Uh, from Grandpa."

Roger Hesterfield looked down upon Sheilah Quinn as she handed the subpoena to Muncie. One of the great advantages of being the judge on an elevated bench, getting to look down on everyone. Now, though, he was puzzled.

What are you up to, Sheilah? I've cut you to the bone on everything you've thrown up, and now you risk annoying me further and the jury further still. Why?

Peter Mendez was calling his next witness. Devol, the customer that night, was no longer pregnant. Too bad for the prosecution — makes a better impression on the jury to see somebody, especially a female victim, struggle a little taking the stand.

Then Roger looked at Sheilah's client. Guilty as sin, a record as long as your arm, detailing a typically delinquent youth "maturing" into a blundering career criminal.

Shifting in his chair, Roger's right hand brushed against the side-bar panel containing his revolver. He'd gotten the idea for putting it there from . . . *And Justice for All*, a movie in which the actor Jack Warden played a haywire judge who wore a concealed .45 when presiding over trials. But try doing a fast draw from under a robe while sitting down. Roger had, and he didn't like his odds. No, much better to have the weapon within arm's reach and always at the bench with you. Just in case of trouble.

Which was the same reason that years ago Roger had put a steel liner on his side of the bench and platform that faced out into the courtroom. From the gallery, the whole bench area looked rock-solid, like a raised minifortress of thick polished wood. But, in fact, it was all hollow inside — just a big exposed desk behind the facade that everyone else saw. Not much more protection for the presiding judge than a pine board, really, should some homicidal maniac ever smuggle a 9-mm past the metal detectors and start firing away. And so, over a long weekend, Roger Hesterfield had installed the steel lining himself.

No need to involve the county commissioners in my little "bench improvement" project. Those political midgets would only think I was paranoid.

Roger looked down again at the defendant, Dios or Diaz, or whatever his name was. Wouldn't be that hard to push on the swinging panel and take out my revolver. Pop the two-bit bandit from here and damn the consequences. But that also would mean the end of this trial, and the loss of my best reason for postponing that dago bastard Giordano's version of a wrecking ball. No, better to let the trial run its course, even permit Sheilah to recall some witnesses if she thinks it will help. No rush to judgment here.

"Objection," said Sheilah Quinn, standing.

"Overruled," replied Roger Hesterfield, not conscious of even having heard the prosecution's question.

Gerry O'Toole sat on the corner of Frank Sikes's desk. "So, how was your dinner after last night's appetizer?"

"Appetizer?"

"Our floater, lying on a bed of brown grass."

"Ger, don't you ever get tired of stiff jokes?"

"They keep me young and carefree." O'Toole looked down at the file in front of his partner. "What've you got there?"

"Giordano," said Sikes.

"Again?"

"More like still."

"What're you doing, Frank, memorizing it?"

"I just think there must be something we missed."

"Yeah, well, the only thing I miss is having your kind of time to go back over made cases. I mean, unless it's slipped your mind, the captain's still after us about that niece who allegedly killed her uncle to get his rent-controlled apartment."

"I remember, Gerry."

"And how about the father who more than allegedly gouged out his own son's eyes, claiming the poor kid was possessed by a fucking demon."

"I remember that one, too."

"Not to mention this new happy horseshit I read about in the paper this morning."

No response from Sikes.

O'Toole squared himself on the desk corner. "Well, let me enlighten you anyway. Seems there's now a booming new business in companies that buy up the life-insurance policies of the terminally ill."

Frank did look up this time. "What?"

"I shit you not. Let's say some poor bastard's dying of cancer or AIDS, whatever. There're companies now that'll say to him, 'Hey, you got this hefty policy' — fifty K, say — 'on your life, premiums all paid up, and you're damned sure gonna die before the year's out. So, why don't you make *us* your beneficiary, and meanwhile we'll pay *you* cash to kind of cushion your last days.' "

"And that's legal?"

"Apparently. At least the government regulators haven't caught up with it yet. The companies are calling it 'viatical settlement' — don't ask me what the fuck *viatical* means in Latin, though. Back in grade school, Sister Bluto of the Bullwhip never did teach us much about —"

"Gerry, we have one of these 'viatical' cases yet?"

"No, and we won't —"

"Then —"

"Unless some company realizes it made a bad fucking deal, decides to speed up the decedent's demise some —"

"Gerry! "

O'Toole looked as if he'd just been slapped. "What?"

"Why don't you wait until we do have one, and meanwhile leave me in peace to work on Giordano?"

O'Toole pursed his lips, now like a little kid about to cry. "We even know if Mendez is gonna retry Ketterson?"

"Not yet."

"Candidate for higher office like our pal the

DA, you're gonna have to come up with some-thing he can't fucking ignore."

"That's what I'm trying to find, Ger. Some-thing new to give him."

"Yeah, well, Mendez has to jump into the water with Sheilah the Shark again, you better find a new dick and balls to replace the ones she bit off him last time."

Frank Sikes bit his own tongue instead, grin-ning at a joke he somehow didn't find all that funny.

Good Lord, can this be how salesmen actually make a living?

Arthur Ketterson flexed his cramping hand, then put his seventh quarter in the coin slot of the pay phone. The first six homes "David Mills" tried had all been willing to check their rosters, but none had a male resident named Quinn. ("Mr. Mills, we do have a Sally Quinn, if that might be it?" "Uh, thanks, but Grandpa seemed pretty certain his army buddy was a male.")

Arthur punched out seven more numbers on the keypad. Surely there must be some computer device by now that can do this sort of thing for you.

"Devonshire Rest Home."

A male receptionist, assertive.

"Great," said Arthur in his most ingratiating Mills tone. "I wonder if you can help me?"

Leaning against one of the pillars of the new

courthouse building, Rudolph Giordano was just thinking about forcing down some lunch when Nick, his foreman on the site, came over.

"Rude, I'm getting complaints from the DA's office about plaster dust."

"Plaster dust in the *new* building?"

"Yeah. It's on account of our prep work for those air-conditioning units."

"The little pony ones going into the interior conference rooms?"

"Right. The DA's office says the vibration's —"

"Fuck the DA. Let him live with a real problem for a while, see how he likes it."

"Yeah, but his secretary's really ragging our guys about it."

"So, they can't take a little ragging, the fuck they doing in construction work?"

Brushing angrily at the chalky powder on his sleeve, Peter Mendez said, "You've called them?"

"Only hourly," replied Veronica.

Peter didn't appreciate sarcasm from his secretary, particularly when he had just thirty minutes before resuming the Diaz case back in the First Session across the park. "And they still can't stop this stuff" — Peter waved his free hand at the air — "from wafting down on us?"

"I don't know."

"What do you mean?"

Veronica said, "I mean, I know word processing. I even know voice mail, you ever want to use it. I don't know 'wafting.' "

Peter tried to take a normal breath. Need to jog again, burn off some of this excess —

At which point, the telephone rang. "Hold on," said his secretary into the receiver, then to him: "It's Mort Zussman, urgent as usual."

Madre de Dios, thought Peter. Now what? "I'll take it in my office."

Once behind his desk, he lifted the phone. "Mort, I have to be back on —"

"I called three lawyers this morning, guys who made pledges for money we need now. Only thing is, they heard you at that bar association thing last night."

"And?"

"And they're welshing on their pledges."

"What?"

"They think your shit looks weak, Petey, and I got to say, you can't blame them after the way the media played up that hung-jury mess in the *Ketterson* case."

"But —"

"What I'm saying here is, come up with a good one, Petey. Something that makes you look like a winner in a hurry."

"Mort, there's nothing —"

"Think of some new angle — hold on." Muffled noise offline. "I'm gonna have to take this other call."

"Mort —"

"Petey, look. It's from a deep pocket who

307

might make up some of the difference we lost this morning. But I got to tell you, word gets around that the rats already on board are shinnying down the anchor rope, you might as well kiss Election Day good-bye."

Hanging up the phone, Mendez dug into the bridge of his nose with the thumb and forefinger of his free hand. "Hey?" he said.

From outside the office, Veronica said, "Hey what?"

"Get me that guy who represents the West Shore in the assembly. The hell's his name?"

"The law-and-order fanatic?"

"Yeah."

"Agonian, Robert. But why —"

"Just get him on the phone, okay?"

A moment passed before Peter Mendez heard his secretary say, "Okay."

"Muir Creek Convalescent Center."

"Hey, how you doing? My name's David Mills. . . ."

Gerry O'Toole left Frank Sikes at the station and went out to hit the medical examiner's office. Within five minutes of being alone again at his desk, Frank was back into the Q&A with Ketterson.

Q: Now, directing your attention to earlier this evening —

A: Do you mean last night, Sergeant? It is

308

after twelve now.

Q: [Pause] Yes. Last evening. When did you pick up Ms. Giordano for your dinner date?

A: I do wish you wouldn't use the word *date*. It's so —

Q: When did you pick her up, Mr. Ketterson?

A: [Pause] Approximately seven-fifteen.

Q: You looked at your watch, then?

A: Not that I recall. But our reservation at Chez Jean was for eight, and I always like to arrive a scosh early.

[Stenographer's note: Detective O'Toole said something indecipherable.] A "scosh," Detective. Meaning just a little bit. Early, that is.

Q: When you picked up Ms. Giordano, was anyone else there?

A: No. She said her mother was visiting a relative, and her father was just . . . out.

Q: Where in the house did you go at that time?

A: The only places in the house I've ever been — the foyer and the living room.

Q: You've never seen the rest of the house?

A: No.

Q: Not even a bathroom?

A: I pride myself on . . . control, Sergeant.

Q: All right. When you arrived there last evening, was Ms. Giordano ready?

A: No, actually she wasn't, quite.

Q: Not quite?

A: No. Jessica had suffered some sort of shoulder injury before I met her, and that somewhat restricted the movement of her left arm.

Q: And?

A: And she asked me to clip and zip her, so to speak.

Q: Give me that again?

A: "Clip" and "zip." Clip her brassiere in the back, and zip the zipper of her dress.

Q: [Pause] So, you handled her bra?

A: Well, that sounds rather vulgar, don't you think? I merely clipped the little metal gadget in the back. [Pause] Sergeant, don't you have any more questions?

Frank Sikes looked up from the transcript of the Q&A. Did they have more questions for Arthur fucking Ketterson? You bet, but to play it safe, they Mirandized him then and there, which with the glory of hindsight proved to have been the right play. Because the readable latent on her bra belonged to Ketterson's left thumb.

Only tell me this, Artie: If you're going to kill the girl, why leave a murder weapon you know you've touched unwiped when there isn't another of your fucking prints in the whole fucking house?

Sheilah Quinn completed her cross-examination of the liquor store's female customer with the same litany regarding a subpoena served to ensure continuing attendance. Sheilah also had been watching Peter Mendez, who looked as though whatever he ate for lunch had given him food poisoning. That may be why — at only 3:30 — Hesterfield said it made sense to stop for the day.

Once Old Bailey ushered the jury out of the courtroom, Sheilah squeezed the shoulder of Pablo Diaz before another bailiff led him away. Gathering her papers, she thought, At least this gives me a nice jump on getting back to the office and over to see Dad.

Sheilah turned to ask Mendez if there was anything out of the ordinary on for the next morning, but, like Roger Hesterfield, he was already gone.

"Valley Nursing Home."

Arthur Ketterson had by now grown thoroughly sick of dropping quarters, of deepening his voice, of observing the flotsam and jetsam of humanity flow through the Goodwill store. "Hi, this is David Mills. I'm just in town, at the airport. . . ."

Good Lord, he thought as he continued talking. I've gotten to the point where I can actually say all this without even having to think about it.

"One moment, please," said the voice on the other end of the line.

A pickup truck pulled into the nearest parking space, belching a foul gray-blue smoke. *Too bad the plebians inside it can't afford a garage. They'd die from the fumes in just the time it took to close the —*

"Sir, we do have a John Quinn, though I'm told he goes by 'Jack.' "

Arthur spoke almost reverently. "And his daughter's an attorney?"

"We have a Sheilah Quinn listed as next of kin."

Eureka! "Hey, thanks a bunch. Can you tell me his room number?"

"One oh seven. First floor has three different wings, but once you're here, the security desk can guide you."

I think not, somehow. "And your visiting hours?"

Arthur made a note of them — mainly because he was planning to avoid them — then hung up. Patience and perseverance had finally paid off, but only after wasting most of a day.

Was I wrong to proceed alphabetically? I managed finally to find one of Sheilah's "complications," though not until the V's. Perhaps this is a lesson, even an omen. Toward being more intuitive.

So, what should be my next step? Jack Quinn has been located, but he's decidedly stationary. Probably better to engage a moving target first. And learn from today's lesson/omen by reverting this afternoon to the end of the alphabet.

Or very nearly the end.

Arthur Ketterson thought long and hard before coming up with a workable strategy. Then he scooped the few remaining quarters into a pocket and found himself fairly whistling on his way into the Goodwill store.

TWELVE

"What happened to your trial?" asked Krissie Newton.

Sheilah stopped at the reception desk to skim through her pink message slips. "Judge let us off early, if not easily."

"Tough day, Sheilah?" asked Etta Yemelman, standing in the doorway to her office and slinging the knapsack over one shoulder.

"Tough enough." Sheilah looked from the message slips to her watch. "You're leaving at four again?"

"Yes, and don't bother to ask."

"I just worry about you."

Etta stopped with her arm halfway through the other strap of the sack. "Why?"

"The way you ride the subway at all hours. Alone."

"I'm rarely alone on the subway, Sheilah. And besides, this time of day, what is there to worry about?"

I'm really growing attached to this concrete throne, thought Arthur Ketterson, sitting on the bench across from Sheilah's office building for the second afternoon in a row. Can't understand how one could actually sleep on it, though. Hardly long enough, and very unyielding.

A panhandler — the same one from the day before — walked toward Arthur, then veered off to hit up a clergyman, who waved the poor wretch away. Amazing.

Not that a callous shepherd would ignore one of the lost lambs. No, rather that the lamb didn't think I was worth the trouble of begging. Though one can't really blame him, and a tribute, actually, to my shopping skills at the Goodwill store.

Arthur looked down at himself. Jogging shoes worn past the tread, faded blue jeans, and flannel shirt. A baseball cap fit snugly over the dark brown shag-cut wig, distorting his head shape considerably. Some old aviator sunglasses completed the disguise. Twelve dollars cash for the entire ensemble. Arthur had even copied a way of walking from one of the miscreants on line in front of him at the store's cash register. A sort of rolling gait, like some pimp —

Wait a minute. Is that *she?* Yes, no doubt about it. The knapsack and the athletic shoes both.

Smiling, Arthur Ketterson stood and began to parallel the Persimmon Queen as she walked down the street.

"Your Honor?"
Roger Hesterfield glanced up from the issue of

Penthouse he was enjoying at his chambers desk. "What is it, O.B.?"

"Mr. Giordano again."

Shit. "O.B., I told you, I don't want —"

"He has one of the county commissioners with him this time."

Shit and double shit. "One minute, then show them in."

Roger Hesterfield looked longingly at the bottom drawer of his desk, but he left it closed as he put the magazine under some files to the side of his blotter.

"Can I, like, take off now?"

Sheilah Quinn turned away from her computer. "As far as I'm concerned."

From the open door of Sheilah's inner office, Krissie motioned toward her boss's monitor screen. "You working late tonight? "

"Not too."

"I'll lock the door, but you sure you're gonna be all right?"

"Why wouldn't I be?"

"With that Ketterson guy on the loose?"

"I talked with him over a drink, and I think the message got through. No contact from him today, right?"

"Right. But it wasn't great for me being alone here yesterday when he showed up, and I'm not even the one he was after."

A little chill? Probably just a draft coming over the windowsill. Then Sheilah thought about

Etta, riding the subways fearlessly. "Krissie, what's there to worry about?"

For an old crone, the Persimmon Queen had a certain bounce to her step, striding down the other side of the avenue as though she owned it. Then she crossed the street toward Arthur, causing him to stop and gaze with feigned interest at a window display of telescopes and binoculars. After the woman turned into some sort of kiosk, it was a moment before Arthur realized she'd gone down into the subway. BING SQUARE STATION, a sign read in large letters.

Walking again, Arthur felt a surge of real interest this time. He'd heard stories in the Admin Unit about what other inmates had done to people down there. And of course there was the media's constant barrage of muggings, rapes, and killings. Arthur even remembered the story of a homeless man who'd electrocuted himself by urinating onto some sort of power rail, the stream of one's liquid waste apparently being a highly effective conduit for electricity.

Descending the filthy, sticky stairs between graffiti-desecrated walls, Arthur wondered what other experiences his new emphasis on intuition might bring him.

Incredibly, after they'd read Arthur Ketterson his Miranda rights, the guy was willing to keep talking. Still at his desk in Homicide, Frank

Sikes read the rest of the transcript.

> Q: We do have some more questions, Mr. Ketterson. Did Ms. Giordano mention anything that was bothering her?
>
> A: Beyond her shoulder, do you mean?
>
> Q: Yes, beyond that.
>
> A: I don't recall anything. She wasn't particularly happy, still living at home.
>
> Q: And why was that?
>
> A: Jessica said it somehow "cramped her style." Which was her expression, of course.
>
> Q: What did you think she meant by that?
>
> A: I believe her parents kept the girl on rather a tight leash, but I never inquired.
>
> Q: Why not?
>
> A: None of my business, really.
>
> Q: [Pause] So, nothing happened during your dinner with Ms. Giordano at Chez Jean?
>
> A: Nothing? I wouldn't say that. We had a rather pleasant talk. Feel free to check with the waitress, who kept trying to insinuate herself into our conversation.
>
> Q: When did you leave the restaurant?
>
> A: A scosh — a *bit* after ten.
>
> Q: And where did you go from there?
>
> A: Jessica wanted to continue on for a drink, perhaps some dancing, but I was a little fatigued, and so I drove her straight home instead.

Q: Straight to her home?

A: Well, her parents' house, technically, I suppose.

Q: And then?

A: I escorted Jessica inside to the living room, and we said good night.

Q: Just "said"?

A: I beg your pardon?

Q: Just *said* good night? No kiss or hug?

A: Oh, she might have pecked me on the cheek.

[Stenographer's note: Detective O'Toole said something indecipherable.] This cheek, Detective. Under my eye.

Q: Did you hear anyone else in the house?

A: No, but then, I wouldn't have expected to.

Q: Why not?

A: As I said earlier, Jessica had told me both her parents would be out late.

Q: How did you enter and leave the Giordano home?

A: How? By walking, of course.

Q: Which door or doors, Mr. Ketterson?

A: Oh. I used the front door.

Q: The front.

A: The main entrance, at the street side of the house, Sergeant. Perhaps I could draw a picture for —

Q: You didn't use the back door, Mr. Ketterson?

A: No. Why should I?

Q: Never used it?

A: Never. As I'm sure you noticed, the back yard borders on a hiking trail that comes out a few blocks away. So, unless one is of a mind to wander through the woods for a ways, there'd be no reason to use it.

Q: How do you know that?

A: Know what?

Q: About the backyard?

A: Oh, very good again, Sergeant. If I haven't been other than in the living room, you mean?

Q: How do you know about the backyard, Mr. Ketterson?

A: Why, Jessica told me. How else?

Q: [Pause] So, when did you leave Ms. Giordano?

A: Last night?

Q: Last night.

A: Ten-twenty-five, ten-thirty. I really wasn't clock-watching.

Q: You said earlier that the two of you left the restaurant shortly after ten?

A: Correct.

Q: You allowed forty-five minutes to get from her house to the restaurant, but it took you only twenty or so to make the return trip?

A: Correct again.

Q: Mind explaining that to me?

A: Not at all, Sergeant. You see, we had a reservation at Chez Jean, and I like to be punctual. In the early evening on a Saturday, one must allow for downtown traffic, finding a suitable parking space, et cetera. By contrast, on the drive back, there was no particular time Jessica had to be home, no parking concerns, and rather less traffic after ten P.M.

Q: So . . .

A: So, I should say twenty or twenty-five minutes was about right for . . . the return trip.

Q: All right. After you dropped Ms. Giordano off inside her house, where did you go?

A: [Pause] Back to Woodmere, of course. As I told you, I was fatigued.

Q: What time was that?

A: Again, Sergeant, I wouldn't have had cause to look at my watch, but it's approximately one-half hour from Woodmere to Jessica's house.

Q: You've timed it?

A: Timed the route, do you mean?

Q: Yes.

A: Certainly. Especially the first few times we went out.

Q: Why?

A: So that I would be punctual. There are a number of cultural events for which we wouldn't have wanted to be late.

Q: And last night, when you got home. Your butler was there to greet you?

A: Naturally, Sergeant. That's part of his job.

Q: [Pause] That's it from me. Gerry?

[Stenographer's note: Detective O'Toole said something indecipherable.]

A: So, I'm free to go?

Q: For now, Mr. Ketterson. For now.

A: Oh, deft twist, Sergeant. My compliments."

Christ, thought Frank Sikes, rubbing a palm over his forehead. Artie, my boy, you are one weird fuck. And you're so dirty, I can smell you. So, how come I can't seem to nail you? There's an easy answer to that one, isn't there?

Closing his eyes, Frank Sikes tried not to think of Sheilah Quinn.

Closing her eyes, Sheilah Quinn tried not to think of Frank Sikes.

Our time at the inn is on my mind — never has left it, really, despite two days of being in court. Very hard for us to get together during the week, though, and not exactly a cinch even come the weekends. On the other hand, Frank's divorce can't go on forever, and it won't be till he's completely quit of his wife that I'll know for sure whether there's a future for me with him.

No, that's not right, either. I know for sure now.

Opening her eyes and smiling, Sheilah went back to the computer screen.

Arthur Ketterson could not believe that he'd nearly lost her.

It wasn't having to cross the street after the old crone, nor having to go down the stairs, but rather the waves of humanity swelling up at him from below. And then Arthur had to stand on line to buy a token from some cretin with too-high a forehead and squirrel-like cheeks who was sitting on a stool in a booth surrounded by glass windows thick enough to be bulletproof.

When Arthur finally put his token into the slot at the turnstile, the Persimmon Queen was already awaiting her train, near the yellow-striped edge of the platform. There were perhaps fifteen or twenty other people arrayed in clumps around her, many of them glancing nervously at two young Negroes, both of whom were swearing raucously, Arthur noted. One was normal enough — discounting a rather plateaued haircut — but the other suffered from some wild rash or skin disease that caused the flesh around the eyes and lips to be almost pink and virtually translucent. Arthur thought that if Africa had circuses, this boy would be the clown.

The two young Negroes moved toward the old crone, and Arthur did the same, subtly. Which wasn't hard for him, as the other patrons moved away with the boys' approach. It reminded Arthur of a nature show on the Admin Unit's television monitors, the crowd like a herd of wildebeest, trotting nervously away from prowling lions. But the Persimmon Queen, though clearly aware of the two blackamoors, seemed determined to stand her ground, even leaning over the tracks to look into the tunnel — presumably the direction from which her train would come.

Arthur leaned over, too, close enough to have tapped her on the shoulder. But instead, his attention was drawn toward the little warning signs, white lettering on a red background, identifying the third metal runner, the one farthest from them: LIVE RAIL — EXTREME DANGER.

Leaning back again, Arthur Ketterson felt a tingle of improvisation dance up his spine.

Flipping ahead in the Giordano file, Frank Sikes reached the medical examiner's autopsy report. At least the fifth time overall that he'd read it, but the content didn't get any more helpful. The pathologist, Dr. Emil Dinetti, had established time of death using as absolute brackets "last seen alive" at the restaurant with Arthur Ketterson and "first found dead" by the victim's mother. That window gave the defendant no alibi, despite his butler's testimony on when he had arrived back at the estate that night and how calm he seemed to be. The decedent died from strangulation, the bra wrenched violently around her neck, even fracturing some small bones in the throat. She'd thrashed as her clothes were being torn, but forensics didn't find any skin scrapings or pulled hair follicles under her nails, and no blood, semen, or saliva from the killer — which let out any hope of doing a DNA test, much less getting a match.

Then Frank went through the statements provided by the defense prior to trial, the women Arthur Ketterson had dated in the past. A beautician, a schoolteacher, a nurse. Not to knock any of those fields, but having read their statements and watched them testify, it was hard to see why a guy with Ketterson's money and status had singled them out. No great beauties, not much social standing.

Then Frank thought about Sheilah Quinn being with his own self, and he shook off the parallel.

But still, why was Arthur Ketterson the fucking IV dating these women? They all agreed there'd been no sex, one of them even hinting the guy might be gay. They're inappropriate prospects for marriage, and he never lays a hand on them.

Frank Sikes leaned back. What the fuck were you doing with these women, Artie?

Etta Yemelman looked into the tunnel again.

Partly because she didn't want to be late for her computer class. But also partly because Etta wanted to keep an eye on the two young boys, who made her nervous and seemed to scare the hell out of everybody except the tall, scruffy man on the other side of her.

The same boys from last time, she thought. No mistaking that pigmentation problem on the one. Oh, the abuse he must have suffered all his life, from every side, thanks to such an affliction.

Etta shook her head just as the boy with the flattop jostled the other, causing the boy with the odd pigmentation to bump into her.

"Yo, watch it, gramma," from the strangely pink mouth.

Etta noticed several of the other people waiting on the platform turn toward the boy and then turn away again. She felt even the tall man edging off a bit.

To the young black who'd spoken to her, she said in a low, even voice, "I'm sorry, but you bumped into me."

"You trying to —"

Flattop broke in. "Gramma, just watch it, he say. You watch it, everything be cool."

Etta turned away from them herself, and she felt the tall, scruffy man edge back closer again as she leaned over the track, watching for her train.

Willing it to come soon.

"Judge, please understand our position," said the chubby county commissioner in a nasal whine that Roger Hesterfield had detested from the first moment he'd met the man a decade ago.

Leaning forward in the chambers chair until it creaked from the strain of his bulk, the commissioner continued. "Mr. Giordano has a contract with us. He's already been delayed —"

"Mr. Commissioner," said Roger, "delays are

a part of life. I am conducting a trial in the court-room outside that door, a very serious criminal matter in which a young man is charged with —"

"Hey, I get to charge something, too, Judge," said Rudolph Giordano, slouching against a file cabinet. "I get to charge five thousand per day delay damages, you don't give me access here to do my dismantling before I plant a hundred-twenty pounds of dynamite."

Melodramatically, Giordano pulled a little electronic device like a television remote from his pocket and pressed a button on it with his thumb.

Some kind of detonator, thought Roger. The hallowed courtroom in which I delivered *the* dynamite charge to countless juries is itself to be destroyed by *a* dynamite charge? Will this degra-dation never end?

Roger reined in his emotion. "Mr. Gior-dano —"

"Can't you just move your trial to the new building, Judge?" asked the commissioner, the nasal voice now wheedling, "We've got court-rooms aplenty over there."

"This trial is being conducted in the First Ses-sion, and here it will stay."

The commissioner stood slowly, regretfully. "I'm afraid I can't allow that."

Now Hesterfield boiled over. "How dare you suggest —"

The Commissioner raised his hand as a stop sign, so like Hesterfield's own trademark mannerism that it stopped him cold. "Judge, I don't have any choice. I'm responsible to the taxpayers, and I'll do what I have to. This is too big a deal to leave our tails exposed to what the media could do to us, wasting five yards a day of tax-revenue money in this budgetary climate. And besides, you have to move sometime, right?"

As Giordano followed the commissioner out the door, Roger Hesterfield fumed futilely. Impotence. Not a characteristic trait for a man like me. Nor a tolerable one.

He tried to gauge if his blood alcohol was already too high for one more drink before driving home. Maybe, maybe not, but give yourself the benefit of the doubt on the question.

A reasonable doubt. In fact, beyond a reasonable doubt, the same standard I have to use in judging the scum of the earth who come before me.

What's good for the goose is good for the gander, right?

What more can I ask, thought Arthur Ketterson? The African Clown bumps into the Persimmon Queen, then taunts her, and enough other people notice it to be perfect corroboration. I'll never have a better chance.

Edge closer again to the old crone. She's aware of me, but, given the competition, not afraid of me. Good. Next, I must wait . . . wait . . . wait until she leans once more over the tracks. There.

Enough prelude; now for the opera itself.

My palm flat under her knapsack. A single forceful push, and — voilà, she's launched!

Lighter than I'd have imagined, though that just might be the adrenaline talking. The Persimmon Queen's trajectory irreversible, her limbs pinwheeling madly, her screams echoing off the station walls.

Arthur turned around, fiercely. "You pushed her!" he yelled at the two black teenagers, using his David Mills voice. Blue and yellow sparks erupted behind him, mirrored visibly before him in the glass-enclosed advertisements for theater and vocational schools. Over the crackling and thumping — I wonder: Her hands, her feet? — Arthur yelled again. "Hey, these two kids pushed that old lady onto the tracks!"

Now other men were yelling and other women screaming, the two blacks running pell-mell for the stairs that led up and out of the station. Arthur was close on their heels, but not too close, having no desire to actually catch them. In fact, if he had to say it, their flight cleared a convenient path for him through the throngs of commuters stumping down the stairs. For what would no doubt be a rather delayed ride homeward, the poor drones.

As that thought occurred to him, Arthur Ketterson reached the top of the stairs and got a last glimpse of the two black youths sprinting across the avenue as though being chased by the Devil himself.

"Agonian," said the voice on the telephone.

"Bob, this is Peter Mendez from —"

"Hey, Petey. How's the boy?"

Political hacks. They all speak the same language. "Building toward the attorney general's chair, Bob."

"That's the ticket. Never show them you're scared."

Scared? He knows I should be scared? "Bob, about that death-penalty case last month, *Jervis*."

A hesitation on the other end of the line. "The one that pinko twat lawyer beat you on?"

Mendez cringed but plowed forward. "I think we need to make a stand on this issue."

"You're preaching to the converted, boy. I was one of the sponsors of the statute she shot down, remember?"

No, but I should have. "How could I forget, Bob? I still can't believe our supreme court invalidated your language."

Another hesitation. "What do you mean, 'my' language?"

"But I thought you said —"

"I said that I sponsored it, Petey. Got the puppy up on its hind legs and walked it through the process. But I didn't draft the fucking thing. That'd take days, boy."

The representative of the people. Madre de Dios. "Well, I still think we need to show strength here, Bob. Shared strength."

"What exactly would we be sharing, Petey?"

"I was thinking about a press conference. You, me, and anybody else you can find to stand with us."

"Generally speaking, you're going to call a press conference, it's kind of nice to have something to announce."

"How's this? We announce a joint initiative to introduce and pass a new death-penalty bill, replace the one our high court gutted."

A third hesitation. "I'm just a poor servant to my constituents, Petey, but I thought the way the judges fiddled their decision on the thing, we couldn't just pass another bill."

Not polished, Agonian. But not stupid, either. "Here's my take on that, Bob. We call the conference, announce the initiative, but fill in the details later."

"Like after Election Day."

"That's what I'm thinking, too."

This time Agonian hesitated longer than the first three times combined.

Mendez said, "Bob?"

"Okay, boy. I'll call Sharon Craig, Chuck Laviolette, maybe one or two more. Have your people — Sussman, right?"

"Right."

"Have Mort get in touch with my people on the details."

"And the sooner the better."

"Hey, Petey? You're the guy calling me, right?"

331

Mendez swallowed some pride. "Right, Bob."

A grunted laugh. "Let's hope we get a good one, just before our stand-up there."

"A good one?"

"Yeah. Maybe some fucking crackheads on a drive-by, acing a six-year-old in the cross fire. Something good like that, get the public back on our side."

Our side.

Peter Mendez cringed again. Something he was doing a lot of lately.

Closing the Giordano file, Frank picked up the ringing telephone. "Homicide, Sikes."

"Dispatch, Frank. Transit police just called one in."

"What've they got?"

"Vic's a female, white and elderly. Looks like a couple of black kids pushed her onto the third rail at Bing Square station."

Lovely. "Any ID?"

"On the perps, nothing definite. Wallet in the woman's knapsack says she was a lawyer."

Frank could picture his department's chief, the label "highprofile" coming out of his mouth. "You got a wallet, you also got a name?"

"Yeah, wait one." A flipping noise. "It's Yemelman, Etta."

Oh shit. No.

"Frank?"

Sikes didn't say anything into the receiver.

"Frank, you want a spelling on that?"

"No. No thanks. Be right over."

Or almost right over. Frank Sikes hung up the phone.

Goddamn it anyway.

Arthur Ketterson made sure to control his stride, but in a natural way. Just another poor slob, laid off by the recession, with no place to go and therefore in no hurry to get there. He could hear an ambulance siren behind him, approaching Bing Square station from the opposite direction. Arthur had been circumspect in leaving the BMW half a mile away, but he genuinely regretted that he daren't stay, watch the further chaos reign before him.

Suddenly, Arthur realized he was parallel with Sheilah's office building across the street. A temptation: Should I go up there, hint to her how I've begun to uncomplicate her life?

He'd suppressed that urge completely when a nondescript sedan screeched to a halt outside the main entrance. From the passenger's door tumbled one of the homicide detectives — that light-skinned Negro — who ran into the building.

Good news travels fast, thought Arthur Ketterson, beginning to whistle as he continued on toward his car.

"Sheilah?"

She'd risen from behind her desk at the knock on the corridor door. Hearing his voice, she was surprised, but pleased.

As Sheilah swung the suite door open, Frank looked apologetic.

He said, "I would have called first, but —"

"I planned on working a little late, anyway." Trot out the coy smile, girl. "Trying not to think of you."

Now Frank looked pained, which didn't seem right. "Sheilah —"

"How about if I blow off the rest of the afternoon and we drive out of town for a nice dinner? Thai, maybe, or —"

"Sheilah!"

An authority voice? "What's the matter?"

As Gerald O'Toole pulled the sedan up to the subway station, Frank Sikes bailed out of the front passenger seat, almost before the car had stopped moving. In the back, Sheilah Quinn tried to open her door but found she couldn't.

After Frank yanked on the handle, she stepped out, only vaguely aware of the people and things around her. An orange-and-cream ambulance, its EMTs chafing at the curb, one smoking. The white-and-blue panel truck belonging to the medical examiner, a gurney being lowered from its rear doors. Yellow tape with POLICE LINE: DO NOT CROSS stretched from lampposts and street signs and even the antenna of a parked police cruiser. Uniformed officers kept the rubber-neckers back from the entrance, but they let Sheilah through as Frank guided her by the elbow, a touch she'd so craved half an hour before but now hardly felt.

Sheilah found herself going down the stairs. Her head buzzed, and her eyes swam a little, as though she'd had too much wine on an empty stomach. There were strobelike flashes from below somewhere. Crime-scene photos, the lawyer part of her mind told the rest of her.

Then Sheilah was on the platform, officers milling around in slightly different uniforms. Why would their . . . Oh, transit police, right. It's a subway station. The cops looked at her, then at Frank before parting to allow them to pass.

They approached the edge of the platform. A peculiar burning smell hung in the air.

Frank squeezed her arm. "Wait here."

Moving to the edge of the platform, he spoke to people Sheilah couldn't see, down below on the tracks. "Sikes, Homicide."

"Frank, good to see you. Find anybody for an ID yet?"

"I have the decedent's partner here."

"Partner? She was a lesbian?"

"Negative," said Frank coldly. "Partner from her law firm."

"Oh. Well, it ought to be okay. Face didn't catch much."

Frank came back to Sheilah. "You going to be all right?"

"No. But let's get it done."

Frank brought her to the edge of the platform.

What Sheilah saw: On the tracks, an orange

shroud with some lettering on it that was upside down from her perspective. Then, sticking out from under the hem, a pair of running shoes. Surrounding the shroud were three men and a woman, one of the men with a camera, another with a brush, the third tagging and sealing small items into plastic bags. Next to the tagging man, the woman seemed to be cataloging things from a knapsack.

Etta's?

"Ready?" said Frank to Sheilah.

A nod.

"Okay," he called down.

The brush man drew the shroud down to the breasts. There was Etta's face in left profile, the eye open but opaque, the lips parted in that "drink it in" expression you have when taking a breath of fresh air in the mountains. Her hair was wrong, though. Dark, like . . . charcoal.

Sheilah closed her eyes, but only long enough to say, "That's Etta."

Frank took her elbow again to lead her away, but Sheilah stayed where she was. "I'd like to go down there, hold her hand."

Frank looked onto the tracks.

The brush man said, "I don't think that'd be too good of an idea."

Sheilah shook her head. "I mean, when you're all finished with the . . . the forensics. I can wait."

The brush mall coughed. "Miss, we figure your partner used her hands to try and break her fall. They're what hit the live rail."

Sheilah heard the words but couldn't understand what he was saying.

The man swallowed and coughed again. "Your partner, she doesn't have what you'd call hands anymore."

Sheilah turned abruptly and began walking away.

"Spiraling," Arthur Ketterson said out loud, shifting gears. "My thoughts are literally spiraling upward."

Only a few more miles to the estate now, and he conceded that adrenaline must still have something to do with his mood. Nevertheless, though, this effort marked the first time Arthur had attempted an improvisation since that night with his own mother, and it had worked beautifully, even . . . perfectly. The police will be breaking down doors, searching for the African Clown and his friend, while I'll be home, sitting in Mother's Dell, celebrating my . . . diversification.

Arthur smiled, then glanced at his speedometer and lifted his right foot slightly off the gas pedal. Celebrate this spiraling feeling, too, but heed your speed. It wouldn't do to get a ticket and spoil such a triumphal day.

Frank Sikes hoped the fresh — well, open — air on the sidewalk would help. "You want a patrol officer to drive you home?"

"Can't you?" asked Sheilah Quinn.

"Gerry and I have to stay."

"Gerry?"

That's what I was afraid of, thought Frank. She's not all there yet. "My . . . partner."

"Oh, right. No."

"No?"

"No, Frank. I don't want some cop driving me home, having to make small talk."

"Sheilah —"

"Just hail me a cab, okay?"

"If there's anything I —"

"There isn't." Frank heard her tone change. "Thanks, but I've got to go home, make some calls about . . . all this."

"I'll try you later."

"If I don't answer, don't be worried."

Walking outside the yellow tape and flagging a taxi, Frank Sikes knew that he would. Worry, that is.

As the cab pulled away with Sheilah Quinn in the backseat, Gerry O'Toole's voice called out from behind him. "Frank?"

Sikes turned around.

O'Toole said, "We might have something here."

A man was standing next to Gerry. A token clerk, given the uniform, with a high forehead and puffy cheeks.

Sprawled a little in the lawn chair, Arthur Ketterson realized that the spiraling feeling still

338

hadn't left him, though he was sure the adrenaline must have worn off by now. He held out his hand parallel to the ground.

See, no hormonic tremors. But still that sense of exhilaration. Why, do you suppose?

It was nothing sexual, of that he was certain. And therefore not at all like the others, Diana and her successors.

So, what then was it? The exhilaration of accomplishing something extemporaneous? That sense of improvisation, of devising the plan as he went along? Or perhaps simply the very . . . diversity of killing other than by strangulation. As though Arthur were an athlete who, having mastered one sport, transcends it by competing in a new event. Competing and winning, crowned a champion once again.

"That must be it, Mother," said Arthur aloud before glancing tenderly at each of the trees in the dell. Then another realization struck him. Apparently, diversification carried a concomitant drawback, as well.

Loss of control. As, for example, not being able to control any disposition of the body.

A pity, thought Arthur Ketterson, his right hand fluttering up to his cheek. The old crone would have fertilized a first-rate persimmon tree.

"And so this tall white guy, he's chasing up after them. These two black kids blow right by my booth like they was in the Olympics or something."

Frank Sikes said, "Can you describe them?"

"I suppose so. But the one kid, I recognized."

"You did?"

"Yeah," said the token clerk, standing off to the side with O'Toole next to him. "Him and a friend of his, they're in the station all the time."

"So you figure they work or live in the neighborhood?"

"Work? I doubt it. But one of them lives around here, definitely."

"How do you know?" asked Gerry.

"How? I seen him, that's how."

O'Toole and Sikes exchanged looks.

"Saw him where?" said Frank.

"Coming out of his house. Well, this building over on Sampson that has like offices on the bottom and apartments on top, you know?"

"Which kid is this?" said O'Toole.

"The one with the funny face."

"Funny face?" said Frank.

"Yeah." The clerk made his hands into fists, then raised them. "Like this much space around his eyes is pink instead of black, and he's got the same kind of ring around his mouth, too."

Frank looked to O'Toole. "Pigmentation problem."

"I don't think so," said their witness.

Frank came back to him. "Why not?"

"Kid was at least five eight, maybe more."

Sikes wondered if he'd missed something. "So?"

"So he wasn't no pygmy, is what I'm saying here."

Gerry O'Toole had to turn and clamp a hand to his mouth to keep from laughing as Frank Sikes got the block address where the token clerk had seen the kid leaving a building.

Sheilah hung up the phone after her — what, eighth call? The answering service for the law firm was easy, and the night board at the DA's office said Peter Mendez would receive her message, but there was no acceptable way to reach Roger Hesterfield until morning through Old Bailey at the courthouse. Etta's rabbi was terrific, saying he'd arrange things the right way with a good funeral home, not to worry. Krissie Newton, on the other hand, took the news a lot harder than Sheilah would have guessed. Maybe youth, maybe Krissie just caring for Etta more than either of them ever let on. Sheilah knew she herself had.

Quigley was trying to worm his way onto her lap again, the way he had the whole time she'd been on the phone, even though Sheilah had fed him first thing. Now it was time for a bath and a glass of chardonnay — but just one.

Carrying her glass to the bathroom, Sheilah ran the water in the tub for five minutes and the spa for five more, no reappearance of the blood-colored water. Really was just a freak condition Sunday night. Thank God for that, at least.

Once the bath was drawn, she sprinkled in

341

some of the juniper-scented oil, which began to bubble from the aeration and to smell soothing, restful. Climbing into the tub, Sheilah eased her body under the surface of the warm pulsating water, then reached for her wineglass.

"Etta, Etta. Why did you have to take the goddamn subway?"

After one sip of the chardonnay, Sheilah Quinn decided not to wait for the ten-minute beep from the spa's motor before starting to cry.

THIRTEEN

It was a busy Wednesday morning, but whenever the board in front of her at the answering service allowed, Terri Como found herself thinking about that Rudy Giordano guy. Not just his tragedy, either, although it was really something, the daughter getting killed and all while she and Rudy were getting better acquainted in the rear seat of his car. Terri's roommate had been entertaining a new boyfriend at their apartment, so she couldn't very well have taken Rudy there. And just her luck he'd left his wallet back at his house. Even a crummy motel would have had a more comfortable bed than the bench thing in the Caddy.

What she recalled of the experience, anyway.

Terri had gotten drunk that night and sure couldn't remember everything, especially since she'd winked out for a while. Then Terri thought of watching Rudy at the wheel as he was driving, those real supple Italian gloves he was wearing. He had strong hands, Rudy; she'd noticed them in the bar. Strong but nice, and she remembered thinking, It wouldn't be the worst thing in the world, he felt me up a little with those gloves on. Terri had touched them, and

Rudy had touched her, here and there. But something about that pale buttery leather just — Hey, this kind of thinking, is it kinky or what?

Then one of the coded buttons on her console lit up. Pressing it, Terri said into her mouthpiece, "Law offices."

"You don't sound at all like Krissie."

Cultured dink. "This is the answering service, sir." The light for another button came on. "Please hold." *Click.* "Law offices, please hold." *Click.* "Now, would you like to leave a message?"

"Can you tell me when Sheilah Quinn will be in?"

"Not today, sir."

"Why is that?"

Another light. "There's been a death in the firm. Please hold." *Click.* "Law offices, please hold." *Click.* "Yes, sir?"

"Do you have the name of the funeral home involved?"

Terri gave it to him. "Any message for Ms. Quinn?"

"Yes. Please extend Arthur Ketterson's deepest condolences."

So, a sympathetic dink. Familiar name, though. "I will, sir."

Click. "Thank you for holding."

An impatient grunt. "This is Presiding Justice Roger Hesterfield —"

A fourth light. "Please hold."

"Now, see here —"

Click. A self-important dink. Gonna be one of

344

those crazy fucking days — pardon my French. *Click.* "Law offices."

"Our guy lives over a lawyer?" said Gerry O'Toole from the driver's seat, the unmarked sedan parked against the curb.

Frank Sikes squinted from the passenger's side, the sun glaring off the first-floor picture window. " 'J. Leroy Washington, Esquire,' " he read.

"You sure this is the right block?"

"The token clerk said the kid came out of a building with some offices on the ground floor."

"And our guys staking it out last night didn't see anything?"

"So they said."

"How long we gonna wait for this kid to show himself?"

"Long as we have to," said Frank.

"Fuck that."

"Hey, Gerry? The alternative is we go up there and knock on some doors. In which case, somebody who knows the kid tells him his crib's been found, which means he won't be coming back to it."

O'Toole nodded. "Yeah, well, I'll give you that. But this is a new one, even for me."

"How do you mean?"

Gerry turned. "A killer who lives above a lawyer?"

"Can't beat the convenience factor, though."

"Convenience?"

345

Frank Sikes grinned. "We do collar the kid, you can read him his rights on the stairs, and he can retain counsel before we even leave the building."

Annoyed, Roger Hesterfield hung up after speaking with Sheilah Quinn's answering service. No real information available beyond funeral arrangements that he couldn't care less about. Etta Yemelman might have been a judicial colleague once upon a time, but he'd never seen eye-to-eye with her, and certainly wasn't about to invest the next morning in her burial.

Sheilah had called O.B. at the crack of dawn, advising him she wouldn't be in court due to the murder. A revolting crime Roger had missed the previous night because he'd passed out before — or, more likely, merely slept through — the late news and hadn't looked at a newspaper until arriving in chambers that morning. Hesterfield'd already tried Sheilah at home, twice, but the phone had just rung ten times, her tape machine not picking up the calls. And here he was trying to do the bitch a favor by granting a longer continuance than she'd likely request.

A stroke of genius, that, if I do say so myself. Always take advantage of the opportunities life offers. Here, a couple of colored street urchins kill the partner of a defense attorney. *The* defense attorney in a trial that the presiding justice would just as soon see drag on a bit, postponing that dago sadist's goddamned enthusiastic wrecking ball. Perfect solution? No, but at least a delay that will continue the case for several days, buy myself more time in the one place I truly love.

Roger Hesterfield looked around his chambers. At the bookshelves and the walls. The plaques and the photos. The furniture and even the slightly worn rug.

Truly, truly love.

Sheilah Quinn sat on her couch, wearing jeans and an old fisherman's knit sweater. Quigley was curled up in her lap, half-purring, half-snoring.

He seems to sense how sad I am, and he's trying to make up for it. Whether empathy or sympathy, cats can surprise you that way.

The phone rang again. Five, seven, nine times before whoever it was gave up. Again. It probably wasn't completely professional to turn the tape machine off, but she really didn't want to speak to anyone, nor even hear other voices.

Except maybe Frank's. One of the calls might have been his.

She decided to try him at Homicide, see if there'd been any progress.

"Well?" said Gerry O'Toole, sliding in the driver's side with a bag of convenience-store coffee and muffins.

"Nothing so far."

"Christ, this stakeout shit's for the birds. I don't know how the guys in Narcotics stand it."

Frank Sikes fished out a coffee and a corn muffin. "Or the FBI. Agent once told me they sometimes sit on a suspect for months, around the clock."

"Those Feebs, though, they're strange to start with. I ever tell you about the time I went to one of their weddings?"

"An FBI wedding?"

"Yeah." Gerry bent back a triangle on the plastic cover for one of the coffees, then slurped from it. "My wife was good friends with the girl this special agent was marrying, so we got invited. And believe me, Frank, it was four-plus strange."

"How do you mean?"

"Well, first of all, the Feebs are all so fucking young. I mean, they look like college kids. How can they handle real criminals?"

Frank thought, Because at Quantico they get taught about a hundred ways to kill somebody. "What else?"

"Second thing, the minister — oh, he was bland, very fucking bland. But he was wearing this ridiculous toupee, and he had a mustache and these thick, thick glasses — like he was in the Witness Protection Program and came out only for Bureau weddings, you know?"

Frank laughed.

Gerry slurped some more coffee. "And the photographer. Somebody said he was an FBI lab guy? Well, alls I know is, he seemed kind of confused to be taking pictures of live people, like he

348

couldn't get over not having a chalk outline on the ground to go by."

Frank laughed again.

"And then, when the bridal couple gets in the limo after the ceremony and it starts to pull away? I expected the ushers to fucking run alongside the doors, like they did in that Clint Eastwood movie."

Frank frowned this time. "You mean the *Line of Fire* thing?"

"Yeah."

"Gerry, that was Secret Service, not FBI."

"So what?" More coffee still. "They're all fucking feds, aren't they?"

Frank was about to toss in the towel on the entire conversation when the doorway next to the office of J. Leroy Washington, Esquire, opened about a foot and a fairly unusual face peeked out at the street.

Putting his coffee on the floor mat between his feet, Gerry O'Toole said, "Now, who the fuck might this be?"

While lying in his mother's bed, propped up by a bolster behind his back, Arthur Ketterson had dialed the funeral home that the woman at Sheilah's answering service had given him. Dialed it twice, in fact, but the number had been busy both times.

Frustrating, especially if I'd been a genuine mourner.

Arthur salved his frustration by alternating his

attention between watching the television bulletins and reading the newspaper Parsons had fetched. Neither, of course, had ever recounted his past efforts, Arthur being careful in his choice and study of targets before taking and . . . recycling them. Now, as he would have expected, the broadcast media was more vivid, the print more comprehensive. Some of the television camera point-of-view shots were strikingly evocative, capturing images he himself had observed while being at the scene. No, while *creating* the scene, or at least creating its significance. The news sources confirmed that police were seeking "two youths, both African-American." However, neither source provided any funeral information.

Arthur wracked his memory. He was certain the Jews had some odd ideas about burial. Inexplicably, his mother once had a Jewish friend, and when the friend died, Arthur seemed to recall the body had to be in the ground by the sunset following death, or some such confusing custom.

That would mean the funeral would be . . . today, Wednesday. However, Arthur was also certain that there would have to be an autopsy on the old crone, even though the cause of death was crystal-clear.

He shrugged resignedly. I suppose you can't really blame the authorities for being thorough.

After all, someone did murder her.

Arthur Ketterson sensed the corners of his

mouth twitching upward as he turned back to the front-page story about his improvisation in the subway station.

"Delta three, Delta three. I have a land patch for you. Do you copy? Over."

The dispatcher's voice squawked over the radio just as Frank Sikes and Gerry O'Toole opened their doors from inside the sedan. The black youth with the pigmentation disorder, who had stepped onto the sidewalk, realized what was happening, and he wisely bolted down the street.

"Fuck," said Gerry O'Toole, getting back behind the wheel. "I hate the ones who can run."

Frank Sikes took off after the kid.

"Delta three, Delta —"

O'Toole grabbed the hand mike. "Break, break. This is Delta three. We are in pursuit of a homicide suspect, twelve hundred block of Sampson, heading west on foot. Pursuit is by both unmarked car and plainclothes on foot. Request assistance, all officers in the vicinity. Description of suspect to follow. Copy. . . ."

As he spoke, Gerry O'Toole put on the siren, squealing the tires a little as he drove toward his partner.

"Thanks anyway," said Sheilah Quinn into the telephone.

"Any message for Sergeant Sikes?"

Sheilah thought the dispatcher sounded har-

351

ried. "Just tell him I was calling about the Etta Yemelman homicide."

After hanging up, Sheilah tried to think of something to do.

The office is out of the question right now. Maybe go see Dad, if I can keep from crying.

Then she remembered how her father had seemed the last time she'd visited him, and Sheilah Quinn decided to think about it a little more first.

Old Bailey stuck his head in the door. "Your Honor, District Attorney Mendez is here."

"Show him in, O.B."

As Mendez entered the chambers, Roger Hesterfield thought, Hell, sallow cheeks, bags under the eyes. Peter must be hitting the sauce harder than I am.

"Sit down, Peter, sit down."

Mendez wasn't in the chair before he began. "About the Diaz case —"

"Yes," said Roger. "Tragedy for poor Sheilah, don't you think?"

"Are we — is Your Honor going to grant her a continuance?"

"Certainly for today. And given the magnitude of the horror — indeed, the insult to our profession — I thought next Monday might be best."

Mendez looked stricken. "You mean not resume *until* Monday?"

"Correct, Peter. What's wrong with that?"

"Your Honor, the election is coming up, and

I'd hoped to be finished with this matter by —"

"Yes, well. We can't let personal agendas dictate our souls' proper response to one in need, now can we?"

It was a moment before Mendez replied, "No, Your Honor."

"And besides, Peter," said Roger Hesterfield magnanimously, leaning back in his chair, "this way, you get kind of a jump on your campaigning."

Mendez nodded, but not terribly convincingly.

They were in a trash-strewn alley, the kid still writhing a little against the restraining hold Frank Sikes had on him, when Gerry O'Toole caught up to them.

O'Toole unclipped his cuffs and then closed them around the kid's bony wrists, a tattoo of a golden hornet on the left one. Homemade jobbie, but pretty good.

"Hey, sport," said O'Toole, "who did your tattoo?"

"Fuck off, motherfucker."

"Ah, it's to be that way, is it?"

Winded from the chase, Frank said between gulps of air, "What's your name?"

"Fuck you, too."

O'Toole said, "This skin problem you got — around your eyes and mouth? — it reminds me of a raccoon, only in reverse, like."

The kid glared at him.

"So how's about we call you 'Rocky,' you know?"

"The fuck's Rocky?"

"From that Beatles song — 'Rocky Raccoon, he —' "

"My name's Charles Rooten."

"Pleased to meet you, Charles." O'Toole shook three of Rooten's fingers on the cuffed right hand. "This is Sergeant Sikes, and I'm Detective O'Toole."

"Motherfuckers, you ain't got shit."

"Ah, the language a body hears nowadays." O'Toole glanced down at Rooten's wrists, his golden hornet, then winked at him. "Hey, Charles, I'm thinking your little bug tatt' just hit the windshield of life without parole."

"Fuck you."

Frank Sikes, his breathing approaching normal, said in a monotone, "You have the right to remain silent. Anything you say can and will . . ."

Arthur Ketterson was nearly out of bed, but he wanted to be sure there was nothing more he should be doing. The funeral home's number had finally been free, and the person answering — female, but still a perfect dirge voice — told him Ms. Yemelman's funeral was scheduled not for that Wednesday afternoon but, rather, at 10:00 A.M. Thursday morning. Arthur asked the dirge person if she were sure of the timing, as he believed that Ms. Yemelman was Jewish. The dirge person said she was Jewish, too, and "Believe me, sir, it's tomorrow."

Arthur hung up without thanking her.

But now he wished he hadn't. Hung up, that is. Arthur could have asked the dirge person if he should send flowers. Although, given his gift to Sheilah last Friday, might that be . . . gilding the lily?

Arthur laughed. Not just a pun, but a double pun, since lilies were traditional at funerals.

At Jewish ones, though?

Arthur began to wish he'd paid more attention during those comparative religion classes in college.

Like God handing you an extra three days, thought Roger Hesterfield.

Plenty of paperwork to do, and the more done now, the less to carry forward on that dark morn when I'll finally have to vacate the First Session. But it's only Wednesday, so I've got plenty of time for the paperwork, too.

And not the worst idea to finish early, squeeze in nine holes before dark. However, sure as Carter made Little Liver Pills, I leave an hour early and there'll be some television reporter there with a camera crew to capture the moment.

That would be all I'd need. Seen to be stalling with the liquor-store case, and then caught playing hooky, as well? No, better to sit here and kill some trees doing the county's paperwork.

Stay here until that dago bastard Giordano —

Some pounding from above, and plaster dust began falling down onto Roger like a flurry of snow. He suddenly found all his good feelings dissipate, and tears began to fill his eyes.

"Goddamn plaster dust," Roger Hesterfield said out loud, wiping his eyes with the back of one hand while reaching for a case file with the other.

From a chair in the interrogation room, Charles Rooten watched the two pigs come back in. After they'd brought him to the station, they'd left him alone for a while, like maybe half an hour.

Motherfuckers trying to mess with my mind. Well, fuck you. People been messing with me my whole life, account of what God done to me, my colors and all. Besides, fucking pigs don't got shit. They did, I be reading a warrant or something by now.

Leaning against the wall, arms folded, the white pig said, "So, Charles, you remember us?"

"Yeah. Beavis and Butt-head, right?"

"He's O'Toole," said the black pig, who talked like a white pig. "I'm Sikes. And, turns out, you're not a juvie."

"So?"

"So we get to charge you as an adult, Charles. Which is going to make me very happy."

"Myself," said the white pig, "I'm almost giddy. You know what 'giddy' means, Charles?"

The black/white pig put his palms on the table, leaning forward on them. Getting into my face from like maybe a foot away. Most times people do that to me, they want to make fun account of my colors. But this pig don't mean for to do that, uh-uh.

"Who pushed her, Charles?"

"Don't know what you talking about, man."

"Bing Square subway station, Charles."

Like maybe six inches away from my face now, motherfucker.

"Yesterday afternoon, Charles, four-fifteen."

"I told you, I don't —"

"About twenty people saw you and a playmate have a fight with the woman, Charles."

"Wasn't no fight."

The white pig. "What was it, then?"

"Honkie gramma was dissing me."

"Dissing you how?"

"Bumping her old bones into me. Wasn't being polite to my person."

The black/white pig. "And for that, you pushed the woman onto the tracks?"

Close enough to kiss me now, the mother. "I didn't push her, man. Darnell —"

Shit.

The black/white pig smiled, backed off some.

Shit, shit, shit. Got to cool your tongue, boy. Got to be cool all over.

The white pig now. "Darrell was your friend, right?"

"Didn't nobody push the gramma, man."

357

"People say they saw you push her, Charles."

"Who say that?"

The black/white pig. "Did you, Charles? Did you maybe just push her because you thought she was dissing you, get yourself a little elbow-room?"

"I didn't see nobody push her, man."

"Then why'd you run, Charles?"

"We didn't run. We was being chased."

The white pig again. "Chased, is it?"

"By this crazy dude."

"Crazy how?"

"This dude, he wearing sunglasses inside the subway, but he don't look high or nothing. And he starts yelling at us, when we didn't do nothing."

"That's not the story the other witnesses gave us."

Oh yeah? Charles had a brainstorm. "Well, how about the crazy dude? What's his story say?"

The white pig glanced at the black/white one, who said, "We're not talking to him now, Charles. We're talking to you."

A grin. Charles felt a grin come over his face wide enough to light up the whole fucking room. "You don't have him, do you? You don't have the dude say we pushed the gramma."

"It doesn't matter —"

"It matter to me, man. I'm not saying nothing more."

The white pig softened up his voice some. "Charles —"

"Gerry," said the black/white one. "Let's talk outside a minute."

At her hall closet, Sheilah Quinn put on a coat over the sweater and jeans. She hadn't decided to go see her dad yet. Just wanted to take a walk, clear the head a little.

But before leaving her apartment, Sheilah turned on the tape machine. Get Frank's message if he called back.

Arthur Ketterson hefted the tiny cassette recorder in his hand and said, "Should I or shouldn't I?"

Not a difficult decision, really. The more Sheilah bears now, the more grateful she'll be when I recount my efforts for her later.

Dialing Sheilah's home number, Arthur waited for the outgoing announcement and the beep before pressing PLAY and holding the speaker up to the receiver.

The woman answering the medical examiner's phone wasn't sure if she could disturb him, but she told Frank Sikes she'd try.

A minute later, a raspy voice came on. "Dinetti, and this better be good. I'm halfway through a twelve-year-old got knifed in her schoolyard."

"Emil, it's Frank Sikes. We have one of the kids we think pushed the old woman onto the subway tracks last night."

"Congratulations."

"Thanks, but we just picked him up; we don't exactly 'have' him."

"Meaning, did I find anything in the post that might help?"

"You got it.'

"Well, there wasn't much beyond what you guys could see at the scene. I'm sorry the woman had to wait for today, but I've got them stacked like cordwood back there."

"Emil, just —"

"And I'll deny this if anybody ever asked, but I try to do the Jewish ones first, their people like to get them in the ground sooner, only I just couldn't till —"

"Emil. Please?"

"Right, right." Frank could hear the clatter of clipboards, the ruffling of papers. "Okay, we've got Yemelman, Etta. White female, age seventy-six by her wallet identification, though the muscle tone and all was still pretty —"

"Emil, can we cut to the bottom line?"

Clearing of throat. "Cardiac arrest, precipitated by electrocution. Some abrasions consistent with the fall onto the tracks. And of course the disfigurement to hands and —"

"But everything else tested normal."

"Down the line. Like I said, woman must have taken care of herself, given her age."

"And no question she was pushed."

"Hey, Frank, that's more your side of things than mine, you know?"

"I know, but —"

"But given the distance from the edge of the platform to that third rail? I'd say either she was pushed or she tried to broadjump the tracks with a good running start. Which way would you bet it?"

Despite the fresh air — thanks to a twenty-mile-an-hour wind behind her — the walk wasn't helping Sheilah much. She found herself missing whole blocks, occasionally focusing on older women, at least any who displayed a mannerism remotely like one of Etta's. And the lawyer in Sheilah began to poke through the blues haze: the need to go over Etta's calendar for appointments and deadlines, to find another competent trusts and estates attorney in order to refer her clients appropriately, to . . . clean out Etta's office.

Then she saw an older man striding toward her, not quite racewalking, but arms swinging at his side, like a soldier in a parade. He reminded her of someone, too.

Jack Quinn, marching every Memorial Day, the dress uniform carefully pressed, the medals pinned over the left breast. The other members of his VFW post would be in step around him, heads high and hands waving to the wives and children applauding along the curb.

Sheilah turned around at that point, bundling up her coat against the wind and heading directly for her car.

"About ready to pack it in for the night, Your Honor?"

Roger Hesterfield looked up from the case file, to see Old Bailey standing stolidly in his doorway. Good old O.B. — no, saying "old" first made "O.B." redundant — but he was good, all right, like a faithful dog. Always the same expression — "pack it in." Always the same deference of "Your Honor," regardless of who was or wasn't around to hear him.

"Your Honor?"

"Sorry, O.B. Lost in thought."

"Well, don't stay too late, huh?"

"I'll try not to."

"Yes, Your Honor."

As the door clicked shut, Hesterfield sighed, saying aloud, "We've worked together for almost twenty-five years, and he can no more imagine calling me 'Roger' than dropping his trousers and mooning a jury. Why aren't there more men like O.B.?"

"Hold him? Hold him on what, Gerry?"

"Jesus, Frank, we know this Rooten kid's dirty."

"Yeah, just like we 'know' that Ketterson's a killer, but at least with him, we have a finger-print."

"Twenty people on that platform said Rooten and his friend argued with the lady seconds before she goes over."

"And not one of the twenty saw either of them push her."

"Frank —"

"Not one. Even Charles himself says he didn't see anybody do it."

"Great source, Frank. What about the tall white the token clerk saw chasing them?"

"Gerry, you want to arrest and ask Mendez to go to the grand jury on the hearsay statement of an unidentified bystander, who himself takes off immediately after the crime?"

O'Toole seemed to give in. "Not even if it wasn't an election year." Then he shook his head. "So, what next?"

"We know our boy Charles was one of the kids. There's a reason this Darnell was the other, and we have a minimal description to go with the first name. So I say we turn Rooten loose."

"Turn him loose?"

"And then, it's either stake out young Charles's crib to watch for Darnell or beat the bushes trying to find him."

O'Toole chewed on the suggestion. "What you're saying is, we snag Darnell . . ."

"And try to sell him on Charles saving his own ass by giving up his friend."

"After which, we hope Darnell flips over on Charles instead?"

"Unless you've got a better idea."

O'Toole chewed on it some more. "You know how I feel about stakeouts, right?"

"Okay, so we beat the bushes. Concentric squares around Rooten's building, use the name 'Darnell' to try and flush the friend."

"Great way to waste a couple of days."

"Which brings us back to the stakeout."

Gerald O'Toole rubbed his face with the heel of his hand. "So we waste a couple of days."

Sheilah Quinn took the nurse's call button from her father's left hand and laid it beside his pillow. Wrapping her own hands around his, she felt a little squeeze in return, and Jack Quinn opened his eyes, smiling at her.

Something rose and glowed inside Sheilah's chest. "Good to have you back, Dad."

The other hand tapped once on the bedsheet.

From the doorway, Lucille Wesley said, "Jack been better today, lots better since you was here Monday."

"I can see it."

"Like I told you. The tough ones like Jack, they can rally, surprise you sometimes."

Sheilah half-turned. "Thanks, Lucille."

As the aide nodded in acknowledgment of their signal and closed the door, Sheilah thought, How can I not tell him?

Her father's right eyebrow arched a little, the eyes beneath it aware, concerned.

"Dad, I, uh . . ."

One tap.

"It's about Etta."

One tap more.

"She's dead."

Two taps, repeated three times over. Jack Quinn's eyes filled a little but stayed open for Sheilah, for his only child and daughter, who now, if only temporarily, needed him again more than he needed her.

Before dinner, Arthur Ketterson sat in his lawn chair at the center of the dell, an aperitif in his hand. Thinking, I have to be careful not to rush things.

No, like this modest little sauvignon blanc, each experience should be savored for its own value, even if that value is relatively lower on the scale of pleasure. Otherwise, one cheapens the next experience. Mother's way of putting it was: "Arthur, after a meal, never eat again until you're hungry. Follow that advice and you will remain slim, and always enjoy."

So apt, as always. Roughly translated, that advice counseled Arthur to rest tonight in preparation for tomorrow's culmination of the current experience, the funeral procession of the Persimmon Queen.

But thereafter?

Well, that second dose of Roger Hesterfield's taped voice for Sheilah should prove a nice touch, but as furtherance of our relationship, it's rather insubstantial. Yes, action of a greater . . . intensity is definitely in order, and soon.

Smiling, Arthur took a sip of the aperitif, just enough to register that there was something washing over his taste buds beyond saliva. Savor each experience for its own value. Mother, you taught me well.

So very, very well.

—

Back in the apartment, Quigley reminded Sheilah that she'd gone straight from her walk to her car and then to the nursing home without feeding him. After plopping the canned stuff into his dish, Sheilah walked to the bedroom. Since leaving her dad, she realized the best thing she could have done was to go talk to him, even if that didn't really mean talking with him. Jack Quinn simply found a way, as he usually had, of making her feel better about the world.

Folding the sweater after pulling it off, Sheilah noticed the message light blinking on her tape machine. She walked over to the night table and pressed PLAY, hearing Roger Hesterfield's voice again, scratchy like the last time, saying . . .

Sheilah mashed the STOP button. That bastard, that incredible *bas*tard! It's the same message. He's reading a . . . a *script* to me.

Yanking the sweater back on over her head, Sheilah ran to the front of the apartment, spooking Quigley from his dish as she grabbed her car keys off the kitchen counter.

Through the torn shade, Darnell Fuquay peeked out from his stepmother's living room. The Man was down there, talking up the shit-brained old lady live across the way. There be two of them, a white bread and a brown, but they the Man, no question about it. Don't have to see no badge to know it, they little notebooks out, pointing to things in them.

366

Ever since I heard on the street that Charles got took off by the police, I been by this window, keeping lookout and keeping cool. Safer to stay in the crib, you dig? No need for running, less Charles give you up. And he your friend, homeboy. Friends don't give you up to the Man.

Only now the old lady nodding. She old, like the white gramma done fell on the subway tracks. But now she be pointing, too.

Pointing up at his stepmother's window.

Jumping back from the shade like it had caught fire, Darnell couldn't believe what he seeing.

No reason for the Man to be on this block. That subway station, it two avenues over and one street down. No way the Man onto him so quick.

Not without Charles give me up.

Raging, Darnell ran as fast as he could back through the apartment to his step's bedroom bureau — where she kept her "rainy day" money. Then, the roll of bills in the pocket of his baggy pants, he went to the kitchen window.

That's the one with the fire escape outside it.

From behind the wheel, Sheilah Quinn caught him in her peripheral vision. He was walking to his Mercedes behind the old courthouse as she roared up to the front of it. Slewing the Miata into the curb at a fire hydrant, Sheilah leapt out and ran toward him.

Roger Hesterfield became aware of the pounding of soles against macadam behind him, thinking, "Odd place for a jogger."

As the steps came closer, he decided he really ought to turn around.

And got slapped across the right side of his face. No, *slapped* didn't quite capture it. *Clouted* might be more accurate. Roger Hesterfield was nearly knocked off his feet.

From less than a yard away, Sheilah screamed at him, "Don't you ever, *ever*, call me at home again, do you understand?"

The judge put a hand to his burning cheek. "What in the world?"

Sheilah turned and ran away, screaming over her shoulder, "Ever . . . ever!"

Roger Hesterfield rubbed his cheek, thinking, "How did she even know I was calling her about the continuance?" Then confusion was replaced by a welling vitriol. Under his breath, he said, "Cunt, that's the last favor you ever get from me. And this time, I mean it."

In his basement workshop, Rudy Giordano could hear the kitchen floorboards creaking above him.

No matter how solid you build a house, you're still gonna get some of that, expecially after fourteen years of settling. But at least the creaking sounds mean Rhonda is up and cooking something for dinner. She still spends every fucking night on the couch, though, losing herself in the photo albums.

Losing herself like I lose myself down here, with the puppets.

Rudy looked at the half-assembled figure on his workbench. He'd started out years ago by making the marionettes out of cloth, but they were too hard to control during a show, even if you stuck lead in the joints. Papier-mâché was classy, but real fragile: It couldn't take the metal eyeholes for the strings, to allow freer movement of the puppets' limbs and heads.

Rudy picked up the torso of the marionette he was fashioning now. No, in the long run, wood is your best bet for material. You can carve it yourself, hollowing out most of the body to reduce overall weight before adding hinged joints for elbows and knees, rotating ones for neck and shoulders.

As Rudy used a sharp knife to cut into the chest area of the puppet in his hands, his mind shifted back to what that cop/carpenter had told him about autopsies, about how the pathologist did the same thing to human bodies, too . . . Jessica.

All the fucking lawyers in that courtroom, keeping me from getting real justice, from seeing that fucking Arthur Ketterson pay for —

"Rudy?"

Why can't the fucking legal system be like my puppet shows, huh? I could manipulate the control bars, make everybody move so that everything comes out right in the end, instead of —

"Rudy!" yelled Rhonda again, now from the top of the cellar stairs.

"What?"

"Supper's ready."

"All right," he said to the marionette.

"Rudy, I can't hear you."

"I'm coming, I'm coming."

Reluctantly, Rudy Giordano laid the wooden torso and carving knife back on his workbench.

FOURTEEN

It was Thursday morning, about 9:30, when Veronica said, "Mort Zussman, on two."

Cradling the telephone receiver against his shoulder, on the call he was already taking, Peter Mendez had barely looked up before his secretary's head disappeared around the doorjamb of his office. He glanced at his watch and couldn't see how he'd be able to make the services for Etta Yemelman on time. Mendez knew Latino voters listened to Latino lawyers for opinions on whom to pull the lever for, come Election Day, and he assumed Jewish voters acted in similar fashion. Even if they didn't, though, there were enough Jewish lawyers to be a sizable voting block in and of themselves, and Peter was sure many of them would be at the funeral.

Mendez said into the phone, "Look, I've got to take this other call. Ten to fifteen, your guy serves maybe eight. That's our best offer."

"Then prepare for trial, Peter, because that's where we're headed with this one."

Peter pressed the second button on his telephone. "Mort?"

"Yeah, we —"

"Mort, can I call you back in say an hour?"

A labored sigh from the campaign manager. Madre de Dios, I hate that sound.

"Petey, Petey, you're the one called me yesterday, remember? On how I'm supposed to shoehorn a press conference into tomorrow morning, now that you got this time off from your trial there?"

"Yes, but —"

"Well, how the fuck you gonna appear at these kind of things, we don't talk about them before they slide by?"

Peter tried to ignore what the face of his watch was telling him. "Okay, Mort, okay. Go ahead."

"Can I give you a lift, Your Honor?"

Roger Hesterfield's eyes never left the file in front of him. "To where, O.B.?"

A pause. "Judge Yemelman's funeral."

"I'm afraid you'll have to go without me."

"Your Honor?"

"Just too much work to do here. Etta was a good judge. She'd understand."

Another pause. "Yessir. By the way, you going to need any cartons ?"

Hesterfield did look up this time. "Cartons?"

"Yes, sir. To pack up the chambers in."

"That won't be for a while, O.B. Perhaps quite awhile." Roger gestured over his paperwork, saying, "And now?"

"Yessir."

As Old Bailey closed the door, Roger tried to remember the last time the bailiff had responded to him as just "sir," instead of "Your Honor." Ah, well, I'm indulging myself in skipping Etta's funeral, and every indulgence has its price.

At which point, Roger Hesterfield thought of Sheilah Quinn, and he felt his cheek burn, as though she'd just slapped him again.

Sheilah Quinn stood next to Krissie Newton at the graveside while the rabbi read words in both English and, she guessed, Hebrew, seeming to alternate every other sentence. He'd already conducted a quiet, relatively nondenominational service in the funeral home, announcing the attendees that there would be a brief reception back at the temple, Etta having no known survivors to host one. Though he hadn't actually mentioned that last part, everyone nevertheless knew it to be true.

Sheilah suddenly was aware of the rabbi standing in front of her, asking if she'd care to lay a flower upon the casket. It felt like something a family member should do, but Sheilah stepped forward anyway, taking a stem and laying it so the petals pointed toward Etta's head. As Sheilah stepped back, some of the scent of the blossom stayed with her, which might be the most one could hope for from a ceremony for the dead.

The rabbi concluded the service by reminding everybody of the reception. As Sheilah turned away from the grave, a hand lit lightly on her shoulder. She was surprised to see it belonged to Frank Sikes.

Waiting until the rest of the mourners moved out of earshot, he said, "How're you doing?"

"Not great, but holding up. I didn't see you at the funeral home."

"I was outside, watching who showed up."

Sheilah nodded. She knew the investigating officers on a suspicious death often covered the funeral of the victim, just to see if anyone they didn't know about appeared without good reason. "Any progress in finding the boys who did this?"

"We found one."

Thank God. Maybe some early closure on this. "Will he give up the other?"

"Not so far," said Frank, "and anyway, we had to cut him loose."

Sheilah almost drove the heel of her hand against her ear. "You what?"

"We could put him at the scene, but nobody saw him — or the other kid, for that matter — push your partner."

Lawyer interested in justice lost out to friend mourning the deceased. "I can't listen to this."

"Sheilah —"

"Not now, Frank. Not now."

As she walked away, she could feel Frank Sikes watching her.

"Hey, Rude?"

Rudy Giordano turned. "Now what?"

Nick stopped, spoke more carefully. "Those pony HVAC units finally arrived for the interior conference rooms in the new building."

"About time. How long to put them in?"

"Three, four days. They only go sixty pounds each, but the installation and balancing's kind of tricky."

"You check the invoice against the specification?"

"Yeah. The supplier guarantees one'll chill a twelve-by-twelve room down to an igloo in thirty minutes. Supposed to be quiet as a mouse, too."

"Good," said Rudy. "Maybe we can get on with the demolition of the old place now."

"Hey, speaking of old, you hear about a broad got pushed onto the subway tracks?"

"From the news, yeah."

"Well," said Nick, "I saw in the paper where she was the law partner of that Sheilah Quinn from your case."

"No shit?"

"No shit. Burying her this morning, I think."

"Even better. Let a lawyer go to a funeral of somebody close. Join the real world for an hour."

As Nick walked away, Rudy Giordano tried to remember who had said something like that in his presence recently.

"Can't you go any faster?"

The state trooper kept her eyes forward,

already weaving in and out of the heavy traffic. "Not safely."

Peter Mendez checked his watch for the fourth time in the last ten minutes. He knew he'd missed the preburial service, and now he was afraid they'd be pulling up to the gravesite as everyone else was returning to their cars.

"Forget the cemetery, then."

The trooper almost looked at him. "Forget it?"

"That's what I said. Go right to the reception at the temple."

"Yes, sir."

"And put your siren on, will you?"

This time, the trooper did look at him. "To a funeral?"

Peter Mendez didn't return the look. "You can kill the thing two blocks away so nobody'll know it was us."

The driver had the funeral home's limo waiting at the cermetery's winding one-lane road. As he got out from behind the wheel to open her door, Sheilah Quinn passed the last tree and felt a hand on her shoulder again. She turned, ready to apologize to Frank Sikes for being abrupt at the graveside.

Except it wasn't him.

"Jesus Christ," she said.

"No, but I'm flattered, Sheilah."

She took a breath. "What are you doing here?"

Arthur Ketterson folded his hands in front of

his crotch, like a schoolboy about to recite a poem. "Sorry, not a good time for jokes, I suppose. But I called your office yesterday morning, and —"

"What are you doing here?"

The man stiffened. "I came to pay my respects, and I thought here at the cemetery might be more appropriate than the funeral home. I'd met your partner just the once, and then only briefly, but I could tell she had a strong influence over you."

Which seemed an odd way to phrase it, Sheilah thought. Unless I'm so out of sync that I can't spot "odd" today.

Ketterson shifted his feet, now standing with his hip cocked in front of her. "I truly didn't mean to intrude on your grief, even if it is mixed with relief."

Now he's talking in . . . rhymes? "What do —"

"I know you two had to have been somewhat close, despite what you said over our drink at the hotel."

I must be out of sync. "What I said?"

"About how harried you were, working for her."

"I didn't say that I was 'harried.' I just mentioned I had responsibilities toward her, as my partner."

"Oh, sorry again. I must have misunderstood." Ketterson glanced toward the limo. "Well, I've probably kept you long enough. Please, if I can do anything, let me know."

He extended his hand, and Sheilah had been accepting so many of them that morning that she very nearly took his as well before remembering. Remembering how Ketterson had held her hand the first time she'd met him.

As though it were something to eat.

Sheilah Quinn just thanked him for his concern instead, then continued on to the open door of the limo. Thinking, I'm not out of sync; Arthur Ketterson is just a chronic weirdo.

"Yo, Darnell," said Charles Rooten from the other end of the line. "Glad you called, homeboy."

"Uh-huh," said Darnell Fuquay, hunched against the pay phone near an alley known as the "Arson Mall," account of you could buy any kind of gun you want there. Darnell had always heard "arson" went along with fire, not fire*arms*, but somebody else told him it stood for what the army called the place they kept their rifles and shit.

"Where you at?" asked Charles.

Darnell couldn't believe it, his own "true friend," trying to find out where he was already, he could give him up to the Man again, save his own shiftless ass. "Heard you got yourself a ride to the police."

"They don't got shit on me, homey."

On *me*, Darnell noticed.

Charles said, "Homey?"

"Uh-huh."

"No lie. I see this hole in their shit, and I drives through it. Stuffed those motherfuckers like a slam fucking dunk."

"They let you go?"

"Had to. Couldn't hold no brother beats them playing his own lawyer."

Honkie gramma who fell on the tracks was a lawyer. Darnell saw it on the TV. And a Jew, to boot. Police think they got a homey killed a Jew gramma lawyer, they gonna cut him loose when he be his *own* lawyer?

"Yo, Darnell?"

"Yeah?"

"What's the matter, boy?"

"Nothing, man. Just glad for you. Relieved, like."

"Yeah, same here. How's about you come over?"

"Your place, man?"

"Yeah."

How dumb this dumb fuck think I am?

Charles said. "We go out, find ourselves some shit, smoke it up for the good feeling."

"Not today, man. Got something else to do. Tomorrow for sure, though."

"Tomorrow? When tomorrow?"

When. Can you believe this shit? "Afternoon. I call you first, let you know."

"Darnell, everything be cool?"

"Frosty, man. I see you tomorrow afternoon."

Hanging up the pay phone, Darnell thought he'd turned the setup around about as nice as you please. I tell that motherfuck tomorrow, no way Charles be expecting to see me today.

Taking a quick look around for the Man, who might be camping outside the Arson Mall — you never knew — Darnell Fuquay slipped into the mouth of the alley. His hand was inside the pocket of his baggy pants, gripping the roll of his step's rainy-day money.

Like it was the handle of a bad-ass Uzi or something, you dig?

"This is Roger Hesterfield."

"Roger," said the voice at the other end, a voice that always made Hesterfield cower. The chief administrative judge of the superior court, a fifty-year-old black who'd actually been promoted on merit and, therefore, someone Roger couldn't intimidate.

"Yes, Chief."

"Roger, I'm getting some serious flak from the county commissioners on your not being out of the First Session by last Friday."

"They've been harassing me, too, Chief. I —"

"So sorry, Roger. I didn't mean to imply they were harassing me. More imploring me."

"Imploring you?"

"Yes, to use my good offices to get you out of there and over to the new building."

"But, Chief, I'm in the middle of a trial that had to be continued, this Etta Yemelman thing —"

"Yes, I'm aware that one of your litigators was in partnership with Etta. A fine woman, and a responsible jurist. I was at her memorial service this morning. Hoped to touch base with you about this there, as a matter of fact."

Shit, the escalating price of indulgences. "Chief —"

"I understand the trial is a garden-variety armed robbery and doesn't reconvene until Monday, by your order?"

"That's right, Chief, but —"

"Which gives you all the rest of today, tomorrow, and the weekend to pack up and move over, Roger, so as to resume the armed robbery Monday next in the new courthouse. Can you do that for me?"

"Chief —"

"Pretty please," with no "imploring" tone to it.

A battle lost. "Of course, Chief."

"Excellent. I'll inform the commissioners you'll be out before Monday, and they'll pass that good word on to the contractor. Thank you, Roger, for your . . ."

Hesterfield knew what he was going to say.

". . . indulgence."

As Roger hung up the phone, O.B.'s knock sounded from the courtroom.

"Yes?"

The door opened. "Just wanted to let you know I was back, Your Honor."

"Good, good." As the door was closing, Hesterfield said, "Oh, O.B.?"

"Your Honor?"

"Those cartons you mentioned earlier?"

"Yes?"

"Can you get them here tomorrow?"

"Will do, Your Honor," the very slight smile on the loyal bailiff's face not noticed by the preoccupied jurist.

In fact, as the door clicked shut, Roger Hesterfield was too preoccupied even to wonder how the chief justice, just returning from Etta Yemelman's funeral, could have known the exact nature and continuance date of the Diaz trial.

The reception at the temple was held in a multipurpose room with high clerestory windows and a polished hardwood floor. The tables held some wine and soft drinks, buffet items — obviously homemade — interspersed. After thanking the rabbi for all his help, Sheilah Quinn asked who had set up the buffet. He pointed out three women and one man, and she sought out each individually.

There were fewer people at the reception than at the service that morning, but somewhat more than had been at the gravesite, which Sheilah couldn't quite compute. A number of people she hadn't met earlier came up to her to express their condolences, while others just nodded to her, paper plates or plastic glasses in hand. Then Sheilah felt yet a third hand on her shoulder, nearly shrugging it off violently before she heard Peter Mendez speak her name.

He followed with, "I just wanted to tell you how sorry I am."

"Thank you, Peter." Fighting through the slight fog she still felt, Sheilah asked, "Do we have a continuance date on Diaz, by the way?"

"Yes." He hesitated. "Hesterfield wanted to start again tomorrow, but I insisted on Monday. For your sake."

"Thanks," she said, thinking of the incident in the courthouse parking lot and figuring the extra day was Roger's way of apologizing to her. "When I saw him yesterday, he didn't mention that."

Mendez tensed, almost as if he'd been caught in a lie. But Sheilah couldn't think what it could be, especially since she'd spoken the words neutrally, no hidden meaning or even irony to them.

"Well, then," he said. "Again, I'm sorry about your loss."

Sheilah Quinn watched Peter Mendez nod absently, still tense, then move off into the crowd, shaking hands. Being seen, and, she guessed, hoping to be appreciated, as well.

FIFTEEN

After leaving the temple, Sheilah Quinn headed the Mazda Miata, convertible roof still up, toward her apartment. Halfway there, she changed her mind.

All morning, everyone had gone out of their way to be nice to her, but she'd not felt comfortable, even though the unfamiliar trappings of Etta Yemelman's religion had been very subtle. Sheilah didn't think — couldn't think — of her partner and mentor being in that subway station, in that funeral home, in that grave.

A change of lanes, then a turn signal toward the left. To spend some time with Etta where things would feel comfortable, where Sheilah Quinn thought of her as . . . being.

Timing, thought Arthur Ketterson, was crucial, but not always plannable. Was that a real word, he wondered? Arthur could recall his mother using it, but then she used a lot of words that surprised him when he came to understand the other contexts in which people said them. For example, Mother believed her best "affairs" — what she always called dinner parties — had a "happening" aspect to them. A happening, as in the old hippie/rock culture. Mother always was a remarkable amalgam of the lofty and the low.

For the most part, however, I do believe in planning. But the convergence of the old crone and the subway station could not have been anticipated so exactly, even by me poring over a schedule of track routes and arrivals. Nothing printed up by the Transit Authority could possibly have encompassed the two Negro convicts-in-waiting, either, providing me with both the perfect scapegoats and the perfect escape for myself.

No, I have to trust more endeavors to extemporaneous timing, especially since it seems to be working so well. But first, a little exercise, perhaps. To focus the mind.

Candy said, "Well, now, little brother, what kind of piece you have in mind?"

The skinny man stood in a doorway of the Arson Mall, sizing up the homeboy with the fade haircut in front of him. The skinny man was partial to the nose candy over smoking crack, and so he went by the street name "Candy." At thirty, Candy was one old motherfucker for this kind of trade, and he knew it.

"Uzi," said the homeboy.

Candy stroked his chin. "Uzi machine gun?"

"There another kind?"

The older man didn't like the attitude in the boy's voice. "As a matter of fact, little brother, there is." Candy let the put-down soak in some.

Homeboy coming for to buy a piece, chances are he ain't carrying at the time, otherwise he don't need to spend his money on my goods. "How much cash you got?"

"How much you asking?"

"For the Uzi — and don't you worry none, I knows where I can get you —"

"How much?"

No, Candy didn't care for the boy's attitude one bitty bit. Bumped his price some for it. "Four hundred."

Homeboy look like he got hit by a bus. "Four?"

"Too high for you, little brother? Got me a three-eight-oh semi for two, extra clip throwed in."

The homeboy reached toward a pocket in his pants. Money pocket, Candy figured, and the boy musta count it seven times afore he come shopping.

Boy said, "Give you a hundred for the thing."

Candy laughed. "Hundred don't get you no three-eight-oh, little brother."

"What do it get me?"

Candy stroked his chin some more. Boy's serious, smell of blood be on him already. "Hundred get you a revolver, six shots. Only thing is, I don't got no extra bullets for it."

The little brother said, "I'm good enough, won't even need all those six."

Candy nodded, then turned to the door behind him, knocking in a rhythm that ended abruptly. Thinking, *This homeboy gonna be superbad, once he grow up.*

If he grow up.

Exhaling, Sheilah Quinn opened the door to Etta Yemelman's office.

Inside, everything looked as it should. The diplomas, both undergraduate and law, framed and spaced on one wall. Her spare umbrella and a light raincoat hanging from an old coatrack that Etta had brought from her chambers upon retiring as a judge. The portable typewriter she used to make notes on five-by-eight cards. The only living thing a spider plant, which Etta always swore made the room fresher by absorbing carbon dioxide and giving off oxygen.

Taking a breath now, Sheilah realized that despite the plant, the room already smelled musty, as though it'd been closed for a week instead of just part of one day. Then she felt a little chill.

What would Krissie — or Frank — feel, coming into my office if I died?

Sheilah Quinn tried to shake that off.

Then tried again.

Gerry O'Toole made his lips flutter, nearly singing his next words. "I fucking hate fucking stakeouts."

Sitting in the passenger's seat of the unmarked sedan a diagonal half block from J. Leroy Washington, Esquire's picture window, Frank Sikes said, "I believe you're already on record about that."

"Yeah, well, underline it or something."

"You think of a better place for this Darnell to try for?"

"Other than his own? No."

"And he shows up there, I think his step-mother'll call us. She was pretty pissed about her 'rainy day' money. Knew how much it was, down to the dollar."

"Don't blame her," said Gerry. "I'd be — whoa, what appeareth now on yon horizon?"

They both watched a black kid, midteens, walk down the sidewalk. Hands jammed in the pockets of a baggy sweatshirt, head up, determination in his stride.

"Right haircut," said Frank.

Deepening and rounding his voice, Gerry said, "Will our lucky contestant choose door number one, door number —"

Without hesitation, the kid drew a hand from the sweatshirt and yanked on the knob next to the lawyer's window, going inside.

Opening the sedan's door, Gerry said, "I think we have a winner."

Frank stayed his partner's arm. "Let's wait a few minutes, see if they come out together."

"Why, Frank?"

"To cement the relationship. And the ID."

O'Toole fluttered his lips again, then said, "Okay," clicking the car door shut.

Thwock. "Fifteen love."

Dressed in casual slacks and another Polo shirt, Arthur Ketterson IV sat halfway up the wooden bleachers on the sideline, watching Larry, the tennis pro, serve to what looked like quite a competent player.

Until Larry served, that is.

Thwock. "Thirty love."

Arthur had heard rumors that the women at the club were simply mad for Larry, and one could certainly see why in a moths-to-the-flame sense. The muscles of his tanned legs bunched and stretched like cords of fiber. There was grace in his movement around the court, all body parts shifting in elegant, perpetual balance. Even the striking disproportionality of his serving forearm — being noticeably larger in circumference than his other one, as though he'd borrowed the former from a man twenty pounds heavier. Add in the skimpy shorts over tight buns and Larry made quite a package.

Thwock. "Forty love."

Arthur had always believed the absence of talk among males about other men's bodies to be a good practice. Latent homosexuality and all that. But such consensus didn't reduce the pleasure of observing a tennis pro cavort and lunge, especially when there was no hint of impropriety in acting the role of spectator.

Thwock. "That's game. Let's take a break."

As Larry came to the side of the net, he made a

show of noticing Arthur for the first time, which seemed disingenuous of him. Surely even a tennis professional's concentration wasn't exclusionary of everything — and everyone — around him.

"Mr. Ketterson," Larry called out. "How are you?"

"Quite well, thank you."

To his rather winded opponent, Larry said, "Be right back," then jogged easily over and up to where Arthur was sitting. "Interested in another session?"

Just the slightest whiff of something there. Greed, thought Arthur. A manageable quality. "Yes, Larry, I would be. If you have some time after this match."

"Technically, no. I've got another club member on for two. But" — Larry looked around conspiratorially — "for you, I can call her and break it, no pro-*blame*-oh."

Arthur tried not to wince at that last cliché. "Excellent. An hour from now, then?"

"Looking forward to it already, Mr. Ketterson. We'll put you through your paces."

And with that, Larry winked before jogging back to his opponent.

Arthur stood and began walking in the direction of the locker room to change. No pro-*blame*-oh. He shook his head.

Moths and flames notwithstanding, I don't imagine the club women stay with Lunging Larry all that long.

Sheilah Quinn found herself moving slowly around Etta's office, touching the little artifacts that defined the older woman so clearly. The framed certificate of her appointment to the bench, marking the beginning of her judicial career. The bronzed gavel, a gift from Sheilah and all Etta's other law clerks through the years, marking the end of that career but not retirement, a concept the proud older — but never old — attorney had found abhorrent. "What would I do, Sheilah, can you tell me that? Watch soap operas? Take senior citizen buses to the casinos? What?"

No, Etta would never have retired. It might have been nice, though, if she could have spent more of her later years with Irv, whose face smiled up from a Lucite frame on Etta's desk. Sheilah had met him over dinner at their house the week she started as Etta's clerk. Irv Yemelman had been a kindly, huggy-bear of a man, the sort you would once imagine as a girlfriend's father. The sort Sheilah now thought of as someone with whom to grow older — but not old herself, either.

Touching the frame above the smile, Sheilah Quinn sighed. Tomorrow, I'll have to put these things in a box — lovingly.

Sitting behind his chambers desk, Roger Hesterfield pried his eyes away from the accumulated mementos of a career. Can't trust the movers with them, can't trust anybody. Except

Old Bailey, of course, who *is* trust. Coined the term, practically.

The man's knock on the door. "Yes, O.B.?"

He stuck his head in. "Your Honor, I got those cartons for you a little early."

Roger Hesterfield felt his eyes closing, willed them to reopen. "Thank you, O.B. Bring them in."

"Oh, and since you're not holding court tomorrow, I switched shifts with Vinnie, so I'll be on the desk downstairs, four to twelve, in case you need help with anything."

Touching, the man sacrificing his Friday night for my convenience. "I appreciate that." Hesterfield began shuffling papers on his desk. "There's a memo here somewhere about how to get them moved to the new building."

"I've got that covered, too, Your Honor. Saturday morning, early, I'm going over there, check out your new digs. Then I'll come back here with a handcart, move everything like it was crystal glass."

Sacrificing half his weekend, as well. "O.B., thank you."

"Glad to do it, Your Honor."

As the door closed, Roger Hesterfield looked around the room again, and the thin veneer of good feeling applied by Old Bailey's fealty evaporated like morning mist on an August pond.

Sitting against a handrail on the granite wheelchair ramp in front of the new courthouse, Rudy

Giordano made check marks in pencil on the punch list for the building. Not much more to go, but best to have the guys working the first part of next week here, no question.

In the old days, when he was growing the company, Rudy would put in a four-to-twelve shift himself, even a midnight-to-eight, although the noise level that accompanied construction could set neighbors from half a mile away against you. Then, once Jessica was born, he tried not to be gone from the house as much, especially as she was growing up. Never wanted to be one of those fathers who missed his daughter's childhood.

But now Rudy thought about Rhonda, back at the house. The photos, the times with Jessica they brought back, crushing him like . . . a drill press, was what it was. Crushing him every day, morning, noon, and night.

Tearing his mind away from that, Rudy considered what he had to do over at the old courthouse. Plenty of work, especially with stripping that bastard Hesterfield's little suite there. Take down the chandeliers, the wainscoting, even save the benches, that kind of stuff. No sense in blowing everything to smithereens along with the building when the dynamite finally gets planted. Lots of restoration places pay through the nose for the real thing.

Not to mention the satisfaction I'll get from doing everything with my own hands. Maybe even get to see that old fart Hesterfield squirm as I do it.

Yeah, a four-to-twelve tomorrow didn't seem like such a bad idea, except that Rudy was supposed to be meeting Terri Como at that fern bar around six. So maybe work some of the weekend instead. Tell Rhonda he had to be on the job site all day Saturday — except for the puppet show — and Sunday, too, then spend part of the time with Terri instead.

Yeah, it had possibilities, that kind of plan.

"You been timing how long our Darnell's been in there?" asked Gerry O'Toole from behind the wheel.

"If he is 'our Darnell.' " Frank Sikes glanced down at his watch. "I make it two minutes."

"Long enough that if they were coming out, we would have seen them by now, right?"

"I'd say so. Let's go."

It helped that their car doors were open, but both Gerry and Frank would later swear to the Shoot Team that they believed the three crumping sounds from inside the building would have reached them anyway.

"Good-bye, Etta."

Closing the door to her partner's office, Sheilah moved into her own. The flowers from Arthur Ketterson were beginning to wilt. No, that wasn't fair, was it? Some of them had drooped or discolored, but most were still pretty perky. And pretty . . . well, pretty.

Using her thumb and forefinger to pinch off

the dead and the dying, Sheilah felt better. The arrangement looked smaller, but stronger now. Lesson there, girl, a lesson from Etta, really. Not one to dwell on today, though. One to come back to.

Then Sheilah picked up her telephone, checking in with the answering service. Roger Hesterfield was on there, the bastard, with an unctuous message about continuing the Diaz case till Monday, just as Peter Mendez had said at the temple that morning. Just as Sheilah hadn't given Roger the time to say the prior afternoon when she'd slapped him outside the old courthouse.

The extended continuance was a mixed blessing: in a way, getting back on trial tomorrow would have been better, a distraction from Etta, the way working has been a distraction from the nursing home and Dad. Sheilah shook her head. No, being on trial tomorrow would be better only for me, not better for my client.

Among the other condolences with the answering service was Arthur Ketterson's, just as he'd said at the cemetery. Such a weird guy — face it, disquieting even, sometimes — but an empathetic streak in him, too. Some people are hard to read, I guess.

No messages from Frank Sikes, though after the way Sheilah had cut him off about the suspects in Etta's death, she couldn't really blame him.

Dripping perspiration, Arthur reached for the

towel draped over the end post of the net. He watched Larry jogging around the court, gathering up the six new balls they'd used over the last hour. Extraordinary, thought Arthur. The man doesn't look as though he's even broken a sweat. As Larry bounded up to him, the worst you could say was that a lock of hair had fallen across his forehead.

"Great match, Mr. Ketterson."

Arthur mopped his face with the towel. "Thank you, Larry. You certainly kept your promise."

A distressingly vacant look from the blue, blue eyes. "My promise? "

The physique of a god, the retention span of a gnat. "Yes. Your promise to . . . 'put me through my paces,' I believe?"

"Oh, right." A different look now, some kind of twinkle in the eyes. "Maybe later — after we're cleaned up, I mean — we could have a drink."

Arthur was caught off guard. "A drink?"

Larry brushed the errant lock of hair with the middle finger of his serving hand. "And maybe after that, you could . . . put me through my paces."

Arthur dropped his towel, could feel the blood surging into his features. "Get out of my sight."

"Hey, I'm —"

"Now!"

"Mr. Ket—"

"Or would you rather I had you fired."

Not really a question. Larry backed away, mumbling "Sorry" over and over again.

Arthur sensed a trembling beginning at his ankles. Knew it would work its way up through the shins, knees, and thighs. Ever northward until he quaked with rage.

Stalking stiffly toward the clubhouse, Arthur Ketterson pulled a white cotton tennis sweater over his head, preferring to drive home drenched rather than chance an encounter in the locker room.

Taking the stairs back toward the street, Darnell Fuquay couldn't believe how well it went down in Charles's crib. Every step, he replayed in his mind what happened. Like there was a VCR hooked up between his ears, you know? He could hear it, see it, *smell* it. Sah-tis-*fac*-tion. The last of Charles, starring in every scene.

Charles opening the door to Darnell's knock and his "Yo, homeboy? It's me."

Charles, his eyes inside those hooky rings all innocent, friendly even. "Hey, homey, thought you wasn't coming by till tomorrow?"

Charles, his eyes changing some when Darnell flat-handed him in the chest, pushing him back toward the TV tray from where the motherfuck was eating some kind of marshmallow-shit cookies.

Charles snapping at him. "The fuck you doing, man?" Just before Darnell showed him the business end of the piece.

Charles freezing then, putting both hands out, his eyes doing jump-ups. "Homey, don't —"

Charles taking the first bullet just about where Darnell pushed him, center of the chest, driving him back a step.

Charles trying to say something, only Darnell can't hear the motherfuck, account of the noise from the gun messing with his ears.

Charles taking the second bullet, lower, folding him up some on his way to the floor. Eyes squeezed shut, like a little baby crying cause he shit his pants.

Charles taking the third, back of the head, down by his neck, rolling over the way a little baby do, too. Eyes open now, blood coming out the mouth like somebody broke a jar of it inside his throat.

Charles dead on the floor, motherfucker never gonna give another homey up to the Man. Close the door on that shiftless piece a shit, let him rot to his bones in there.

Then, as Darnell hit the second landing, he saw the two pigs was with the old woman across his street yesterday. He never did hear them coming up the stairs, though, not with the way the shots in Charles's crib done fucked with his hearing. The white one was first on the one side of the steps, the brown one hard behind him on the other side.

They saying something, too, but Darnell not hearing them. Busy aiming his piece for the second time in a minute, thinking, Damn good thing I didn't waste all my bullets on that piece a honky-eyed shit upstairs.

Then Darnell got punched when there wasn't nobody there to punch him. Strong punch, too, like a professional boxer. And it took him back some, his elbow bouncing off the step behind his body, only he didn't feel nothing. Trying to raise the piece again, another punch. Hard in the mouth, felt like. Except Darnell couldn't feel it, neither. Not really.

Trying to bring the piece up once more, this time getting punched three, four, five —

Not fair, man, the pigs got all these invisible boxers working for them.

Sheilah Quinn locked the corridor side of the office door and dropped the key case into her handbag. She hadn't moved five steps toward the elevators when she heard the phone ringing behind her. The answering service picked up, though, and Sheilah went on, thinking, I hope Dad's sharp again tonight.

Arthur Ketterson tried not to let his fury infect his driving. First that whore at the trial, the one I paid to fly in from Seattle. Now Larry, the tennis pro at a club that costs the earth to —

Arthur sensed the BMW slipping away from him and mustered all of his concentration to refocus. Mother's advice: Control, control. "Castle walls, Arthur. Maintain those castle walls."

But he had to do something. An . . . antidote to this nonsense. A sexual conquest was out of the question, given his mood, if nothing else. Better to address an issue — any issue — that already was on the agenda.

Suddenly, Arthur brightened. Timing over plan, again. Treat that revolting incident at the club as an omen. An omen for his next step into uncomplicating Sheilah's life.

Arthur looked down at his clothing. Best to stop home first and shower. Then change into something a medical-supply store would find less memorable than tennis togs.

Arthur Ketterson felt himself smile, and the perfect joy of mastering the Beemer, of being in control generally, began to reassert itself.

Our unit was into Germany, some farm land just before the Elbe River, when we found a spread looked like any other, except that most of the barn was burned. An accident, I figured.

Well, it was no accident.

No, inside that barn were over a hundred people — men, women, and children. Jews, maybe, but the Germans, they'd . . . machine- gunned these people. Sweet Jesus, the bodies piled up against the doors, the fingernails gone from their hands as they'd tried to burrow into the dirt floor, away from the bullets or . . . the fire. Because after the Germans shot these poor devils, they set fire to —

"Grenade! Grenade!"

I jerked my head up then, saw the German soldier

400

who threw it. One of those goddamn potato-masher things, would have looked like a mallet except the handle was stuck in the wrong end of the tin-can head. I fired three rounds at the soldier, saw him —

Then a flash in front of me, and . . . nothing.

"Not much you can do, child," said Lucille Wesley. "God will take him soon."

Sheilah Quinn looked down at her father. Squeezing his hand barely got a tremor, nothing like the awareness he'd shown just the day before, when she'd unloaded the whole Etta tragedy on him.

How could I have been so selfish, so inconsiderate? Here he is, staring death in the face every day, however benign the surroundings, and I lobbed in the ugliness of the outside world to try to make myself feel a little better.

"Lucille, has he been like this all day?"

"All day. Fact is, last night with you is the onliest time I seen Jack perk up for I don't know how long."

Sheilah searched her own memory, found it faulty, but also knew she couldn't disagree. Squeezing her father's hand again, Sheilah tapped a finger against his cheek and then ran her fingernail down along it. No response at all this time.

She turned her head toward the door. "Can you look in on him once in awhile?"

"Always do, child. You take your time with him now."

As Lucille moved up the corridor and away, Sheilah squeezed Jack Quinn's hand one last time, then replaced the nurse's call button in it. "Dad, I'll see you again soon, okay?"

But given the way the week had gone so far, Sheilah Quinn wasn't sure she believed that herself.

Opening the driver's door to the unmarked sedan, Gerry O'Toole said, "Shoot Team finished with you?"

Frank Sikes looked up at him. "Just about, I think, but they said to hang around anyway."

O'Toole slid in behind the wheel. "I was slow back there. Being closer than you, I should have put the first one in him. I told them that."

Frank rested his head against the whiplash protector mounted on the bench seat. "You're welcome."

A very small laugh. "I said these kids were dirty, remember? Said it five times over."

"Turns out you were right, too. Doesn't mean I wouldn't have liked to talk to Darnell about the Yemelman thing, though."

"Good thing we had a set of Fuquay's prints on file. My jaw shot pretty much ruined his good looks."

Frank didn't reply, but above his right ear, a female voice said, "Okay." The brass in charge of the Shoot Team was standing next to the sedan, holding a clipboard in her hand. "Tentative call pending the lab work: WDR."

Meaning "within departmental regulations," a righteous shoot.

A pat on the roof of their car. "You guys are cleared from here."

Gerry and Frank said thanks, meaning it, and watched her move back to her own people.

"So," said O'Toole, "I could use some whiskey."

"I'll join you, but just for one."

"Jesus, you rationing yourself or what?"

"I want to go back over the Giordano file."

"Frank, give me a break, huh? And give it a break, too. Arthur fucking Ketterson is probably still floating around on cloud nine from the hung jury there, and he's too fucking flaky to think about going anywhere for a while."

Sikes looked over. "One drink, Gerry. And I want to find a pay phone first, okay?"

From the medical-supply store, Arthur Ketterson drove almost sedately toward a part of town that, though unfamiliar to him, seemed genteel. Well, perhaps not authentic gentry, but at least the homes enjoyed decent-sized lots and there were a number that wouldn't look suspiciously incongruous with a shiny BMW adorning their curbs.

Arthur picked one such house and parked in front of it. Reaching into the backseat for the vinyl backpack he'd so carefully filled in his bedroom at Woodmere; Arthur also brought to his lap the bag of items he'd purchased from the medical-supply store. Opening the bag, he took out the white laboratory smock first. After shrugging into it — no mean feat in a bucket seat — Arthur removed the length of thin black tubing, too, arranging it in a side pocket of the smock so that the tubing bowed up and out. Like a stethoscope, he believed.

And wished others to believe, as well.

Then Arthur left and locked the car, swinging the backpack into place between his shoulder blades and enjoying a fleeting memory of the old crone, strolling for the last time toward the subway station. Then he refocused. Concentrate on the things at hand.

For the five remaining blocks to Valley Nursing Home, Arthur Ketterson practiced and eventually perfected that "Out of my way; I'm on a mission" walk he'd seen so many doctors affecting over the years.

Within five minutes after stepping through the apartment door, Sheilah Quinn was running the bath in her tub. The tape machine on the bedroom night table glowed six messages back at her, but she decided they could wait.

The sound of the air burbling through the water barely allowed her to hear the telephone ring. Somehow, Sheilah thought it might be Frank, but she was too much into the bath to jump up, towel off, and hope to run into the other room before the phone stopped ringing.

Besides, Frank, it might be nice to hear your

voice on my tape as many times as I want to. The way the machine will let me, just before I go to sleep.

". . . before you heard about it on the news. This probably closes the thing out, Sheil, but if you don't think so, give me a call."

Frank Sikes hung up the pay phone.

"You get who you wanted?" said O'Toole through the open car window.

"Not quite. How about that drink?"

"We're halfway there."

Just outside the main entrance of the nursing home, Arthur Ketterson looked around. No one in sight. Excellent. He pulled a manila file from the backpack, leaving the clasp unfastened so the top would flap behind him as he walked.

Strode, really. On his mission.

Marching across the lobby, his nose in the opened file, Arthur was positive he got a better look at the somnolent security guard than the guard did at him. After glancing at the white lab coat and manila folder, the incompetent buffoon never even raised his eyes toward Arthur's face.

There were little signs indicating which corridor led to which room numbers, including 107. Without breaking stride, Arthur veered into the wing he wanted, just in time to see an enormous Negro matron wearing a pink uniform disappear into what seemed to be some sort of employee lounge. Walking past the doorway she'd used, Arthur confirmed the enclosure's purpose.

A bit farther down, he found Room 107. Pausing just a moment, Arthur looked up and down the corridor. Not a creature was stirring. Excellent again.

He opened the door and, being careful to allow for the backpack, slipped into the room.

It was that trite motif of hospital-*cum*-Holiday-Inn that Arthur assumed such places attempted to project. There was a chair next to a bed, an ancient and terribly gaunt man lying under the sheets, inert.

Silently, Arthur settled into the chair. A dragonfly lighting upon a lily pad, he thought to himself.

First thing I remember is looking over to the next cot in the field hospital. I'd been hit, I knew, but nothing like the poor devil next to me. Head bandage, all kinds of tubes. Draining him, from the angle of them.

My own wound didn't hurt much, just like somebody'd whacked you with a baseball bat. But it was shrapnel, and tore off a hunk of skin as well as doing in a couple of ribs. The doctors were pretty good about coming around, especially with all the GIs they had to look after. And at least I'd be getting better, going home without much except a close call and a scar to remember it by. Not like the poor devil —

Wait a minute. Who's this with the funny hair? A new doc coming to check on me?

After popping two sleeping pills, Sheilah Quinn played back the tape messages. A teary one from Krissie, saying she'd be in the next day, a few more condolences, and a couple of computer-dial hang-up calls from telephone solicitors. The new message was Frank's voice all right, sounding a little down, talking about finding one of the suspects in Etta's killing, even more down about the other one getting shot. But solid, reassuring her that he was fine, though indicating she might have trouble reaching him by phone before the next morning at the station.

Not adding, I need you tonight, Sheil. Damn, why can't men just say that when they mean it?

Or even just say it, whether they mean it or not.

Sheilah turned off the machine. Shook her head over the entire tragedy of Etta's death, all the lives it had darkened. Or ended.

Then Sheilah Quinn went to bed, thinking that at least the world couldn't turn any worse tonight.

Taking the call button from the ancient's hand, Arthur Ketterson marveled at the latent strength remaining in the fingers. Before that, he'd spent a good two minutes watching the man's eyeballs moving under their lids. Time well spent, too, like watching an aged dog on its porch, having a dream.

However, when Arthur squeezed the hand, the

ancient's eyes opened suddenly, searchingly. Perfect. But is he visually aware of me, as well?

Arthur passed his free hand back and forth in front of the man's face. Yes. Yes, he definitely follows my movement.

"So," said Arthur, lowering his hand and shrugging his shoulders to allow the white smock to drape without wrinkles, "Sheilah tells me you were quite the war hero."

Back at his desk in the squad room, Frank Sikes set his mug down next to the telephone. He considered dialing Sheilah's home number again, then thought, What if she's trying to get some sleep? He let it go.

Opening the Giordano file, Frank started with the embarrassed — and embarrassing — statement O'Toole had taken from the Como woman. Pretty obvious what Rudolph Giordano had been after in that bar.

Which only reminded Sikes of what bothered him the most about the case. What was Arthur Ketterson after in dating those other women who testified for him? If they were "below his station," and it wasn't sex, and he didn't kill them, what the hell could they possibly have done for him?

Pulling on the mug of coffee, he kept reading.

Goofy-looking guy for an army doctor, though. And not just the haircut, either. No insignia, no sense of . . . command. Doctors have to be officers — at least all the ones I've seen are. Plus the guy's way of talking is off, too.

And how the hell does he know Sheilah? She isn't even born yet.

Padding toward the refrigerator in his stocking feet, Rudy Giordano could already taste the next beer.

Rhonda yelled to him from the living room. "Rude, when you get back, there's this wonderful shot of Jess from her First Holy Communion."

Giordano stopped just shy of the handle on the fridge. Nobody can live like this, nobody.

The voice again, pitched too high. Rhonda's way of trying to carry around corners. "Hey?"

Rudy Giordano thought once more about that Terri broad. Second thoughts, kind of.

Oh, she was good-looking, all right, with the big hair and earrings, that easy, trashy way some women just seem to have naturally. And sympathetic to my problem, you think about her setting up another date with me for tomorrow night. But too much of a risk to see her again in that bar, and then maybe over the weekend to boot?

"Rudy?" Rhonda pitching her voice even higher, like a fucking air-raid siren now. "Rudy, you hear me?"

Uh-uh, thought Rudy Giordano, hearing Terri Como's voice instead. Maybe not too much of a risk at all.

Fluffing up the extra pillow, Arthur Ketterson said, "My temporary associate, Mr. Willie T. Eggers, instructed me on this procedure. It's quite simple, actually."

Arthur looked into the ancient's eyes. Truly aware, however impaired he might be. His eyes weren't like my others, though, the women. Even the Persimmon Queen, who'd have been about his age, too. No, this war hero was a man who'd known death, most likely had even dispensed it himself.

A man who knew what was coming.

Arthur gripped the pillow firmly at each of the long ends. As he lowered it toward Jack Quinn's face, Arthur peered over the top, trying not to lose those knowing eyes until they were absolutely, positively blocked by the pillow itself.

Then Arthur could feel the crabbed hand clawing at the sheets, the legs shuddering, the chest heaving. Willie had said the technique would "get by" as a heart attack, and my now personal observations would lead me to — Wait. Have we already . . .

The tremors quieted, and a stillness descended over the bed. Arthur counted to thirty, then lifted the pillow very carefully, as he remembered once raising a toy bucket while making a sand castle at the beach. Then Arthur looked down. And smiled.

The ancient's eyes were open — bulging, even — but no longer aware. Just . . . glazed.

410

Now like all the others. A deep sense of satisfaction enveloped Arthur at that moment, the inherent universality of all things human shimmering within his soul.

Sheilah Quinn awakened with a start, too groggy to remember at first where she was, then unable to remember what in her dream had disturbed her. Instinctively, she reached out for Mr. Fuzzums but couldn't find him.

Couldn't find him. "Quigley. Quigley did something . . . to . . ."

Then the pills overtook her again, and Sheilah rolled onto her side, dropping back into sleep.

"Peace at last, peace at last."

Arthur Ketterson remembered a line his mother once read to him: "Old soldiers never die; they only . . . fade away."

To be absolutely sure here, however, I should check neck and wrist for a pulse.

Both nil. Excellent beyond excellence.

Arthur slipped the spare pillow back on its side of the bed. Then he arranged the nurse's call button so that it was almost, but not quite, in Jack Quinn's left hand. Arthur pictured the real doctor coming by — probably the next morning — to pronounce the ancient dead. "See that button there? So near and yet so far when the old ticker finally went crazy on him."

Arthur returned to the present. I'd like to spend more time here, enjoying the sense of peace I've brought both this husk and Sheilah, once she finds out yet another complication has been excised from her life. But tarrying too long around any corpse is unwise. Unwise in the extreme.

Reaching around to his backpack, Arthur opened the flap and took out the stuffed teddy bear from Sheilah's apartment. He tucked the tattered toy into the space between the ancient's elbow and rib cage, as though the man had fallen asleep . . . hugging it.

At least that's how the staff should see it. Sheilah, on the other hand, would have to wonder how her beloved keepsake had made its way from her bedroom to her father's deathbed.

One complication deleted, another added. Sheilah, my Sheilah, how you'll thank me for all this. Eventually.

And soon.

Then Arthur gathered himself, took a last, admiring look at his handiwork, and slipped quietly from the room.

Lucille Wesley figured she'd just about had her fill of the white trash sitting and smoking at the end of the lounge table. For the last ten minutes, Orville been bragging on hisself with one of the other janitors. Bragging on how, the last place he worked, he took cigarettes off a resident he found dead one night in her bed.

"They weren't no good for her, anyways," said Orville, getting a big laugh from the other.

Lucille stood and left without a backward glance. Walking down the corridor, she thought she might stop in, see how that old soldier Jack was doing. At his room, she pushed open the door, looked toward the bed, then sucked in a breath. Turning on the light, she moved slowly to the bed.

"Jack, Jack." Lucille touched his left hand. "You had yourself a harder living than many, and a harder dying than most. But you be in heaven now, forever and ever, Amen."

Then Lucille noticed the stuffed animal, which she'd never seen before. Old raggedy thing, too. Now, where did . . .

Her eyes went over the bed, stopping on the spare pillow. Picking it up, Lucille examined both sides of its case. Mucous or phlegm stains.

She put just the tippy tip of a finger on the edge of one yellow blot. Still damp, but how . . .

"Oh no." Thinking back to seeing the daughter that other night, the pillow in her hands. "You poor child." Then looking down at the bed again. "You gots to forgive her, Jack. She just couldn't stand for you to be like you was no more."

Glancing at the damp stains once more, Lucille wavered, then made up her mind. Going to the other bed, she swapped pillows so a clean one would be next to Jack's head when the doctor got called. Which could wait awhile, maybe till morning even. Let the lawyer woman go home, get herself some sleep.

If she can.

Then Lucille picked up the stuffed teddy bear. Poor raggedy thing, all right. Like a present her daddy give the child when she was just a little tyke.

Cradling the animal in the crook of her arm, Lucille Wesley thought, I leave this here in Jack's bed, it going to be thrown out. Or worse, stole altogether, the white trash they got working this place. Better I save it for the daughter, for when she able to appreciate it again.

Lucille Wesley moved toward the door. Turning once, she said, "You rest in peace now, Jack," before reaching for the light.

SIXTEEN

A disaster, thought Peter Mendez on Friday morning, sucking vigorously on a maximum-strength Sucrets to prepare his voice for the outdoor press conference. A fucking disaster, that's what this is going to be.

Shifting from foot to foot on the steps of the new courthouse — which Mort Zussman had insisted would make a "great backdrop for the stand-up, Peter" — Mendez could see Robert Agonian at the curb. The representative for the West Shore was trying to lever himself out of the backseat of a Pontiac driven by a younger guy with similar features, maybe a nephew on the legislative tit. But Mendez hadn't yet seen the other two reps Agonian had promised him, and there was no sign of even Mort himself.

The fuck is he? Peter shot a look at his watch. It was 10:10 A.M. We told the media 9:30 sharp for the stand-up.

And, wouldn't you know it, the media is here on time for once. Not many print people: They like to have their chairs, sit down and take notes.

But Mendez counted three radio and two television stations, one a network affiliate, the other a local independent struggling with a couple of cast-off, has-been anchors and three or four on air reporters who didn't have the looks or voices for a major market.

The media's champing at the bit, and we're not ready for them. Great, Mort. Just fucking great.

"So," said Frank Sikes into the telephone receiver on Friday morning, "the doctor thinks it was a heart attack?"

"Sometime after I left him." Sheilah's voice sounded listless, distant. "In his sleep, though. Dad never pressed the nurse's call button."

Frank thought of some old-age homes he'd visited where the staff wasn't so attentive. Their attitude: Best to let the disoriented elderly leave us as soon as possible.

He said, "Well, at least we have your partner's situation squared away."

"The black — the African-American kids?"

Despite the memories of yesterday's shoot-out, Frank felt a rush of warmth from the week-end at the inn. Everything she's been through the last few days, and she's still trying to —

"Frank?"

"Sorry, Sheil. Yeah, we figure a kid named Darnell pushed her, and after Gerry and I picked up the other kid, Charles, this Darnell decided his buddy was planning to rat him out."

"So Darnell goes over to shut Charles up."

"With a Saturday night special."

"Jesus, Frank. I'm really glad you're all right."

"The question is, Are you?"

"No." A tiny laugh. "No, but I will be. It's just been . . . quite a week."

Gerry O'Toole brought a coffee to Frank's desk, cover still on the cup to keep it warm. O'Toole pointed to the phone, but Sikes shook his head as he said into the receiver, "When's your dad's wake?"

"Don't come, Frank."

That sounded odd, almost as though she was embarrassed to have him in the same room with her. Sikes waited until O'Toole began walking across the room before he said, "Why not, Sheil?"

"Because with the *Ketterson* case still hanging fire, it wouldn't look right. And besides, my father outlived his generation. I'm just having a viewing today for the few friends left, then a simple cremation tomorrow."

"Cremation."

"So I can keep him with me a little longer."

That sounded even odder, but he'd already asked her if she was okay. "You going to see if Hesterfield will grant another continuance in the armed-robbery thing?"

"No," she said firmly, almost shouting it. "I've asked that bastard for my last favor."

"Sheilah, how can you prepare a case with what's happened to you?"

"Frank, if I don't have something to do, I'll go nuts. I've already called Krissie, and she knows to tell people I'll be working home today."

Best not to push too hard. "Call me if I can help, huh?"

"With the armed robbery?"

"Not what I meant."

"I know. And thanks."

Hanging up the phone, Frank Sikes noticed the Giordano file again. He moved the coffee Gerry'd brought him aside and, feeling a little bit like a traitor to the woman he'd just reassured, opened the folder and started reading.

Roger Hesterfield shunted a file off to the growing pile on the corner of his chambers desk.

There's enough paperwork to take me through the rest of the morning. Until two or three, in fact, if I milk it. And why not? Go out of here the way I lived here, doing —

Hesterfield stopped. Funny, I was thinking *lived*, not *worked*. This place has been more of a home to me than my house. Is that what's making it so hard to move out of the First Session and into the new courthouse?

He glanced over at the empty cartons O.B. had brought him.

Opening the next file, Roger Hesterfield realized there was more than enough paperwork to take him deep into the afternoon.

"What do you mean, they're not coming?"

Robert Agonian, who was already out of breath from climbing the Mayan pyramid of courthouse steps, didn't seem to like the way this candidate was expressing his gratitude. "Whyn't you say it a little louder, Petey? Hear it as the lead for the retirees tuned into the nooner news."

Peter Mendez struggled to control himself. Have to lower my voice. "But, Bob, you promised me that —"

"Whoa, whoa. I said I'd try to get Sharon and Chuck, but your guy Zussman gave my people less than a day to coordinate this. That's not much time, you know?"

Mendez knew Agonian was right, but one of the radio guys — Chinese-American, and a law graduate with a baritone voice like an opera singer — was already tapping the face of his wristwatch, and a woman from the local independent was looking back to her TV truck, shrugging at the techie who'd been waving to her.

Got to get this show on the road before the media hits the road. "Okay, folks," said Peter Mendez in a commanding tone. "We're ready to start. I'll be speaking first, followed by Representative Agonian, whom I'm sure you all already know."

Quigley sprawling over her lap like an organic electric blanket, Sheilah Quinn began writing things down on a checklist. More to do for her father's funeral than she'd realized talking on the phone to Frank, and this time she didn't have a rabbi to help her.

Dad, Dad. I don't blame you for not staying religious after Mom died, but for this, a friendly priest might have helped, you know?

Sheilah looked back down at the checklist. *God, how am I going to handle this?*

Having slept until 10:15, Arthur Ketterson was sitting at the dining table, a farmhand's breakfast half-finished in front of him. He needed the fuel, after last night's exertions, both physical and intellectual. But he found his mind wandering from the eggs and sausage to his next step.

Certainly the "natural" passing of just another nursing-home ancient wouldn't be newsworthy enough to trigger media coverage. That means I'll have to contact Sheilah's office, and be told about the current tragedy the same way I "learned" about the old crone. On the other hand, it might look suspicious for me to call again on the morning after another "complication" has slid off Sheilah's shoulders.

But perhaps not suspicious at all if I was inquiring as to how she's holding up after her partner's demise, and when I might contact her toward my own case, which, after all, is still dangling from some thread in the judicial system's loom.

Yes, that's it.

"Is everything satisfactory, sir?"

"Yes, Parons. Just fine."

"Thank you, sir."

420

Arthur Ketterson did, in fact, like his breakfast. But he liked being subtly oblique even more.

Rudy Giordano waited for the wave of nausea to pass. Standing next to the construction trailer outside the new courthouse, he looked at all the shit that had piled up over the course of the project. Remnants of new carpeting, some six-by-ten pieces, some even bigger. Ruined bathroom fixtures, either delivered broken or busted up by ham-handed laborers carrying them in. Scrap heaps of cracked stones, noncomplying lumber, strip linoleum. And the sledges, pry bars, and other hand tools that stayed stacked behind the trailer as the crews finally wound down on this job, just four or five spare hard hats left.

Four or five. If only I'd stopped at that many drinks last night.

But no. Rhonda and her fucking photo albums. I'm coming to work earlier, staying here later, all to avoid her. Then last night, going out for a few pops, kind of a warm-up to seeing that Terri broad tonight. Finally having something to look forward to, something —

Wait a minute. Who's that yelling? Familiar voice, too.

". . . followed by Representative Agonian, whom I'm sure you all . . ."

Mendez. That fucking DA, the lawyer who couldn't win at poker with a pat fucking hand.

Forgetting the way his stomach felt, Rudy

Giordano walked around to the front steps of the new courthouse.

Frank Sikes popped the cover off the coffee. It always came back to the same question. Why these other women, Artie?

He took a sip from the cup, then rubbed his left eye with the knuckle of his index finger, like a little kid cranky after too short a nap. But the answer didn't come.

Why does a person spend time with people he doesn't seem interested in?

Frank saw that a couple drops of coffee were going to slide off the lid and onto the desk. Better move the cover . . .

"And therefore, Representative Agonian and I intend to sponsor a bill that will restore the death penalty to our commonwealth, a punishment which truly fits the crimes of —"

"Then how come you couldn't get that for my daughter?"

Peter Mendez didn't believe his ears. At first, though the voice was rough and sort of offstage, he thought it was a Johnny-come-lately reporter, believing that by now the press conference was into questions from the audience. But even a tardy reporter should know better than to interrupt a candidate's answer to another reporter's question.

And then Peter's eyes picked up the source of the voice. Picked it up just as his ears were recognizing whom the voice belonged to. A few of the reporters were turning toward the man in the hard hat at the bottom of the courthouse steps, also recognizing him, whispers of "Giordano," and "You know, the guy whose . . ."

Peter thought, I can't believe this is happening to me.

"Well, what do you say, '*coun*selor'?" Rudy Giordano's voice, carrying some in the open air. "How come you couldn't get the kind of justice you're talking about here for my Jessica?"

Have to salvage this. Somehow. "Uh, we'll be happy to take questions, but not until after Representative Agonian presents his prepared remarks."

Seeing Giordano wave a hand and stomp off in disgust, Peter smiled brightly for the cameras. He glanced hopefully just once toward the jowly pol next to him.

Agonian then cleared his throat and said, "I believe District Attorney Mendez has put forth the issues as clearly as anyone could. Now, if you'll excuse me?"

Peter felt the smile die on his face as Agonian waddled down the steps.

The Chinese reporter/lawyer said, "Mr. Mendez, how can you ask the *legislature* to pass another death penalty bill when the state supreme court in the *Jervis* case — a case you yourself argued and lost — invalidated the *concept* of capital punishment on a state *constitutional* ground?"

Peter Mendez closed his eyes, trying to make time stop.

Sheilah felt Quigley awaken and jump down off her lap. Once on the floor, he shook himself the way a wet dog does and began to stretch. Front legs flat out like a supplicant first, then straightening his shoulders before stretching the back legs, too, one at a time, yanking each rear paw forward a little, as though it had been caught in a snare.

"Quigley, you are a caution." Then Sheilah shook her own head. I'm fixating on my cat because I don't want to get started doing the things on this checklist.

She set the completed list on the end table before getting up herself. All right, girl, you know the drill. Go to the kitchen and make some tea. Then come back in here and start with the phone calls.

. . . cover? "Cover." Sure, *as* cover.

Frank Sikes stared at the lid from his coffee cup. You spend time with someone you aren't interested in as cover for what you are interested in. Or for who you're interested in, and when you're interested in them.

Think about it. The time frame for Arthur Ketterson dating these other women might give some indication of what he was using them as cover for.

Frank went back over the statements of the

424

defense witnesses in his file, but all three women had been vague about exact dates, like "Arthur and I dated each other for a couple of months last year." He thought he remembered their trial testimony being more specific, though.

Fuck, what's the use of it?, thought Rudy Giordano.

That wimp prosecutor, ranting on about how he's gonna bring back the death penalty. "A punishment that truly fits the crime" — I let him get that far. Fucking hypocrite, there's no such thing as justice in this world. Not in a court-house, not even in my *own* house.

Before Jessica . . . died, Rudy could have divorced Rhonda. No grounds against her, but in the bars, he'd heard a lot of guys talk about no-fault divorce. *Irreconcilable differences,* Rudy thought the magic words were. Only problem was, Rhonda would hire some kind of lawyer, who'd clean him out but good, take everything he'd worked for, built up over the years from his own sweat and blood. Which had always kept Rudy from pursuing the divorce angle.

Now, it was hard to see any way out. Given what had happened, he couldn't dump Rhonda, but he was also scared shitless that living with her and her grief — not to mention his own guilt about that night — would drive him crazier than she was.

"Am I crazy?"

"You say something, Rudy?"

His foreman was standing behind him. Snuck up somehow.

"Never mind, Nick." Christ, can't wink out like this, not on the job and all. "What's left on the punch list there?"

Wild-eyed, Peter Mendez grabbed the stack of pink message slips off his secretary's desk.

"How was the press conference?" asked Veronica.

Peter began scanning the slips. Mort, you fucking deserter, where the fuck are you?

"I said, how was —"

"A fucking crucifixion, all right?"

"What?" said his secretary.

Mendez glared at her. "Our supreme court won't let me execute criminals behind prison walls, but that doesn't stop the media from nailing me to a cross in broad daylight."

"Are you all —"

Peter shook the clutch of message slips like a rattle. "I don't see anything in these from Zussman. Didn't he at least call?"

"Not since I've been in. You want —"

But her boss was already headed for the door to his inner office. "Get him on the line for me. Now!"

"You want any other calls?"

"Only in the event of murder," he replied, harshly closing the door. Slamming it, just about.

Picking up the phone, Frank punched in a familiar number. "Sergeant Sikes, Homicide. Is he in?"

Frank thought the DA's secretary — Veronica? — hesitated a moment before saying, "One moment, please."

A click, then a harried "Mendez. What do you —"

"Your office got daily transcripts on the Ketterson trial, right?"

"Dailies? Yes, all the good they —"

"You still have them in your office?"

"Yes, but —"

"I'll be there in fifteen."

"Hey, O.B. Really appreciate your switching with me for tonight, what with it being a Friday and all."

Old Bailey looked up from the magazine he was reading — *Outdoor Life,* an article about deer hunting. O.B. thought that if he read the article carefully, he might understand why people would go into the woods and intentionally hurt the poor things.

"Glad to do it, Vinnie."

"Oh, and don't be too surprised, the phone goes out on you."

"The one at the security desk?"

"Yeah. Something got screwed up in the wiring, account of they been switching the numbers over to the new building. And, except for the desk, the rest of the old system's gonna be dead as of Monday."

"Thanks, I'll remember that."

The younger man nodded to the magazine. "Be sure you bring plenty of those with you, too."

"You afraid I'm going to be bored, Vinnie?"

"Hey, I been on that desk downstairs four to twelve every — what, three, four nights? Other than the rats, nobody but *no*body, is around."

Good, thought Old Bailey. He'd felt just a little bad telling the chief justice about the Diaz trial continuance and all the problems with Judge Hesterfield not wanting to move to the new courthouse on time. It'll be good to have a nice, peaceful night for helping His Honor pack those boxes, make it up to him.

"Law Offices."

No life to the voice at all. "Krissie, is that you?"

"Yes." The voice cautious now. "Who's this?"

"Arthur Ketterson, but you don't really sound yourself."

"There's been, like, a death in the family."

"Yes, I'm so sorry. I saw Sheilah at the funeral of . . . Mrs. Ettelman?"

"Yemelman." Krissie's voice skipped a beat. "Etta Yemelman. But I mean there's . . . Sheilah's father died last night."

"Oh, I'm even sorrier. Was it sudden?"

"Heart attack, they think."

"Well, I'd say to give her my condolences, but I already left that rather inadequate message with the answering service last time. I wonder, do you know which funeral home will be used, so I might send flowers?" though he had no such intention.

"Yeah, I got it right here."

As Arthur Ketterson took down the name and address, he found himself smiling in a less than controlled way.

Fanning a fistful of pink messages in one hand and holding his telephone in the other, Peter Mendez inclined his head toward the bookcase. "Second shelf."

Frank Sikes didn't think the district attorney was looking too good. He moved over to the bookcase, Mendez already on another call. There were a dozen binders of transcripts on the second shelf, but all were labeled, and Frank found the ones he wanted pretty quickly.

"Your secretary said I could go through these at her desk."

Just a nod.

"You might have heard, the Shoot Team ruled the incident yesterday a righteous one. Looks like the Yemelman —"

Mendez waved him off with the hand holding the message slips, yelling into the receiver. "Mort, where the fuck have you been? "

Sheilah Quinn's first phone call from the

checklist had been to Mr. McCoy, the funeral director who'd buried her mother. Sheilah was lucky: McCoy could accommodate her dad on short notice.

Jesus Mary, this is what I call "luck" now?

Shaking her head, Sheilah finished with McCoy and began calling the people she thought would be interested in coming to the viewing, including Lucille Wesley at the nursing home. The switchboard there said Lucille wouldn't be in till later, so Sheilah had to leave a message containing the information.

After hanging up, Sheilah tried to think if there was anything else she could do. Nothing came to mind.

Going to the bedroom, she got dressed. Dressed to stand by her dad once more.

Strike while the iron is hot.

That was an expression Mother said her own mother had always endorsed. Arthur Ketterson wasn't sure of the allusion, but he felt it had something to do with blacksmithing. Forges and anvils and all that.

After obtaining driving directions from the McCoy Funeral Home, Arthur moved to his closet. He selected another of his dark suits, then packed a variety of more casual clothes in his tennis bag. In case a change of uniform might be necessary for any . . . activities later that evening.

It took Frank Sikes about an hour to go

through the trial transcripts for the information he needed. Arthur Ketterson IV had dated each of the women for several months, usually once a week. All three were pretty certain of the beginning and ending points, particularly since they were surprised when Ketterson simply stopped calling. None of them thought her relationship with him was going anywhere, though, and therefore none had tried to call the man herself.

Leaving the transcripts with Mendez's secretary, Frank returned to the Homicide Unit. It took him thirty minutes more to confirm what he already felt pretty certain of: No open homicides involving "true victims" — that is, people who weren't drug dealers, gang members, et cetera — fell within the periods Ketterson had been seeing the women involved.

"Let me guess. Arthur fucking Ketterson, I presume?"

Sikes looked up at Gerry O'Toole. "The guy dated these women who testified for him, right?"

"Right."

"But he seems to have no good reason for seeing them."

"Frank, the guy's a flake."

"Yeah, but maybe Ketterson was using them as cover for something else, like killing a victim the women knew."

O'Toole considered that. "It's a possibility."

"Only we don't have any open homicides that make sense during the time frames."

"How about after he stopped dating them?"

"What do you mean?"

"Maybe Ketterson was using these women as some kind of decoy."

"Decoy."

"Yeah. Date the 'decoy' to attract the real target, then go after the real target later."

Frank stopped, worked it around in his mind. "I don't think so."

"Why not?"

"That angle would tie Ketterson to the later deaths. Be too dangerous for him, leave the women he dated around as witnesses."

"Yeah, but only if somebody found a body, right?"

"Again?"

O'Toole said, "I'm not nuts about your theory, but the dates can tie him to a real target only if somebody finds the real target's body."

"Kidnapping?"

"Other than some child-custody shenanigans, we haven't had one for — what, three years?"

Frank Sikes almost smiled. "Missing persons."

In turn, Gerry O'Toole almost frowned. "That means a visit to Donna the Dominatrix at her computer, right?"

"Right."

"You're on your own there, sport."

"I'm glad it was peaceful for you, Dad."

Mr. McCoy had made sure that Sheilah was

by herself for a while in the viewing room before the scheduled wake hours. Looking down at her father — dressed in his only dark suit, medals and ribbons from World War II pinned on the left breast of his jacket — Jack Quinn's daughter went back over time, through all the benchmarks of a child's relationship with a parent. And then the combat decorations made Sheilah remember something else, something she'd heard on a news broadcast. It was when they were holding the memorial ceremonies marking the fiftieth anniversary of D day a few years earlier. President Clinton at a podium in Normandy to address a group of veterans, most by then in their seventies. Citizen-soldiers who had stormed ashore with her dad, onto those beaches and up the cliffs and across half a continent into Germany.

Sheilah remembered Clinton saying, "We must never forget that when these men were young, they saved the world."

Back in McCoy's Funeral Home, she leaned forward then, over the prayer rail and the edge of the casket, to kiss her dad's forehead. And at that moment, for the first time in a long time, Sheilah Quinn began to cry somewhere other than her bathtub.

Roger Hesterfield found himself unable to concentrate on the file in front of him, instead staring at this aspect or that of his chambers. The curve of the wood, the texture of the ceiling, the way everything felt . . . right. And soon, so soon, it would all be gone. This place is like a tall tree: Takes five minutes to cut one down, fifty years to grow one back. He could move the artifacts to a new setting, but it would never be as right as the First Session and his chambers beside it.

Then Roger Hesterfield found himself starting to sniffle, and he forced his eyes to return to the file.

"Hold me up and fan me quick."

Frank Sikes nodded to Donna. "Good to see you, too."

"I mean, we should get a photographer up here, memorialize this. Homicide, slumming with the lowlifes in MP."

Turning from the computer screen in the Missing Persons Unit, Donna shifted in her swivel chair. Frank couldn't remember ever seeing her *out* of her chair. Fortyish, short, and at least two hundred pounds, Donna looked as though her hips were wedged between the furniture's arms, and whenever she needed to move around the office, her feet, clad always in tennis shoes, would pedal the chair over the old linoleum.

"I need some help," said Sikes.

Donna scratched at her short brown hair, spiked thanks to some kind of mousse. "What with?"

"I want to run some time periods, see anything

you've got by way of missing persons."

"How long are the periods?"

"Two, sometimes three months."

Donna's eyes widened. "You want everybody went over the hill for months at a time?"

"Just the ones who didn't come back."

"Which is most of them. Christ, Frank, any way to make this more manageable?"

Sikes thought about the women Ketterson had dated. "Can you use some kind of search command by gender and age?"

"Yeah, that'd cut it down some."

"Okay, let's start with women under thirty."

"Gonna get you a lot of kids, runaways."

"Can we see how it goes?"

A monumental sigh. "Sure. The fuck else do I have to do, right?"

But Donna turned back to her screen and began attacking the keyboard with something approaching enthusiasm.

"A good man, your father. A good man."

"Thank you for coming."

Sheilah Quinn did her best to greet the older men and women who shuffled into the viewing room. They would sign their names with great deliberation on the next line of the visitation book, then shuffle farther along to speak with her before approaching the prayer rail at the casket. Canes, polio-style braces, even a couple of four-footed metal walkers. Surprised at how many came, despite the limitations on mobility,

Sheilah was glad she'd gone to the trouble of calling them.

"A fine man, Jack was," one said. "But a blessing in the end, I suppose?"

"The last few months certainly were difficult for him."

Each introduced himself or herself to Sheilah, often taking one of her hands in both of theirs. She was taller than all but a few of the men, and the crowd was mostly female, a function of life expectancy, Sheilah guessed. Almost as soon as the next person came up to her, she had forgotten the name of the previous visitor.

"In his sleep, you say? What more can a body ask?"

"Not much, I guess," Sheilah would reply.

Then one man, wearing an off-buttoned cardigan and a two day beard, tottered up to her. Reeking of beer, he had to use one hand on the prayer rail to steady himself.

"I hadn't heard if there's to be a reception afterwards?"

"No, no reception."

A tight-lipped expression. "Pity. Old Jack would have liked his friends to enjoy themselves."

After the man moved away, Sheilah realized she'd been holding her breath.

A block from the funeral home, Arthur Ketterson pulled his car into the curb. He sat for a moment, biding his time, watching the mourners wobble up to the main entrance.

A Frantz Fanon sequel. *The Wretched of the Earth: Our Sunshine Years.* Good Lord, death really is a gift to these creatures. That ancient back in the home was probably thanking me himself as the last frame of consciousness flickered across his brain.

Then Arthur tried to imagine himself old and feeble. Tried, but simply could not. Impossible for a man of his fortitude to descend into such decrepitude.

Arthur was about to get out of the BMW when a Buick, dinged here and rusting there, belched oil smoke going by him. Reminded of his day of telephoning outside the Goodwill store, he waited for the fumes to dissipate. Arthur therefore saw the car park and an enormous Negro cow exit the driver's side. Apparently dressed in her Sunday church clothes, the woman marched ponderously up the drive of the funeral home, carrying a shopping bag.

Something about her gait was vaguely familiar, and Arthur took that as an omen. "Bide your time," Mother would say. "Bide your time."

He sat back into the bucket seat once more.

Donna said, "That any help to you?"

Over her shoulder, Frank Sikes had watched the computer screen display the objective data and photos, often out-of-date, that families or friends had provided on a missing loved one or even acquaintance. Sixteen women under thirty reported in one period, fourteen in another, ten in the third. No apparent pattern or even cross-reference to the ones Arthur Ketterson had been dating and whom Frank had committed to memory.

Donna looked up from the monitor. "Well?"

"No help."

Frank thought about the testimony of that third witness, the one now living in Seattle, and what she'd suspected about Ketterson.

"You know," said Donna, pointing, "the longer this machine is on, the more electricity the city pays for."

Sikes said, "Try males this time."

"Males now?"

"Yes. Under thirty, too."

Donna sighed even harder. "Just like a man, can't make up his mind."

Sheilah Quinn saw Lucille Wesley enter the viewing room, seeming a little nervous. At first, Sheilah was puzzled, then thought, she realizes everybody else is white.

Leaving the casket area, Sheilah moved to her directly. "I hoped you'd be able to come."

"Owed it to Jack, child." Her features were troubled. "Can you and me talk, private like?"

Sheilah was puzzled again, but said, "Sure. Let's just step outside."

Sheilah led the older woman back through the front door. After the closeness created by the cut

438

flowers around the casket, the fresh September air had a cleansing bite to it.

Lucille waited on the front steps until Sheilah secured the door. "Just wanted you to know, I didn't tell nobody."

Huh? "Tell them what?"

"About the pillowcase. I switched it."

"The pillowcase?"

"And it's already in the laundry, child, so you don't have to worry none. Ain't nobody gonna see that mucus and stuff on there, find out nothing."

"Lucille, I don't —"

"Thought you might want this, though." Lucille reached into her shopping bag, pulling out the tattered teddy bear. "Looked like you had it a long —"

"Mr. Fuzzums!"

"Who?"

Sheilah ripped the animal from Lucille's hand. "Where did you get this?"

"Child —"

"Where?"

Lucille's face was blank. "Right where you left it."

"Where *I* left it?"

"Tucked under Jack's arm, after you . . . helped him along."

Helped him . . . Oh God. Pillowcase, mucus. Jesus Mary, no! "Somebody smothered my father?"

Lucille shot a horrified look around them.

"Child keep your voice down. I told you already, ain't nobody gonna find out nothing."

But Sheilah Quinn was already running down the driveway, toward her car, holding the teddy bear against her chest as she fought to breathe despite the daymares whirling through her head.

Roger Hesterfield dropped his last file on the stack, the little slap noise almost echoing around the otherwise-silent chambers. Reaching into the bottom drawer of his desk, he took out the bottle of Glenfiddich, pouring three fingers into one of the crystal glasses. Lifting the scotch as a salute to each wall, Roger tossed it off, refilling the glass immediately. He drew down half that second drink as well before setting it on his blotter and moving, reluctantly, to the closest of the empty cartons in the corner of the room.

Perform this ritual lovingly, old man. One item at a time.

"Whole world's gone to shit."

One hand on his bottle of springwater, Rudy Giordano looked around quickly, making sure that Nick wasn't nearby again, hear him talking to himself twice in one day.

Christ, I'm losing my mind, and my focus along with it. Ever since this fucking nightmare started. And that fucking hypocrite Mendez didn't help any, with his speech at the press conference there. Reminding me of all this, even when I'm not home with Rhonda.

Rudy lifted the bottle to his lips and swallowed another few ounces.

Lunch had helped with the hangover, and at least some of the fluid the booze seemed to soak up had been replaced by the other two bottles of springwater he'd put away that day. There was a time in this country when drinking right out of the tap was like an artesian fucking well. Not anymore, though. Just one more thing that's gone to shit.

Like the rest of the fucking world.

Rudy thought about knocking off early, seeing it was a Friday and all. Maybe check on that sonuvabitch judge, make sure he's cleaning his shit out of the old courthouse. And I've got to go home for a shower and change before meeting that Terri broad at the bar. Rhonda's no problem. Just tell her I'm working late again, let her spend another night with the fucking photo albums while I'm with Terri, making up for some lost time.

"Yeah, that's what I'll do."

From about three feet away, Nick said, "Hey, Rude, you got a minute?" Which caused his boss to jump about three inches out of his skin.

Arthur Ketterson sat bolt upright in the bucket seat as soon as he saw the second woman come through the funeral home's front door. He could tell that the lovely Sheilah and the enormous Negro, now standing on the stoop, were deep in conversation, but he couldn't quite see what the latter had taken from her shopping bag. However, it threw Sheilah into a frenzy.

So much so that the lovely thing is now running pell-mell down the drive, clutching some . . . Of course, the stuffed animal. That was why the Negro cow still on the stoop looked so familiar. She was the one in the hallway at the nursing home, now shaking her head in a tsk-tsk manner, folding the shopping bag.

Arthur watched Sheilah jump into her car and literally screech off down the street. The poor thing can't imagine how her tattered little toy came to be in her dead father's embrace.

Smiling, Arthur Ketterson started the Beemer. Given her state, there's no chance Sheilah will be looking for anyone following her.

And who knows where she might lead?

"Well?" said Donna.

Frank Sikes had watched each missing male under thirty come up on the screen, but none rang any bells, and he couldn't see any connections to Arthur Ketterson.

"Dead end," he said.

Donna scratched the spiky hair again. "You got a suspect in mind?"

"Yeah."

"Male, right?"

"Right."

"How old?"

442

"Late twenties."

"So that's why you had me go through the twenties?"

"That's the age group he was dating."

"But you're not sure if he's straight, gay, or bi?"

"Right."

"Well, the guy's a little questionable, maybe he's into older, too."

"Older?"

"Yeah. Older than he is."

Costs nothing but time. "Okay. Try the same time period, women in their thirties."

"Just thirties?"

"Right. Knowing who he was dating, I can't see going any older than that."

The fortyish Donna gave Frank Sikes a jaundiced look. "That supposed to be funny?"

Gripping the steering wheel until her knuckles hurt, Sheilah Quinn tried to think. Who would kill Dad?

For that matter, who would steal a stuffed animal from my apartment? There's been nothing wrong with the locks, and — Wait. That problem with the water in the tub, that was the night I noticed Mr. Fuzzums was missing. What night . . . Right, right. When I got back from the weekend with Frank, Sunday. But the only person inside while I was gone would have been Krissie, to feed Quigley, and she said everything had been all right. Could somebody have snuck in behind her?

Sheilah Quinn shook her head. It was all so mixed up. How could somebody sneak past Krissie? And that led to other complications, like "no signs of forced entry," as Frank had testified at Arthur Ket—

Ketterson. And *complications*. I used that word with the weirdo over drinks, when I said that between Etta and Dad — Jesus Mary! At Etta's funeral, Ketterson said I should be . . . "relieved." Relieved by what? First Etta, then Dad . . .

No. No, no. Stop and think, girl. Think. If that weirdo killed anybody, it was a twenty-one-year-old woman named Jessica Giordano. The rest of this just doesn't fit with her death. I mean, it was you who nearly got Ketterson off on a murder charge, and then you did get him out on bail. He should be grateful to you, not start targeting people close to you. Everything you've just been thinking is . . . speculation, even fantasy.

And besides, I'm still Ketterson's attorney of record. I can't do anything unless and until I withdraw as his trial counsel. Then — and only then — can I go to Frank with my suspicions, see if any of this makes sense to him.

But to withdraw, I need the trial judge's permission. Which means Roger Hesterfield's permission.

Gritting her teeth, Sheilah Quinn turned east, toward the courthouse complex.

Sheilah, Sheilah. Do you always drive this erratically?

Arthur Ketterson stayed several car lengths behind the little Miata, watching Sheilah change lanes, but not as though she was trying to increase her speed. No, it was more arbitrary, as if she was just taking the next empty slot in the traffic.

And now a veer to the east. Arthur began searching his memory for where Sheilah might be heading, when a large truck cut him off, forcing him to lose sight of her before taking the same turn she had.

"These any better for you?" said Donna.

Frank thought he saw something. "Go back two."

"Go back to what?"

"No, I mean go back two files, or whatever you call them."

Donna pressed several keys at once. "Diana Mayhew, age thirty-three when she checked out six years ago."

"Now forward again."

"How far?"

"To the one we were looking at just now. Hedy somebody." Another couple of keys. "Hedy Porrell. Age thirty-three — no, thirty-four as of her disappearing. You see something?"

"I don't know." One was from the period when Ketterson was dating the first woman who testified for him at the trial, the other from the next time period, when Ketterson was dating the second witness. Addresses in the respective neighborhoods of the two witnesses, which seemed to support his "cover" theory. But there was also something about . . . "Donna, do those two look alike to you?"

"Diana and Hedy?"

"Yes."

"Not really. Same type, I suppose. Dark hair, quasi-good looks."

"The eyes, maybe?"

Donna canted her head this way and that. "Yeah, maybe."

Those eyes, thought Frank. They're what's catching me, too. But why?

"Well?"

"Print me copies of Diana and Hedy, both photo and text."

Donna looked up first. "Will that do it?"

"No. I want to try the third time period, too."

"You know, I get off at four?"

"We'll be done sooner, you print those two now."

Donna's sigh seemed forceful enough to puncture the screen as she pressed a couple more keys.

"It's four-ten, Ms. Quinn. We're all closed up for the day."

Barely breaking stride, Sheilah looked down at Old Bailey, sitting behind the security desk on the first floor and reading some kind of outdoors magazine. "Is Hesterfield still upstairs?"

The bailiff began to stand as she went by him. "You can't disturb His Honor. He's pack—"

But Sheilah was already halfway down the hall.

"Ms. Quinn, go easy on him. Please?"

Frowning, O.B. sat back down, closing his magazine on a story about catch-and-release programs in trout fishing — which had kind of reminded him of the criminal justice system in a lot of ways: the police catch the offenders, and we in the court system release them to be caught again.

O.B. knew the telephone would be faster than chasing Sheilah Quinn. He reached for the receiver, thankful that the dial tone meant the line was still working.

Extemporaneous timing. Again, everything.

Had that truck not blocked his vision before the turn, Arthur Ketterson almost certainly would have stopped short as Sheilah slewed to the curb in front of the courthouse, slamming her door and stomping up the steps. As it was, however, he was able to spot her as he went past rather naturally, Sheilah disappearing inside before he found a good opportunity to reverse direction and park.

I must say, though, that I don't like the idea of losing sight of her, even when it can't be helped. There's always the possibility —

Then Arthur saw a man in blue jeans and a T-shirt, slouching with that construction worker's walk, tipping the hard hat back on his head as the man climbed the same stairs Sheilah had. Familiar face, too.

Arthur nodded. The pig Giordano pater. Checking on his motley crew's progress; otherwise, they'd probably shirk. . . .

Which gave Arthur an idea. No, more an inspiration, really.

Looking around carefully, Arthur got out of his car and walked back toward where the contractor had come from.

He's tanked, the bastard.

"Sheilah, O.B. just called up about you. I'm so —"

"Judge, we have to talk."

" 'Roger,' please."

Hesterfield's words came out "Rajah, pleesh."

Sheilah shook her head. "Roger, I have to make a motion."

"Without notice to your opponent? No, join me in a toast first."

He grabbed the bottle of scotch on his desk, not a lot left in it. Not a lot left on his desk and walls, for that matter. Most of it in boxes on the rug.

Hesterfield sloshed some booze into another glass, extending it to her.

Sheilah weighed her chances of him granting the motion, and, reluctantly, accepted the drink.

Roger Hesterfield raised his own. "To grand old times in a grand old place."

"Can't let you upstairs just yet, Mr. Giordano."

"Why the hell not?"

"His Honor has somebody else with him."

"He's supposed to be out of there by now."

"The packing's almost finished, and then I'll help him with the boxes over to the new building tomorrow in the A.M. Nothing for you to worry about."

"You're sure of that, huh?"

"Positive."

Rudy Giordano was nobody's fool. He didn't trust this fat fuck or the robed sonuvabitch he worked for, but there was no percentage in pushing it now.

Later, maybe. But not now.

Back in Homicide, Frank Sikes sat at his desk, placing the third photo that Donna had printed for him beside the other two. The photos were of uneven quality, and copying hadn't made them any clearer. But there was definitely something about the eyes, about the look of the three women, all early thirties, each disappearing when Arthur Ketterson was dating one of the younger ones who'd testified for the defense at his trial. And each from the time-paired younger woman's neighborhood, one within a block.

Diana Mayhew, Hedy Porrell, and Lorraine

Vouvray. Tell me, Artie, am I right? Did you date the younger ones as cover for getting close to the older, actual targets? To have an excuse for being in the neighborhood, maybe?

But why target the older ones at all?

Frank shook his head, then checked his watch. Ought to call the funeral home, see how Sheilah's making —

Holy . . . shit!

He rearranged the photos, then looked from one to the other fast, focusing only on the eyes. Faster now, and faster still.

No question. These women had the same look as Sheilah. Had *her* eyes.

Frank pictured in his mind the house Jessica Giordano lived in with her parents. A house that he was sure lay within four or five blocks of Sheilah Quinn's apartment building.

Nick reached for the telephone in the construction trailer. "Hey, Rude, how's it going?"

Listening to his boss rail about "that boozy prick in his courtroom," Nick thought Rudy might have kind of a glass-house problem there. Then Nick heard somebody walking around outside, by where they kept the spare hard hats and hand tools.

I could get up, stick my head out, or I could try to calm the boss down some.

Nick settled deeper in the one chair the trailer held. "Rude? . . . Hey, Rude? You gotta take these things in stride, you know? Why don't you try going home and getting cleaned up? Maybe go out for a couple of pops even, take your mind off things?"

Roger Hesterfield felt that last dram of Glenfiddich spread warmingly through his system. Looking — all right, probably leering — at Sheilah Quinn standing there. So attractively distraught, hair spilling down from the bun she'd pinned at the top of her head, not taking much of a hit from her own drink. He felt the warmth spread farther southward, thinking it was a very good sign that Sheilah had finally come around to using his first name. For the first time since that magical Christmas party, so many holiday seasons ago.

"Judge —"

"Oh, Sheilah, how can you have forgotten so soon? It's 'Roger.' You had it right just a moment ago."

Something was giving her trouble. "Roger, I need to withdraw from a case."

"Withdraw?" This was confusing, not consistent with the mood at all. "Has successor counsel been retained?"

"No. There's no time for that."

Hesterfield tried to focus, remember the right phrases and parrot them in the proper sequence. "But Sheilah, surely you know withdrawal is impossible without my permission, and my permission depends on the client being —"

"Will you just listen to me?"

Hesterfield couldn't remember being addressed like that since he'd ascended to the bench. Except by that dago contractor who —

"I have to withdraw, Roger. I may have to provide information about a client to the police."

Hesterfield regained some of his judicial bearing. "Then you can damn well file a written motion, young lady, on notice to client and opposing counsel, and mark it for hearing on a day —"

Sheilah slammed the glass so forcefully onto his desk, Hesterfield was amazed the crystal didn't shatter. "Judge, please!"

The bearing hardened, now like a metal alloy. "I'll see you in court, Ms. Quinn. On Monday, in the new . . . building."

"To hear my motion?"

"No. On the armed robbery, whatever that wetback's name is."

"But Judge —"

"Now get out of here."

"But —"

"Get out!"

Sheilah Quinn spun on her heel and nearly ran from his chambers. At first still stung by her attitude, Hesterfield hesitated before following her through the door. By the time he was into the First Session, she was gone.

The scotch swam through his mind, softening it again. Roger looked around the old lady then. Very nearly for the last time, he realized. The beams like the ribs of a mighty ship, the doused chandeliers hanging from them like the lighting in a palace, just some wall sconces glowing softly in the darkening of late afternoon. The meticulous wainscoting, soon to be pried off and carried away by that dago contractor to line the walls of some wet-bar rec room. Or worse.

Turning and walking back into his chambers, the presiding judge of the First Session shut the door. As he reached for his glass, Roger Hesterfield's hands were trembling so badly he had to use both just to grasp it.

The deep and soothing voice at the other end of the line said, "This is Mr. McCoy."

"Mr. McCoy, Frank Sikes. I'm a police officer."

"Is something the matter, sir?"

"I need to speak with Sheilah Quinn. I understand —"

"Oh, I'm afraid you can't."

"I can't?"

"Ms. Quinn became upset over something, and, well, she left."

"Left your funeral home?"

"Yes, sir."

"Where did she go?"

"I've no idea, sir. But I wouldn't be too concerned."

Sikes found himself staring at the receiver, as though he could see the face behind the voice. "You wouldn't."

"No. This sort of thing can happen to the bereaved."

"You've seen it before."

"Oh, sir, what haven't I seen before?"

It took a moment for Frank Sikes to realize that Mr. McCoy had hung up on him.

No, too rakish an angle.

Laying the pry bar on the floor, Arthur Ketterson sat in the backseat of the Beemer, needing some distance from the rearview mirror to get a proper perspective on how the hard hat looked on him. It was robin's egg blue, the same color as the one he'd seen the pig Giordano pater wearing, which was why Arthur, behind the construction trailer, had picked that particular model from the junk heap of hats, tools — even carpeting. Arthur found it difficult to accept all the waste that went with new public buildings.

Fortunately, the strap inside the hard hat was adjustable, the prior wearer evidently almost a pinhead. However, even with —

Wait. What's this?

Arthur watched Sheilah Quinn emerge from the main entrance of the old courthouse building. Her car was still parked in front — not even the city, apparently, would tow a lawyer — so he hadn't been worried about having missed her while he walked across to the new building. However, Sheilah appeared . . . Yes. Yes, she was leaving the courthouse in a . . . "huff," his mother would have called it.

Then, as Sheilah reached her car, another figure appeared in the main entrance. That circus bear of a bailiff, shaking his head, almost sympathetically. Arthur doubted that obese lackey could have brought Sheilah to such a state. His being there, though, raised another possibility. Indeed, a likelihood, especially given how much time Sheilah had spent inside the building.

Perhaps the Honorable Roger Hesterfield was still at work. Complicating Sheilah's life even more since our drink together at the hotel.

Arthur had assumed that he'd be dealing with the Jolly Roger at the judge's own residence. However, now there might be no need to visit this particular complication's house at all.

Holding the hard hat in his lap, Arthur Ketterson forgot to watch Sheilah Quinn drive away. He was lost in thought, hatching a plan. A hasty one, in that he'd be taking advantage of unpredictable timing, but all the more exciting for it.

And the more creative, given the variety of clothing Arthur Ketterson had fortuitously packed in his tennis bag.

Roger Hesterfield may be an asshole, girl, but you were stupid back there. Stone-stupid.

Sheilah Quinn now had herself a little bit more under control, her lawyerly reason gnawing away at the scare she'd had. You've been under a lot of pressure lately. The *Ketterson* case, your dad, even before Etta —

No! Don't drift. Stop and think.

There's no real proof Arthur Ketterson — or anyone else — went into your apartment, except for Mr. Fuzzums here. If you take the stuffed animal away, there's nothing. The discolored water in the tub was a freak of plumbing after you hadn't used it for a couple of days, and it hasn't happened again. Frank identified the kids responsible for Etta's death. Your father was a sick old man, and the mucus could have gotten onto a pillow by him sneezing or coughing. Or it might not even have been mucus, just some food or drug stain that Lucille mistook for something it wasn't.

Sheilah Quinn drew in a deep breath. Granted, Arthur Ketterson is a client to pass on to someone else, but I can set that ball rolling on Monday, after I resume the *Diaz* case and Roger Hesterfield has had a chance to calm down, too. If he denies my motion to withdraw, I'll appeal, and once I'm out of it, I can tell Frank about my suspicions. Then let the police take it from there.

Sheilah felt something like peace come over her. "And once my mind is clearer, I'll be able to figure out just how Mr. Fuzzums got from my apartment to the nursing home."

She glanced down at the little fellow, then thought again of the man who'd given it to her. Jack Quinn deserved better from his daughter than this.

Sheilah turned again, back toward Mr. McCoy's address.

Frank Sikes hung up the phone after his call to Krissie at Sheilah's office. He'd now left messages for her everywhere he could think of.

I can just sit here, or I can go camp someplace. Like maybe Arthur fucking Ketterson's doorstep. But, if he's got Sheilah, they could be anywhere.

So, shelve that, focus on the other possibility, and follow your feelings. If Sheilah's under her own power, where would she go?

What do you *feel?*

The answer flowed into him. Sheilah would want to be back with her father.

Frank Sikes stood up and checked the board where Homicide kept its car keys, seeing if there was an unmarked unit available.

"Your Honor, everything okay?"

Roger Hesterfield sat slumped in his chair. The anger had worn off, succeeded by a dusky haze. "Yes, O.B. I'm fine, aside from that hotheaded bitch Sheilah Quinn."

Old Bailey flinched at the judge's words, though he didn't believe his immediate superior was in any condition to notice the reaction. It wasn't right to talk about attorneys — or people, period — that way. Judges had to be in control of themselves in order to control the system. "Need help packing?"

A wave of the hand that could have meant anything.

"Well, Your Honor, just give me a call downstairs when you're finished with the boxes, and I'll come back up."

Another wave of the hand that then tried to close on the Glenfiddich bottle and did.

On the third attempt.

Rudy Giordano — showered, changed, and feeling a little less pissed at the world — had gotten only halfway through his first beer at the fern-infested meat rack, so he wasn't worried. Yet.

That's when the bartender remembered to give Rudy a note dropped off an hour before.

The message read:

Rudy,

Got hung up on something. Real sorry, but too much to explain. I'll stop in here next week, maybe see you then.

Terri.

Giordano made a fist, crumpling the note before letting the paper drop to the floor. He downed the rest of his beer, rapping the glass on the bar for another.

No justice in this world, no fucking justice.

Which reminded him of an idea he'd had earlier.

Hefting the pry bar over his shoulder, Arthur

Ketterson cocked the hard hat down over his eyes as he marched up the steps of the old court building. He wore a T-shirt and dungarees — the proper name for blue jeans, his mother had always maintained. Before donning those pieces of clothing, he'd rolled both in the dust. A different form of perfection, the patina of manual labor. Arthur thought he had the slouching walk of pig Giordano pater perfected as well, though so long as Arthur was mistaken for any construction worker, he didn't think there'd be a problem in gaining entrance to the building.

Which proved no issue at all, since the security desk inside the front door sat abandoned.

A rat skittered across the hall, near the staircase, ten feet away. Arthur could understand why the poor preferred not to have the creatures share their abodes. This particular rodent was the size of a dachshund.

On the other hand, one of the nature programs on the television screens in the Admin Unit had shown how remarkably resourceful rats could be. Able to live in any kind of little hole, able to survive on any kind of comestible food. Flood the hole and they could tread water. For *days,* the narrator had said.

Climbing the wide staircase toward the First Session, Arthur pondered his own immediate future. I'll have to disappear after this episode, perhaps for some time. I need a hole, like the rats in that nature program. Somewhere I can hide.

459

Somewhere such as . . Arthur looked around him.

This building. Perfect, in that it's virtually abandoned. And ironic, too, in that a courthouse is the last place anyone would look for a murder suspect already tried there. Which would buy me time to deal with that Mambo King of a district attorney, as well.

And finally, of course, Sheilah herself. To reveal to her how I've relieved her of all those complications, perfected her life. And now will perfect her beauty as well, ensuring that exquisite quality against —

"I thought you all were finished for the night?"

Arthur resisted looking up toward the familiar voice and just kept climbing the stairs, hard hat angled toward the steps ahead of him. No possible way for the lackey bailiff to see his face from the second floor.

"Hey, fella, you hear me?"

In what Arthur believed to be a good-natured blue-collar greeting, he flicked the hand that didn't hold the pry bar, dropping his tone a full octave to the voice he'd mastered on the telephone with the nursing homes. "Boss said to meet him upstairs."

Arthur could hear the circus bear moving toward him on the landing. Just a few more steps to go.

"His Honor's still packing his stuff," said Old Bailey. "You can't start working up here till tomorrow."

"What're you talking about? Tomorrow's Saturday."

Keeping his head down, Arthur reached the top step, seeing the lackey's black tie shoes and white socks on the landing, not six feet away from him.

"So, Monday, then," said the bailiff. "All right?"

Arthur lifted his head as he brought the pry bar off his shoulder in an arc not unlike a good first serve. "I think not."

The obese lackey's face contorted almost as much from terror as it distorted a millisecond later from impact, and Arthur was genuinely surprised when the resulting sound didn't resemble a tennis racket's *thwock*.

"Oh, Ms. Quinn?"

Sheilah had just come out of the funeral home's rest room, thinking, God, if I looked like this in front of that disgusting lech Hesterfield it's no wonder I didn't get anywhere on the motion.

"Yes, Mr. McCoy?"

"While you were . . . out, a police officer called for you."

"Did he leave a name?"

"Yes, it was —"

"Me."

Sheilah turned, Frank Sikes just standing in the open doorway of the home. As McCoy left them, she said, "Oh, Frank. Am I glad to see you."

461

"Same, and for more than the usual reasons."

Sheilah looked up at him. He seems to be searching my eyes. Isn't that strange? "Frank, there's something I can't tell you."

"What a coincidence. There's —"

"Please, hear me out?"

"Sure, Sheil," he said, his voice different now.

"I want you to stay with me this weekend, okay?"

"At your place?"

"Yes."

"But I thought —"

"I know, I know," said Sheilah. "But I can't tell you why just yet. Can you trust me?"

That expression on his face. He seems to be thinking about something else. Then, "Being close to you this weekend is exactly what I was intending."

Sheilah didn't completely follow that, but she was just so glad to get over the hump of not explaining herself that she said, "I have to go back in with my dad."

"Can I . . . pay my respects?"

Sheilah thought about the withdrawal motion she'd be making Monday, after finishing the *Diaz* case. "No reason not to, now."

Roger Hesterfield lovingly lowered the last item, a spare gavel, into the last box. Last item, last box, last drink, at least from this bottle.

As he turned to the Glenfiddich, Hesterfield banged his knee against a panel of the desk.

Cursing, he bent over to rub the bone, staring malevolently at the panel he'd hit.

The panel?

God, that would have been perfect. Just perfect. Come Monday, that dago bastard Giordano tears apart my bench, finds the gun that even O.B. doesn't know about, and I'm —

What was that? O.B., moving around in the First Session, outside the chambers door? Wouldn't do for him to see me taking the gun. No, wouldn't do at all.

Roger Hesterfield waited until he heard no further noise before venturing out into the courtroom.

Frank Sikes sat quietly on one of McCoy's folding chairs in the last row wondering if there'd been more mourners earlier.

Two stooped gray-haired women, similar enough to be sisters, had been chewing Sheilah's ear off for a good ten minutes. Maybe felt they had to, nobody else being in the room right then.

Frank's view of the situation: Better to get Sheilah out of here and back to her place. Ask McCoy for the use of his phone before we leave, order some takeout, pick it up on the way. Then a nice quiet weekend, getting the universe back in order.

So long as I'm with her, I can't see Ketterson trying anything. And those missing persons files have been open long enough, another two days won't matter so much as clearing them entirely.

Though, for that to happen, things would have to go only one way.

And probably not a pretty way, either.

Then an old man on a cane, supported by what looked like his son, came in the door and spent maybe five minutes signing the visitation book. Frank settled deeper into the folding chair, kind of like a stake-out.

Which made Frank Sikes glad that Gerry O'Toole wasn't sitting there with him.

"O.B., are you in here?"

Roger Hesterfield tried to peer through the darkness of the First Session. The chandeliers' switch in the antiquated cavern was all the way across the room, and the waning light from the high windows and the faint glow of the wall sconces created odd, almost-mobile shadows around the walls. Especially near the . . .

"O.B.?"

That is him, isn't it, thought Roger? Slumped into the bailiff chair at the far end of the jury box, his face in one of the shadows.

Hesterfield took another three steps into the courtroom. "O.B.?"

Then another three. "O.B., what's the matter with you?"

Then a final three, almost close enough now to shake the man. "O.B., what on earth is that smell?"

A deep, gravelly voice behind him said, "Involuntary evacuation."

464

Roger whirled, the voice somewhat familiar, the outline of a construction hard hat and some kind of crowbar thrown against the far wall by the uncertain light. "What . . ."

"Evacuation. Defecation. Shit."

Nothing made sense. "Giordano?"

"No, but I'm flattered you'd think so."

A different voice — also familiar, even more so — from the outline now. Hesterfield shook his head. "I don't understand."

The hard hat came off, like a magician doffing a formal stovepipe. "Can't let appearances fool you, Roger."

My God, my dear God. "Ar . . . Arthur?"

"That's right. Now, what's this I've heard about you abusing my chosen counsel?"

Hesterfield felt his bladder about to release. Over his shoulder, he shouted, "O.B.!"

"I'm afraid your bailiff communes only with the angels, Roger."

At which point, Hesterfield's bladder gave way, and he ran for the bench, wetting himself without realizing it, without even caring. Only one thing occupied his mind. If I can get up there, slap the panel, get the gun —

My throat . . . the crowbar . . . choking me.

Hesterfield's back felt pinned against the man behind him as vile lips brushed his ear, the words almost tender. "Not exactly a bra, Roger, but then I couldn't rely on your being a cross-dresser 'underneath it all,' now could I?"

No air . . . the . . . pain!

465

"Can't have you going for that panic button up on the bench, either. Willie T. Eggers told me about such things. You know Willie, though you probably wouldn't remember him. Thanks to you, he and I were next-door neighbors for a time."

No . . . air . . . black . . .

"Look at it this way, Roger. The captain goes down with his ship. You're going down with your courthouse."

. . . No . . .

Arthur Ketterson felt the judge sag, as he'd felt his mother and all her successors do at the comparable moment in their own . . . lives. Releasing his grip, Arthur allowed the body of Roger Hesterfield to ooze onto the floor, settling down almost gracefully.

Then a skittering noise behind him. A rat in the Jolly Roger's courtroom, as well. Lifting his face to the ceiling high above, Arthur laughed. The unbridled laugh of the true professional, a man who was confident that he'd soon reach the pinnacle of his career, successfully concluding the stalking of Sheilah Quinn.

Arthur wanted to see the panic button up at the bench. But first, a star turn for his audience, the presiding rat of the First Session.

Closing his eyes modestly, Arthur Ketterson spun around, hands flapping outward, a smile from ear to ear. "Well, what did you think of the performance?"

SEVENTEEN

Saturday was a blur for Sheilah Quinn, if a relatively benign one, and she registered only a few details.

Frank, being attentive, even doting. Bringing me breakfast in bed. Just toast and juice and tea, but really trying, you know?

And Mr. McCoy at the funeral home, giving me some last moments with Dad before the cremation. I'd already cried out all my tears, though, and that part of my life was closing behind me. People always say the death of a parent takes a year to get over. We'll see.

Finally, I'm surprised to find I'm not worried about Arthur Ketterson. Partly, it's having Frank here. Hate to admit it, but I feel safer with a capable man — and face it, girl, one with police power and a handgun — sleeping next to me. Mostly though, it's just gaining some perspective on things. With perspective, all the suspicions about Ketterson seem less likely, and therefore less real.

After all, he hadn't attended Dad's wake or funeral, as he did with Etta's. Uh-oh, stab of pain there, very real. I knew Dad was going to die; I didn't think Etta would, and certainly not so soon or so . . . horribly. Have to keep sealed for a little while longer the compartment in my mind — and heart — that holds her. But there's still no sign of Ketterson, and no ominous communications from him. Maybe I have him all wrong.

Of course, that doesn't mean I want to continue to represent him.

As Sheilah put the urn with her father's ashes on the mantel in her living room, she thought about going in to work, do that motion to withdraw so it could be presented to Roger Hesterfield first thing Monday, then appeal his denial. If he denied it. Maybe the perspective of the weekend, and the new courthouse, would give even Roger a more open frame of mind. Then she could share her suspicions about Arthur Ketterson with Frank, and let him take it from there.

But instead, Sheilah decided a nice normal weekend off might be better medicine. And so on Saturday night, she and Frank had an early dinner out, then made love. Passionately and intensely, Sheilah needing and wanting more than he seemed to, as her reaffirmation of life, of living.

Sunday, more normality. Brunch at a trendy restaurant, Sheilah treating, then a walk in the park. They took in the last of the outdoor jazz concerts in the late afternoon before returning to her apartment, feeling like a couple.

Despite the funeral, an enjoyable weekend, thought Sheilah Quinn.

468

What a miserable weekend, thought Frank Sikes, lying in bed on Sunday evening next to a dozing Sheilah. They'd made love three nights in a row, and he'd have thought that would have his spirits soaring, but no.

Not that I didn't try. Calling in to the station to take a personal day for Saturday. Bringing her breakfast in bed. Simple stuff, but making the effort, you know?

Which had turned out to be the high point.

At the funeral home, Frank had watched for Arthur Ketterson around every corner. Then the cremation, picking up Jack Quinn's ashes in an urn — the "cremains," Gerry O'Toole would have called them. Sheilah had to pay for the coffin anyway, it having been used for the viewing. Frank'd read about some funeral homes on the coast getting caught for reusing coffins in those situations, selling them over and over again to new grieving families, but the director of this place, McCoy, didn't seem like the kind who'd cheat the bereaved.

Though that wasn't it, really, the funeral and all. It was Sheilah herself. Too many things had happened to her, and Frank could see how detached she was from everything, as if she hadn't connected with her grief yet. He knew Sheilah didn't understand that it was Ketterson, focusing in on her somehow because of her resemblance to the other women in the missing persons photos. In fact, Sheilah had never even mentioned him, like she'd forgotten old Artie even existed. Which might be fine for her mental health, short term, getting through her daddy's funeral and all, but not practical for the long term. No, not practical in the least.

Then the shallow "fun" of Saturday and Sunday: the meals, the walk, the concert, all feeling artificial somehow. Even the lovemaking.

Frank closed his eyes now, Sheilah snoring softly beside him. Without moving, he tried to "feel" her inside him as well as hear her through his ears.

Tried, but couldn't.

EIGHTEEN

Well, it's a new courthouse, a different environment. And only Monday morning, too. Everybody's going to be a little off.

Sheilah Quinn, sitting alone at the defense table, assumed that was the reason why as of 9:30 A.M. there was no Old Bailey, no request to join Roger Hesterfield in his new chambers prior to resuming the Diaz trial. Peter Mendez, now arranging some files on the prosecution table, had mumbled how sorry he was to hear about her father. Thanking Mendez for his concern, she was struck by the bags under his eyes and the hollowed cheeks below them.

Jesus Mary, the campaign must really be taking its toll. Peter looks like he's the one who just lost a parent.

Sheilah used Hesterfield's delay to look around the new courtroom. The floor plan was identical to the old First Session's. Chambers door to the left of the bench, witness stand to the right. A doorway for jury and defendants in custody on the right wall, jury box along it, bailiff's chair and table at the gallery end of the box. Within the bar enclosure, the attorneys' tables were equidistant from the bench, the prosecution closer to the jury, the defense farther away.

However, the similarities ended there. The new woodworking was blond oak instead of the First Session's dark mahogany, and it went only six feet up the walls from the carpeted floor. The sun streamed in through the intelligently placed windows, designed more for letting in light than for holding in heat. All the furniture — the gallery pews, the counsel and jury chairs, even the relatively low judicial bench area — was of the same oak as the walls. Overall, a feeling of airiness, of freedom. Sheilah, somewhat to her surprise, found she loved the change.

Then she almost smiled. Roger must hate it. Takes away the sense of brooding power the old place carried with it. And therefore carried over to him.

The door past the jury box opened, and Vinnie escorted Pablo Diaz to Sheilah's table, taking off his shackles before the jury was brought in. Which would probably still be Old Bailey's job.

Sheilah Quinn made small talk about the change in courtrooms with her client, waiting for the door to the judge's new chambers to open.

Gerry O'Toole said, "Great. Another fucking stake-out."

"Look on the bright side."

"Which is?"

"We're in a much better neighborhood."

Sitting with Frank Sikes in an unmarked Plymouth outside the gates of the Ketterson

472

manse, O'Toole decided that's what he liked most about his partner. The guy feels free to make a joke with me that, between two white guys, might seem . . . racist, somehow.

Frank had given him a summary of what he'd found out about the three missing women, though Gerry still thought his partner's theory sounded far-fetched without any evidence to back it up.

"So, Frank, you figure it makes sense for us to sit here, wait for the flake to come out?"

"Or come back. I asked one of the copter pilots to do a quick flyover an hour ago. No sign of his car on the grounds."

"Don't mean much. What I remember of the house there, Ketterson could probably hide his BMW in the living room."

"Still."

That was what Gerry liked least about his partner. I mean, how the fuck do you argue with "still"?

Pushing the hard hat back on his head, Nick leaned into the double swinging doors of the old courtroom. Only they didn't swing.

Nick put his ear up to the crack between them. Sound of a power tool inside. He pounded on the wood. After a minute, things got quiet on the other side of the door. Then Nick heard a dead bolt snick, and one of the doors opened.

"Christ, Rudy, you okay?"

Nick couldn't believe how his boss looked.

Plaster dust, stains on the T-shirt and jeans. Face streaked with sweat, eyes a little buggy. Like he'd fucking worked ten hours already.

"What do you want, Nick?"

The foreman tried to peer around him into the courtroom, already partially dismantled. "Rude, what time you get here this morning?"

"I came in over the weekend, try to get back on schedule. Fucking judge left his shit piled up in boxes, but at least he's packed. I been working around it."

Nick nodded. "Well, I got some bad news."

"Now what?"

"You know those pony cooling units for the new building there?"

"Yeah?"

"Well, over the weekend, somebody slipped in and stole one of them."

"Christ on a crutch." Rudy Giordano planted his fists on his hips. "How the fuck could that happen?"

"Beats me," said Nick, trying not to remember hearing somebody walking around behind the trailer the prior Friday. "They were secured out by the trailer, and we only had the three of them left to install. Why I noticed it right away when I got in this morning."

"All right. Deal with it."

"Deal with it?"

"Yeah. The fuck we have insurance for? And do me a favor?"

"Sure, boss."

474

"Try not to keep running to me with every little thing. I'd like to get this job done here."

Nick stood stock-still as Rudy Giordano swung the big door shut, the sound of the dead bolt sliding back into place. He was never like this before, thought Nick. His daughter's thing, it's still eating him up.

As the two young bailiffs joked quietly in the corner, Peter Mendez checked his watch against the clock on the wall of the new courtroom. For the fourth time. Almost ten, but still no sign of Old Bailey or Roger Hesterfield.

The authoritarian bastard, he's making us wait for him. Wants us to sweat, reassert his power the first day in the new arena. Bastard!

Mort Zussman had engaged Peter in a real heart-to-heart the night before. "Just where are we heading?" and all that. Not very optimistic now, the campaign manager hedged his bets against the next poll showing the whole effort going into the toilet.

The time pressure, the mental stress. Peter felt as though the top of his head would blow off. And then to be stuck on this piece-a-shit armed robbery as Sheilah tries some kind of . . . I don't know what.

Oh, please God, don't let Hesterfield work us through lunch. I've got to jog today, or I'll go nuts.

"Also, Frank," said Gerry O'Toole, still outside the gates to the mansion. "From what you're saying, Ketterson's using the young ones he's dating as cover for stalking the older ones he's disappearing somehow, right?"

"Right."

"Okay, but in that case, Ketterson wouldn't have killed the Giordano girl, right? He'd have been using her to go after some older woman."

Frank hadn't shared with Gerry his suspicions about Ketterson stalking Sheilah Quinn, but even so, he had no answer to his partner's point. "I haven't figured that out yet."

O'Toole fluttered his lips. "Time you got?"

Frank glanced at his watch. "Ten-fifteen."

"What say we go a-knocking on Little Red Riding Hood's door? If he's in there, maybe the flake's just cocky enough to see what we want."

Frank thought about it. He'd sat around with Sheilah enough over the weekend to be almost as antsy as Gerry. "What can it hurt to try?"

They got out of the car and went up to the very impressive gate, Frank remembering the intercom from their first visit three months before. About twenty seconds after pushing the button on the electronic box, he got a remarkably clear voice responding to some computer chimes.

But not Ketterson's voice.

"Yes?"

That butler, maybe? "Police. Who's this?"

"Parsons, sir. I am employed by Mr. Ketterson."

Parsons, the butler, right. "We'd like to come

up, have a talk with him."

"I'm afraid that is not possible, sir."

"Why not?"

"Mr. Ketterson is out."

"When did he leave?"

"I'm not sure, sir."

"When will he be back?"

"I don't know, sir."

Frank began to feel a little silly, interrogating an electronic box and losing ground to it. "Mr. Parsons, you have any objection to buzzing us in, let us take a look around for ourselves?"

Frank noticed O'Toole stiffening a little. This was the tricky part. The butler says no, then, without a warrant or probable cause, it's back to the car to wait for Ketterson himself.

Maybe ten more seconds went by. Then the voice came back over the intercom. "I believe that would be possible, sir. So long as I might accompany you."

Both detectives jumped a little as a high-pitched whine made the gates vibrate and begin to open.

"This is ridiculous," said Peter Mendez, pulling the cuff of his sleeve back over the watch. "Vinnie, it's ten-thirty already. Can you knock on the door, see what's holding things up?"

Sheilah watched the young bailiff think about it. "I dunno, Mr. Mendez. Maybe you better do that."

She thought, Vinnie doesn't want to spend his

first day in the new building being reamed out on the carpet of Judge Hesterfield's new chambers. And I sure can't blame him.

Mendez rose, walking over to the door. He knocked. And waited. Putting his ear against the wood, he knocked again. And waited again. To the others, he said, "I don't hear anything."

Pablo Diaz whispered to his lawyer. "This like school?"

Sheilah turned to him. "What?"

"Like school, you know? The teacher don't show, you can go home."

"No, Pablo. It's not like that."

Vinnie said, "This is screwy."

Mendez took the handle of the door. When he pulled down on it, the big six-panel swung inward. "There's nobody in here."

Vinnie walked over and entered the chambers. Sheilah got up and followed him. By the time she reached the door, Peter was slightly across the threshold, and the young bailiff stood in the middle of the starkly empty room, palms upward in a shrugging gesture.

"Not just nobody," said Sheilah. "Nothing, period."

"This don't make no sense." Vinnie gave a once-over around the chambers. "O.B. was gonna move the judge's stuff over Saturday morning, after His Honor was done packing up."

Sheilah thought back to her seeing Hesterfield about withdrawing from the *Ketterson* case. "He was finished with the boxes — or close to it — by around four-thirty Friday afternoon."

Mendez looked at her, started to say something, then didn't.

Vinnie shrugged helplessly. "So, what do we do?"

"Maybe you could call the old First Session," said Sheilah. "See if maybe Judge Hesterfield showed up there by mistake. Or habit."

Vinnie shook his head. "All the phones in the old building got disconnected."

"What about the first-floor security desk?"

Vinnie looked at her oddly, almost suspiciously. "That one's still supposed to work, but nobody's on the desk during the day anymore, account of the only people in the building now are the contractor's crew." Vinnie shook his head some more. "And besides, if the judge did show up over there, O.B. would have reminded him to come over here."

Sheilah nodded. "Except O.B. isn't around, either."

Peter Mendez looked at his watch again. "Well, I'm going over there."

Vinnie was walking back into the new courtroom as Sheilah Quinn said, "I'll join you."

Frank Sikes had been inside the Ketterson mansion only twice before, once to take the suspect to the Homicide Unit the night of Jessica Giordano's murder, and once to help execute the search warrant the court had approved. But he'd never been above the ground floor, Gerry O'Toole taking care of things on the second.

Now, as Frank climbed the wide staircase behind O'Toole and Parsons, he could really appreciate the extent of Arthur Ketterson's little cottage. Magnificent, like they maybe have in England or France. I might not be too up on the architecture, but I know enough to recognize a palace when I see one.

Over his shoulder, the butler said, "Is there any particular place you'd care to start, gentlemen?"

"Yeah," said Frank. "His bedroom."

They were led through a living room and into a bedroom off it. The bed looked like an old-fashioned horse sleigh, the Oriental rugs some kind of antiques, probably. Frank sniffed around, then went to the bed. There was something cold, even sterile, about the furniture and the air. "Ketterson sleeps here?"

Parsons seemed to hesitate. "Mr. Ketterson spends considerable time in several of the suites, sir."

"Then let's see those, too."

The next bedroom looked like a boudoir from a black-and-white movie, sort of a courtesan's version of the room Frank and Sheilah had loved at the inn. Mahogany four-poster with a canopy, and curtains you'd have to draw back in order to get into the bed. Lots of little chairs and tables and even a wheeled serving cart. A framed portrait hung on the wall between a couple of sconces. Frank stared at it, thinking, Jesus H. Christ.

"The mother's room, right?" asked O'Toole.

"This was Mrs. Ketterson's suite."

Parsons didn't glance at, or even near, the big painting of a woman looking at a picture of some dancers on a wall.

Gerry said, "And that's her there?"

Without turning, the butler said, "Yes, sir."

Frank was staring at the painting, his mouth nearly hanging open.

"Hey," O'Toole said to Sikes, "what's the matter?"

His partner didn't respond.

"Hey, Frank?" Now Gerry moved toward him. "You still with us?"

"Her eyes."

O'Toole glanced up at the face in the painting. "Looks kind of familiar, somehow."

"The missing girls. Their photos. Dark hair, and eyes just like hers."

Gerry focused on the painting now. "Yeah, but you never showed me the girls' photos, right? So how come she looks familiar to me, too?"

"Think about it," said Frank Sikes. "You've seen her in court a lot."

Nick thought, I don't believe this shit. "Hey, this is a hard-hat area now."

Over the echoing sounds of pounding and power tools on the ground floor of the old courthouse, the young bailiff Nick had seen around the site spoke to him. "You're the foreman, right?"

"Right." Behind the bailiff were two suits, the lawyers from Rudy's case, no question. Nick said, "What's the problem?"

"We need to go up to the First Session, look around some."

"Look around? Are you kidding? The place is being torn apart."

The male lawyer said, "Let's go."

Nick considered making a stand, but he was the boss only when the boss himself wasn't on the job site. "Your funeral," said Nick to their backs.

Sheilah climbed the wide staircase behind Mendez and Vinnie, plaster chunks crunching under her shoes. At the top, Vinnie pushed on one of the First Session's doors, but it didn't give.

Mendez said, "It's locked?"

"Yeah."

Sheilah could hear construction noise inside.

Vinnie pounded on the door. "Hey? Hey in there. Open up."

From the First Session came a muffled "Go away."

"This is the Sheriff's Department. We gotta get in there. Now."

The noise stopped. About thirty seconds later, Rudy Giordano opened one of the doors.

Through it, Sheilah could see a cloud of dust hanging over the room.

Giordano hiked a pair of safety goggles onto his forehead, his eyes and face haggard, even more so as he recognized her, Sheilah thought. "What do you want?"

Vinnie said, "We're looking for Judge Hesterfield."

Giordano grinned. "Yeah, right. He was helping me out with the pry bar. Just went for coffee."

Mendez looked at his watch again. Leaning into the First Session, he spoke to Vinnie and Sheilah. "Come on."

"Hold it," said Giordano, putting out a hand like a traffic cop. Like Hesterfield, in fact, Sheilah thought. "You can't come in here. This is my building now. The contract says so."

Vinnie found some brass somewhere. "We're coming in."

Giordano looked from one to the other, then stepped back. "Just don't send me the cleaning bills. Or the doctor bills, something hits you on the head."

Walking in, Sheilah said to herself, My God, it's like a bomb went off.

The wainscoting had been pried away from two of the four walls, the jagged edges of interior boards showing through. Debris and dust cluttered every horizontal surface, the chandeliers already down on the floor. Several tall ladders were positioned at different places in the room to access some kind of elaborate system of pulleys and wires affixed the ceiling beams and trailing back to the judge's bench. Only the bar enclosure area remained relatively intact, everything ready to go to trial if only a competent cleaning crew would just spend a morning tidying up the rest of the place.

Giordano made his way to the bench, flicking some kind of switch that stopped a low humming sound, then flicking another to bring up light from some lanterns with rubber handles and cages around the bulbs. The effect was eerie, and Sheilah felt a wobbly chill.

The sort of sensation Arthur Ketterson would bring on.

Vinnie picked his way to the chambers door, opening it.

Giordano said, "He don't get his stuff out soon, I won't be able to work around it no more."

Sheilah watched Vinnie look down at the cartons. "Full," he said, "and I'm pretty sure a couple of these things are from on top the judge's desk." Vinnie turned back to them. "This don't make no sense. O.B. was supposed to move all these boxes over to the new building Saturday morning."

Sheilah said, "Mr. Giordano, when did you start working here?"

At first, the contractor looked as though he didn't see how she had the right to ask him questions. Then Giordano said, "Saturday, around noon. Make up for the time the bastard cost me, not getting out of here on schedule."

Mendez said, "But then where's Judge Hesterfield?"

Sheilah looked around. "And O.B."

Vinnie shrugged helplessly, again with his palms up. "What now?"

Giordano motioned them toward the doors. "Nobody minds, you want to discuss this outside?"

In the corridor, Sheilah said, "Vinnie, I think we'd better find a working phone."

The young bailiff grew concerned. "You mean, like, call the judge at home?"

"No." The wobbly chill again. "I mean Sgt. Frank Sikes."

In the downstairs parlor — the word Gerry O'Toole heard the butler use, swear to God — Frank Sikes reached to his belt and turned off his beeper. "Mind if I use your telephone?"

Parsons said, "Would it be a toll call, sir?"

O'Toole grunted out a laugh. This guy's a pip. Gives us the run of the house, then worries about a buck or two of long-distance on the flake's phone bill?

Sikes walked over to a table model on a bookshelf. "We'll leave a quarter under the welcome mat."

After Frank dialed, O'Toole heard him say, "This is Sikes. . . . How long? . . . Somebody call his house? . . . No. No, send a couple of units right now, but tell them to wait for us — they wouldn't know what they're dealing with. . . . Right, give me the home address. . . . Got it. On our way."

Sikes put down the phone. O'Toole knew better than to ask what was up. "Gerry, we've got to go. Thanks for your time, Mr. Parsons."

"A pleasure, gentlemen."

After Vinnie called the Homicide Unit from the security desk in the old courthouse, Peter Mendez led the trio back across the park to the new building. They went up to the courtroom, where Pablo Diaz sat.

Mendez looked down at his watch. It read 11:30. "I can't believe this is happening to me."

Sheilah said, "It's happening to all of us, Peter. But it doesn't have to happen again."

He was distracted by something else in his head, came back to her slowly. "What do you mean?"

"You ever know Hesterfield or Old Bailey to be late for court?"

"No."

"Me, neither. So I'm betting something's happened, and this case is probably going to have to start over before a new judge."

Mendez began counting the days to the election. "That's impossible."

"No, Peter. It's likely. But not unavoidable."

Mendez was thinking, I do not have time for this horseshit. Mort Zussman said I didn't have enough time for the final push as it was. "What do you mean 'not unavoidable'?"

"I mean you've already nailed Borbón on his plea bargain. Let me plead Diaz as just an accessory, sentence of time already served, and we're both quit of this one."

"No way. I need somebody to go down as the gunman."

"Which might not happen, once I recall the two eyeball witnesses after they've gotten a look at Cundo Borbón."

The light began to dawn. "That's the reason you wanted my other witnesses unsequestered?"

"Gold star, Peter. They get a look at Borbón on the stand, get to hear him, and I'm thinking they'll both agree that he's a lot more like the gunman than my guy." A smug smile. "And when Diaz takes the stand, he'll testify he was in the car but didn't know what his friend was going to do."

"But Diaz has priors. I can impeach him with at least some of them."

"Which means the jury will hear about those convictions, none of which involve anything as heavy as armed robbery." Sheilah smiled more broadly. "But the sheet on Borbón — your witness, who I get to impeach before that? Wow."

The world according to Mendez was turning to mud. "Look, even if — for the sake of argument — we agreed on your plea request, Hesterfield would still have to accept it."

"If he shows up, fine. If not, we can get

another judge to wave the magic wand over the deal. Either way, this case is closed out, and you can hit the campaign trail. What do you say?"

It wasn't perfect. It wasn't even very good, not having a vindication of who the gunman was. But it would let Peter get on with what was really important.

A glacial sigh. "Deal. Let's cut the paperwork back in my office now."

Sheilah went over to her client. After a few moments, Peter Mendez watched him nod emphatically in response to what she was saying.

Rudy Giordano flicked the switches again, the power coming back on with a low, steady hum. As he considered what he should do next, he thought about that asshole of a bailiff. "We're coming in." Who the fuck does he think he is? But better to let them in, lose a couple of minutes, get them off my back.

And that prosecutor? The asshole of assholes. He looks even worse than he did last week. No wonder the bitch of a defense attorney whipped his ass.

Well, I'll show them. I'll show all of them. What justice really is.

Picking up another pulley, Rudy Giordano felt good for the first time in he couldn't remember how long.

"Anything?" said Frank Sikes, not expecting much.

On the sidewalk in front of Hesterfield's home, the oldest of the four uniformed patrol officers shook his head. "Car was in the drive when we pulled up. Called in the plate. Belongs to the judge all right."

Frank looked past the Mercedes to the house itself. Everything looked normal. Serene, even.

"Okay. We might have a crazy holding him, or it might be nothing, or something in between. Everybody know what Judge Hesterfield looks like?"

All but one of the uniforms nodded.

To the one who didn't know Hesterfield, Frank said, "You and your partner stay here, back us up. Other two, around to the rear. Don't kick in; just cover the door. Questions?"

None.

Frank nodded. "Call Dispatch, too, get an address on Old Bailey — Christ, I don't even know his first name."

"The judge's bailiff?" asked the senior patrol officer.

"Yeah. We may be going there next."

Frank waved, and the first pair of uniforms moved off to flank the house from a wide angle.

O'Toole said to him, "Kind of wish we had some Kevlar vests in the trunk."

"Ketterson's a strangler, not a gunman."

"So far."

When the patrol officers were out of sight, both homicide detectives drew their Glock 17 pistols and moved up to either side of the front door.

Frank put his ear to the jamb, listening, then shook his head. He pushed the button, a deep chiming audible from inside the house. No response. A second push. Same. Bad vibes from this.

Knocked, hard and then harder.

Worse vibes. Tried the handle, knowing it wouldn't open and not being disappointed.

To O'Toole, Frank said, "What do you think?"

"I never kicked in a judge's door before. You figure it'll feel any different?"

Frank Sikes had to grin. "Maybe a little better than usual."

Gerry O'Toole said, "I could use that," and he squared around, cocking his right foot just above the lock.

Sheilah Quinn stood up from the chair in front of Mendez's desk. "Believe me, Peter, we're doing the right thing here."

She'd extended her hand to shake, but Mendez was already turned away, so she silently withdrew it.

As Sheilah closed his door, she heard Peter Mendez yell what sounded like "Mort!"

Sheilah Quinn hoped he had dialed someone on his telephone.

Back on the road, O'Toole driving, Frank

490

Sikes said into the car's mike, "There was nothing at the judge's house. Nobody, no evidence of a struggle or even a break-in. We had to bust through the front door, so I left one of the units there to secure it."

The dispatcher cleared her throat. "Roger, Delta three."

The traffic in front of them was awful. "You have any traffic advisories might help us?"

"I have them, Delta three, but they won't help you."

Sikes looked toward O'Toole, who gave his little grunt laugh.

Frank keyed the mike again. "How about that other address we asked for?"

"Wait one."

Krissie hung up the telephone for what seemed like the millionth time that morning. People calling about Etta still, people calling about Sheilah's dad. People not knowing about either death and just calling, like . . . like clients, you know? Going ballistic about why the fuck they can't seem to reach their attorneys.

Krissie took a breath, thought about going down the hall. Then she accidentally noticed Etta's closed door, and she reached for some tissues instead.

God, I'm even looking forward to seeing Vinnie tonight.

Of course, it's not gonna be as classy as the scene a week ago Saturday in his uncle's limo.

No, that'd take some doing.

But still, I have to admit, there's something awful sexy about doing it on the security desk of a courthouse.

Sheilah Quinn stopped off for a real lunch at a nice restaurant. She knew she was just postponing the inevitable, going back to the office to deal with what would have piled up while she was gone most of the prior week.

But then I bought myself back some time this morning, resolving Diaz. And think of the prior week I had.

When the waiter came over, Sheilah ordered soup and an entrée, as well as a glass of chardonnay. Less a celebration and more a reward.

A reward for surviving.

The only utensil Peter Mendez held during lunch was his telephone. And the meal consisted of three raisin/chocolate-chip granola bars he found in his desk drawer. After nearly two hours of yelling at Mort Zussman and being yelled at in return, he really was ready to explode.

I've got to get out of here, clear the head.

Picking up his telephone again, this time as if it were a snake that had bitten him before, Mendez pushed one button, then said to Veronica, "Catch my calls. I'll be gone awhile."

He hung up, rose, and went to the little closet in the wall. After opening the door, Peter Mendez yanked down his tie and started pulling his jogging clothes off the hooks.

Rudy Giordano walked over to the old court-room's window and lifted his thermos from the sill. The coffee was long cold, but it was caffeine, and he was feeling a little sluggish now, working straight through the weekend and all. Been awhile since you done that, he thought. Since you wanted to.

What the fuck? Rudy squinted at the dusty glass, rubbed a clean spot like a porthole into it. No question. That asshole of assholes, Mr. District Attorney. In floppy little shorts and a basketball shirt, jogging out from the new building across the park.

That's what I get for my tax dollars? A fucking loser of a civil servant, goes jogging in the middle of the day instead of studying his cases? Where anybody next to a window can see him, yet.

Capping the thermos, Rudy Giordano thought about just how fucked up the order of things had gotten. Then he felt the caffeine hit, that surge of energy that carries you to the next thing.

God bless the fucking coffee bean, huh?

Krissie said, "You're back."
"We pleaded out. We think."
"You think?"
"It's kind of complicated."
"Want your messages?"
Sheilah took the sheaf of pink message slips

from her secretary. "Any from him?"

"He-imm?"

"No. Ketterson."

"Not today, I'm, like, ecstatic to say."

Roger Hesterfield's absence prevented Sheilah from bringing the withdrawal motion formally. Before she suggested to Mendez and Vinnie that they call the police, and specifically Homicide, the pendulum in her head had swung all the way back to Arthur Ketterson, she thinking that he might have gone after the judge. Thinking it, but not saying as much. After all, the weirdo was still her client, and that tied Sheilah's hands about sharing her suspicions regarding Etta and her father. Best to let sleeping dogs lie, at least until she heard what had happened to Hesterfield.

Scanning her messages, Sheilah said, "How are you doing?"

"I'm okay." In a different tone, she added, "It'll be awhile before I'm good again. Everything go all right with . . . your dad and all?"

"Yes."

"I'm sorry I didn't make it, but after . . . Etta . . ."

"Not to worry, Krissie. What happened to her would throw anybody for a while."

Krissie nodded. "Anything you need me to do?"

Sheilah looked at Etta's closed door. "We're going to have to spend some time today, really sorting through her things."

"I figured. I been over the appointment calendar for this week already, got in touch with all the clients we had things hanging with."

"Good." Sheilah scanned the messages some more. "Let me catch up on these."

Walking into her office, she suddenly realized a tremendous sense of relief in not seeing flowers from Arthur Ketterson on her desk.

"A car?" said Old Bailey's landlady. "Oh, no. Poor Stanley lost his license because of the booze."

"Stanley," said Gerry O'Toole, deadpan.

"Yes." The woman had a moon-shaped face under bluish hair and a pear-shaped body under frumpy clothes. "It was what sobered him up, losing his license and all. Hasn't touched a drop in — oh, a year, maybe?"

Frank Sikes nodded. It had taken them forever to get there with the traffic, he didn't want to spend forevermore with the landlady. "When's the last time you saw Mr. Bailey?"

"Let me think. Last week sometime? He's quiet, Stanley is, quiet as a mouse. You never hear him moving about."

Frank said, "Can you let us into his apartment?"

Suspicion crept into her voice. "What's this all about?"

"Mr. Bailey never showed up for work today," said Gerry O'Toole.

"Oh, that's not like Stanley, no."

Frank Sikes nodded. "We're a little worried about him."

The landlady sucked in her breath as she brought a hand to her mouth, but she used the other to fish a key ring from the folds of her clothes.

Peter Mendez had left his watch in the office. He knew some people who trained by timing themselves: So many minutes of exercise equaled so many calories expended. But Peter always jogged a set route, with that nice wooded section in the middle of it, and besides, he had to do enough clock-watching on the job. Also, to him, jogging wasn't training or exercise; it was a way to burn off anxiety.

Of which he'd borne more than his share lately. The campaign was cascading toward the toilet with the speed and consistency of diarrhea, his marriage probably racing it neck and neck. And now he couldn't even seem to litigate competently. Thanks to that fucking Sheilah Quinn.

No. No, bad attitude. I have to try some positive thinking here. With luck, the Arthur Ketterson dragon will keep its head down and the fire in its mouth until well after Election Day. And the Borbón/Diaz fiasco may not even be all that noticed by the media, unless the pregnant — formerly pregnant — witness gets it into her head to be some kind of lightning rod for victims' rights. But she wasn't shot or anything that night at the liquor store, and, with any luck at all, whatever's happened to that bastard Hesterfield will crowd any other aspects of the case off the front page.

Peter heard a motor noise over his left shoulder. Glancing back, he saw the grillwork of a BMW about a quarter of a mile behind him.

Maybe I ought to slow down, hit up the owner of the car for a campaign contribution as he goes by.

Peter Mendez found himself grinning for the first time in what seemed like weeks. Fucking jogging, works every time.

Krissie said, "I'm ready if you are."

Sheilah looked up from her desk. "You're talking about Etta's office, I take it?"

"Like, what else?"

Sheilah looked back down. She'd returned most of the phone calls and had either spoken with the people trying to reach her or determined there was no real emergency. But she still had a lot of mail to sort through.

"Tell you what, Krissie. How about we close down early today, then tackle Etta's stuff first thing tomorrow, when we're both fresh and can spend the whole day on it?"

The secretary looked relieved. "Got my vote."

"Take off when you're ready, and I'll see you in the morning."

After Krissie moved back into the reception area, Sheilah picked up her phone one more time. Dialing the number she knew by heart, she was disappointed when Frank didn't answer.

"Is Sergeant Sikes available?"

"I'm sorry, no. If it's important, I can beep him."

"No. Just tell him" — what, to call me at home? — "just tell him attorney Quinn was curious about Judge Hesterfield."

"Your first name?"

"Sheilah, with a second *h* at the end."

"So, now what?" said Gerry O'Toole from the driver's seat.

After finding nothing unusual in Old Bailey's apartment, they were stuck in more bumper-to-bumper traffic. Possibly an accident or construction ahead, more likely just congestion on the too-narrow roads. And the siren wouldn't help: With all the parked cars lining the curbs, there were no spaces for the vehicles ahead of them to pull into, anyway.

Frank Sikes said. "I don't like that both the judge and O.B. have dropped off the face of the earth."

"Yeah, but we're Homicide, remember? Let Donna and her computer worry about them."

Frank just stared at him.

Gerry noticed, then looked at the car in front of them again. "Okay, so I don't like it, either. But we got file cabinets full of people we already know are dead. Which kind of revives the question of what the fuck we do now."

"You can go back to the office. Just drop me at the old courthouse first."

"You think you're gonna find something there?"

"Never know till you look," said Sikes.

"Yeah, but the judge's car was in his driveway."

"Maybe because somebody wanted us to think he got himself home."

"How about O.B., then?"

"Gerry, somebody — and we're both thinking Arthur Ketterson, right?"

"Goes without saying, that AWOL flake."

"Okay. Ketterson does Hesterfield and O.B., he might go through their pockets, find car keys on one but not the other."

"So the flake knows he's got only the judge's car to move."

"Right. And Hesterfield's driver's license would have his home address on it."

O'Toole clucked his tongue off the roof of his mouth. "Still seems pretty thin."

"Then try this. If Ketterson did both the judge and his bailiff, where's the only place he'd find them together?"

Gerry O'Toole looked over at his partner. "So, I'll drop you at the old courthouse."

Frank Sikes leaned his head against the backrest. They'd moved maybe twenty feet in the last five minutes.

The only place in the city without traffic.

499

Peter Mendez loved this little stretch of wooded road. Close your eyes and the smell of evergreens would make you think you'd gone to sleep and awakened in the wilderness. The gravel on the shoulder really was as smooth as a groomed track, a goddamn soothing break for the fevered brain.

So what if the campaign tanks completely? I'm tired of being a government attorney, anyway, and I can find another job. One that'll pay better, too. Maybe a large firm with a department specializing in the defense of white-collar criminals — alleged criminals, that is. Use my prosecution experience as a calling card. Not to mention my ethnicity, the firm getting to count me in statistical reports to probably a hundred agencies. Yeah, I'd still be watching the clock, but now it'd be for billable hours, which would let me afford a much better clock.

Behind him, Mendez heard the engine again, recognizing it this time for the BMW. Huh, thought the guy had turned off, but — glancing back — no, that's him. Only car on the road, too. Probably retired or independently wealthy, out for —

A sickening feeling came over Peter. He remembered from the testimony at trial that Arthur Ketterson drove a BMW, one of the really expensive sports models. This time, a lingering glance over the shoulder. The BMW was closer now, but Peter couldn't see anything except the flush front, no profile to help him with the model it was. However, he could make out a silhouette of the driver, and he relaxed.

Guy was wearing a hard hat. Peter almost laughed. Can you just imagine it? That arrogant, overbred jerk Ketterson in a hard hat? Probably an engineer or an architect, maybe even the one from the new courthouse project, back there to check on the last few items.

Then the engine revved some, and Peter realized the car was going to pass him. He edged over three feet more onto the shoulder, plenty of room for the BMW to —

Instead of the road and the trees, Peter saw the sky in front of him, which made no sense at all. Then he found himself collapsing into a ball as he flew through the air, like that dive his kids used to make the water spray all around them. The impact of the vehicle was still just a sound, not a feeling yet, the shock disrupting his nerve endings for the first few seconds.

Then Peter landed hard on the gravel, rolling to the point of tumbling, scraping the skin right off his hands and face, elbows and knees. Finally coming to a stop, he tried to get oriented, looking first to his left, seeing his leg —

And wishing he hadn't. The splinter of bone that stuck through the flesh, a gaping, grisly hole where —

Even over his scream, and the rush of sensations that slammed into his brain, Peter Mendez could hear the BMW's engine behind him, revving again.

"I could make better time jogging it."

Gerry O'Toole said, "This shit is no picnic for me, either, Frank."

Sikes looked at the unbending, unending line of traffic in front of them. Still no sense in trying the siren.

"Gerry?"

"Yeah?"

"Drop me at this subway stop up here, okay?"

"You got it."

As Frank got out of the car, he noticed a homeless woman sitting on a piece of cardboard, rocking back and forth with her hand out. As he approached her position, she said in a singsong voice, "Help the homeless at the holidays. Help the homeless at the holidays."

Sikes went by her, thinking, Holidays? Which one's she talking about, Columbus Day?

To his back, she said, "Aw, you're a tight queer, ain't you?" Then, without missing a beat, "Help the homeless at the holidays. Help the . . ."

If Frank Sikes had been in the mood for a joke, it would have felt good to laugh.

Sitting behind the security desk, Vinnie checked his watch. Almost 4:15, and he hadn't seen a construction worker for almost half an hour. Maybe telling Krissie to wait till six was being a little too cautious. He knew he was ready for her, especially with the prospect of the double shift he was working.

Which was okay by Vinnie. O.B. hadn't wanted to leave the judge high and dry, first day in the new building — which Vinnie could certainly understand — so they'd agreed to switch off another day later in the month to make up for O.B. covering for him the prior Friday night. Only thing was, Vinnie didn't like O.B. not showing up at all today. Judge Hesterfield, now, was a different story. Vinnie could give two shits about that drunken asshole. But O.B., he was quality people, and Vinnie worried that nobody could seem to figure out where the fuck he was.

Then Vinnie saw a guy wearing a hard hat, carrying what looked like a rolled-up rug over one shoulder, a pry bar in the other hand. Walking kind of unsteady, too, face under the hard hat down toward the ground, like the rug was a heavy fucker and the guy didn't want to risk tripping with it.

Christ, thought Vinnie. Good thing I told Krissie six o'clock after all. "Hey, how you doing?"

For an answer, the guy just waved the pry bar toward him.

Vinnie said, "I need to log you in. How long you gonna be?"

For an answer this time, the guy wearing the hard hat hit Vinnie in the face with the pry bar, then caught him again over the right ear, going down.

Pitching the last piece of junk mail into the office wastebasket, she picked up the bleating telephone. "Sheilah Quinn."

"Ms. Quinn, this is Detective O'Toole, over in Homicide."

She stifled the urge to ask if Frank was all right. "Oh, yes. I called Sergeant Sikes a while ago about Judge Hesterfield."

"Maybe you could give the information to me."

"Well, it wasn't exactly information."

"It wasn't?"

"No. You see, I was supposed to be on trial before Judge Hesterfield this morning, and I was there when the court officer called the police about it, and I was" — this is going on too long to sound right, girl — "I was just wondering if there'd been any progress."

"Progress."

"On finding the judge. Or his bailiff."

"Well, I really can't comment on that now. You want, I can pass the message on to Sergeant Sikes."

"Do you — did he say when he'd be back, by any chance?"

"No, but for that matter, your office is close enough, you can go over, maybe catch up to him."

"Go over where?"

"The old courthouse. He took the subway, should be there by now."

"Oh. Thanks."

Hanging up, Sheilah thought about the conversation. O'Toole would think it strange if Frank hasn't told him about us, and he probably hasn't, since O'Toole thought I was calling with information about Hesterfield.

As if I'd have information about him. I've tried to have as little as possible to do with him, and the only thing I know that others might not is . . .

Roger's gun, the one he showed me after that damned Christmas party when I was still clerking. Crazy for the man just to disappear like that, and with Old Bailey, too. Which certainly makes it look like foul play, and therefore probably Arthur Ketterson. But what if it really is innocent? What if Roger just packed up and decided to . . . take off? No. Roger wouldn't — what did the hippies call it when I was young? Oh, yeah. Dropping out. No, that's not Roger, but if his gun is gone, then he could have left voluntarily, even though it seems unlikely.

However, if the gun's still in that hideaway panel on his bench, there's no way he would have left without taking it out first. None. Which would give Frank some clear evidence that something unquestionably bad had happened.

Sheilah looked out the window. The traffic was a beast, and she probably could almost walk faster, but then Frank and she wouldn't have a car to ride home in.

Home. Thinking about Frank riding home with her.

Sheilah Quinn decided she liked that idea. A lot.

Frank Sikes went into the main entrance of the old courthouse, thinking, Nobody at the security desk?

He walked over to it. Granted the building was just about shut down, and quiet as a ghost now, but still it was only a little after — what, 4:30? You'd think the sheriff's office would maintain some kind of guard.

Then Frank noticed the phone, a thin film of plaster dust on it. On all the surfaces, in fact, once you looked. Maybe that's why nobody's around. Plaster dust gets into and onto everything, drives you nuts.

He picked up the telephone receiver. Dead. Of course, they've moved everybody over to the new building, they'd have disconnected the phones here, too.

Then Frank thought he heard somebody moving around on the upper floor. Walking down the first-floor corridor, his ears now could pick up only his own shoes, making a crunching, echoing sound as he moved toward the wide staircase.

Crunching. Turning the corner for the first step, Frank noticed that there was crumbling debris everywhere. Then a skittering noise from above him, and Frank looked up just in time to see the back of a head with a hard hat on it disappearing out of sight at the second-floor railing.

"Hey," said Frank, but all he heard was more of the skittering noise and, he thought, the sound of the First Session's door shushing open and closed.

"Hey, who's up there?"

No response again. Cursing the dead phone at the security desk, Frank Sikes drew his Glock and began climbing the staircase, slowly.

Krissie Newton hung up the pay phone in the bar a few blocks from the old courthouse. Fucking Vinnie. Gives me the number at the security desk downstairs; then when you call it, the fucking computer voice tells you "That number is not in service at this time."

Well, he said six, right? Back on her stool, Krissie checked her watch. She had an hour, plenty of time for another peach schnapps drink, a "Sex on the Beach."

Before some "sex on the desk."

Krissie caught the bartender's eye and with her index finger made a circling motion over her glass.

Sheilah, foot on the brake, gearshift in neutral, drummed a thumb against the steering wheel. Her mantra: I should have walked. I should have walked. . . .

Boy, whoever said anticipation makes things better never sat in traffic while thinking it. Then a memory of the last time she drove to see Frank flowed into her mind. The trip out to the inn for that weekend, which now seemed so long ago.

But the sensations it stirred seemed very fresh,

very real, and Sheilah Quinn found herself humming Lionel Ritchie's "All Night Long," despite the fact that the Miata hadn't moved three car lengths in the last five minutes.

Very carefully, Frank Sikes pushed open one of the doors to the First Session. The left door, so the Glock in his right hand could come to bear right away.

Only he couldn't pick out a target. The room was in shadow, the faint light of an autumn afternoon through the high windows not nearly enough to allow him to see well. Frank flipped a few wall switches near the door. Nothing.

Made sense, though. The phone's out, the electricity might be off, too.

As his eyes adjusted to the dimness, Frank began to appreciate how much of the room already had been torn apart. Guywires running up to pulleys in the ceiling beams, the chandeliers down — no wonder the light switch didn't work. And most of the wainscoting was pried off the walls, making the place feel smaller, like that garbage compression chamber in *Star Wars*.

Chamber. Chambers.

Frank looked over at the door to Hesterfield's chambers on the left side of the bench. Open. He moved slowly toward it, noticing the air growing colder somehow. Then he stopped dead.

Somebody was sitting in shadow, the bailiff's chair near the gallery end of the jury box.

Leveling his weapon, Frank said, "Police officer. Who's there?"

No reply. Par for the course.

Frank edged a little closer to the seated figure, dark shoes and white socks sticking out, like the man was stretched back, napping.

"O.B.?" said Frank. "O.B., that you?"

From off to the left, near the bench, a squeaking sound and "I'm afraid he can't hear you, Detective."

Frank wheeled around toward the witness stand, both hands on his gun, legs apart at shoulder width. Combat stance, because he'd recognized the voice. Garbled, like the man had a cold, but no question who it belonged to: Arthur Ketterson.

In the poor light, Frank could barely make out the silhouette, sitting upright in the witness chair, shadows over Ketterson's face and torso, some of the wires to the ceiling beams glinting a little where the shadows ended. The guy's fingers were splayed out on the narrow ledge in front of the witness chair, no weapon that Frank could see. "Hands over your head, Ketterson."

"I don't think so."

"Raise them empty, or I'll shoot you."

One of the wires glinted differently, and a muzzle flash from the witness stand blinded Frank as the sound of a shot reached his ears. The first round struck him in the stomach, a second in the chest. He fell to the floor, his gun clattering away from him.

Even as he passed out, though, Frank Sikes would have sworn that Ketterson's hands had never moved.

Nobody around.

Sheilah Quinn moved past the untended security desk, the plaster dust seeming worse than it had that morning, her heels on the stone floor of the corridor the only sound, like somebody rhythmically snapping their fingers over and over. At the foot of the stairs, she stopped. A scratching, dragging noise from the second floor, but muffled, as though it was behind a wall or something.

"Hello, is anybody up there?"

Then silence before a door creaked open. Somebody coughing while saying "Come on up."

It sounded like him, sort of. "Frank, is that you?"

"Yeah." More coughing. "Plaster dust. But I found something."

"What? "

"You have to see it" — cough — "to believe it."

Looking upward, Sheilah Quinn began to climb the stairs.

Gerry O'Toole pulled a completed incident report out of the typewriter and read it over, correcting by hand the two typos he spotted. Then a glance at the clock over the detention cell.

Five-fifteen. Frank should have been at the courthouse — what, an hour ago?

"Hey, anybody heard from Sikes?"

Different voices called out, "No,"

"Not a word," and "He's your fucking partner, isn't he?"

Gerry O'Toole graciously thanked one and all, then rolled a blank form into the typewriter. Frank doesn't call me in another half hour, I'll swing by the courthouse myself, see what's happening.

Sheilah Quinn pushed open the right door of the First Session and walked in. The room was dark, only a few rays of dying sunlight trickling through the window glass, making crazy patterns of shadows everywhere.

"Frank?"

Coughing from behind the judge's bench.

She began walking toward it, the interior even more dismantled than she remembered from that morning. As Sheilah drew closer to the bar enclosure, she could make out two figures, slumped into chairs at the prosecution table on the right, near the jury box.

"Frank?"

That's when the rubber construction lanterns suddenly came on, not very brightly in an absolute sense, but enough to illuminate the room.

To illuminate a nightmare.

Sheilah sucked in a breath, nearly shrieking. As a lawyer, she'd instinctively looked first to the bench, where Roger Hesterfield sat in his chair. Only his features were grossly contorted, bloated and bluish, the flesh above the cheekbones sagging, making the bugging eyes seem vertically eliptical. A lot of those shiny wires running down from the ceiling around him, some even seeming to be connected to his . . . head?

Stunned, her gaze moved to the witness stand. Arthur Ketterson, wearing a dirty T-shirt, was slumped forward in the chair, his face between his hands on the wooden ledge in front of him. There were dark bruises on the cheeks, and more wires, these obviously connected to his shoulders and hands.

Then Sheilah turned to the jury box. O.B. was stretched out in his chair at the gallery end of it, his skull caved in at the hairline, the flesh around his nose and eyes blackened. More wires.

At the prosecution table, another body, Peter Mendez in . . . a jogging outfit? No wires, but his legs were both broken, the jagged bone sticking through the flesh under the running shorts, his face a death mask of pain and terror.

And next to Mendez, Frank. Oh my God, Frank. Blotches of blood covering his shoulder and his shirtfront and the top of his slacks, bright red blood.

Sheilah moved toward Frank. His chest was moving. Not much, but he was alive. Still alive.

Then Sheilah heard movement above her, on the bench, and turned toward it.

Rudolph Giordano grinned down at her. His

512

right hand held a gun, pointed in her direction.

Giordano said, "I figured I'd have to snatch you off the street, maybe even out of your fucking office. Good of you to just drop by like this."

Sheilah gestured helplessly around her. "What . . . what are you doing?"

Giordano said, "We're going to have another trial. Only this time, it's gonna be a real one. Where that fucking monster on the stand tells the truth. About how he killed my baby."

Sheilah felt a little dizzy, struggled to focus. "You . . . you're crazy."

"Uh-uh. I'm the one sane person in the room. Because I know how everything's gonna come out. The right way, this time."

"I'm leaving, and I'm taking Sergeant Sikes with me."

Giordano frowned. Still holding the gun on Sheilah, he used his left hand to pick up something that looked like a series of tongue depressors, all lashed together with . . . wires running from the ends.

Giordano said, "The judge wouldn't like that. He'd hold you in contempt or something, make me shoot you. Right, Your Honor?"

Giordano waggled the thing in his left hand, and wires glinted over Hesterfield's head. The corpse nodded grotesquely, a garbled caricature of Hesterfield's deep voice saying, "That's right" as the puppeteer's lips barely moved.

When I was downstairs, and thought I heard

Frank's voice, it was . . . Giordano, imitating him.

Sheilah stole a glance at Frank Sikes, still breathing, then took a deep breath herself. *I can't help Frank if this maniac shoots me, too.*

"*Coun*selor?" in Hesterfield's voice again.

Looking up at the bench, Sheilah said, "What do you want me to do?"

Rudolph Giordano smiled. "I want you to do your job. Ask this fucking monster the right questions, get me justice here."

Slowly, buying time to think, Sheilah Quinn moved to the defense table on the left and sat down, trying not to look at the horror surrounding her.

NINETEEN

"It would be a help in examining the, uh, defendant if you could tell me what happened here."

Sheilah wasn't sure that would work, but Rudolph Giordano, still standing on the bench next to the seated body of Roger Hesterfield, nodded. Then Giordano began speaking, giving her time.

If only Sheilah could come up with a way to use it.

". . . and all these months, the system's been jerking me around. You're a lawyer, you should know how that is. And not just about my Jessica, my baby. Even on this courthouse thing here. Judge Roger fucking Hesterfield, not moving out when he was supposed to. This county commissioner I know told me the boss judge gave Hesterfield an order, that he had to be gone — absolutely positively — before the weekend. So, last Friday night, I came back after my crew was done for the day, be sure Hesterfield had cleared out."

Roger cleared out. Sheilah remembered his gun, in the panel at the bench. Might as well be a mile away, even if it was still there.

"Only when I walk in the door downstairs,

there's nobody at the security desk, which seems kind of funny to me. All these weeks, there's been a bailiff down there, usually that young guy come up with you and Mendez to see me this morning." Giordano shook his head. "But last Friday, when I climb the stairs to this floor, what do I hear but the fucking baby-killer, your client. Only he's in the courtroom here, talking to the judge. I kind of peek in the doors just in time to see Hesterfield running for the bench. Ketterson's right on his heels, though, and catches him between the lawyer tables."

Through the horror, through the madness, one thing registered with Sheilah. Roger would have been trying to reach his gun.

The gun's still there.

"But your client," said Giordano, "he's not dressed like a rich boy. Oh, no. The fucking monster's wearing jeans and a T-shirt, with one of my hard hats on his head. And he's got this pry bar, uses it to strangle our judge here. Right, Your Honor?"

Giordano waggled the sticks in his left hand, and the bloated blue face bobbed up and down again. "Yes, Mr. Giordano," in the same garbled voice.

Then the contractor, in his own voice, said, "I used to do puppet shows, for my baby and her friends, learned how to imitate voices pretty good. Even . . . even hers."

Giordano shook that off, continued. "Well, like I said, last Friday I come up from behind, quiet as I can, while they're going at it by the bench. Only I think Ketterson musta heard me, because he turned with his eyes closed and said something like 'What'd you think of my performance?' The goofy bastard, God knows who he figured I was. All I know is, I belted him once on the jaw with my right and followed up with a couple of lefts. He went down easy, the baby-killing wimp. Then I picked up the pry bar and broke his neck for him."

Something's wrong, thought Sheilah. The trial-attorney part of my mind is listening to Giordano differently from the rest of me. Listening to him as though he was a witness, testifying. And something about his "testimony" doesn't ring right.

But what is it? And how can I use it?

"I swear," said Giordano, "that's when I noticed the bailiff over there, the older one. I'm guessing he must have been on the desk downstairs, and your fucking client killed him. Why Ketterson carried him all the way up here, I don't know, but he saved me the trouble."

"Saved you the trouble?" said Sheilah, surprising herself.

"Yeah. A courtroom needs a bailiff, right?" Giordano gestured with the gun. "And a prosecutor. I got him at lunchtime today. Fuckingcivil servant, he's out jogging — probably why he lost my case, too. I even used Ketterson's car, which I spotted a couple of blocks from here as I was taking the judge's car to his own house, throw off

517

where Hesterfield disappeared from while I kept him and the others on ice."

Gerry O'Toole laid the last report of the day in the out-box on top of his desk. Proofread it in the morning, when the eyes are fresh.

Right now, check the watch. Five-forty-five, and Frank never called in.

Okay, so I knock off, drive by the old courthouse. If Frank's still there, maybe we can get some dinner.

" 'On ice'?" Sheilah immediately regretted asking the question. Rudolph Giordano set down the puppet sticks, his hand under the bench. That low vibrating hum came on, then died again quickly as he brought his hand back into view. "Cooling unit, keep the bodies from Friday 'fresh.' " Giordano grinned. "I stole one of my own pony units from the new building across the park, installed it in the bench here — the front's all hollow inside. You wouldn't think that, would you? Then I ran a live electrical line and packed the bodies in like an old-time icebox."

Which means he might have found Roger's gun. Please God, don't let —

"Fact is, I was afraid you all might have noticed when you came tramping in here this morning, looking for Hesterfield."

Sheilah remembered feeling cold, the feeling Arthur Ketterson produced in her sometimes when . . . he'd be in the room. Which he had been, she now realized.

But there was still something off with Giordano's doing all this. Think, girl. For Frank as well as for you.

Sheilah stole a look at the prosecution table to her right. Jesus Mary, his breathing seems so shallow, like it'll stop any —

The sound of a gavel.

She looked up at the bench. The wire above Hesterfield's right hand was quivering, the gavel in the hand poised to strike again. "Pay attention to Mr. Giordano, *coun*selor," said Roger. Almost.

"Yes . . . Your Honor." Use your brain, girl. What's wrong with the program here?

"To carry the DA's body," said Giordano in his own voice, "I rolled him a carpet remnant my crew left at the new building. But coming in with him over my shoulder, that young bailiff was on the security desk. I knocked him out, then hid him down there. I sure as shit don't need two bailiffs up here for the trial."

"Then you don't need Frank, either."

"Frank?"

"Detective Sikes."

A look over at the prosecution table. "Yeah, he came in at the wrong time. Your detective, he probably thought it was Ketterson shooting at him." Giordano gestured with the pistol toward the witness stand. "But it was me, from behind the witness chair there."

519

"Frank's no threat to you now. Let me take him down —"

"No! The detective barged in here. Like he wanted to be part of things. Which is fine; he was part of it from the beginning, anyway. He builds a better case against that baby-killer, I don't need the judge or the bailiff or even you."

"Me?"

"A live lawyer. To ask the right questions, like I said. To get me justice here."

That was it — what was wrong. Giordano had already punished the killer of his daughter. Why would the father want a "trial" now? Why go to all this trouble, killing Mendez and wounding Frank and Vinnie, after he's already had the satisfaction of avenging his family by his own hands? What good does the vindication of a "conviction" do him at this stage?

Sheilah thought back to the trial, the jury coming back hung, the bail argument for Arthur Ketterson. The enraged Rudolph Giordano had gone after Peter Mendez. Not the alleged killer of his daughter, but the prosecutor, who didn't get the father justice. Why would Giordano do that then and all of this now? Unless . . .

My God, could that be it?

"Another?"

Krissie Newton put her hand over the glass, shaking her head at the bartender. It was just about time to start walking to the courthouse, if she wanted to be on time for Vinnie.

520

And she did. At a security desk. That would be a first for her. Maybe for the whole fucking building.

Smiling at becoming a part of history, Krissie took the little money purse from her handbag to settle up the drink tab.

"You're gonna have to bring the Bible over to the witness stand."

"What?" said a distracted Sheilah Quinn, still seated at the defense table.

Rudolph Giordano waved with the gun toward Old Bailey's body. "The Bible. Took me a while to find it, like it was hidden away in a drawer of the bailiff's table there."

Sheilah hadn't seen the Bible used at a trial during all her years in the First Session. "I don't understand."

An edge came into Giordano's voice. "I want this bastard baby-killer telling the truth. I want his hand on the Bible before you ask him questions."

" 'His . . . hand.' "

"Yeah. Only I can't make the bailiff there 'walk' like one of my marionettes. With wood, you can hollow out most of the weight. Can't do that with human bodies, account of the pounds are in the muscles and bones."

Sheilah felt dizzy again, clamped her hands on the edge of the defense table to fight it.

"What's the matter, *coun*selor? You don't like to hear about this kind of shit? Well, let me tell you, it'd be no different from what that medical examiner did to my baby. Hollowing her out, like he was making a canoe, you know?"

Sheilah heard herself say, "I know."

"Okay, then. You go over to the bailiff there and get his Bible."

Sheilah stood, having to lock her knees at first to keep then from wobbling.

"Come on, *coun*selor."

She took a step, didn't fall, and took another, slowly approaching Old Bailey's body at the gallery end of the jury box. The Bible was under his hand, on the telephone table next to him.

The telephone. Tempting, but no hope, not even if it still was connected. Not with Giordano holding a gun on me from twenty feet away.

Reaching for the Bible, Sheilah felt her left knee contact O.B.'s right one. Like bonking into a stone statue.

Old Bailey's distorted head tilted toward her, the jaw slack. "Careful there, Ms. Quinn."

Garbled, like Hesterfield's voice had been, and again coming from the bench, from Giordano. Sheilah knew that — knew it — but the corpse's head movement and open mouth also pushed a small cloud of air toward her face, a hint of what was happening inside the bailiff now.

Sheilah closed her eyes, fought through the gag reflex.

Old Bailey's beyond help, but Frank isn't. Bide your time, wait this maniac out.

She reached for the Bible, nearly jumping as O.B.'s hand lifted away from it, the taut wire glinting in the uneven light.

"He's just trying to be polite, *coun*selor." Giordano's own voice, behind her.

Bracing herself, Sheilah took hold of the Bible, then gingerly walked down the railing of the jury box to the witness stand. She began to place the Bible in front of Arthur Ketterson's body, then actually jumped back this time.

Because Ketterson's eyelids had opened, without any wires attached to them.

"Jesus Mary."

"What?" said Giordano from the bench. "The fucking monster wake up again?"

Now Ketterson's lips moved. "Sheilah," he said in a hoarse whisper. "Help me . . . a doctor."

"I thought . . ." She had to start over, pitched her voice to Giordano. "I thought you'd killed him."

"So did I," said Giordano. "But when I took your client out of the bench cooler here, he opened his fucking eyes and started whining about me paralyzing him. Then he passed out again, fucking baby-killer."

"Sheilah," whispered Ketterson again. "Jessica . . . wanted me . . . sex . . . her house . . . But . . . I didn't . . . kill. . . ."

Sheilah wanted to believe him, because it confirmed what she'd thought of a few minutes before and gave her something to work with, something that might —

"Is that fucking monster talking to you?"

Sheilah whispered to Ketterson, "Act like you've passed out."

"This madman . . . paralyzed. . . . Drilled holes —"

"Arthur, please. Now."

Giordano began moving on the bench as Ketterson closed his eyes.

Loudly, Sheilah said, "He's unconscious again."

Giordano stopped. "Yeah, well, that's too good for him. Put the Bible on the ledge there, by his right hand."

Sheilah did, watching the wire attached to Ketterson's hand grow taut, the hand itself lifting before slapping onto the black book. Then Arthur Ketterson's shoulders lifted up and back into the witness chair, his head lolling.

"I worked on him extra hard, the bastard," said Giordano from atop the bench.

Steadying herself, Sheilah was about to ask what Giordano wanted next when a version of O.B.'s voice rang out. "You swear to tell the truth, the whole truth, and nothing but the truth, so help you God?"

Giordano's idea of the oath or affirmation.

Sheilah turned toward the bench. Now what?

She watched Giordano's lips barely move, a version now of Arthur Ketterson's voice saying, "I do. Promise to tell the truth, that is. Finally."

Sheilah turned her head away.

"Ms. Quinn" — now Hesterfield's voice from

the bench — "start asking your questions."

Sheilah took a deep breath, forced it down into her lungs. I have to do this right. Just right.

To buy us the chance.

Fucking city and fucking traffic. No better than it was a couple hours ago.

Behind the wheel of the unmarked sedan, Gerry O'Toole glanced at his watch. Be awhile before I can get to the courthouse complex. Maybe I'm wasting my time even trying to match up with Frank. He found something, he would have called it in.

On the other hand, where am I going in this traffic anyway? May as well stick to the original plan.

Close question, though. Close fucking question.

"Now, Mr. Ketterson, you testified that you picked up the decedent —"

"Use her name," said Giordano from the bench to her left. "It was . . . Jessica."

Sheilah addressed the witness stand, trying not to look at Ketterson's face. "You arrived at the Giordano house by seven-fifteen P.M., correct?

"Yes," said her client's voice from the bench, the wired hand at the witness chair fluttering up to his cheek in a caricature of the Ketterson gesture.

Sheilah tried to tamp down her revulsion.

Can't get deflected, girl. "And was there anyone else in the house at that time?"

"No."

Sheilah stopped. "Don't you mean that you didn't see anyone else?"

"No." The hand dropped abruptly, almost bouncing off the railing in front of the chair. "I mean, nobody else was there."

"But you didn't go through the whole house, right?"

"Objection," said a version of Peter Mendez's voice.

Reflexively, Sheilah turned toward the prosecution table, immediately sorry she had as her eyes went to the broken legs.

"Sustained," said Hesterfield's voice from above.

Sheilah turned back to the witness stand. "Mr. Ketterson, you testified that you helped the — Jessica with fastening her bra in the foyer of the first floor; then the two of you went out to dinner. But that means somebody else, somebody you didn't know about, could have been elsewhere in the house, maybe —"

"Goddamn it, there wasn't anybody else, okay?"

Ketterson's voice from the bench, but not his speech pattern or rhythm. Sheilah was on the right track, began to *feel* it.

"All right. You testified that after you two left the restaurant, you drove Jessica back to her parents' house, correct?"

"Correct." Just Ketterson now from Giordano.

"And you went inside with her."

"Yes."

"And then what happened?"

"I followed her up to her bedroom and killed her."

Sheilah turned away from the stand, walking toward the defense table, just as naturally as though this were a normal trial. But what she really wanted to do was look at Frank, who seemed to be breathing even more shallowly, almost . . . randomly. Not much time left.

"I don't think so," said Sheilah, turning back around.

"What?"

Ketterson's voice, the hand fluttering up to his cheek again.

She kept her distance from the stand. "I don't think you followed Jessica to that bedroom, and I don't think you killed her. I think she asked you to have —"

"Objection!" came the Mendez voice.

"Sustained," said Hesterfield's voice once more, but with effort, Sheilah thought. Good. Go for the throat. Now.

"Jessica asked you to have sex with her, didn't she?"

"No! Jessica was a good girl," a little of Giordano creeping back into "Ketterson's" voice.

"I think Jessica knew both her parents were going to be out late, and she saw a chance to bed the rich boy, to get her hooks into him."

"You don't know what you're talking about!"

Half Ketterson, half Giordano.

"Get her hooks into him, so she could get out of that house."

"No."

"Jessica couldn't wait to get out —"

"No. No! She loved living in that house. I built it for her."

Now just Giordano.

Sheilah kept addressing Ketterson's body. "Like you played puppet games with her?"

"Not *with* her. *For* her."

"That collection of puppets in Jessica's room. Not her collection. Yours. Jessica wanted out of the house, but you wouldn't oblige her, would you?"

"I told you. I —"

"You left her, Mr. Ketterson. And she went up to her room."

Sheilah sensed Giordano hesitating behind her, not sure of which voice to use now.

He got as far as "You don't —"

"But since you didn't go through the house after dropping Jessica off, Mr. Ketterson, you couldn't have known that somebody else really was in the house then."

"No, there —"

"Somebody Jessica didn't expect back so early. Somebody who had to come home for something, maybe using the hiking trail behind the house and the back door so his car wouldn't be spotted out front."

Sheilah heard Giordano, in his own voice, say, "I needed cash . . . for the hotel . . . that Terri broad . . ."

Sheilah didn't completely recall the Como woman's statement alibiing Giordano, but she couldn't stop to explore it. "The same somebody who overheard Jessica offering herself to you, Mr. Ketterson."

"Stop it," said Giordano's voice.

"Somebody who couldn't stand to hear that his little baby — the one he played the puppet games with — would do something like that."

"Stop!"

Sheilah looked up at the bench. "Betray him like that."

"Shut the fuck up, you fucking bitch!"

Rudolph Giordano kept the pistol in his right hand but wedged the puppet sticks under the lip of the bench before coming down off the back of it. Sheilah tensed and stepped away, but Giordano went directly to Ketterson, grabbing the right shoulder of the T-shirt, bunching the fabric. Sheilah moved toward the side bar as quietly as she could, hoping Ketterson would keep his eyes and mouth shut.

Giordano began screaming into the paralyzed man's face. "Tell the truth, you goddamn sonavabitch! Tell the fucking truth about how you chased my baby up to her bedroom, and when she wouldn't talk about it with you, when she . . . laughed at you . . . Tell the truth."

Sheilah froze as Giordano looked over and spoke to her. "Make him tell the truth! He tore off my baby's dress and pulled off her bra and choked the fucking life out of her."

"Without leaving fingerprints?" said Sheilah.

Giordano let go of Ketterson, the taut wires keeping the man's torso upright in the chair. "What?" said Giordano.

"Ketterson did all that — and scattered the puppets around her body — without leaving fingerprints? When he'd already left one print on the bra from helping Jessica at the beginning of the evening? No, whoever strangled your daughter was wearing gloves, and just by luck didn't smear Ketterson's earlier print."

Giordano looked down at his hands, flexing the fingers of the one not holding the gun. "My driving gloves . . . Jessica wanted to fuck that monster . . . in the house I built for . . ."

Sheilah used Giordano's distraction to move closer to the side bar.

He said to his hands, "I never . . . never meant to . . ."

Rudolph Giordano's legs seemed to buckle under him. He sat heavily onto the floor at the foot of the witness stand. Staring down, down into his own private corner of hell.

Sheilah moved up to the bench and leaned over the side bar, pushing on the panel she thought was the right one.

From the floor, Giordano's voice said, "What're you doing?"

The panel didn't give. Shit. "I need some . . . paperwork here."

"What?"

Sheilah didn't like the sound of panic she began to hear in her own voice. "Some paperwork to . . . clear this whole thing up for all of us."

Sheilah pushed on the next panel as Giordano said, "Paperwork?"

This time, the thin wood flipped around, and the small revolver came into her hand.

Giordano started to stand up. "Where did you —"

She pointed the weapon at him. "Please, drop the gun."

Giordano stared at the thing in her hand as though he'd never seen a firearm, as though he wasn't holding one himself.

Sheilah spoke louder, trying to keep her voice firm. "Mr. Giordano, just drop the gun."

He looked once around the bar enclosure, seeming to see it for the first time. Then his face hardened, and he began to raise his weapon.

"Please, no," said Sheilah.

As the muzzle of Giordano's pistol kept coming up, Sheilah fired, and Hesterfield's revolver bucked in her hand. Then a second shot, and —

Sheilah lost count as well as her aim, the index finger acting on its own. When she felt no more bucking from her hand, she stopped pulling the trigger and made herself look at the floor.

531

Giordano was down, his gun six feet away from him now, the man crawling back up toward the bench as blood soaked through the left side of his shirt.

Arthur Ketterson opened his eyes. "Sheilah . . . bravo. . . ."

Ignoring him, Sheilah dropped her empty gun and rushed over to the prosecution table. "Frank?"

No response, but he was still breathing. Barely.

"Sheilah . . ." Ketterson's voice cracking now. ". . . help me!"

She ran to the telephone by O.B.'s body. Call 911. Ambulance. Picked up the receiver. Dead. Of course, that's what Vinnie had said that morning, as they waited futilely for Hesterfield at the new courthouse. But the security desk downstairs, that phone should still —

"Sheilah!" from Ketterson again.

She turned at a different noise, realized she couldn't see Giordano anymore.

Frank's gun. If he has that, too. Oh God.

Sheilah ran toward the bench now, stopping short as Giordano pulled himself up, one hand on the back of Roger Hesterfield's chair, blood running down the contractor's arm onto the corpse.

Giordano said, "You think you won?" More blood came burbling through the only bullet hole she could see, high in his chest.

Mind spinning, Sheilah chose her words as

532

carefully as she could. "Nobody . . . won, Mr. Giordano."

"Wrong, *coun*selor."

She watched him reach for . . . Frank's gun? No, just a device like a television remote.

Giordano turned the device toward his face, then pushed once with his thumb, as though hitting the power button. Grinning, he turned the device again so that now its display faced Sheilah. "See?"

Ketterson said, "What does . . . the madman . . . ?"

Sheilah moved closer to the bench. "I don't understand what I'm supposed to see, Mr. Giordano."

"This little window here." The contractor's voice began to falter, his eyes crossing. "It shows . . . how many seconds."

"Seconds? "

"Remote detonator. . . . Way I set the thing . . . you can't stop it."

Sheilah couldn't say anything.

Even with the other hand on Hesterfield's chair, Giordano began to teeter. "I wired the building . . . with dynamite for demolition. Gave myself . . ." — he was swaying now as he squinted at the device's window, grinning some more — ". . . three minutes."

And then Rudolph Giordano fell like a marionette with its strings cut.

Just outside the front door of the old courthouse, Krissie Newton thought she heard a rivet gun going off inside somewhere. Shit, the construction guys were still working — that'd sour anything with Vinnie.

Might as well say hello, though, maybe work something out for later. She opened the door. No Vinnie. Picked up the phone. Dead all right. No wonder I couldn't —

Then Krissie heard the vague sound of voices, from the second floor. Maybe Vinnie's up there with the work crew, shagging them out.

That's when she heard something else. Like a little puppy whimpering. Behind the desk somewhere.

Krissie went around it, didn't see anything. Except the phone cord, ripped out of the wall. No wonder the fucking line was —

Then the whimpering sound again, from the closet there. She opened the door to it.

"Vinnie. Ohmigod!"

Dropping down onto her knees, Krissie Newton couldn't believe a person could lose that much blood and still be alive.

Sheilah Quinn lunged for Frank Sikes, taking him by the lapels. "Please God, Frank. Get up! Help me get you up."

Just a moan.

Arthur Ketterson said, "What . . . are you . . . ?"

She pulled her lover to his feet, stumbling into him before steadying his weight against her.

A louder moan, but Frank seeming to come awake, too. "Sheilah?"

"We have to get out of here." She got his right arm up and around her neck. "Come on."

Behind them, Ketterson said, "You can't leave me!"

Block him out, girl. No time to save anybody else.

She began to lead Frank like a clumsy dance partner down the aisle of the courtroom.

"Sheilah," said the hoarse voice, "after I . . . uncomplicated . . . your life?"

In spite of herself, she turned her head toward the witness stand.

Ketterson attempted a smile. "The old . . . crone . . . your father . . . Hesterfield. . . ."

What she'd feared about her dad, but . . . Etta, too? Sheilah repressed the emotions welling up inside by thinking, Jesus Mary, how many seconds did I just waste?

"Sheilah!" Came the hoarse screech behind her.

As she banged through the double doors to the corridor, the lawyer heard her client begin to cry.

Reaching the top of the staircase, Sheilah felt Frank stop, weaving now and even harder to support.

"No . . . can't," he said.

"Frank, we don't have time!"

"Let me . . . sit down. . . ."

"Frank!"

"Kind of . . . slide . . ."

Sheilah forced herself to focus, then helped lower him onto the top step, Frank with his legs out like a child on a saucer sled. Sheilah guided him down the stairs, cushioning the jolts from each step as best she could.

Finally, they were at the bottom, on the first floor. As Sheilah tried to get Frank back to his feet, he passed out again. Gasping for breath, she realized she'd have to drag him along the granite corridor.

Still a block away, Gerry O'Toole wasn't sure he could believe his own eyes.

By the curb at the foot of the steps leading to the old courthouse. A woman holding up a guy in a bailiff's uniform, him covered in blood, her trying to wave down cars, the drivers swerving around them.

Naturally. They're just fucking citizens of this great metropolis. They don't want to get involved.

But what the fuck is going on?

O'Toole changed lanes, horns blaring all around him, then knifed the unmarked into the curb at an odd angle, more horns as he got on the radio. "Break, break. Dispatch, this is Delta three. Officer down! I say again, officer down. Old Courthouse, front entrance. Old courthouse, front entrance. Now, now!"

As he replaced the mike, he could hear the dispatcher start an all-units broadcast, which would include EMTs, too.

Gerry watched the bailiff collapse, the woman — looked like a teenager, for Chrissake — riding down to the sidewalk with him. As O'Toole got out of his sedan, she began yelling, "Ohmigod, I think he's dying. Help him, will you? Just help him!"

Gerry ran over there, the corner of his eye registering somebody else way at the top of the steps. Another woman, business suit, coming out the courthouse entrance.

Hauling something behind her. What's she got, a . . . mailbag?

Sheilah yelled down to the people at the curb. "Help me, please! I can't lift him."

She kept dragging Frank, her hands under his armpits, Sheilah's own arms feeling as though they were going to pull from their sockets. A heavy man in a sports jacket was coming up the steps, two at a time. Familiar, but she couldn't try to place him now.

Sheilah began to pull Frank down the concrete stairs, not worried so much about cushioning him as just getting him away from the building.

Then the other man's voice erupted next to her. "Christ, Frank?"

He began to swing Frank up, fireman's carry over his shoulder. Frank's partner, Gerry —

"What the hell's happening here?" said O'Toole.

"Hurry," said Sheilah. "The whole place is about to blow up."

Or in.

As they hit the bottom step, Sheilah felt it shaking beneath them. Then, reaching two other people at the curb, Vinnie, his face bleeding badly, and . . .

Krissie? What was she —

Thumping noises caught up to Sheilah, shaking even the sidewalk enough to make her have to shuffle both feet, as though she were on the deck of a ship in a storm. After the thumping noises came a deep rumbling from within, the building beginning to fold and crumple on itself, the window frames and pillars dissolving toward the center as a massive mushrooming cloud of dust rose up from the foundation.

As O'Toole lowered Frank to the sidewalk, Sheilah Quinn heard Krissie say, "Vinnie, be glad you can't see this. I think it's an atomic bomb."

TWENTY

Frank Sikes had lost count of how many times he'd relived it. Seeing Ketterson sitting in that witness chair, the courtroom shadows now not blurry, but sharp as a crime-scene photograph.

Ketterson talking, me leveling my piece on the asshole, telling him to raise his hands. Then the shots . . . the impact . . . the pain. But I swear his hands never left that —

"Frank?"

Sheilah there, somehow, pulling on my jacket. Making me walk with her when I could barely stand. Hey, what's the rush?

"Frank, are you awake?"

And then those stairs, Sheilah saying we had to get down them. Slide one at a time, like a little kid on a snowy hill. Only the pain . . . Hard to breathe. . . . But Sheilah's hand, holding mine —

Wait a minute. Doesn't feel like the . . . courthouse. Where are we?

"Frank, can you hear me?"

"Sure . . ." He made his eyes open. Sheilah, sitting on . . . his bed?

She leaned over him, her lips brushing his cheek, her eyes . . . wet? "Oh God. Thank you, thank you."

Frank tried to swallow, help him talk to Sheilah, but his throat was so sore. He didn't think Ketterson had gotten him in the throat. "What . . . happened?"

"It's a long story. How do you feel?"

Bundled up and fragile, all at the same time. "Okay. . . . Why?"

"Why? Because you got shot."

He tried to nod, stopped because it hurt too much. "Ketterson."

"No, Frank. Rudolph Giordano."

"Giordano? "

"I'll tell you later." Different tone to her voice. "The doctors said it was touch-and-go for a while there."

"Doctors?"

"You're in Mercy Hospital, Frank."

Hospital. Sure. I got shot, right?

"Gerry and I have been kind of switching off, making sure there'd be somebody in the room if . . . when you came out of it."

"Where's . . . Gerry?"

"Checking on Vinnie. Fractured cheekbone and a bad concussion, apparently, but they say he's going to be all right."

Vinnie? Vinnie who?

"Frank?"

"Still . . . here."

"I'm going to let you get back to sleep in a second. But first, I want to know if you can feel this."

A squeeze on his hand, almost like something

electric coming from Sheilah, running through him. "Sure . . . I can."

"Good," she said, brushing his lips this time with her own. "So can I."

Frank sensed that his mind was drifting, but he knew what Sheilah Quinn meant, too. And Detective Sgt. Frank Sikes also knew he now had a very important reason to wake up again.

ABOUT THE AUTHOR

Jeremiah Healy, a graduate of Rutgers College and Harvard Law School, was a professor at the New England School of Law for eighteen years. He is the creator of John Francis Cuddy, a Boston-based private investigator.

Healy's first book, *Blunt Darts*, was selected by *The New York Times* as one of the seven best mysteries of 1984. His second work, *The Staked Goat*, received the Shamus Award for the Best Private Eye Novel of 1986. Nominated for a Shamus a total of eleven times (six for books, five for short stories), Healy's later novels include *So Like Sleep*, *Swan Dive*, *Yesterday's News*, *Right to Die*, *Shallow Graves*, *Foursome*, *Act of God*, and *Rescue*. His last Cuddy book, *Invasion of Privacy*, was also a Shamus nominee, and his current novel, *The Only Good Lawyer*, appeared in February 1998.

Healy has served as a judge for both the Shamus and Edgar awards. His books have been translated into French, Japanese, Italian, Spanish, and German. Currently the North-American vice president of the International Association of Crime Writers, Healy was president of the Private Eye Writers of America for two years. He has written and spoken about mystery writing extensively, including the Smithsonian Institution's Literature Series, *The Boston Globe* Book Festival, and international conferences of crime writers in New York, England, Spain, and Austria. Healy has participated in eleven World Mystery Conventions ("BoucherCons"), serving as banquet toastmaster for the 1996 event. This past July he was a Guest of Honor at the Dallas mystery convention.